THE VIOLINS PLAYED BEFORE JUNSTAN

The Celwyn Series Book 1

The Violins Played Before Junstan

Lou Kemp

4 Horsemen
Publications, Inc.

Violins Played Before Junstan
The Celwyn Series Book 1
Copyright © 2022 Lou Kemp. All rights reserved.

4 Horsemen
Publications, Inc.

4 Horsemen Publications, Inc.
1497 Main St. Suite 169
Dunedin, FL 34698
4horsemenpublications.com
info@4horsemenpublications.com

Cover by J. Kotick
Typesetting by S. Wilder
Editor Joseph Mistretta

Library of Congress Control Number: 2022939114

Print ISBN: 978-1-64450-626-4
Audio ISBN: 978-1-64450-624-0
E-Book ISBN: 978-1-64450-625-7

Table of Contents

Acknowledgements:

MANY THANKS AND LOVE TO MY daughter, Charmaine, who supports me no matter what, even when I got a third cat. Thank you to friends Anita, Nikki, Debbie, Peggy, Norm, Benjamin, Karen, and Chris P. for their support and advice. Thank you to Lorin Oberweger of Free-Expressions for her wonderful editing of Farm Hall, and to John Helfers of Stonehenge Editorial for his patience and expertise in editing the Celwyn series.

Cast of Characters

Jonas Celwyn: Immortal magician and provocateur

Professor Xiau Kang: Automat, medical man, scientist

Bartholomew: widower from Juba, friend to Kang and Celwyn

Annabelle Pearse Edmunds: heiress and ward of Uncle Celwyn

Captain Patrick Swayne: Friend to Celwyn, loves Annabelle

Mrs. Elizabeth Kang: tolerant and beautiful wife of Kang

Zander: an orphan rescued on the way to Prague

Ricardo: Chef Ricardo of Tellyhouse

Mrs. Thomas: formidable Housekeeper of Tellyhouse

Jackson, Selkirk, Stephen: porters on the train
and in Prague

Edward Murphy: their driver and head of security

Angus Sully: footman of Tellyhouse and a leg-
endary bad chef

Telly: an orphan rescued on the way to Prague

Suzanne: deceased fiancé to Celwyn and sister
to Patrick

Francesca: head of Prague's notorious coven

Delgado: Vampire who killed Suzanne and Telly

Mrs. Karras: disciple of Delgado and
enemy of Celwyn

Prince Leo: thief and old friend of Celwyn

PART I
Lies

And now there came both mist and snow,
And it grew wondrous cold:
And ice, mast-high, came floating by,

— Samuel Taylor Coleridge,
The Rime of the Ancient Mariner

Chapter 1

San Francisco, 1876

LATE IN THE EVENING, THICK RIB-bons of fog moved like a living animal, breathing, then thinning to vapor before revealing the shadows between the wooden barrels that lined the docks. Beyond the Opera House's silhouette, oily glimmers of the bay cut through the darkness, only to be obscured by the fog again.

As Celwyn neared the docks, he heard virulent cursing above the commotion from a carriage as it charged down the cobblestones toward him. When the coach drew level, the driver raised a whip above his horse. On its descent to the horse's back, the tip suspended mid-air and snake-like, the whip shimmied out of the coachman's hand.

The man steered the hackney to a stop. As he slithered out of the high cab, the whip followed him, wrapping around his ankles, lifting him feet-first into the air. His cursing echoed to screams as he disappeared into the night sky. A moment later, a splash could be heard, and a satisfied smile crossed Celwyn's lips; he couldn't stand to see anyone mistreating an animal. The horse trotted down the street, rather jauntily, back toward the stable yard as the magician stepped around a snoring drunk and into Salty's tattered and dingy atmosphere. Celwyn could have sworn it was the same drunk he stepped over last night.

The place was half full, the gas lights dim, and as quiet as it would get. Just inside the door sat a priest who regarded Celwyn with the boldness of King George as if he knew him, as if he knew him, yet Celwyn would have remembered the little elfin ears, long black hair, and vaguely Asian eyes. The eyes glittered an invitation.

Oh, really? The magician thought it odd to discover a priest in a saloon—in his experience they were more likely to drink their whiskey by candlelight in the church vestry, elbow-to-elbow with the spiritual mice. Curious, he placed his top hat on the table and settled into the chair opposite the priest.

Beads of sweat decorated the bald head of the bartender as he rushed forward with a shot of whiskey on a tray. He deposited it in front of Celwyn and whirled to run back behind the bar.

The priest aimed a thumb at the publican. "Well-trained. Just like a seal at a waterfront show."

Celwyn paused and then picked up his glass. He recognized that voice. A fortuitous coincidence? A few blocks away, St. Marks provided excellent places to eavesdrop, such as a false wall behind the altar. This morning the Monsignor of St. Marks and this same priest had discussed some unusual incidents occurring during Mass. It was not a coincidence that the same man should be sitting here.

"I do not need to know how you caused the bellowing of bulls during services." The priest made a distasteful face, like the air around them suddenly smelled of rancid cabbage. "I only need to know that it was you who did the deed. The flute music you added probably had meaning for you, but it was in poor taste."

The magician tensed and sat back. *He has no idea of what I can do if provoked.* Celwyn eyed him as he finished his drink and speculated how much effort it would take to lure the priest outside and snap his neck. The man obviously couldn't appreciate the purpose of music. He also reeked of cloves.

"Your ensuing act was more violent." The bugger smiled. "The Monsignor has suggested I take the matter to the police."

Celwyn stood, throwing some coins on the table as he turned to go. Perhaps it was time to return to the Continent. He could almost taste the oranges in Seville. He could take one of the new excursions to the Pyramids, and a smile went with that as he imagined how entertaining it would be if one of the depictions became animated. His enjoyment was interrupted as the priest got to his feet, and Celwyn noticed he did so in a somewhat stiff manner. Perhaps his joints needed oiling. But there was nothing slow about him as he trailed the magician out the door and into the fog's moist embrace.

Rehearsed peals of well-paid feminine laughter emanated from the brothels lining the street. The priest did his best to keep up as Celwyn strode along. They detoured around a dapper gentleman who'd just been tossed out of one of the betting parlors and rolled across the boards. He tried to stand, but a pair of roughs poured out of the parlor doors and set about beating him.

"Shouldn't you do something about that?" Celwyn asked, hooking a thumb at the attackers as they started to kick their victim. "It's a priestly duty, I believe."

"No." The priest started walking again. "I am not a priest."

How curious. Celwyn waved a hand, and a strong wind arose, blowing the attackers down. They scrambled up again only to be knocked head over heels farther down the street. "Why not?" Celwyn asked as he rejoined him. "You're dressed like one."

They stopped in front of an alley redolent with fish and horse manure. The gaslight overhead painted his companion's face, and Celwyn noted the man's skin had the consistency of bleached leather, like it needed a good pinching to give it some color. Celwyn straightened his cuffs. Not everyone could be as handsome as he. Nor as elegant.

They stood next to a particularly foul-smelling pile of rubbish. The man's delicate little nose didn't even twitch as he said, "Mr. Celwyn. Yes, I know your name." His voice held reluctant admiration. He eyed

Celwyn as a butcher would a carcass before carving. "You are much more refined than I expected. And I know of your particular talents. Your sense of right and wrong seems to be even stronger than your disagreements with the clergy."

The conversation and the man had become tiresome. If he knew so much, he would have to know how dangerous Celwyn could be. Yet again, the little man tickled the magician's displeasure.

"Murder one moment, acts of gentle kindness another. Whims," the priest sneered.

Celwyn grabbed him by the throat and lifted him to eye-level. "Not whims." Celwyn shook him like a cat would a rat. "Evil should be punished."

A tremendous force exploded under Celwyn's hand, and then the other man was standing a few feet away, nattering along as if the magician hadn't been about to throttle him.

"For hundreds of years, you have performed heroic acts, acts of mayhem, and then disappeared to do it all over again."

Celwyn stepped closer until their chests nearly touched. The priest stared back, not afraid at all.

"And pray tell," Celwyn started, finding that phrase appropriate, "what do you think I am?"

"A supremely gifted magician. As immortal as you are amoral."

Celwyn brought his hands together, struggling for control.

"*What do you want?*"

"I have a proposition for you: help me capture a wicked man." He spoke slowly, playing his best card. "A person much worse than anyone else you've hunted and killed."

Celwyn rubbed his face. "Gad, this place smells." Next to his foot lay a half-eaten dog. "Couldn't you have asked me this at Salty's? It is a hell of a lot warmer in there."

They began walking up Van Ness Avenue. Celwyn asked, "Who is this person you seek? For that matter, who are you?"

"Xiau Kang is a powerful criminal. He departs for China tomorrow. If we are successful, you will be rewarded and can continue on to Singapore." As they crossed the street, the bells of St. Mark's echoed through the ocean air and into the night, her spires visible above the brick buildings nearby. She was a grand lady, gothic and tall, yet less than thirty-years-old, unlike her sisters in Europe.

"When we reach the island of Junstan in the China Sea, I'll take custody of Kang, and you will receive enough gold to make your stay in Singapore a long and pleasant one. It's a mysterious and beautiful city," the priest continued.

Payment wasn't a motivation. "Why can't you catch him yourself?" They reached the steps of St. Mark's and sat down.

The man glanced to the side, not meeting Celwyn's gaze. "It will take all of your skills of illusion, your cunning, and more to subdue him."

Celwyn yawned. "And what will you be doing?"

"Helping, of course."

The magician regarded him. He looked skinny, peculiar, and seemed more of an intellectual than capable of pummeling someone if needed. For several minutes, Celwyn thought about his own level of boredom and the unknown and wondered how depraved this Kang could be.

The other man stood and opened the church's heavy door. "You may call me Talos. Do not mention my name once we board the ship."

"Why?"

"It would only make things more difficult. You see," he paused, and his eyes again glittered like broken crystal in the sun, "Kang is my brother."

———

Celwyn felt, more than knew, it would soon be dawn. No hint of pink filtered through the higher panes of the rectory windows, yet faint sounds of stirring in the kitchen below could be heard. In another second, he determined he was not alone in his makeshift bedchamber below the rafters. The magician had become accustomed to the rats but found Talos' smirk as annoying as the stench of cloves that clung to the man.

"Excellent. I'm glad you have awoken." Talos jumped off a crate and beamed at Celwyn. "We must get to the docks. The *Zelda* will sail soon, and we have much to talk about along the way." He clapped his hands. "Make haste."

As Celwyn pulled on his trousers, he wondered if Talos had any idea how close he had just come to flying off the church roof. But no, the man chattered on.

"...voyage of several weeks. Keep that in your boot." He handed Celwyn a short knife with an ornate ivory handle. "I have sent a trunk of rather elegant clothes on ahead to the ship for you. Of course, I will be the passenger with seasickness who stays in his cabin and out of my brother's sight."

Chapter 2

DAWN PAINTED THE TALL-MASTED ships of the harbor with a watery hand as scores of sailors in wide-legged uniforms winched cargo aboard barques, transports, and barquentines. The magician inhaled the salty air and, with it, a reminder of how much he adored the sea. Like a mating or dying sea lion, a moaning foghorn resounded across the bay. The sound competed with a crate of squawking chickens as it was lowered into the hold of a nearby barque. Celwyn approved: omelets.

Talos led the way toward a throng in front of a pristine barquentine. The *Zelda,* white with a band of blue and her three-story-high masts, spread great expanses of freshly laundered canvasses. Celwyn admired ships, especially elegant ones. He expected to discover a worthy gentleman's parlor aboard and, perhaps, a decent game of poker.

Talos had wandered on ahead. Celwyn scanned the area and discovered why Talos had disappeared; at the rear of the crowd stood a similar man with elfin ears and gleaming eyes that didn't seem to rest until they encountered Celwyn's gaze. One of the most beautiful women the magician had ever seen held the man's elbow. Her hair was the color of a darkened flame, and her skin shined a healthy glow as she murmured at who had to be Xiau Kang. He continued to return Celwyn's stare as he ushered her forward.

Celwyn presented his ticket to the purser and his own trunk to a porter. He had excellent taste in his wardrobe, but it would be interesting to see what Talos had provided, "I say, who is that gentleman in the beaver hat?"

The purser raised his chin and squinted. "You must mean the Professor. He's traveled with us before."

Chapter 3

As the *Zelda* sailed west, Celwyn stood on the leeward deck, letting the restless wind buffet him. In the distance, thick opalescent clouds gathered near the horizon. The magician sighed. It appeared they were about to encounter a storm. Maritime logic dictated that they would navigate around the worst of the tempest but would not sit still to let it overtake the ship.

Two of the fussier passengers, Mrs. Pearse and her niece Annabelle, clutched parasols and minced their way along the rail to join him in his perusal of the sea. Celwyn wrinkled his face in annoyance. Their arrival could be a social call, but he suspected that the aunt viewed him as a wealthy prospect for the fair-haired, comely niece who did her best to bat her eyelashes at him while holding on to her billowing hat and the rail. The aunt's voice reminded him of fingernails sliding across glass.

Mrs. Pearse sighed. "Traveling is such a bother, is it not Mr. Celwyn?"

"Yes, ma'am, it is."

So far, Celwyn had exercised a modicum of restraint with Mrs. Pearse. If he weren't careful, he'd endure hearing an oft-repeated story of how she had found a live fish nestled in her trunk nestled with her flowered frocks.

He bowed to the niece. "You are looking well today, Miss Annabelle."

"Thank you. The First Officer reported that the ship will encounter a storm tonight, and we will be confined to our cabins." The niece frowned, and her perfectly formed brow crinkled. "Is this true?"

Celwyn felt a twinge of sympathy for her. Being trapped with her aunt in a small cabin while the wind roared and her aunt howled wouldn't be pleasant. He debated how much to say to the niece, but then it occurred to him that the situation could be useful. "That is one option the Captain has. However," he assumed a worried expression, "I would suggest that we all stay in the salon. There are less than a dozen of us."

"Why?" Mrs. Pearse asked. A gust of wind slammed the *Zelda* broadside causing the dowager to lurch back to the rail and hold on.

"The salon is located in the center of the ship. It will receive less water from the waves." Celwyn stood taller. "And we can offer each other encouragement if the storm becomes too frightening."

The magician considered himself nothing, if not devious, and that was not bad: sometimes it was useful. If Mrs. Pearse convinced the Captain to utilize the salon, Kang would remain there for the evening. The magician had tried for days to invent a way of getting into the man's cabin without interruption. He intended to take his time to search it and then have a conversation with him.

Luncheon was a simple affair with the last of the fresh vegetables, a fair claret, and an overly cooked roast placed before them. As he sampled the wine, Celwyn observed the other passengers at the next table. Colonel Gilliam's luxuriant mustaches and ice blue eyes missed nothing. He furrowed his brow as Mrs. Pearse leaned closer, resting her shelf-size bosom on the table. Beside him, Mrs. Caruthers tucked a strand of gray hair under her flowered hat and debated whether to dump her water on Mrs. Pearse's well-displayed bosom.

The young Tarrytons ate as if their final meal aboard the *Zelda* had just been served. Mrs. Tarryton nearly resorted to picking up the roast beef with her fingers when she couldn't cut through it fast enough. Heavens! What about propriety and etiquette? Celwyn had heard the Tarrytons were on their way to a diplomatic posting in Hong Kong. He tapped his nose and Mrs. Tarryton began to snort as she ate.

The magician turned his attention to the passengers at his table, who were trying to ignore the snorting. For the first time since they sailed, Kang and his wife had been seated with him.

Elizabeth Kang's hand lay close enough that Celwyn could have touched the emerald she wore. He resisted the urge to do so and continued to eat parslied potatoes. Her perfume reminded him of a lilac field nestled high in the Irish mountains.

Across the table, Kang ate with quiet efficiency. It was time that Celwyn knew what the man was thinking. One of the many talents that Talos had alluded to is the ability to invade another man's mind. While there, Celwyn could add another secret, explore thoughts, and discover fears. It also made a perfect opportunity for inserting a new wisp of mystery or useful morsel of scandal, depending on his mood.

As Celwyn turned toward Kang, the man looked him in the eye and barely shook his head. Celwyn pushed forward to enter Kang's thoughts. Nothing happened. The magician tried again. Nothing! Kang's lips twitched as he nibbled a roll.

Celwyn cursed and behind him a row of bar glasses shattered. The candles throughout the room dimmed until he controlled his anger, and then burned even brighter than before. A few of the passengers reacted appropriately with gasps, but Kang continued to eat, not missing a beat.

Fine. It occurred to Celwyn that even if he could not read Kang's thoughts, perhaps getting to know his wife better would be just as useful. Of course, with decorum and modesty. The magician had been accused of many things, some of them true, but he'd always been a gentleman.

"Please pass the salt, Mrs. Kang."

As she handed it to him, Celwyn directed his attention to her, entering her thoughts as easily as a warm knife through butter. "*...storm ... lifeboats ... Mrs. Pearse's pushiness ... her double chin ... Kang talking about his brother...*" Celwyn listened and within minutes knew much more about the Professor. Enough to confirm that Talos had lied.

Elizabeth Kang stole a look at Celwyn while silently noting how handsome she thought him, especially the curve of his jaw. The magician looked away so that she wouldn't notice the air of satisfaction he wore. He hadn't even had to suggest the thought to her!

Throughout the rest of the afternoon, the hammering of boards over the windows and doors rang across the deck. Barrels and other unsecured storage had been taken below. The clanking of the chains in the yardarms grew louder with the increasing gales. More telling, heavy crates from the cargo hold were wrestled up to the deck and tossed overboard. He hoped the passengers didn't register the significance: dumping expensive cargo overboard indicated extreme danger lay ahead.

When Celwyn entered his cabin, he found Talos sitting on the bunk and reading a newspaper. Cloves again. He pinched his nose and crossed to the desk.

"This storm could blow us off course a great distance," Talos spoke without looking up.

Celwyn said nothing but realized with Talos so near, he had an opportunity. What more did Talos know? With a deceptively blank expression, Celwyn attempted to read his thoughts.

Damnation! Celwyn gripped the desk trying for control. Two times in one day, he had failed at such a simple undertaking. How could both brothers thwart his attempt?

"Is there something wrong?"

Celwyn waited until he could control his anger before asking, "Do you have a ship following us?"

"Yes." Talos folded the newspaper and began examining his nails. "All you must do is deliver Kang to me when the time comes."

"I thought we were to do this together." Again, Celwyn eyed him, wondering how much effort it would take to throttle him. Probably one hand could perform the deed.

"You should be more worried about how you will subdue Kang."

"I won't allow the passengers and crew of this ship to be hurt," Celwyn said. "Played with, yes. Hurt, no."

Talos stood and walked to the door. "At the right moment, attack, or cause an illusion, or whatever you do. Just be sure Kang is restrained. That is the surest way to ensure their safety." The ship dipped low and a collection of toiletry bottles beside him toppled off the dresser. "Assuming we make it through this storm."

Celwyn replaced the toiletry bottles without touching them and resumed thinking about the situation.

Chapter 4

NINETEEN BELLS RESONATED across the deck. As the *Zelda* sailed into a wall of rain, the staccato pattering grew to a pounding cadence. The iridescent foam of the roiling waves contrasted starkly with the blackness of the night. One by one the waves extinguished the running lamps until only the signal lamps on the bridge glowed, swinging side to side like death knells.

In the distance, a flicker of lightning decorated the darkness. As the First Officer ushered Celwyn into the salon, a ridge of seawater topped the railing and flooded the deck.

The magician had seen livelier parties at funerals. Most of the passengers huddled on the sofas in the center of the room except for Annabelle who paced the room fore and aft, holding a cigarette and a full glass of red wine that dribbled down her satin skirts with each swing of her hips. Kang and his wife sat side by side across from the Tarrytons. The magician acknowledged Kang with a nod as Mrs. Pearse's voice shrilled, "We are going to die!"

Annabelle patted her aunt's shoulder and tried to stem the flow. Celwyn crossed to the bar and poured a large quantity of sherry. When Mrs. Pearse took a breath for another outburst, Celwyn handed her the glass. "Drink that." It wasn't a request.

She gulped and bleated, "The ship will sink!"

"I cannot swim," Mrs. Caruthers moaned. "We will all drown!"

Colonel Gilliam's eyes bounced from passenger to passenger, growing more frightened by the second.

Celwyn frowned. A distraction was in order.

They didn't notice when he lit the fireplace behind them, bringing warmth and, hopefully, cheer. As if it had been there all along, he produced a spirit board from behind the bar while planting the idea in Mrs. Pearse's mind that it would be entertaining to ask it when her niece would marry and what the spring fashions would bring. He also added a strong desire for chocolate cake in Mrs. Caruthers' thoughts.

With a bit of help from Celwyn, the notion of lighting candles and summoning spirits occurred to the other passengers. Celwyn reclined against the bar and watched their conversation evolve: they decided to ignore the noise outside. With his help, all night long they would disregard the fury of the rain as it pounded the roof of the salon like hundreds of symphony drums.

A few minutes later Celwyn shut the salon door behind him while the passengers closed their eyes to concentrate on the unnamed spirits.

Seawater had stopped draining from the scuppers, sloshing leeward and back again along with the rhythm of the waves. It took less than twenty steps to reach Kang's cabin, and when the ship shifted to starboard taking the water with it, Celwyn opened the cabin door and slammed it shut behind him. From his pocket he withdrew a stub of candle, lit it, and began to explore.

The Kangs had been assigned an excellent room. A velvet settee, a carved wooden dresser, and tall, ornate pianoforte made the room livable. The magician added a vase of red roses and bowl of chocolates next to the bed. Just as he congratulated himself on his thoughtfulness, he nearly tripped over the bedpost: an opaque eye stared back at him from atop the pianoforte. He looked closer. A small, iridescent blackbird with silver-tipped feathers sat, twisting its head from side to side, inspecting him. After a moment, it soared upward with languid wings moving just fast enough to keep it aloft. As he watched, it descended and resumed its position atop the pianoforte.

Although somewhat fascinating, considering his own predilections, Celwyn had things to do.

He began to tour the room, examining various items, noting the type of shoes Mrs. Kang favored and the silk of Kang's ties. For a "professor," he appeared quite wealthy. The magician speculated what Kang's real purpose could be. Earlier, his foray into Elizabeth Kang's mind confirmed Talos had lied to him: Kang wasn't a criminal. But what was he?

On top of the desk blotter, Celwyn discovered a bound collection of papers with a single walnut placed on top. Again, a strange discovery, but he found the Professor odd, too. The pages contained numbers, drawings, and what appeared to be alchemy. On the final page Kang had written "*correction to Dalton's theory.*" *How interesting*, the magician thought. The last line read, "*...suppress this discovery until such time as the world is ready for it. Until it is used for forthright purposes, not for war. I believe in the good it can do...*"

Celwyn stood still for several moments trying to understand the quixotic lists of numbers. His gifts did not extend to science; more accurately, they extended to bending the laws of science. From outside, the calls of the crew faded as the reverberation from the thunder grew louder.

What could be more perfect than nature and music together? Celwyn nodded, and the pianoforte began a tinkling baroque ballad that fit the atmosphere perfectly. He enjoyed the play between numbers and power, for that was what music and the storm represented. Even more appropriate was the contrast of elements; he produced dozens of candles and lit them.

What was keeping Kang?

Another ten minutes passed before the cabin door opened, and a cold gust of wind blew in, along with the man. He staggered to a halt and held out a scrap of paper. "I believe this was from you?" Kang wiggled the paper. "Inviting me to my own room?"

"Yes."

He studied Celwyn as he lounged by the desk. "I trust you are comfortable?"

"Except for a spot of whiskey ... to warm our souls." The magician rubbed his hands together and produced a bottle.

Kang stared and then accepted a glass. It didn't take him more than a half-second to process what he saw and mentally shrug. "Are you armed?"

"Only with the knife your brother insisted I carry," Celwyn murmured as he held an imaginary baton high, conducting the music emanating from the pianoforte.

"It is time we talked." Kang crossed the room to sit at the pianoforte. For a moment, he watched the keys as they continued to move and play the music. "I've surmised why you are here."

"Then you know your brother engaged me to capture you." Celwyn eyed him. "Why?"

Kang shrugged. "Because in an altercation between us, he would lose. But bring in someone such as yourself, then the odds are in his favor."

The magician poured two more glasses and extended one to Kang, "To civilized discourse." After a few sips he added, "You are not the supreme criminal he indicated, or fundamentally evil from what I can discover." The ship stopped swaying and then began a slow tilt leeward. When the vessel righted itself, he continued, "My reasons for helping your brother are dwindling."

Kang began to pace the room in short, precise steps. "I have heard of you. In 1373, the first recorded instance attributed to your magic were the images of Anubis in the clouds above Chartes. Then came the khamsin in Algiers, where you turned the dust storm to water. It was only later I learned your name."

Celwyn raised his glass in salute. As he tossed the walnut in the air and caught it, Kang gazed at it as if it were the devil's toy. "Where did you find that?"

Celwyn pointed at the manuscript. Kang hesitated, frowned, and then continued speaking while staring at the walnut.

"I can appreciate the moral point of view that drives what you do, at least I think I do, and that Talos has probably asked you to ... uh ... disable me. Is this true?"

"Yes."

"How?"

For a long moment, Celwyn thought about what he surmised, and the lies Talos had told him. Like the American cowboys say, it was time to switch horses mid-stream.

"It didn't make a great deal of sense: I was to cut into your chest and find what he called 'the source of your power.' Then I was to remove it." The magician lifted his hands palms-up. "That wouldn't make you very useful afterward, would it?"

Kang unbuttoned his shirt and undershirt. He tapped a nail on a pale leathery chest, and a distinct metal clank answered back.

Perhaps Celwyn was speechless, although he would deny it. Several moments passed before

Kang's superior smile finally got on his nerves. "You are made of metal?" Celwyn asked.

"A type of metal, yes." Kang held out his arm, and the bird swooped downward from the pianoforte to land on his wrist. "Many centuries ago, near the Mar Maggior, the Black Sea, artificers made automats for wealthy kings and princes and for their wars and amusement. Our strength is remarkable. We are mechanical, similar to a sophisticated clock as it were, but with much more ability. Like a chess piece that can think on its own and has come to life. The artificers built bears, lions, and other animals, too."

"Ah." Celwyn looked at the bird, right in its diamond-like eye. "Come here."

The creature tilted its head one way, then the other, shaking itself before streaking upward in a blur. Then it plunged again to land on the desk beside Celwyn. As it waddled closer, Celwyn tilted his head, one way and then the other, mimicking the bird. The bird hopped on to the magician's shoulder.

"Qing fancies you."

"Of course." Celwyn stroked the bird's feathers. "Why does Talos want you captured?"

"Hatred. Brotherly jealousy. Who knows?" Kang rebuttoned his shirt. "The artificers who made us are long dead. Perhaps he wants replacement parts." A smile did not appear with the last statement.

"You can't die … if you are not alive."

"Over the years, we acquired many traits, such as the feelings of love and the ability to grieve. That is part of living, wouldn't you say?" Kang nodded, agreeing with himself. "Talos may have also begun to feel greed. He could want an army of automats again for war. Only this time, he would want something spectacular to guarantee he would win."

"Such as your discovery?" Celwyn extended a long finger to point at the portfolio of papers on the desk. As he did so, the ship began a sickening slide toward starboard. Kang gripped the pianoforte as the wind roared like howling devils chased the ship. He raised his voice above the tumult.

"If you've read my study, then you know that it is a design for a weapon the world should not have right now. If ever." The wind rattled the cabin door. "For years, I have had more science at my disposal than my contemporaries." Kang rose and faced Celwyn. "If Talos builds a weapon from my discovery, many will be dead or wish they were."

The ship stilled, and the wind quieted. "Why are you traveling to Singapore when you know he hunts you? Why board this ship knowing he is probably here?" Celwyn shook his head and stood up. "Your wife was very worried about encountering him earlier."

"You spoke to my wife?" Kang's voice sharpened, and his brows lowered.

"Not with words." The creaking of the ship resumed as it twisted against the wind. "*Why* are you here, sir?"

Kang stared at his hands a long time before whispering, "Because he killed my wife's father, trying to lure us back." He added even more softly, "He is now poisoning her mother. Slowly." Kang gripped the magician's arms. "Promise me you will protect Elizabeth," he implored Celwyn.

The man did not have to beg. The magician patted him on the back. He planned to do more than protect what was dear to Kang. Celwyn removed a small brown object from his pocket and offered it to Kang. "Care to partake?"

"Peyote?"

"Of the finest kind."

"On me, it would be a waste, without effect."

"True." The magician popped the disk in his mouth and began to chew.

"It would help if you knew more about Talos," Kang murmured.

Celwyn's brows rose. "Do tell."

Over the next hour, the storm had worsened ten-fold. "Damn!" The wind stole Celwyn's hat, carrying it away into the night. The magician watched Kang stagger up the deck against the squall and enter the salon.

With one graceful movement, the magician gained the lowest spar of the main mast. The rain blasted the ship, bringing the first chill of arctic cold. High above, a few brave sailors remained in the rigging, dodging the canvasses that blew upward off the masts like enormous wings. The Captain and First Mate manned the bridge, holding onto the wheel as another wave swamped the ship from bow to stern and the *Zelda* dipped lower on the leeward side, the waves licking the deck rail. Then she righted herself, spinning clockwise in the wind. A row of lightning arose beside the ship like an illuminated stage.

Celwyn loved the sea. Even more, he prized a fierce and flamboyant storm.

The magician raised his hands, conducting the expanse of lightning as it gyrated, dancing to an unheard melody. He bowed, and the thunder boomed directly overhead, threatening to bounce him off the spar. Celwyn laughed, relishing the display of so much beauty and power. But with a sigh, he knew it had to end. He closed his eyes and spread his arms wide, holding them steady until the winds calmed.

When he opened them again, the *Zelda* floated on a hushed sea so calm not a ripple crossed the glass-like surface. The rain continued to fall, silently turning to snow.

Chapter 5

UNDER BANKS OF LOW CLOUDS, dawn bled orange and pink on the edge of the horizon. Chunks of ice as big as small boats floated in the snow surrounding the ship, and a towering iceberg glimmered just off starboard. Many more icebergs loomed out of the shadows. The wind had returned in the night, and the *Zelda* had been blown far north where the ice grew as high as castles. Masses of her canvasses draped off the mainmast and into the water while fragile threads of ice formed a crystalline spider web above the bridge where the Captain and First Mate began to stir.

The salon door creaked open, and the passengers stumbled onto the wooden boards. From below decks, the first of the sailors poked their heads out and joined the others. The Tarrytons made their way to Celwyn at the bow, and the others followed. Kang escorted his wife with a watchful eye.

With her hair undone and a general air of dishevelment, Annabelle resembled a drowned cat. She opened and shut her mouth several times before pointing at the ice. Already, the crew unstrapped long poles from the bulkheads. Just as they took their positions at the rail, First Officer Gray arrived with a deep bow and reassurances.

"They will push us away from the ice. The others," he turned and issued orders, "will get the ship ready so we can catch the first breeze out of here."

Celwyn sighed. It would take hours to get the sails set and underway. The crew would require some unexplainable help. And enough wind to set them on course again. He twirled his finger, and a mound of lines began to separate and straighten.

Mrs. Pearse appeared at the magician's elbow, seeming invigorated or still tipsy from the night before, wobbling like a marionette even on the calm deck. She looked beyond Celwyn with the glassy-eyed stare of one of the drunks on Cannery Row.

"Officer Gray, what *is* that?"

Through lowered clouds, the shadows had darkened and became distinct against the background of mountainous ice floes. Another ship drifted out of the mist, floating toward the *Zelda*.

Mrs. Pearse began to scream.

The cabin door under the bridge flew open. Talos stepped out with a pistol in each hand. Without hesitation, he shot Officer Gray through the heart, and before the body hit the deck, he turned the gun on Mrs. Elizabeth Kang.

Just as quickly, Kang stepped in front of her. The bullet ricocheted off of him with a solid clang.

The *Zelda* lurched starboard as a loud rending ripped along the leeward side of the stern: Talos' ship had run into them. A row of deadly cannons, all capable of punching a fatal hole in the *Zelda,* became visible as hundreds of small men with black hair and elfin ears swarmed the deck of the other ship. They chattered, identical in voice and words. Kang regained his feet just as the other ship floated away again.

Annabelle pulled a still screaming Mrs. Pearse across the deck to join the other passengers hiding behind the bulkheads. The *Zelda's* crew retreated to the far end of the stern, leaving Talos, the Kangs, and Celwyn alone on deck.

Kang held Elizabeth behind him as he faced his brother. Although the automats couldn't stop glaring at each other, it was the magician that Talos addressed.

"Mr. Celwyn, would you be so kind as to do what we agreed upon?" Talos smiled a smile of triumph. "We have reached that moment."

Celwyn's hands flexed as he continued to study the other ship.

Talos growled, "*Now,* Mr. Celwyn, or my crew will blow holes through this ship, and the passengers will die."

"Because it is your *brother* who is evil?" Celwyn murmured.

Talos' laugh echoed in the cold air.

"You must desire bloodshed, Mr. Celwyn. That is unfortunate because—"

Celwyn breathed deeply. He opened his hands, and a deluge began, a veil of rain so thick nothing could be seen. From across the water, a storm of violin music commenced: five notes repeated softly and growing into a crescendo surrounding the *Zelda*.

As the rain cleared, five tall men encircled Talos, all of them Celwyn. The music became deafening, reverberating until the walls of ice surrounding the ships cracked, the sound like gunshots that repeated, causing new fissures as more of the towering icebergs split open. All of the Celwyns moved closer to Talos. Each of them moved deliberately, orchestrated to confuse, illusions designed to kill. In a swarm, they covered the automat like insects. He fought them until one cut through his shirt and removed a metal disk.

As the violins grew quiet, the illusions faded into a gray mist, dissolving into the frigid air. The magician handed the disk to Kang.

"Thank you." Kang bowed.

"My pleasure."

The flurry of activity on the other ship increased as Talos' automats threw lines across to the *Zelda*, ready to board her. Still, others stuffed cannons with explosives.

"Excuse me." Celwyn turned to the *Zelda's* mast and in seconds used magic to climb high to the eagle's nest.

The magician faced the other ship.

As if pushed by a celestial hand, Talos' ship spun away and began to move toward the ice. Celwyn concentrated his gaze on the other ship's mainmast. With a tremendous roar, the mast exploded into flames. The burning canvasses blew upward as he propelled the other ship into the immense field of ice. Celwyn shook his fists, and from the belly of the other ship came a rumble, and then its magazine detonated. The heat from the conflagration began melting the nearby ice floes. In moments, the ice refroze, and the last of the automats became still inside a crystal tomb of ice. The echoing of ice explosions repeated into the distance as great walls of ice fell into the sea and the displacement of water flew even higher.

The iridescent bird hovered above Talos' body and then soared high, orbiting the *Zelda*, flying between the masts and streaking upward again, diamond eyes glittering.

A moment more and Qing landed on Celwyn's shoulder as the violin music began again.

Forlornly, triumphantly, in celebration of the sea.[1]

---

[1] This portion of this story first appeared in the Mystery Writers of America anthology *Odd Partners*, edited by Ann Perry. A few years earlier, Celwyn was introduced with "In Memory of the Sibylline" as part of a previous MWA anthology, *Crimes by Moonlight*, edited by Charlaine Harris.

Chapter 6

CELWYN SLUMPED TO THE FLOOR OF the eagle's nest as Qing swooped by overhead, just a sliver of a shadow across the ship. One of the bird's feathers drifted down and into the magician's lap, the metallic tip twinkling in the cold morning light. His exhaustion after magic equaled the effort of making it. He sat still until he could stand again.

Far below, the crew of the *Zelda* ran across the deck in a high state of excitement. Their chatter floated upward.

"Look! The other ship, she is frozen!"

"Mon Dieu! Why did she blow up? How did she move so fast into the ice? How? Who did it?"

Mrs. Pearse's high-pitched voice could have cut glass. "Annabelle! What *is* this? What... what—"

Annabelle helped her aunt to stand. Colonel Gilliam took Mrs. Pearse's other hand to steady her. Although a bit aged, the old boy appeared still capable of chinning himself a dozen times. They joined Kang and Elizabeth as they stood over Talos' body, wearing perplexed expressions. In Celwyn's opinion, it shouldn't be that difficult to decide how to dispose of the body.

He shimmied down the mast and landed flat footed on the deck. Several of the crew, Annabelle, and others backed up. Their thoughts reflected the fear in their eyes as they looked at him seemingly for the first time.

What is he?

He must be a devil!

Instead of listening to hysterical squawking, Celwyn immobilized the crew and passengers, except for Kang, as he dusted off his coat and turned to the ship. The damage to the masts appeared serious but repairable. In seconds, they looked new again.

As tiring as the last hour had been, the ship needed to be free from the ice before he could rest. A few minutes more, and he'd raised the main canvasses out of the water and attached them to the spars again as the lesser sails once more fluttered in the breeze. He removed the block on the crew and passengers after Kang pulled Talos' body to the side and over the rail. Elizabeth Kang heard the splash, and her face registered relief as it disappeared from sight in the dark depths. The magician wondered what a fish would do if it were expecting a delectable nibble for dinner and found cold metal instead.

Celwyn sighed. With each movement, his exhaustion grew, but a last chore remained. In one sweep, the magician included the crew, the Captain, and all the passengers of the *Zelda* in a strong suggestion they couldn't ignore (apart from Kang and his mechanical brain): none of the events of the last few hours would be remembered. They wouldn't see Talos' ship entombed in the ice, and they would once again enjoy their voyage. Celwyn blew out his breath and a stronger breeze whipped around the ship, inflating the sails as the crew scampered up masts, and the Captain bellowed orders.

Qing hopped along the rail toward the magician. He twisted his head to each side, seeming to wait for an invitation.

"Come along. It is time for a nap."

⌣

As the sun set, a panorama of dark crimson and cerulean blue painted the horizon, and a light wind ruffled the waves as a reminder of how playful the sea could be. The *Zelda* creaked and rocked in rhythm, slowly plowing forward toward Singapore as the crew lit the running lamps, and their light reflected across the water before dissolving into the gathering darkness.

The salon door scraped open, and Celwyn entered, inhaling the yeasty scent of rolls and fried fish. Their culinary fare would gradually become more limited over the next few days. Already water rations had been cut back. On a brighter note, the wine supply seemed quite healthy and varied. He sampled tonight's offering: dry, with earthy tones.

This evening the Kangs occupied his table along with a dithering Mrs. Caruthers, who already appeared to be tipsy, as evidenced by her inability to focus and remember his name. She was also missing one pearl earring. The magician hoped it hadn't ended up in her soup.

"My dear Mr. Shelton, do you know how many more days it will—" she hiccupped, patted her mouth with her napkin and continued, "be until we arrive at our des—des—" she tried again, "destin—"

"Destination? I believe it is another five to six days," Celwyn said.

Dinner continued uneventfully until Mrs. Caruthers tried to spear the last piece of fish on her plate. The piece inched away from her fork. She blinked and narrowed her eyes. The piece was back next to her roll, where it had started.

Kang leaned closer and said in Celwyn's ear, "Must you?"

Celwyn shrugged. "Perhaps a competitive game of cards this evening would alleviate my boredom?"

"It could," Kang said. "Let's have a cigar outside first." He kissed Elizabeth's cheek. "Excuse me, my dear."

As the magician rose, Mrs. Caruthers pulled at his sleeve. "Will you return later, Mr. Sheldon?"

Celwyn patted her hand. "Of course I will, Madam." He silently suggested that she retire for the evening after she finished her fish.

Other than a pair of crewmen in the yardarms, they were alone on deck. Celwyn drew his coat closed. The chill of the ice fields had been left behind, but the wind wanted to embrace him with icy hands. To the south in the far distance, he could just spy a faint light. Kang saw it too.

"Daniil Island?"

The magician thought about it. "Possible."

Kang handed him a cigar and lit his own. "I've never visited that area but understand it is still wild and the food unsanitary."

"It also has a fairly active volcano." Celwyn squinted. "That could be what we are seeing."

A moment passed in compatible silence while they puffed on excellent tobacco, the only sound the gentle slapping of the waves against the hull.

"Tell me, have you always wandered the world aimlessly? Do you have a family?"

The magician laughed, noting the hollowness of it. "Is there a Mrs. Celwyn? I can just hear the introduction: 'become enamored of Jonas Celwyn if you enjoy danger and odd occurrences every day.' No, there isn't anyone."

"Was there someone once?"

Celwyn noticed his new friend was a perceptive and persistent little bugger. He stared into the vast darkness, no longer seeing the distant light of what might be Daniil Island's volcano.

"A long time ago, I was in love. Betrothed and deliriously happy. She died."

Kang relit his cigar and waited. The magician couldn't remember telling anyone this story, but he relived it every time he saw a woman with the same auburn hair and musical laugh—and when he realized the profile he had glimpsed wasn't Suzanne.

"Sometimes beauty is a distraction from the quality within. Sometimes that is all one looks for. Suzanne had the special internal quality and intelligence that made her beauty more intense, even more than what observers saw. Particularly so when she smiled at me." He eyed the automat. "At times when I'm reminded of her, or especially morose, I torture myself with her image." The magician opened his hand, and a few feet away, a transparent image of a woman appeared, hovering a few inches off the deck. Her diaphanous dress blew softly in the breeze as she leaned over the railing.

"Blimey!!" More expletives came from the rigging above, and one of the sailors pointed.

Instantly the image disappeared.

"And that is a demonstration of how sea myths are born." Kang rolled his eyes and waited a moment in case the sailor decided to come down and check further. "She was beautiful. Where did you meet?"

"In London at Prince Albert's charity horse race. Suzanne was quite small and couldn't see through the guards standing in front of her. I moved them out of her way." Celwyn hesitated as he remembered. "She sent me a look. Somehow, she knew I'd done something. We spoke and were never apart for more than a few hours after that."

Kang flipped his cigar butt into the sea, and they heard a brief sizzle. "What happened?"

Celwyn studied the water as it rose and fell, to and fro, the years blended into a continual loop. Faces swam by and faded again. Through it all, the pain still pierced his heart as intensely as if it had occurred only moments ago.

"Suzanne knew of my talents and the unpleasantness that sometimes surrounded me. Did I mention I composed an opera for her?" The magician glanced at Kang, who regarded him intently.

"It wouldn't surprise me."

So light as to be barely ascertainable, the melody from a flotilla of oboes passed by them and out over the waves again.

"One evening, Suzanne witnessed an unfortunate incident where a man died very near the Notre Dame cathedral. Right at her feet." Celwyn once more inhaled the sight as clearly as the night it happened. "Because of the circumstances, it became necessary to break the man's neck. After he fell from my grasp, she looked into my eyes and said she had to leave. To get away from me." The magician swallowed the emotion that threatened and whispered, "At that moment, she hated me."

"Why did you kill the man?" Kang asked as one of the waiters came out of the salon and threw a bucket of liquid over the side.

Celwyn shrugged. "He was a crazed opium addict who had accosted us and held a knife to her heart. Breaking his neck was merely a reaction. But she said she couldn't be with me ... because I killed." The magician's voice deadened. "There's more. Even before that, a fine mist had grown between us. I suspected she was already a beautiful sun in someone else's sky. Just a feeling, mind you."

"And?"

"She had developed a way of blocking her thoughts when near me … so that I couldn't read what she was thinking."

"You shouldn't be reading her thoughts."

"I know."

They had begun a promenade around the deck and neared the stern. Raucous singing echoed from the crew's quarters below decks.

"When did she die?"

"A few hours later, courtesy of a disgruntled vampire, Charles Delgado. He'd attempted an attack weeks before," Celwyn breathed deeply. "And the night she left me, he succeeded." Kang didn't need to know that when the magician had found her, she'd still been alive or that he had tenderly kissed her for the last time. If Celwyn told him of this, Kang would ask why he didn't save her. That would be another story for another time, and only when the magician felt ready to tell it.

From his silence, Kang probably assumed something as maudlin as what Celwyn hadn't said. "What happened to the vampire?" he asked.

They had finished the circuit and once again leaned over the starboard rail, the cold spray from the waves brushing them with a light touch. At least this part of the story Celwyn enjoyed.

"He met an untimely end in a most spectacular manner. Most of Paris saw him descend from the Black Tower trussed like a rotting sausage in a net.

As the sun rose on high, he turned to flame above the crowds." Celwyn's expression burned also. "A pity, though. I really should have taken my time to kill him."

Kang eyed Celwyn like he would one of his experiments. "And since then, you've wandered the world seeking adventures? Sometimes inventing the adventures?"

"An excellent description."

"That is all?" Kang asked. "You do not have a vocation? Saboteur, composer, or...?" He slapped the magician on the back. "Elizabeth is waiting, and I must retire for the night. It would do you good to employ restraint and patience, my friend."

"Why?"

"So that you don't draw the wrong kind of attention. As an example, there could be another vampire who might wish to avenge Mr. Delgado. If Talos and I knew of you, others do also."

Chapter 7

SEVEN DAYS AFTER DEPARTING THE ice fields, the *Zelda* sailed into the Bay of Singapore under a hot and cloudless sky. The crew had made amazed comments about how the entire time strong wind had filled their sails.

Celwyn took off his hat and enjoyed the view from the bow, the breeze lifting his hair and whistling around the deck. To the north, hundreds of colorful taipans, small skiffs, and larger vessels decorated the harbor like colorful confetti had been tossed across the water. In the port itself, the dock workers appeared tiny compared to the ships as they winched cargo aboard them. Rows of buildings lined the wharf, and behind them, clusters of houses covered the hillsides amid lush greenery. The magician inhaled deeply. Something smelled intriguing, too; spicy without being overwhelming.

Just as he came to that conclusion, Mrs. Pearse arrived at his elbow. As usual, she held a parasol decorated with bows and lace to match her flowery frock.

After pleasantries had been exchanged, Celwyn asked, "May I inquire why are you traveling to Singapore, Madam?"

Her jowls twitched into a prim and determined smile. "Annabelle will be presented to Colony society at their Spring Ball. Of course, she will be betrothed within a month's time." With a twirl of her parasol, she strolled a few steps toward the stern and back. "It will be a grand occasion, and she will wear the latest fashions and a strand of pearls the Queen herself has lent me. My late husband was related to her, of course." The woman's thoughts continued in a tumble of self-importance mixed with worry.

I should have been a duchess... There had better be no more talk from Annabelle about becoming a nurse. Or a singer! Or any other horrid idea... I must remember to buy the right color gloves...

The woman's internal dialog reminded him that he'd heard Annabelle crying as he walked by their cabin earlier. He looked around for Kang, his new conscience. He wasn't in sight. Celwyn controlled the urge to meddle in the old woman's plans. It really wasn't his affair. However, Mrs. Pearse's parasol somehow flew out of her hand and rolled toward the salon. The magician pretended not to see it. She waddled after it. Every time she reached the parasol, it rolled away again. The magician had been told before that he was easily entertained. A true observation, of course.

An hour later, the passengers prepared to disembark as twin tugboats towed the *Zelda* to the dock. The Kangs joined Celwyn at the rail, shading their eyes from the sun as the breeze fluttered Elizabeth's hat and brought a becoming blush to her cheeks.

"What will you do in Singapore, Mr. Celwyn?" she asked.

The magician gestured toward the city. "Patronize the museums, the art galleries, and perhaps tour a few of the gardens. I'm fond of many varieties of jasmine and heirloom roses." He watched a red and orange sampan inch away from the dock. "Then I'll arrange for a carriage to Skudai and board the *Royal Victoria* heading west. My destination is beyond Constantinople." Celwyn detested humidity. "Paris … is a possibility."

"Interesting prospects." Elizabeth winked at Kang and kissed his cheek. "I must freshen up before we disembark. *Au revoir* for now, Mr. Celwyn."

Kang watched her walk away and said, "We owe you a great deal. I've taken the liberty of securing a suite for you at the Raffles Hotel. It is named after Stamford Raffles, founder of Singapore."

"Thank you for your generosity." The magician bowed to Kang.

As he spoke, Colonel Gilliam strolled by with a disdainful look at the automat and a sneer for Celwyn. This could be because the magician had not allowed him to cheat at cards last evening. Kang had probably done little besides not appearing to be a privileged Englishman. Celwyn wiggled his nose, and the Colonel's suspenders snapped and his trousers dropped to his ankles. The older man's choice in underwear had a patriotic flair with bright red, white, and blue stripes. As Mrs. Pearse rounded the corner and skidded to a stop, her shriek could have been heard in Jurang Park five miles away. Colonel Gilliam hustled away, holding his trousers as high as they would go, with Mrs. Pearse flinging another invective at him.

Kang stared at the magician.

"Did I grow another nose?" Celwyn asked.

"I've been wanting to ask…" Kang still stared. "What occurs when someone you know ages and dies? How difficult is it for you to watch that?"

The magician sighed, turning an irritated look upon automat. "I'm not sure what you want to know, but if I've stayed too long in one place, I do become involved with the people there. If I become fond of someone, I try not to be."

"Because you know they will eventually die and leave you."

Celwyn glared. "Damn it! Do you think I haven't looked at people and wished they could live?" He gestured, and a row of crates on the dock toppled over. "I wrestle with how much I should interfere with destiny, or time, whatever you would call it. How can I not?"

"Indeed."

"Don't 'indeed' me." The magician half-smiled and stared at the crates until they again sat upright to the shock and consternation of the dockworkers beside them. A few scratched their heads. A few more ran for the nearby trees as fast as they could.

Kang said, "I understand a bit more about why you have traveled so much. Because it becomes too painful to stay, perhaps."

"Perhaps."

The *Zelda* blasted her horn three times and kissed the dock with a solid bump. The activity below the ship increased as dozens of crewmen secured the lines, and more of the crew ran across the deck. After a few minutes, a collection of waiting officials climbed the gangplank.

Kang eyed Celwyn. "If you can restrain yourself from extravagant displays before you leave the city, perhaps your journey will be uneventful." He nodded to Mrs. Caruthers as she brushed by and lowered his voice. "I only make the suggestion because I would propose that we travel with you, and I would prefer a quiet trip. Our eventual destination is Paris also. This is, of course, after we ascertain Elizabeth's mother has recovered."

The frantic activity on the dock continued, and they watched an overloaded cart of boxes tip forward, spilling melons across the quayside road.

"This proposal is most welcome." Celwyn was surprised at how much enjoyment he felt at the prospect of the Kangs' company. He pointed at the melons. "That wasn't me. I look forward to your companionship on the journey. Is your wife aware of how long and difficult it will be?"

"She is. While still a child, she lived in Bangladesh and then Singapore before moving to San Francisco. I met her there years later." They watched the workers chase and corral the melons. "She has always wanted to travel the other way, west across the British Indian Empire."

"It is settled then."

The sun rose higher as the noon hour approached, and the colorful scene below became more intense. Instead of the odor of fish rot found in most ports, Celwyn inhaled ginger and something very green and fresh overlaid with the clean saltiness of the bay.

Beside him, Kang lit his pipe and seemed to finally relax. Gone was his intense scrutiny of everything and the jumpiness that characterized his vigilance. His jacket appeared recently pressed, and he wore a cream-colored cravat that had most likely been tied by his wife. Celwyn had no one fussing over his appearance and made do with a looking glass. Nonetheless, he knew he must find a barber in Singapore before embarking on the next leg of his journey. He rubbed his chin and contemplated possibly shaving his beard, but the ladies seemed to appreciate it — such a dilemma.

As the two men watched the various goings-on from the deck, all of a sudden, an itching sensation crawled up the magician's back like a line of erratic fire ants. Celwyn swiveled. Behind him, the Captain huddled with a collection of dock officials over a manifest. Nearby, several of the porters smoked as they lounged against the bulkhead, awaiting word to begin moving the passengers' trunks. The sensation stopped, and immediately Kang tensed.

"What is it?" Celwyn murmured at him.

Kang dropped his pipe and took his time picking it up. Just as Celwyn had, he scanned the area behind them. "I could say nothing, but you should know." He continued to stare at the variety of people behind them. "A long time ago, I battled someone evil, much worse than Talos. That was the last time I felt the same frisson of unease I experienced just now."

Celwyn glanced behind them again. "It isn't just your fancy. I felt it, too."

"If we had tails, they'd be raising right now."

"What does this man look like?" the magician asked.

"I do not know."

"Nonsense! How can you not know?"

Kang lowered his voice and drew the magician to the side, further away from the crew and others. "Weeks ago, I thought it couldn't be true, even that, perhaps, it was you who'd left that walnut in my cabin after we sailed from San Francisco."

"A walnut? I saw it. And your suspicious looks."

"Considering your talents and the antics of my brother, you can't blame me." Kang shrugged. "The evil I mentioned has a habit of leaving a trail of walnuts as an obscure form of a calling card: only those familiar with him and his deeds would recognize the significance." His eyes darted around the deck. "And be afraid."

Celwyn studied each of the faces of those close by and then transferred his scrutiny to the dock immediately below the *Zelda*. "Tell me more about him."

"It is said that wealthy and powerful forces from industry hire him. However, he usually has a personal agenda. Some say it was he who sunk the *Merrimack* during the American's civil war. On the Continent and in Asia, there are court intrigues in which he participates—in fact, he seems to relish those the most. Most recently, his activities have centered on stealing something valuable."

"Such as a new weapon for war?" Celwyn watched a man as big as a walrus, and shaped like one, sidle up to the porter stationed at the bottom of the gangplank. His suit looked so tight; it was a wonder he could walk. When he whispered something in the porter's ear, the porter's expression of annoyance changed as he turned pale and began licking his lips. The walrus man smiled and trudged up the gangplank, which sagged under his weight. Celwyn had a premonition that they would encounter him before too long.

He faced Kang.

"Have you hidden the description of your weapon?"

"Yes." He tapped his chest. "I am well padded."

Celwyn studied Kang with a raised brow. Not a very original solution, but it seemed better than leaving it in his cabin. "Could you recreate everything in it if you had to?"

"It would take quite a while, but yes, even without my notes. Let us talk of something else."

"All right. Do you smell that?" the magician asked.

"What is it?"

"Nutmeg. It is from a nearby plantation."

"It makes the city even more enchanting," Kang said.

They studied the imaginative costumes of the vendors and a half-dozen solemn monks standing beside as many donkeys. Well-dressed women sported hats that seemed to favor ostrich feathers, and the ornate uniforms of the military officers displayed so many medals and ribbons they could have tipped over from the weight. On the dock, much of the aristocracy remained hidden inside ornate carriages. Celwyn counted at least five other ships, either disembarking or embarking, along with the *Zelda*. The quay made a hive of bees seem rather dull by comparison.

Into the fray, a long scream split the air followed by shouts and running steps across the boards of the *Zelda*. Kang and Celwyn ran aft and turned toward the leeside cabins. The screams increased in pitch and volume as they pushed into the crowd.

Kang yelped. Out of the corner of his eye, the magician saw him tumble face first over the rail. Celwyn whirled. He stopped the automat's fall just inches above the water and quickly tossed a rope to him in case there were observers. As he hauled him back up, Celwyn hoped that, amid all the commotion, no one had noticed that nothing had suspended Kang above the water before he grabbed the rope.

Celwyn pulled him by the collar over the rail and back onto the deck. "Who pushed you?" he demanded quietly, certain this was no accident.

Kang straightened his jacket and tie while assessing the nearby crew and passengers. "I do not know, but they were quick and strong. Oh, my." He pointed. "It appears the excitement is centered on your room."

"Curses!" Celwyn kept Kang in front of him as they elbowed their way forward. Beyond the Captain's rather large stomach, the magician could see through the open door of his cabin, which he had closed, and the pair of boots, toes up, on his bed. Under normal circumstances, the internal chatter in others' minds could be regulated to a dull hum in the background, but give them a dash of bloody mystery, and an uproar always ensued. Even Mrs. Caruthers' demure and scattered internal voice became as piercing as a hot poker.

The magician shook his head: the public would be surprised at the language some of the most innocent, well-bred people knew. Colorful profanities, animal habits, and husbandry, along with a lack of knowledge of anatomy, were common. The clamor became so loud Celwyn couldn't think.

"Please!" he admonished them and stepped around the Captain. Kang leaned around his other side and froze.

Colonel Gilliam lay on the magician's bunk with his throat slit. Blood dribbled off the bedclothes and inched its way across the floor as the ship rocked at anchor. The man's eyes remained wide open in dread of what he last saw. Celwyn noted that either the colonel or another intruder had been rummaging through his things: one of his dress shirts lay halfway out of his traveling trunk.

A syrupy voice, and foul breath reminiscent of rotting eggs, came from right behind the magician.

"Is this your room, Sir?"

Not often did Celwyn encounter someone as tall as he. The magician backed out of the room, putting a bit of distance between himself and the walrus in the tight blue suit. Kang stayed close by, likely still aware of his recent tumble over the side. Celwyn hadn't forgotten his unplanned dive either, and between that and the murdered man in his bed, it seemed prudent to keep track of Kang. Of all things, he had become fond of him and did not want to lose him. Kang raised an eyebrow, indicating what Celwyn didn't know.

The magician spied the brim of Elizabeth Kang's hat edging closer through the crowd. He pointed. Kang grasped her arm and turned her away from the cabin.

Celwyn bowed. "Jonas Celwyn lately of San Francisco. Yes, it is my room."

Walrus man's double chins rivaled those of Mrs. Pearse, and they jiggled as he bounced on the balls of his feet, a typical pose of a boxer or brawler. Celwyn suspected the latter.

"Mr. Celwyn, I am Lieutenant Dooney, chief authority of the city police." His brogue thickened the air. "We seem to have a fine mess here, wouldn't you say?"

The crowd behind them had grown, and nearly all the ship's porters, crew, passengers, and officials had gathered outside the cabin along with their noisy thoughts. Some became audible to all.

"You know, the Colonel cheated at cards."

"...he pinched my derriere as I sat down to dinner..."

"Why was he in Mr. Celwyn's room?"

Lt. Dooney used a fingertip to lift Gilliam's collar and let it fall. "Captain? Please come here."

The Captain didn't come into the room but stopped in the doorway, where he had no trouble viewing the body.

"Can you identify the diseased?"

"Yes. It is Colonel Gilliam." The Captain had seen the blood and turned as green as if he had a bad case of seasickness.

"Were you aware of any animosity against him? Any disagreements?"

The Captain wouldn't meet the magician's gaze and cleared his throat.

"I heard he cheated Mr. Celwyn at cards."

The magician snorted. Not likely. The urge to pin the Captain's hat to his ears became an attractive idea.

Kang had come closer, coughed, and spoke up in a clear voice loud enough not to be ignored.

"If I may? Colonel Gilliam attempted to defraud most of the passengers at cards, one at a time. Please interview them. If that is the criteria, everyone is a suspect. I also wouldn't consider his antics as a motive for something this extreme."

The policeman peered down at Kang. "And you are?"

"Professor Xiau Kang, traveling with my wife." As he spoke, Kang shot Celwyn a *be patient* look.

Celwyn swallowed the inventive idea he had just decided upon. It was going to be a bother to have a voice of reason at his elbow, but logical. It would be a more pleasant stay in the city if he weren't harassed by the constabulary.

Mrs. Tarryton's voice, without any oinking as before, broke into his thoughts.

"Then why was the Colonel in Mr. Celwyn's room?"

She had ducked around the policeman's rear end to share her observation. When she saw the body, she retreated and hovered behind her husband.

"That is an excellent question, Madam. Perhaps Mr. Celwyn will accompany me to our headquarters where we can discuss it."

That will not happen. As Lt. Dooney reached for his elbow and Celwyn readied himself to set fire to his hand, a vision in pink chiffon and lace inserted herself between them. Annabelle hooked an arm through the magician's and bestowed a deceptively sweet smile on Lt. Dooney. "I'm sure that won't be necessary."

The policeman tried to bow but couldn't do more than bend forward. "Miss."

Annabelle looked up to Celwyn with a love-struck glint in her eye. "My betrothed, Mr. Celwyn, has other plans for this afternoon."

Although unexpected, this could prove interesting. Celwyn deposited an appreciative peck on his newly betrothed's cheek.

Lt. Dooney wedged a pencil between his fingers and posed a notebook under his nose. "Your name please, Miss?"

"Annabelle Pearse Edmunds." She waited for him to laboriously write each letter. "My uncle is the American ambassador for Singapore. You wouldn't deny him the pleasure of meeting his new nephew-in-law, would you?"

Lt. Dooney licked his lips. "There is a dead body in his room."

"Do you know anything about it?" Annabelle asked Celwyn.

"No."

She batted her lashes at the policeman. "There you are. We really must be on our way. It is nearly noon now."

As if they'd rehearsed it a dozen times, and with the Kangs in front of them, Annabelle and Celwyn strolled toward the stern, ready to descend the gangplank. The magician could feel Lt. Dooney's stare burning the back of his head and clearly hear his unspoken opinion of Annabelle's figure. His doubts about Celwyn's pedigree did not sound very inventive either.

Oh drat: Dooney intended to send a telegraph to Rome inquiring about Mr. Jonas Celwyn. The magician's stay in Singapore would have to be a short one.

Chapter 8

AS THEY APPROACHED THE GANG-plank, the Kangs awaited them. Annabelle dropped her hand from the magician's arm and replaced the adoring look she had granted him with something else.

"Mr. Celwyn, I'm fairly certain you did not murder that man. However, it may be best that we leave here before that oaf becomes tiresome. I understand from Elizabeth that you intend to take a coach to Skudai, and then board the *Royal Victoria* traveling west. Please book passage for me also."

Celwyn looked at Kang. He shrugged and looked at Elizabeth.

"What about your aunt?" Celwyn asked.

Annabelle stamped her foot. "To hell with my aunt." She lifted her skirts and stepped onto the gangplank, allowing the magician to steady her against the roll of the ship. "I assume that your gratitude for my assistance in dealing with the police will extend to spiriting me out of the city before my aunt discovers I am gone."

Kang smirked as he escorted Elizabeth ahead of them. Celwyn ignored him.

"As you wish, Miss Annabelle," the magician said. She hadn't any way of knowing he required no assistance in dealing with the police. But the automat did and found the situation amusing. No matter. They could either depart before Annabelle attached herself to them or send her back on the first carriage returning to Singapore when they were safely away from Lt. Dooney.

Of more interest seemed to be the attempt on Kang's life and the conveniently placed corpse in the magician's quarters. Furthermore, it didn't seem to occur to anyone that Lt. Dooney had arrived *before* the body had been discovered.

From high above the bar of the Raffles Hotel, a crystal chandelier as large as a small boat bathed the room in warm light. Chinese, Malay, and English art covered the walls, shaped the furniture, and painted conversations. The magician especially admired the enormous, gilded mirror behind the bar that afforded him a view of everyone in the room without turning around. The establishment only served men, guaranteeing that he and Kang would not have to explain their plans to Annabelle until they were ready. As he sipped a fine Courvoisier, the magician moved to make room for the automat on the next barstool.

Kang glanced behind them and then at each of the occupied tables before addressing Celwyn.

"We must talk." The mechanical man appeared more preoccupied than usual: the waiter had to ask twice what he wanted to drink.

"About the attempt to kill you, or who butchered Colonel Gilliam?"

The automat swallowed air and said, "I am afraid."

A tanned gentleman with silver hair settled into the seat next to Kang. Then a Pakistani in a flamboyant suit of flamingo pink and green joined him. They delved into a deep conversation about the recent antics of a Judge Bao from the Di Gong An story collection. The magician's interest peaked: this threatened to become fascinating, but Kang finally began speaking.

"I can't be sure if I am the target or if you are, but my analysis concludes that the killing of Gilliam and the attack on me are connected. It could be a test to see what you would do if I were threatened. To see what you are capable of."

"By whom?"

"The evil I alluded to earlier on the ship." Kang tossed back his drink. "I won't call him a man because he isn't one. It has been more than a hundred years since my last encounter with someone I knew as Jax. Unlike you, he isn't immortal in a physical sense. But the essence of him assumes a human physical vessel for as long as he chooses. Then he leaves that vessel to occupy another, and then another. That would make him extremely versatile for a multitude of activities."

"And undetectable because no one knows what he looked like."

Kang blinked several times before saying, "He could be anyone, even a woman."

"Or a Singapore policeman." Celwyn surveyed the room and verified that the conversation at Kang's elbow continued as they discussed someone called Moriarity. In his own experience, fiction was sometimes the actual truth. "But it wouldn't be logical for Jax to assume so obvious or public a personage."

Kang thought a moment. "Or would it?"

The possibilities threatened to give the magician a headache. For several minutes they sat and watched the clientele of the bar amid the clink of glasses. Bursts of laughter emanated from a gathering of university lads in the corner. As Celwyn watched them he asked, "Do you think that Jax is after your, ah, discovery?"

Kang shrugged and sipped his whiskey. "It could be something else. He could have been engaged by one of your enemies. Or mine."

That would broaden the field of suspects significantly, Celwyn mused. He wondered if it was a personal animosity or a professional one. Over the years, several other magicians jealous of his abilities had tried to eliminate him. On a different front, a few women had thought of him as their exclusive property and held grudges long after each affair had concluded.

"Or it might be someone who hired Talos and now wishes to finish the job of killing you," Celwyn said and waved for refills. "You are aware that I would have no problem in dispatching any of our enemies, but we must identify them."

"And protect Elizabeth." He eyed the magician with a glint of amusement. "And your new ward, Annabelle."

Celwyn made a face. "Thank you for the reminder."

"It would be prudent to make a plan for our defense."

"Where is Qing?"

"In my suite upstairs. Why?"

"Have you trained him for anything?" the magician asked as he studied the crowd.

"No, but he is very intelligent."

"He could be useful." The magician thought about the possibilities. "Perhaps to let us know when we're being watched. Or in case of an attack." Celwyn could picture Qing swooping in to give someone a good peck on the nose.

"You should arrange that with him." Kang smiled. "Beware: he has his own peculiar habits."

"As do we all." Celwyn slid a glass over to the automat. "But I suspect it won't be as easy to rid ourselves of Annabelle."

A bark of laughter erupted behind them. Through the haze of cigar smoke, Celwyn spied the Captain of the *Zelda* deep in conversation with one of the men who had boarded the ship just as she docked. His companion had the vivid red hair of an Irishman and flushed face and bulbous nose of a confirmed drinker. "That is a Lloyds of London investigator."

"How do you know that?" Kang protested. "How can I be as useful as you when I can't read someone's thoughts?"

"You have the extremely logical mind that I lack. The Lloyd's insignia is just peeking out of the right side of his shirt collar. See it?"

Kang squinted. "Yes. You must have excellent eyesight."

"I do."

"Conspiracies. Conspiracies," Kang said. "Do you think it is a coincidence those two are in the same bar and hotel as we are?"

Celwyn held up a finger, signaling for him to wait, and strode to the frosted windows overlooking the street. As he appeared to gaze outside, he stood much closer to the men. After a few moments, he returned, patted a yawn, and said, "You don't want to know what they're conversing about: it would destroy your faith in someone of authority. And no, it isn't a coincidence. Both of them are curious about us."

The hotel concierge rushed into the room wearing an impeccable white plantation suit, a delicate carnation in his lapel, and a broad smile for Kang. He bowed. "Professor Kang, your travel plans have been confirmed. Mr. Celwyn, yours and your niece's also. Please let me know if I can be of further assistance."

Celwyn murmured a suggestion in Kang's ear and blocked the room's view of the concierge and Kang.

"Sir, if you would be so kind as to let us know if there are any inquiries about our destination, it would be appreciated." The concierge didn't bat an eye as Kang handed over a collection of coins. "And you will be further rewarded if you can identify whoever is curious about us."

As the concierge departed, Kang slid off the barstool and shook his trousers down. "I've got to take Elizabeth to see her mother. It would be best to get this over with. The old woman hates me, and if we are to disembark soon, she needs to visit with her now."

Kang walked through the ornate doors of the bar and the Captain and the Lloyd's investigator both pretended interest in their drinks as he walked by. No matter. Celwyn had already decided to shadow Kang to his rendezvous at his mother-in-law's. It would be instructional to see who else followed him.

Chapter 9

THE PORT OF SINGAPORE HAD GROWN over the years. Much of the commercial district displayed stately brick buildings with colonial columns, and the residential streets portrayed a variety of cultures and architecture, such as some fine Tibetan-style houses behind manicured trees. Celwyn stopped and admired the Parliament House with its three stories of glorious pillars and buttresses. As he continued on, the business district gave way to taller buildings and intricate passages between quaint streets. Whiffs of donkey mixed with rose gardens.

After twenty minutes, the Kangs mounted a short flight of steps to a well-kept house behind ornamental gardens.

From between two buildings further down the street, Celwyn leaned against a wall to keep watch. For an hour, no one approached the house or even glanced at it. He backed away and went to find the tailor shop in the maze of shops he'd just passed through. A bolt of crimson velvet in the window called to him, promising the possibility of a new smoking jacket.

When he was ready to return to his observation post, for reconnaissance purposes, he joined a group of students standing on a nearby corner, chattering like magpies about their evening plans. Their blue uniforms reminded him of Edinburgh's elite school, Barnaby's, and his own notorious youth. He had learned early on that a magician's life never would be dull but full of poetry, music, and justice.

As they neared Oxbow Street, Celwyn faded back into the doorway of a shop selling women's gloves and thanked his customary luck he hadn't walked a mite faster. Lt. Dooney had just turned onto the street, waddling purposely forward with a pair of smaller policemen in his wake.

The magician frowned. Under no circumstances did this bode well. Celwyn side-stepped down a parallel avenue, counting houses. In seconds, he had vaulted a wall and entered the rear yard of the house where Kang and Elizabeth should be. As he mounted the steps of the back porch, Elizabeth's voice came through clearly, with more patience than Celwyn would be capable of, as she explained to Lt. Dooney that they had no idea of where Celwyn could be, and that it was preposterous for anyone to disturb her mother like this.

The policeman persisted. Then Elizabeth's mother joined in, her voice shrill with annoyance as she addressed the intruders in old school English. Lt. Dooney growled something disrespectful at Kang and became more aggressive, suggesting the Kangs accompany him to the police station.

When faced with an opportunity to provide a distraction, the magician always tried to make it appropriate and tasteful. Of course, music would accompany the scene to make it memorable, too. He was reminded of one of his favorite quotes from Victor Hugo: *Music expresses that which cannot be said and on which it is impossible to be silent.*

Silent it would not be. A solitary deep cry could be heard from the front yard of the house. Then a chorus of loud braying arose in harmony, accompanied by the rich tones of French horns. The raucous noise and horns increased in volume: a duet of sorts.

Celwyn entered the house from the rear. If he had been privy to the automat's thoughts, he would wager that, at the moment, Kang probably decried his methods but also appreciated that the magician must be nearby.

The magician's view through the parlor provided an excellent picture of the house's front yard. A dozen water buffaloes milled about, all extraordinarily fat, and because the magician couldn't resist, the face of each one resembled Lt. Dooney to a degree. When the buffalos brayed, the French horns resounded. Lt. Dooney rushed out the front door to join the other policemen as they waded into the herd. Celwyn increased the volume of the horns.

Kang turned and saw the magician standing in the parlor. He rolled his eyes and nodded before glancing at Elizabeth, who gaped open-mouthed at the scene outside. Despite the nurse's remonstrations, her mother hobbled to the window and cursed the policemen in loud and colorful Mandarin. Kang's wide-eyed expression showed that he'd never heard his mother-in-law like this before. With an amused smile, he pivoted and joined Celwyn.

In a low voice, he said, "Thank you. I believe that cretin intended to arrest me to get to you." He watched the spectacle unfold in the yard. "It would be best if we left Singapore at once. Elizabeth wants to stay with her mother. I told her it may be for an extended time." He couldn't help but peek at the scene in the yard. "She will be safer here until we return without whoever pursues you. Or me." One of the larger water buffaloes slapped Lt. Dooney in the face with its tail. "I assume this display will end after we leave?"

"Of course."

"Then let me say goodbye to Elizabeth."

While he was doing so, Lt. Dooney slipped and fell in the growing mess in the front yard. The two policemen tried to lift him, but he fell back again accompanied by indelicate sound effects. The magician wondered, *My my, how did that happen?*

Kang returned and tugged on his arm. "Enough theatre, Jonas. We must depart."

As they made haste up the neighboring street toward the harbor, Kang asked, "How long will the water buffalos remain?"

"A few more minutes, then the garden will return to its former beauty, which may cause further consternation."

They increased their strides. Celwyn asked, "Who knew you were here?"

"I told the hotel desk."

Celwyn raised a brow at him. "We must be a bit more circumspect until we're on the train."

Kang snorted. "You, of all people, telling *me* to be less noticeable?" He trotted faster. "The police will be watching the hotel. How will we get back inside?"

"With our ingenuity." Celwyn loved to dress up. Costumes could be nearly as much fun as magic.

"We do have that."

"There are many vendors between here and the hotel. We'll find hats, spectacles, and other items. Or I can make things, too." He sighed. "Because we're leaving in a hurry, the jacket I ordered will have to be cancelled."

They crossed the street in front of a bicycle cart. The driver had stacked a dozen hats upon his head becoming a movable vendor of haberdashery. Kang made a point of checking the streets behind them before speaking. "It will be helpful if we enter the hotel from different doors and not at the same time."

The magician had decided upon a matronly woman's costume, one flowery and fluffy in honor of Mrs. Pearse.

Hours later, they dined in Kang's suite with the lights turned low. Qing sat on the table between them, preening and admiring his reflection in the silverware. Once, heavy steps stopped outside the door. Celwyn held a finger in front of his lips, signaling quiet, as someone tried the handle and found it locked. A few moments more and the heavy steps continued down the hallway.

Their request for secrecy seemed to appeal to their waiter's sense of intrigue, for he provided post-prandial cigars and a wink without being asked. Alone again, they smoked and enjoyed a delightful view of the harbor at night.

Qing sat on the magician's shoulder. When he puffed on the cigar, the bird hacked in his ear. Celwyn gave the mechanical bird a look. "Is this one of his annoying habits you mentioned?"

"Just one of them," Kang said. "Back to our current dilemma. Are you sure Annabelle will journey with us?" A myriad of lights from the boats twinkled across the water like the sky had been inverted onto the water, and a parade of barges cruised by in silence. Against the darkness, the music from several party boats seemed jarring and immediate. "Is she still intent on escaping her aunt?"

"Wouldn't you be?" Celwyn said. "I talked with her when we checked in here, and she made her own reservations for the *Royal Victoria* under a false name. I cancelled the ones we had made for her."

Kang relit his cigar and asked, "That is helpful. Are we to pretend not to know her or be the type, and gender, of traveling companions that would not meet with society's approval?"

"A complicated dilemma."

Kang shrugged. "We do make rather an odd pair."

The magician stared at the water for a moment. "Where have you traveled?"

"If you mean by water, not far enough. To Japan and Singapore, then back to the Americas." Kang thought for a minute. "I enjoy traveling across the north Atlantic and braving the elements there. But, on a very big ship, mind you."

"I hear there are several new ocean liners under construction now. I prefer comfort too. Not bouncing across to the Jersey Islands in a toy boat with a crazy captain who drinks more than he eats."

Kang laughed. "*You* get seasick?"

"I certainly did that time. We were being shot at by Nelson's British forces, and my inebriated French companions didn't help any. The crew missed the appointed passage through the rocks, and I had to use magic to keep us upright and out of the water."

Kang lit another cigar. "Pretend I can understand how magic works. Describe what you can do and can't do."

"Could you be more specific, please? It is more of an art than the science you are used to." Celwyn had heard requests similar to this before, the last being from a one-eyed jailor in the Black Tower of Paris as they played cards in one of the cells all night. Glassmort lost so much money that night that he tried to leave the magician locked in the cell.

"I'm not interested in the parlor tricks common conjurers perform. I can tell the difference between them and someone such as you."

Across the water, a cannon boomed. Just once. Perhaps a warning from one ship to another. Celwyn regarded Xiau through lowered lids. As much as he nagged him, his new friend had a very open mind to phenomena and things not easily explained. As he should, considering his origins weren't exactly normal either.

"On a purely physical level, all I can really say is that if I want something to occur, it does. As quickly as I desire it to, usually. For instance..." Celwyn stared at the lamp on the table by the window until it undulated, snake-like, and then subsided. "But could I do that to something across the harbor? Yes and no. I would have to know it was there to manipulate it. I prefer to see what I intend to do."

"And for intricate magic?"

Celwyn smiled. "Ah, there is an interesting subject. It involves many things, some of which I can explain, and others I have done so long I do not question. You are referring to the way I overcame Talos?"

Kang nodded solemnly.

"I promise to explain another time when I am not as tired. Or try to."

"One last question: can you sense danger?"

The magician shrugged. "Not as well as I would like. I'm very observant, but sometimes that is not enough."

"It would be useful to know who killed Gilliam."

"When I checked, generally, no one's thoughts nearby sounded guilty. And I didn't have time to enter each person's mind at the time." Celwyn tried to remember who stood close to the cabin. "My money is on one of the crew who is inhabited by Jax."

"We'll see." Kang stood. "I'd best call a valet and get packed. We leave very early tomorrow."

Celwyn hadn't unpacked. Even though weary, he spent a restless night pouring over the maps of the Orient, the Himalayas, and points west.

What would their journey bring?

Celwyn removed the spectacles from his disguise and his face reverted to its normal state as he strolled outside. From a vantage point at the corner of the building, he stood and waited, moving down a bit further after another aromatic reminder of how much cleanup horses entailed. Only minutes remained before the departure time when Kang's carriage rolled to a stop next to the scheduled departures. His trunks must have been full, judging from the coachman's reddened face and grunts as he unloaded them. Qing stuck his head out of the magician's coat, squeaked a greeting, and then burrowed back inside as the magician approached.

"Good morning. According to the ticket seller, we share the carriage with two others, and Annabelle, if she arrives in time," Celwyn said. The activity in the yard seemed to increase by the moment with overloaded carriages disgorging group after group of passengers. Many of the travelers brought multiple trunks, indicating long journeys. "When you remove that mustache, be sure to get the glue too."

"I will, and good morning." The Professor bowed. "It is a fair distance to Skudai," Kang said as he ripped off the elaborate mustache, lit his pipe, and studied the crowd through puffs of smoke. "I really don't want to climb aboard until we have to; the trip is going to be long enough as it is."

"Agreed." Celwyn nodded absently as he scanned the road leading into the carriage park. The city appeared fully light now, and the street teemed with residents crisscrossing the avenue on their way to market or other worthwhile activities. "It is a four-hour ride, and the *Royal Victoria* departs from Skudai at sundown. We should be able to luncheon at our leisure if all goes well."

The automat handed the magician a flask. "To warm the soul on a dreary morning."

Celwyn gulped and then nearly spit. "This isn't whiskey—"

"Of course not, it is coffee. Courtesy of the hotel staff."

The same ginger-haired gentleman from Lloyds of London that they had observed talking to the *Zelda's* captain walked by, doing his best to hide his face behind his bowler hat. He climbed into their carriage.

"Isn't that interesting?" Celwyn asked.

A Japanese porter strode by, announcing two minutes to departure. At that moment, two things happened simultaneously: Annabelle arrived in a one-person coach which could barely move with its mountain of trunks, and in the distance, another carriage and team of horses rounded a corner nearly on two wheels, racing toward them. Annabelle's driver picked up speed and then lurched to a stop in a hail of flying gravel.

"The plot thickens like bad oatmeal," the magician said as he urged Kang ahead of him. They hustled Annabelle into the Skudai coach and toted her trunks while the driver strapped them onto the roof. Seconds more, and they climbed inside without ceremony.

"Good morning," Celwyn said and noted that Annabelle's traveling hat had even more feathers than the elaborate plumes the coach horses wore. What more, with its lightweight cloth and lace, her costume bespoke summertime, not winter near the Himalayas. By late afternoon she would need to change into something much warmer. She nodded at the other two passengers and greeted Kang and his own worthy self.

As they started moving forward, both Annabelle and Celwyn fingered the drapes aside so they could peer out, hopefully without being seen. "Oh damn," she said with a frown.

Kang peeked. "Indeed." He dropped the drape back in place after seeing the other carriage barreling into the station under billowing clouds of dust. Mrs. Pearse bellowed, leaning halfway out the carriage window with a red face and shouting at her driver. To make matters more interesting, an entourage of police wagons with wailing sirens trailed Mrs. Pearse's transport. It would be interesting to know if the old lady tipped off Lt. Dooney.

Celwyn and company's carriage picked up speed and passed through the gates as the police drove in. The magician flipped a wrist, and the gates closed and locked behind them, trapping their pursuers inside. He dumped over as many nearby crates as he could find in front of the gates for good measure.

Kang and Annabelle both watched the carriage terminal recede with audible sighs of relief.

Celwyn said, "The border for the Idoh province is less than an hour away." He could have added that they would pass through there before the police found a qualified ironworker or demolition man to blow the terminal gate open. More frustrating would be the moment when they discovered there was nothing wrong with the gate after his magic dissipated.

Annabelle nodded, and the frown across her brow smoothed out. She even offered them a tentative smile. "I believe my new life has just begun, Uncle Celwyn and Professor. Thank you for offering to accompany me."

That last tidbit of information may have been for their fellow passengers. Directly across from Celwyn sat the Lloyd's man, as quiet as a devious mouse. He had immediately buried his nose in a thick ledger as the carriage began to move. At close quarters, the man's aftershave reeked of lemons and something less desirable, and his reading glasses seemed to be for show only—they did not appear to be very thick. Celwyn checked the stranger's thoughts: they concentrated on numbers, dates, and ships overdue. *Interesting.* Again he wished he could silently tell the automat things he should know.

The magician noted the swollen and reddened knuckles on the Lloyd's man, which indicated someone used to fisticuffs. In contrast, the man's pristine white shirt fairly glowed within the darkened coach.

Annabelle didn't seem to mind at all the other passenger who sat opposite of her. He was of Indian descent with a great deal of glossy hair, lively eyes, and judging from his ornate costume, he hailed most likely from the Topol province—if Celwyn remembered his visit there correctly. He tugged on his embroidered vest and smiled at everyone, introducing himself before they could catch their breath.

"Sree Jayarama, at your service. I am fifty-three years of age and own my own carpet company in Delhi. It is a beautiful store, and I invite you all to visit!" His contagious smile made even Celwyn's mood a bit lighter.

The automat introduced them, ending with his own, "Professor Xiau Kang, of San Francisco."

After the pleasantries had been exchanged, the magician turned to the Lloyd's man.

"And you, sir?"

Seconds ticked by before the man decided to raise his eyes from the ledger in his lap and face the others. His gaze did not appear friendly, as if he thought they all collectively smelled. In contrast, his voice sounded as smooth and as mellow as a fine single malt scotch.

"Pleased to meet all of you. Miss." He kissed Annabelle's hand. "James McAlistair at your service." Although his voice sounded calm, the level of anger behind his eyes drew his brows down until they nearly touched.

Despite his words, the thoughts Celwyn heard from the man were not charitable toward Annabelle. He itched to teach the man a lesson without attracting attention. Perhaps after they arrived at their destination. Xiau would be proud: the magician could practice patience.

Kang asked, "And what is your business in Skudai, Mr. McAlistair?"

"I'm on my way to Barcelona. New ships with new accounts."

Kang and the magician exchanged a look that plainly said: *horse feathers.*

Chapter 10

THEIR COACH ARRIVED IN THE CITY center of Skudai just before noon. As they decamped from the coach, the magician waved goodbye to their jovial companion, "*Au revoir*, Mr. Jayarama." Celwyn ushered his charge forward. "It is time we talked."

They walked away from the lineup of carriages and followed the other passengers toward the terminal. When they ducked into a nearby alcove, he told Annabelle, "The Professor will join us when he finishes arranging for our luggage." From here, Celwyn could see the automat as he haggled with a porter with the same enthusiasm as most women he'd seen display toward cabbages at the market.

Annabelle blinked up at him with inquiry, not irritation. "'Why did you and the Professor introduce me as 'Miss Carter'? Why lie to the other passengers?"

"I thought it best if we are to assist you in escaping your aunt." Celwyn wished Kang would hurry up. Making explanations to women wasn't his forte. Either he had to tell her she was in danger or prevaricate. "I applaud your ingenuity on your escape. However, Professor Kang and I are not chaperones, nor are we—?" The magician paused as she decided on tears or bravado.

The tears won. Celwyn handed her his handkerchief, a fine piece of linen that she would probably ruin. "You should be aware that hysterics will not sway me. We will protect you and arrange for a companion to accompany you back to Singapore or wherever you wish to go. However, our trek will continue across a great distance, eventually to Constantinople and then to France. It is an arduous journey. And a long one."

Kang re-joined them, noted the tears, and ushered them further back from the walkway. The magician checked behind them. In the middle of the yard, the red-haired Lloyd's agent lurked not too far away. As Celwyn watched, the man drifted even closer to stand behind a tree and near enough to hear them. McAlistair hadn't said a word throughout the rest of their journey out of Singapore, conveniently asleep during conversations about destinations. Yet here he stood eavesdropping.

The magician waved a hand. A swarm of bees descended from the tree above the Lloyd's agent, chasing him inside the terminal building.

"How old are you?" Celwyn demanded of Annabelle.

Her chin went up. It was a finely chiseled chin with a strong line of stubbornness.

"I will be twenty soon."

Thank god, Celwyn thought. It wouldn't do to be suspected of kidnapping a child.

The chin rose even higher, and a glint of determination entered her eyes. "I do not require watching or pampering. I have adequate funds. You do not have any responsibility to me." She included the automat in her speech. "In fact, I will continue my excursion with, or without, you and the Professor."

From beside Celwyn, Kang hid a smile as he turned away to watch another coach arrive, finding the magician's new role of duty humorous.

Celwyn knew when to throw in his cards. He bowed. "Miss Annabelle, please accept our apology. We have a responsibility, even by proxy, and have no intention of abandoning you." Celwyn gestured at Kang. "The Professor and I are gentlemen of the highest order and would be honored to escort you until our paths diverge. Both of us are at your service." He elbowed the automat and bowed again. "There will be no more discussion of you returning to Singapore unless you desire it."

After Kang's bow, and assurances, she handed the soggy handkerchief back to Celwyn with a satisfied smile. "Thank you. I believe it would be a good plan to find an establishment where we could have our luncheon. And then," she favored them both with a determined look, "I need to explore the shops here. I left a majority of my wardrobe behind in Singapore in an attempt to deceive my aunt."

Qing nuzzled Celwyn's neck and gave him a friendly peck. He was probably smirking as broadly as Kang.

"But of course. It will be our pleasure."

Many hours later, a trail of clerks and porters followed them to the train. Hat boxes and parcels had been piled on the arms of each man in the procession. Two more porters toted new traveling trunks. One boy ceremoniously balanced a tray of chocolates on outstretched palms and followed the others. As their party approached the train, she blew her horn, signaling the all-aboard.

The *Royal Victoria* was considered a long train with at least thirty cars, several of which were sleeper cars in first class. Celwyn and company planned to occupy the last one before the luggage car and caboose. The magician would be in the first cabin and be the initial line of defense if needed, then Kang, and then Annabelle. The magician had a feeling that in a test of action and determination, Annabelle would fare quite well. Even so, at night, he'd place a layer of protection over the entire car to be sure Jax kept his distance.

Kang boarded the train, muttering about organizing his desk. Annabelle announced she needed to buy periodicals and entered the terminal. This left the magician outside, between the ticket seller and the train, as clouds of steam from the engines swirled around the worried, bored, or excited travelers to the unknown. In the middle of it all, a woman cradled a beribboned and whining small dog in her arms. From all directions, porters pushed carts of mountainous luggage from the arriving coaches toward the train. In front of the terminal, shouts of vendors peddling maps, tobacco, and tea competed with the bedlam.

Celwyn patted his pocket. Yes, his tea pouch was there. It should last until the city of Chiang Rai, where he expected to acquire a quantity of tea and some interesting mushrooms to supplement his store of peyote, which had become rather depleted.

Something alerted the crowd, and a coach sped into the train station at full speed just as a small child jumped out of its pram. The mother screamed as the child raced in front of the horses. With a shout, an African, as broad as he was tall, sprinted in front of the speeding coach and scooped the child into his arms as it thundered by without stopping.

The child yowled in fear, and several bystanders came running. They hadn't seen the man rescue the child and set about beating him with their umbrellas and fists. Celwyn blocked the blows until the child's mother finally got between them to cease their attack. The magician approached and listened to the men who had attacked, to what they said and thought. Some of their motivation was born of their dislike of Africans. The woman thanked the hero profusely and led the child away.

Minutes passed, and to Celwyn's right, the queue at the ticket counter grew thinner. The African man who had performed so heroically approached the ticket counter. At nearly seven feet tall, he appeared imposing and inspired respect on several levels. Yet Celwyn had no trouble hearing the disdain in the ticket seller's tone as he shook his head and told the black man to move aside.

The magician controlled his anger. Kang would be proud. Celwyn approached the ticket seller and inquired, "Are there still seats available for this train?" It would have been much easier to resolve the encounter with this oaf using a modicum of violence. But instead, he used tact—of a sort.

"Yes, Sir. First-class or coach?"

"First class. One."

When the African's frown deepened and he would have turned away, Celwyn touched his sleeve as he handed over the fare and extracted the ticket from the counterman's grubby hand. He told the ticket man, "You are lucky you don't find yourself hanging upside down in that tree without your trousers." He handed the African the ticket.

The black man's smile sparkled. The magician touched his hat and, with a wave, strolled toward the train car. Kang couldn't say he'd attracted attention. Or at least Celwyn thought so at the time.

Once aboard, he headed to his cabin, threw his hat inside, and verified both of his trunks had also arrived. Then he walked next door. He had barely rapped on the door when Kang jerked it open, drew him inside, and almost closed the door on his foot.

"My, aren't we nervous today?"

The automat peered out the window of his room and sat down, motioning the magician to do the same. The sun had already started its descent, and the light in the train yard faded with each moment. Still, Kang's attention remained on the crowd outside. A newsboy shouted and held up his wares just outside their window.

Celwyn asked, "Are you looking for Jax or Annabelle?" He shuddered, thinking, *What if Mrs. Pearse anticipated our move and is also aboard the train?*

"Jax," Kang added, "I'm sure we'll know for certain when Annabelle returns. Oh—" He shoved the window high and offered a coin to the newsboy. He brought the newspaper inside and, in a second more, said, "Well. We seem to have a problem."

After he handed the paper to Celwyn, the magician had to agree.

Murder!!!

Singapore police have issued an arrest warrant for a Mr. Jonas Celwyn for murder. Although rumored to be affianced to Miss Annabelle Pearse Edmunds, niece of Ambassador Edmunds, it appears that Mr. Celwyn is wanted in Portugal for defacing Church property and mayhem. Lieutenant Dooney of the Singapore police reports, 'I want to question Mr. Celwyn about the murder of Colonel Arthur Gilliam on the Zelda, which yesterday arrived in the Port of Singapore. Colonel Gilliam's throat had been slit open like a pig's. Consider Mr. Celwyn to be dangerous, and alert authorities if you should encounter him.' Mr. Celwyn is described as well over six feet tall, muscular, strong of face, well-dressed, and whiskered.

Per Lieutenant Dooney, Miss Annabelle Pearse Edmunds is also missing and may be in danger. It is possible that Mr. Celwyn kidnapped the young woman.

Kang folded the paper and scrutinized the crowd again. "At least there weren't pictures of you."

"None of the water buffalos either."

"Amusing."

"But there was a blurry picture of Annabelle." The magician wondered how much higher their threat of discovery had risen. He stuck his head out the cabin window and checked outside for their new ward.

"It is just more evidence that you shouldn't call attention to yourself."

"You nag me." Celwyn rubbed his chin. "I should shave off my whiskers before we encounter the rest of the passengers. It wouldn't hurt to somehow disguise Annabelle either."

As he got to his feet, the last call for the all-aboard sounded, and here came Annabelle, loaded with at least five more packages and her parasol. Just as she located the correct train car and pivoted toward it, a general cry went up from inside the train station across the yard that she had just left. Through their open window floated excited shouting and the kind of commotion that didn't bode well.

"Come on," Celwyn said, and they bolted out of the cabin and down the hall. "I'll get her inside while you find out what is going on."

"Good idea until you shave," Kang said. He hurried down the steps and ran toward the terminal building. The magician leaned partially out the door and tugged on Annabelle's parasol without touching it until she looked up.

"Over here, please," he called and hooked a finger at her. As Celwyn backed into the shadows of the car, she approached wearing a perplexed frown. Behind her, the conductor strode by, calling the last all-aboard.

"Hurry." Celwyn ushered her inside. "Down the hallway, last door, we'll join you in a moment."

"Now, just wait—"

He gave her a little nudge forward. "No. We do not have time. Unless you want your aunt to know you're here." Celwyn put the newspaper on top of her packages as she glared at him and stalked down the hallway.

Where is Kang? Celwyn could hear the ruckus in the train station as the voices of the crowd grew into a loud cacophony of fear and speculation.

"...knotted under his left ear..."

"...looked like he saw a ghost..."

"No robbery! ...look at that ring and gold fillings..."

"Where are the police?"

Kang shoved his way out of the terminal doors and ran back through the dense crowd, elbowing a few others to let him by. The train's wheels squealed and began to turn. Celwyn leaned out, extended an arm, and pulled him inside.

"Nothing is ever dull with you, Jonas." Kang shook himself and straightened his tie.

A fond compliment. The magician liked it, and he liked Kang.

"Anything for you, Sir." The magician led the way down the corridor. "Let us confer before Annabelle has to be entertained."

"An excellent idea. And a spot of whiskey for the road wouldn't be amiss either."

Celwyn stopped himself from opening his cabin door. "It would be more congenial to imbibe in the club car but not as private." He eyed Kang. "I take it someone was murdered at the station?"

The train gathered speed, and its whistle shrieked.

"Oh, yes there was." Kang glanced at Annabelle's door. "Do you think we could keep our voices low enough in the club car?"

"We can certainly try," Celwyn said as they turned around and backtracked to the main part of the train.

Chapter 11

DEEP LEATHER CHAIRS, THICK cigar smoke, and the aroma of aged liquors amid the rustle of newspapers—hopefully not the most recent editions—greeted them in the first-class club car. The car appeared half-full, and the temperature a bit stuffy. Celwyn removed his coat before sitting down across from the automat.

"Christophe designed your vest?" he asked.

"No." Celwyn signaled the barman. "It is just something I had made the last time I was in London. Although it is of a fine brocade, I imagine we'll still need to discuss what you saw in the terminal."

"I suppose so." The automat turned to the windows and back again.

Celwyn wasn't particularly surprised at what happened in the terminal. A pattern had developed regarding Jax. Their whiskeys arrived, and Kang downed half of his before the magician finished sniffing his glass. Perhaps, he could make this easier for the automat.

"I can venture a guess as to who was murdered in the terminal."

"How do you know it was murder?"

The magician spread his hands open. "Do you forget my abilities? My hunch is that it was our friend from Lloyds, Mr. McAlistair."

As Celwyn spoke, the door opened, letting in the clanging of the train and a party of four well-padded men in bankers' suits and top hats. One sported a monocle, and another a pince-nez on a delicate gold chain. The sun had nearly set through the windows, and the chain twinkled in the golden light. The other two men observed Kang and the magician as if they were intruding in a private car rather than outlaws on the run from the police in a public car. Obviously, they thought the former more of an affront. The tallest of the bunch led the way to a table at the rear.

In a low voice, Kang asked, "How did you know it was our loquacious friend from Lloyds?"

"Follow the pattern as it seems to be following us: Colonel Gilliam is murdered by Jax, and Lloyd's McAlistair conveniently trails us to the hotel in Singapore and then in the carriage to Skudai. Now he is found dead in the train station." Celwyn frowned as he thought the pattern through to the next logical step. "This presents a problem."

Kang started to wave for another round and stopped. "It certainly does." He sighed. "Jax could be inside anyone at this point. And on the train with us."

It was Celwyn's turn to sigh. "Let us discuss something more pleasant. Perhaps the Brazilian rainforests. Have you ever visited there? Or the Pacific Ocean along the coast of Washington. The Strait of Juan de Fuca could favorably compare with—"

Kang gulped the rest of his drink. "I can't concentrate right now, Jonas. Let's return to our cabins."

Like anyone who walks between the seats on train cars, they were observed. To Celwyn, it felt as if they paraded naked on a stage under the kind of searching scrutiny they did not need at the moment. They made their way quickly through two coach cars and several others, including the dining car.

As they reached the door leading to their compartments, Kang asked, "Do you think we could avoid Annabelle a bit longer? Perhaps until dinner? We have no answers for her, and I am not a very good liar. Or so Elizabeth says."

Celwyn laughed as they stepped through into the last car and then abruptly stopped as they rounded the curve in the hallway. Annabelle stood there in a lacy afternoon gown, puffing on a cigarette. Her glare could have lit a second one.

"Apparently not," Celwyn murmured.

"Good afternoon, Miss Annabelle."

She ground out her cigarette under her toe. "Where have you been?"

Kang and the magician glanced at each other like two boys caught sneaking out after curfew. Kang ventured, "The club car."

"Of course. Women do not have that option." She eyed them. "I read that newspaper article—"

Celwyn rubbed his face, always an indication of annoyance. At least he wasn't breaking glasses or tossing things out windows. "Even though it isn't considered proper because of your gender and status, it would be better if we conducted the rest of this conversation in private." Celwyn opened his cabin door and motioned them inside. As he rang for the porter, he invited them to sit.

How much to tell her? As little as possible. Anything about Jax?

As Celwyn debated, Qing hopped out of the adjoining lavatory and stopped in the middle of the cabin. He squawked a greeting at Kang, then at the magician, before training his gaze on Annabelle. His eyes glittered. Celwyn knew what that meant; he was interested. Annabelle's mouth opened and closed again. She appeared ripe for an outburst. Just then, there was a knock, and the porter announced his arrival.

"James, from room service."

Celwyn looked at Annabelle and put his finger to his lips. Kang scooped Qing into his arms as Celwyn opened the door partway, just enough to place an order for coffee and drinks.

"Thank you, James." He shut the door as the train slowed, tilted to the right, and chugged around a curve.

Once seated again, the magician looked at Qing, who obediently hopped over to be petted. Annabelle regarded him.

"Is that the same bird from the ship?"

Qing squawked at her. If Celwyn knew him, and he was beginning to, Qing was considering a peck at her earrings. Celwyn laid a hand on his back.

"Yes, it is," Kang said in a friendly tone. "We are delighted to travel with you and defend you if necessary, but from reading that newspaper, you know we have attracted the attention of the police."

Not to mention a metaphoric and evil entity, Celwyn thought.

Kang continued, "We also sympathize with your desire to escape your aunt. But the situation requires some finesse by all of us if we want to continue our journey in peace." Annabelle wanted to debate the situation, specifically to know why they were in danger.

A short time later, the porter knocked. Celwyn motioned Annabelle to go into the lavatory. She looked ready to balk, but his glare propelled her into the loo. Even if propriety didn't interest her, it was one of the things Celwyn appreciated about Victorian times. Over the years, he had enjoyed the favors of many women. Now, he used discernment and limited his attentions. He would not contribute to the demise of Annabelle's reputation.

"One moment," Celwyn called. When the lavatory door closed behind Annabelle, he invited James inside to set up the refreshments. After the porter had left again, Annabelle stalked out of the lavatory and across the cabin. As she sat down across from Celwyn, she regarded their whiskeys, then her innocent cup of coffee.

"Is this the best you could do?"

"Yes," Celwyn responded. "Ordering three drinks for two is more difficult to explain, and it calls more attention to us than the extra pot of coffee. Drink up," he said with a smile.

"I dislike propriety." Annabelle grumbled a bit more but dumped cream into her coffee. She tasted it and drank.

"It isn't just the appearance of respectability. You have read that newspaper story. We need to alter our appearance unless you want your aunt to find you and drag you back to Singapore." Celwyn stroked his beard. "For my part, I will be clean-shaven before dinner." Kang couldn't get taller, and he couldn't grow whiskers. "That leaves you," Celwyn told her.

Annabelle narrowed her blue eyes at the magician like she would when presented with a misbehaving child holding an ice cream. "Exactly what did you have in mind?"

Qing hopped along the back of the sofa toward her. Although Kang insisted that the magician spoiled Qing, he didn't agree. Celwyn didn't have the heart to divert him from his amusements.

But to business: neither Kang nor Annabelle knew the extent of the magician's background, although Kang wouldn't be surprised by any of it. Celwyn arose and opened one of his trunks. "Do you have a turban?" he called over his shoulder as he rummaged through the trunk.

"Yes."

"Wear it when you aren't in your cabin." Celwyn sat down again and handed her a vial of dark liquid. "When you return to your cabin, please use this. Soak your hair in it tonight and the following nights. Over the next few days, it will darken your hair. We will need to purchase more of this concoction when we reach Chiang Rai."

"All right." She nodded. "In my quest for a new life, it isn't too much to ask. However, my new wardrobe is decidedly far eastern. I just bought hair clips and some heavy jewelry."

It seemed she had entered into the spirit of their adventure, which Celwyn considered a victory. "Excellent. Apply as much eye paint as possible. It will age you and add to the subterfuge we want to achieve."

Kang said, "I agree. This will work."

"One more thing would be helpful." Celwyn noticed Qing had almost reached his goal. Annabelle's earrings dangled only a few inches away. He shrugged; she would have to learn to deal with Qing in her own way.

"And what would that be?" Annabelle regarded them with the level of distrust she would if someone offered her an apple with a worm poking out of it.

"Languages and linguistics are useful. An American southern accent is distracting. You should acquire one as soon as possible."

Qing attacked the earring, getting his beak on the dangling piece of gold. Annabelle jumped, spilling coffee on her lap.

"I *do* declare," she drawled, "that bird is annoying!"

It seemed odd, but as soon as his company had departed, Celwyn yawned and needed a nap —and he never slept during the day.

When he awoke, he experienced a frisson of disquiet, of uneasiness.

Someone else had been in his room, he sensed it, yet he could see that nothing had been disturbed, and his trunks were still locked. Celwyn had been so tired that he hadn't put a block on his door. His own personal magical protection, always in place, seemed undisturbed and did not require his attention. Which was good, for when he looked down, his sense of unease grew.

His shirt had been unbuttoned by his neck, and he felt a strange, sticky saliva on his cheek. Why?

And who had drugged him?

Chapter 12

"I AM SURE," ANNABELLE KICKED THE bed next to her and muttered to herself, "I am not staying in this room just because something *might* happen."

She shoved the tray aside from her breakfast and dug through her trunks until she found a scarf to wrap around her head. Some of her protectors' precautions made sense. Above all, she had to hide from her aunt and her ill-conceived idea of forced marriage. Annabelle grabbed her cigarettes and peeked out the door. All clear.

It took only a minute to tiptoe by Uncle Celwyn and the Professor's cabins. Both doors were shut, and she wasn't about to knock. With luck, she would have a pleasant morning walking the train, stopping for a smoke, and when she felt tired, she could sit in the observation car and perhaps meet a few fellow travelers.

Everything went well until she opened the door to the dining car and saw her protectors huddled at the far end at a table with a teapot. She closed the door and backtracked. A clandestine cigarette it would have to be. So far, she'd not encountered too many passengers on the platforms between the passenger cars, and with luck, none of the prudish stuffed shirts would discover her there.

After she arrived on the platform before her car, it took some effort to raise the window, but Annabelle managed to get it above her head, letting in the clamor of the train. The breeze hit her square in the face, the air warm and wet. As she watched the terrain, she tried to be unbiased, but the landscape held no interest for her at all: just long stretches of fields and nothing more. She lit a cigarette and leaned out the window to see what lay ahead. In the distance, she could just detect a range of snow-capped peaks through hazy clouds.

"Hey—"

Strong hands lifted her further out, propelling her through the window. For once, her wide bustle became useful. She was wedged in the window as she struggled and kicked. Annabelle screamed and then heard a most welcome sound.

"*Stop that!*" the Professor yelled.

Whoever had a hold of her pulled her out of the window and flung her forcibly at Kang. They tumbled into the corner. She turned in time to glimpse the back of someone in a big hat and heavy coat disappearing through the door toward the front of the train.

She scrambled up at the same time as the Professor. Both spoke at once.

"Are you all right?"

"Are you all right?" The Professor held her steady in front of him and nodded. "You seem to be."

"Who was that?" Annabelle's voice shook in anger as she demanded, "Why did he do that?"

The Professor looked through the door to the main part of the train, gazing as far ahead as he could, and shook his head. He slammed it and said, "I do not know, but this illustrates another reason for us to be vigilant." Kang opened the other door that led to their cabins and bowed. "If you are certain you are all right, I'll escort you back to your room."

As Annabelle accepted his arm, she still shook from the shock of her ordeal. "Thank you. Must we tell Uncle Celwyn about this?"

The Professor patted her hand. "Yes, we must."

***

"...Mount Ashawan's elevation is..." Kang read from the train's brochure.

Celwyn could see little of the mountain or anything at all in the darkness they sailed through, just a suggestion of fog and occasional rocks as large as the train engine reflected in the *Victoria's* lights. The aroma of roast beef and clinking of silver contrasted with glimpses of stunted trees and the gradual sensation that the train had begun a long climb. Every time they crossed a trestle, the water in the crystal goblets would slosh back and forth and then settle into a slow rocking motion again. Although not as wonderful as a sea voyage, alone at night on a train climbing through desolate snow-covered mountains had a certain charm. An adventure painted with danger, perhaps. What lay ahead?

For that matter, Celwyn wondered what he would do once they reached Paris. The city of beauty, of consummate evil, and the bittersweet memory of Suzanne. He remembered the internal music of the city itself, which brought a wisp of an idea. By the time they arrived in Paris, it might blossom.

Kang closed his menu and handed it to the waiter. A Mrs. Trenton sat next to him, one of the dowagers who loved her port and could have been Mrs. Caruthers' twin sister. After their introductions, she couldn't believe her good fortune to be seated with them for dinner and said so. Kang possessed a quiet kind of attractiveness, which became even more irresistible to the woman because he displayed no interest in her. In contrast, only inches away, on the magician's right, sat a treacherous reminder of what he and Kang had found earlier in the observation car.

It had been after five in the afternoon, and as Celwyn knocked on Kang's door, it occurred to him that Annabelle really couldn't be trusted to stay in her own cabin. That thought drove him to the next cabin and rap on the door. Nothing.

Kang stuck his head out of his room and saw the magician's expression. They had begun to think enough alike that he didn't have to ask Kang to watch for the porter before he unlocked the door, and they entered Annabelle's room.

Their spoiled little princess had flown the coop.

"Wonderful," the magician growled.

Kang sighed. "It's worse than that. This morning someone tried to push her out the window on the platform between the cars."

"Who was it?" the magician demanded. He faced the automat with a glare.

"I couldn't identify him."

"Why didn't you tell me? Was she hurt?"

"I planned to tell you but assumed it would scare her enough to make her behave. I *did* plan to tell you," Kang said. "She was shaken up. That is all."

"Bah. It doesn't appear she learned her lesson. Where would she go?"

Kang poked around the room and checked inside of the hat boxes, for what the magician didn't know. "There are few places other than the dining car. And I'm betting she won't be pausing by the windows between the cars again very soon. My presumption is that she will either be in the observation car or try to sneak into the men's club car."

"You know I'd never hear the end of it if I kept something like this from you."

"Pfft." The automat slipped out the door and blinked at him. "Probably, but of the two of us, you are more likely to be secretive."

"Hush, Xiau," Celwyn said it fondly as he relocked the door, and they headed toward the front of the train, passing through the rest of first-class, the dining car, and approached the club car. A quick glimpse through the cigar smoke revealed no outraged males or feathered hats. When they reached the observation car with its walls of glass, a dark worry replaced their initial relief. It contained two occupants in a shadowy corner: Annabelle and a woman who made the hair on the back of Celwyn's neck crawl. Even as they entered and walked closer, he recognized a dhampyr.

"Hello, Uncle and Professor," Annabelle called. Celwyn could read the uncertainty in her eyes as they drew near. "I just met a new friend."

The woman turned to them and opened her languid eyes.

"Good afternoon. I am Mrs. Madalene Karras."

A woman of perhaps forty years or older, with the kind of cold beauty that didn't age, regarded them. Swirls of ebony curls framed high cheekbones, ruby lips, and lashes that canopied eyes of impenetrable steel. The smirk she wore could have been an all-knowing response to the magician's perusal or one that indicated she expected to be admired. A fur-lined wrap barely contained her plump breasts, and she wore full length gloves. Which would seem odd during the day... Celwyn felt the cold emanating from her. There was only one explanation for it.

"May I offer myself as a companion to your niece on your journey? It is unusual for a young unmarried woman to travel alone, even with the able supervision of her," she paused long enough to let them know she doubted the label, "uncle." She favored Celwyn with a flirtatious twist of her lips. "No matter how handsome."

The magician acknowledged her compliment by touching the brim of his hat. Qing squirmed inside his coat, another barometer of caution. The woman's overall appearance declared that she was a woman of the world. Compared to her, Annabelle resembled a baby gazelle who hadn't yet learned how to stand.

"This is Frederick Oliver, of Seattle," Kang announced as they sat down in the chairs opposite the two women. "I am Professor Chang, also lately of Seattle."

Manners dictated acceptance of the offer. At least for now. "Miss Dolly is my sister's daughter." Celwyn indicated Annabelle. "Mrs. Karras, we would welcome any help you can offer my niece, wouldn't we, Dolly?"

Annabelle's glare was just for Celwyn, then she turned it into a beaming smile and said, "But of course. I look forward to it."

"You introduced yourself as—"

Annabelle flipped a hand. "Just a nickname. My legal name is Dolly." She rolled her eyes at the magician.

Mrs. Karras asked her, "May I inquire as to your destination?"

Celwyn interjected, "We plan an extended stay in Venice."

"Oh, really?" Kang murmured under his breath.

If, he was capable of letting Celwyn enter his thoughts, he wouldn't be treated to surprises when the magician had to improvise to match situations they encountered. The magician could have just told him silently.

"What will you do in Venice, Miss Jackson?" Mrs. Karras asked.

The *Royal Victoria*'s engines changed tempo as she began a steep descent. In the valley far below, hundreds of lights twinkled from a sizable town. It made a picturesque scene and timely distraction, and the pause long enough for Annabelle to prepare a response. Celwyn didn't appear to be the only one proficient at improvising.

"I would like to attend the university there." Annabelle favored the table with a serious look. "St. Maria's has a nursing and medical program. It is possible I'll also explore acting."

Celwyn coughed, and if he'd been drinking a beverage, he would have choked. Acting was *not* a profession respectable ladies embraced. If Mrs. Pearse felt like skinning Celwyn alive now, she would be even more indisposed to him if he allowed Annabelle to frolic with nubile and handsome actors. Kang snickered into his sleeve while pretending to rub his nose.

Annabelle said, "My trust provides for a leisurely life, but there must be more worthwhile adventures. I plan to escape matrimony."

The magician maintained a fixed smile. Mrs. Pearse would fillet him after she skinned him.

Mrs. Karras blinked several times in horror. "Forever?" One would have thought Annabelle wanted to be a warlord in the wilds of the Sahara. The older woman adopted a resolute tone. "Regardless, it is my duty to help chaperone a young woman traveling on a journey such as you propose. I will be available until we reach Baghdad."

Celwyn tapped Annabelle's shin with his boot.

"Err... thank you, Mrs. Karras. That is very kind of you."

The magician sighed inwardly, pleased that their subterfuge had worked.

It only lasted a moment until Celwyn caught the intense assessing gaze from the woman to Annabelle. It took control to suppress the shudder that nearly overwhelmed him. The magician had seen the same cold appraisal of Suzanne by the vampire who had eventually killed her. The revulsion he felt toward Mrs. Karras sickened him.

He glanced at the automat, who stared back at him and mouthed the word "Vampyr."

And now, a few hours later, Celwyn sat next to the vampire, trying to eat his dinner.

If it weren't for Kang's annoying and repeated nagging about control in front of others, Celwyn would deal with this quickly and return to enjoying his journey. Instead, he endured Mrs. Karras sitting much too close. He'd already wedged his chair against the wall and couldn't move any further away, which was the woman's intention. Her satin dress afforded everyone a grand view of her cleavage and elegant neck. Worse, her perfume went right up his nose and tickled his senses and libido. Celwyn squirmed. Even of more interest, he had yet to remind Kang that in his experience, there was never an occasion when he encountered just one vampire. Usually, he found several of the nasty creatures together.

From across the table, Mrs. Trenton launched into a lengthy description of the grandchildren that she expected to see when they reached Bangladesh. It seemed her son had a small import business there. As their waiter served the soup, the Professor encouraged her dissertation with questions every time her recital faltered: for dinner conversation, they couldn't very well ask a vampire about her past or relatives. To Celwyn, Mrs. Trenton provided a neutral background as he inhaled leeks, ginger, mushrooms, and lemongrass, with a hint of succulent pork. The steam from the soup bathed his face, still a bit sensitive from its recent shaving.

The magician perused the dining room, which now appeared full. Each table had an assigned waiter, and the noise level grew higher as the train rumbled across a rough patch. As soon as it settled again, the *Royal Victoria* began a steep descent. A quick check across the table confirmed that Kang's nervousness had returned. With a trembling hand, he let his soup spoon clatter back in the bowl.

Celwyn doubted it was the trajectory of the train that upset him. He raised a brow in inquiry, but the automat shook his head. Beyond his shoulder, the magician caught a glimpse across the aisle at a man in military dress.

Could it be? When Celwyn leaned forward to more fully study the man, Mrs. Karras' knee rubbed against his thigh. Not accidentally. *Oh bother!* Celwyn had been the object of lust from both female and male vampires before, and it never ended well. He either killed them or had to flee to avoid their advances.

Celwyn eyed Kang and sighed. He supposed that his new friend would object if he tipped Mrs. Karras' chair over into the aisle. Just then, fortune smiled. The train braked hard, coming into a curve. When it accelerated out once more, Mrs. Karras' chair had been relocated until it would be difficult for her to rub knees with the magician again. At the same time, Celwyn managed a clear, direct look at the military man.

Everything in the dining car dimmed, from the noise to the red of the roses on the tables. Celwyn could still hear Mrs. Trenton reciting the long list of her grandson's scientific endeavors and remained well aware of Mrs. Karras' bosoms blocking his view of the salt and pepper bowls, but for a fleeting moment, most of those details disappeared.

The man across the aisle wore the amulets, medals, and uniform of a British Army captain. He appeared to be about thirty years of age, very blond, thin, muscular, and most likely on his way to the continued military conflict in Punjab where Suzanne's brother Patrick had been posted years ago. Yet, Patrick should be more than fifty years old at this point, not the younger man a few feet away. Right now, he appeared the same as when Celwyn saw him last.

Patrick's expression hardened as his glance around the room encountered Mrs. Karras.

For pity's sake: all of this transpired while Celwyn attempted to dine. A blissfully unaware waiter placed the magician's plate in front of him with a bow. It smelled divine. The vegetables appeared fresh and delectable as the juice from the roast mingled into their sauces. The magician chewed slowly, wondering what Mrs. Karras had to do with Patrick. The most obvious answer did not occur to him until a bit later.

By the time they finished their plates, Celwyn knew Mrs. Trenton's grandchildren's' names, their preferences in pets, academic potential, and had counted the fine line of freckles across Mrs. Karras' collar bone on their trip downward. Kang regaled the table with a description of the construction of the London Bridge. When he paused for the removal of their plates, Mrs. Karras spoke.

"And where is your charge, Miss Dolly, this evening?"

"She felt the need to rest and planned to dine in her room," Celwyn answered. The waiter distributed dessert cups of sorbet on the table and poured coffee.

"Perhaps I should stop in later and check on her."

The magician's spoon stopped in mid-air. Then he put it back in the bowl. Even if her words sounded innocent, in her tone he heard a distinct dare: to determine if they knew of her vampiric interest. The automat recognized her words for what they were and the potential for danger. He pointed at Mrs. Trenton with his eyes, and Celwyn obediently blocked her hearing.

Professor Xiau Kang addressed Mrs. Karras in a quiet voice unmistakable in its menace.

"You should know that we know you for what you are and will not allow you to harm our charge."

As he spoke, Celwyn laid a heavy hand on top of the vampire's cold one. "Do not test us."

A low, throaty chuckle escaped her lips. Then a vicious hiss.

"Then stay out of my way." She removed her hand and stood. As she swept by, Patrick wasted no time throwing down his napkin and following her.

Celwyn couldn't let a challenge like that go. As he stood, Kang nodded him ahead while he performed the social niceties with their waiter for the occasion when someone fled their dining table during the dessert course.

As he passed out of the dining car, the magician sidestepped the maître'd and, at the last table, was pleasantly surprised to see the black gentleman who'd been initially refused a fare for the train. The man stopped sipping coffee when he saw the magician rushing out the door. He got to his feet, also. Celwyn nodded a quick greeting and increased his stride: he had realized where the vampire must be going: to Annabelle's cabin in the last car. There was no time to waste if Mrs. Karras intended to harm her.

From behind him, the black man said, "Allow me to accompany you, Sir."

The magician threw him a smile and said, "Why not?"

They tailed Patrick and Mrs. Karras through the first-class sleeping cars. As they exited one car and entered another, they began to trot as the glimpses of the top of Patrick's head became fewer, and Celwyn couldn't see Mrs. Karras at all. She must be flying along in front of them.

They arrived at the open platform between the last two cars, where a brisk wind tried to blow them back inside. Directly in front of them, Mrs. Karras faced Patrick, snarling at him because he blocked the door into the last car and Annabelle. As Celwyn stepped onto the platform along with his new, seven-foot-tall acquaintance, the *Victoria* slowed through rows of vegetation that lined the tracks and then chugged through a village. Seconds more and they entered the country again, leaving the glow of welcoming lamps behind as darkness again swallowed them.

Mrs. Karras slapped Patrick hard. It rocked him, but he continued to hold her at bay.

"Get out of here, Jonas. This is between us," Patrick yelled.

The vampire flung Patrick against the rail. He would have gone over if he hadn't spun to the side. She pulled him down by his hair and planted a foot on his chest, pressing hard. Almost immediately, his face turned purple. She was crushing him.

A deep growl escaped from her as no lady would do.

"You cannot harm me, or stop me, if I want the morsel called 'Dolly.' Her eyes glowed red and her bosom heaved. When the black man reached for her, she twisted away from him. "As for you," she looked down at the gasping Patrick, "I made you, and I can destroy you."

Patrick wheezed and tried to pull her foot off of his chest.

Kang's restraint or not, Celwyn had had enough.

The wind whipped around them as the magician raised the vile creature into the air, petticoats and all. She dangled eight feet above the platform, screeching and clawing at the air.

"Patrick, did she help Delgado kill Suzanne?" he asked.

Patrick rasped, "No, at least I don't think so." The black man helped him to his feet. "She was waiting for me when I went after Delgado, and … she seduced me, and then—" He touched his neck.

"Put me down!" the vampire shrieked at Celwyn.

"What was Delgado to you, Madam?"

"Put me down, and I'll tell you!" Her fangs were out, and saliva dripped off her red lips.

That answer wasn't comforting. For the first time in years, a small doubt crept into Celwyn's thoughts.

"Is he still in Paris?" he asked as if it didn't matter.

She laughed, which told him little except that he would learn nothing from her and spend the rest of the trip fearing what she would do to Annabelle and others.

"*Au revoir*, Mrs. Karras," the magician said and tossed her off the train. They watched her sail high in the air, and if it weren't for her white petticoats, they wouldn't have been able to watch her roll down a long incline like a discarded puppet as the train chugged ahead, gaining speed.

Kang had arrived in time to see the vampire's departure and sighed. "Jonas, you know she will be after us now."

"True, but we should be well away by the time she finds another train."

Patrick's eyes bulged as he dusted off his uniform. "But did you hear what your friend said? She will come after you."

Celwyn shrugged. "It is of no consequence. She thinks we are going to Venice."

"Wonderful," Kang said, his sarcasm on display.

The magician grinned and slapped his back. "Have cheer, my friend. It will be a while before she finds us."

A deep voice rumbled from behind them. "If I may: I am Bartholomew from Juba in the Sudan. If there is danger, I am at your service." He bowed.

"Jonas Celwyn." The magician bowed in return. "I am pleased to meet you again. This is Professor Xiau Kang and Captain Patrick Swayne." The handshakes they exchanged hid some of their fears: they now were soldiers in arms.

"I will not allow any harm to befall your party," the big man said.

"It is very much appreciated. Let's get out of this wind," Celwyn suggested and waved everyone through the door and into their car.

Patrick said, "I will have to leave you when the train stops in Kanpur. I am with the Queens'—"

Annabelle rounded the corner at full steam and collided with him. From the expression on Patrick's face, it appeared that he had just seen an angel.

Annabelle's expression indicated that she no longer abhorred marriage.

Oh ... my, Celwyn thought.

Chapter 13

X IAU SAID, "THE PLOT THICKENS like—"

"Must you?" Celwyn growled. If he had wanted to become a father, he would have said so. The magician couldn't anticipate all of the dangers in the world and spend his time protecting Annabelle. Yet he knew that he would.

Bartholomew must have observed undercurrents of humor and frustration because he tactfully looked the other way.

"Uncle?" Annabelle asked.

Bloody hell. And could Patrick keep their secrets?

"Miss Annabelle Pearse Edmunds, may I present Captain Patrick Swayne?" Celwyn watched a spellbound curtsy and equally transfixed bow exchanged.

Annabelle smiled as demurely as she could—which wasn't terribly much considering she held a cigarette in one hand and a full glass of wine in the other. For his part, Patrick appeared speechless.

"Miss Edmunds and Mr. Swayne, this is our friend Mr. Bartholomew." Courtesies were exchanged.

The automat reached for Patrick's hand. "I am Professor Xiau Kang, a new friend of Mr. Celwyn's."

Bother. Celwyn realized that more conversation would be necessary, and they couldn't fit everyone respectfully into his compartment. For his part, Patrick just stared at Annabelle with his mouth open.

"I must retire for the evening, Mr. Celwyn, but we will find time to converse on the morrow. Good night, Miss." The big man bowed to Annabelle. "Professor." Bartholomew shook Kang's hand and then Patrick's. Smiling with a measure of polite sympathy, he headed back to the main part of the train.

"Annabelle, Patrick is an old acquaintance of mine, and we were just stopping by to retrieve a few cigars before we adjourned to the club car. I'm sure you understand." The magician urged Patrick and Kang toward the exit door. "I'll meet you there."

For the second time in a day, they entered the club car. This evening the room appeared full, and amid the flurry of activity, the porter found them a table at the end of the bar. Patrick had shaken off his stultifying look of *amore,* at least for now. He also seemed none the worse for wear from his altercation with Mrs. Karras, except for a tear in his uniform jacket. Celwyn wiggled a finger, making it as good as new, as he leaned back in his chair, and they observed the other guests.

"Are any of them vampires?" Celwyn asked, gesturing to the room. He usually could recognize the vermin, but it wouldn't hurt to have a professional opinion. From Patrick, he felt some of the cold of a vampire, but not to the full extent. The little mysteries from over the last hour or so began to make sense.

Patrick studied the other tables. "No, and it is good to see you again, too, Jonas."

The magician acknowledged that he lacked social graces sometimes. "My apologies. The Professor and I are under a bit of a strain at the moment."

Kang retrieved their drinks from the bar and handed them around while the magician signaled for another round, knowing it would be a wait with this much activity.

Patrick sipped and said, "I've had times like that also."

"At the risk of being rude, may I summarize your situation for the benefit of the Professor?" the magician asked.

"Certainly."

Celwyn leaned back and pursed his lips. "Mrs. Karras had the expectation of your loyalty, or your fear of her, to compel your allegiance?"

"Yes."

"Because she tried to make you a vampire? Now that I am closer, I can see certain signs that she didn't succeed completely. This happened when you attempted to avenge your sister's death by Delgado?"

Patrick's tone sounded as bitter as un-ripened lemons. "Rightio, Jonas. She stopped short of that, but I have some of the traits."

"Such as youthfulness. Tell me about what happened afterwards?" Nothing would surprise Celwyn, considering his own abilities and longevity, but that day he *saw* Delgado burn. It was not possible that he'd survived.

Patrick shrugged and sipped. "Magdalene kept me around like a cat who toys with a sick mouse until she tired of me and sent me back to my unit in Kanpur. You can imagine it was an unpleasant surprise to find her on this train."

Interesting. Kang must have thought so also because he asked, "Tell me, Captain, since you boarded this train, what had Mrs. Karras done or said? Are there any clues to her plans?"

Patrick gazed at his glass and thought for a bit, then looked up again. "She seemed to be ignoring me. But she also kept watching the last few train cars. Apparently, the ones where you and Miss Edmunds have compartments."

Celwyn thought a moment and told the Professor, "It doesn't appear that our deception with false names and camouflaging Miss Edmunds' tresses will be necessary any longer. The danger from the authorities fades with each mile we travel west, and Mrs. Karras had no idea who she was."

"I beg to differ." The Professor kept his voice fairly low and leaned forward to say, "Annabelle's aunt, Mrs. Pearse, will probably not give up, and she will pester the police to pursue us."

Patrick retrieved another round of drinks and sat again. "Why is her aunt interested?"

"Because Miss Edmunds is escaping an arranged marriage, not one of love."

Patrick's expression became thoughtful.

"You stated that there are no other vampires on the train. Do you have any ideas why Mrs. Karras was on it?" Kang asked.

"I didn't know before, but I do now that I see you. She's been living in Skudai the last few years and probably heard of you from the newspapers since they are delivered there daily." Patrick looked at the magician. "Even I had read about you the day before I boarded the train. And the allusions in the article about strange and odd occurrences confirmed it was you. Mrs. Karras probably deduced the same thing."

"She knew who you were all along," Kang said.

Celwyn shook his head. "If so, why did she challenge me about feeding on Annabelle? To prove her superiority?"

"It wasn't just that if you want my opinion." Patrick verified none of the nearby patrons were listening and continued, "Mrs. Karras is beholden to Delgado: she was made a vampire by him. And she is fiercely loyal."

"Just wonderful." Kang threw up his hands.

"I'm not liking this," Celwyn said. The bottles behind the bar started to shake.

The automat agreed. "Neither am I."

"She probably wanted to prove her worth to Delgado by killing you," Patrick said and frowned at them both.

Was it true? Did Delgado still roam the streets and boudoirs of Paris? Celwyn cursed his luck and felt his temper rise at the same time. *No.*

"I loved your sister," he told Patrick. "I killed the man who murdered her. He did not survive that day!" The glass door behind them began to crack as Celwyn stared at it.

Kang glanced at the other occupants. "Keep your voice down, Jonas, and stop looking at the door."

The magician's glass shattered in his hand, spraying his trousers with mediocre whiskey. "It cannot be!"

The emotion once more drew Celwyn back to that horrible night in Paris after Suzanne had died.

The Hotel Corbeau occupied more than half of a block in the older bohemian quarter. Legends of daemons, vampires, and witches permeated the businesses on the street as much as the city itself. While some proprietors shuttered their doors and windows at dusk, others proclaimed themselves open for anything, such as the Le Pub Fang and the Sorcière Boire. Center to it all, the Hotel Corbeau's five stories of dark wood, stained glass, and lively suspicion made it irresistible to morbid romantics and a few fallen angels.

After he closed Suzanne's sightless eyes, Celwyn had headed to the hotel intent on revenge and in a high state of anguish. Because he was distracted, it took a little time to trap and remove the various sycophants, hotel staff, and other vampires making up Delgado's entourage, but one by one, he'd locked them in the basement and made sure their cries could not be heard. The most difficult to catch had been a dandified daemon named

Francoise. For the vampires, iron restraints had been necessary.

It would be dawn soon, and as the magician waited for Delgado to arrive, he couldn't stop reliving Suzanne's last words to him. He would have his revenge.

The door to the downstairs parlor whispered open. A dark-haired man a bit taller and broader than Celwyn entered, his face shadowed, his eyes glowing like a cat's.

Delgado wore a tuxedo, well-pressed and made, and with his high cheekbones and handsome features, he could easily be a part of a court or any aristocratic gathering. Instead, he hunted there. From what Celwyn had discovered, nubile princesses found him irresistible—until they could no longer breathe, their necks bloodied, and their illusions of love destroyed.

Delgado stopped short just inside the door.

"Gardner? Robert?" He moved as fluidly as a panther as he toured the room. "Interesting." Delgado sniffed the air. "Ah, I have a visitor. I wonder who it is."

The vampire walked to the opposite wall, nodding to himself, glancing behind the sofas and hiding places, including the heavy drapes. Celwyn had made a point of leaving his scent over every chair, pillow, and drape.

From his perch atop the chandelier, the magician observed his target. Now that his quarry had arrived, Celwyn's resolve strengthened: it was merely a matter of how he would do what he needed to do. Direct touch-to-touch destruction would be the most satisfying but also the most difficult.

The magician dropped to the floor behind Delgado.

Without turning around, the vampire sniffed the air again and smiled. "Ah, Mr. Celwyn. It is time we finally meet. I recognize Suzanne's perfume on you."

A hurtful taunt intended to distract the magician.

In a whirl so fast he couldn't be seen, the vampire swerved to the side, knocking Celwyn across the room and into a bookshelf. The magician blocked his assault with a solid punch in the stomach that lifted him over-head. He flung Delgado through the window to the courtyard far below.

The vampire came back in the window before Celwyn had even turned, again attacking. The magician had fought vampires many times before, but this felt different. Delgado was much faster and stronger than the others. No matter.

They slammed into walls and furniture and rolled into the hallway. The magician found not only was he challenged, but he felt a loss of control as his grief gnawed at him, distracting him. Celwyn told himself that even if Delgado were stronger, it wouldn't make him more intelligent.

The vampire slammed a vase across his face. Blood covered his eyes, and Celwyn's anger rose.

"You're bleeding, Magician." Delgado taunted him. "Allow me to taste you," he purred as he tried to pin Celwyn to the floor.

That wouldn't do, *Celwyn thought. Not at all.*

Their struggle escalated until the magician felt the vampire becoming even stronger. He flung the magi-cian into the ceiling, and Celwyn's resolve weakened. He tried to attack, but the vampire deflected his blows and once more pinned the magician to the floor, crushing him, his eyes burning into Celwyn, attempting to mesmerize him. With a supreme effort, Celwyn used magic to elevate Delgado off of him and fled.

Across rooftops they raced, leaping from building to building. Delgado ran much faster, swifter than the human eye could see, yet he couldn't find Celwyn, except when the magician wanted him to. The breeze blew in the direction Celwyn went, denying his scent to the vampire to track him. The magician's ribs were broken and his pain great, but his resolve had returned. Delgado would pay. Every time the vampire stopped running, a low whistle from the magician would attract his attention, and they'd be off again. Building by building, Celwyn drew Delgado closer to the top of the Rubicon Bath House.

When he arrived on the roof, the vampire found it empty. For several minutes, Delgado paced, growling, becoming careless as he searched the roof for Celwyn. Each shadow seemed to shift with the pale moonlight and then glow bright as day as Celwyn threw brilliant illumination between them. He separated himself and blew several of his own images across the rooftop. The images surrounded Delgado, walking slowly around him.

"Show yourself, coward!" Delgado shouted. The vampire cursed, and dogs howled from the street below.

Celwyn inhaled, and the music began. Sad and forlorn, Suzanne's opera played for her, for Celwyn's love of her, echoing across the night air. In the distance, under a shifting mist, the Seine glimmered like an otherworldly *snake. The magician wiped the blood from his face. His arm hung loose from the fight, but it wouldn't stop what he planned to do. In fact, having his enemy think of him as weak or wounded worked very well.*

Celwyn stepped from the shadows and moved to the edge of the roof.

"Aha! I knew you would show yourself," Delgado said, cocking his head to the side. "Your lover used to play that music on her phonograph. For hours and hours, until dawn. Then she would cry. Why? You couldn't satisfy her?" The vampire floated closer to the magician, dancing in the air and circling the magician so close he could have reached a hand and touched Celwyn's hair.

The thick, spicy scent of the vampire covered Celwyn, and bile rose in his throat.

The infinitesimal fraction of the moment had to be timed, *Celwyn reminded himself. It must be perfect, to anticipate when Delgado would strike.*

"You are much stronger than I expected," Celwyn said and took another step backward toward the yawning blackness below.

"And you, much weaker. You are little more than a common human. Useless."

Anger would make the vampire a bit more reckless.

"Suzanne loved me," Celwyn said. "She laughed at you."

The vampire lunged so quick Celwyn didn't see it, but he felt the whoosh of air beneath his feet as he elevated, and the vampire ran underneath him and off the roof.

As Delgado started to fall, Celwyn used magic to cinch the iron net he'd readied and closed the top, trapping the vampire. Delgado struggled and snarled as

Celwyn tightened the net still further and sent it to the top of the Notre Dame Church, ready for the morning's conflagration.

When Celwyn opened his eyes again, years had passed, and he was back on the train with Kang staring at him after an apparently repeated question. "Do you know for certain Delgado died?"

"I watched the net catch fire."

"I sincerely hope I'm wrong, Jonas." Patrick added, "Perhaps Delgado did die years ago." But his uncertain expression belied his words.

Kang eyed him and said, "If you don't mind me asking, you are not a real vampire?"

"No," Patrick replied. "I have some of their blood but do not satisfy my hunger with others' blood. A good claret and filet are more to my taste." He nodded at each of them in turn. "Miss Edmunds is not in danger."

"Noted, but your reassurance is not necessary," Celwyn said.

"Is Miss Annabelle a close relation to either of you? I ask since you are ostensibly chaperoning her."

The magician nearly smiled: there would be only one reason to ask: Patrick was already thinking ahead to possible marriage to Celwyn's "niece."

The Professor said, "No, not to either of us. She is an obligation that we have assumed in order to help her out of a delicate situation. Our objective is to keep her in new hats and good health until we reach Paris."

Patrick expelled a long breath, and his smile grew wide. He was a good-natured lad; Celwyn remembered that about him now. At the time, the magician only had room for his own grief.

"If I may, I would like to call upon Annabelle in Paris once I am able to."

"We would be honored but would caution you that she is as headstrong as she is beautiful." Kang wiggled his empty glass and glanced at the bar.

Patrick said, "That makes the challenge more interesting. How will I find you in Paris?"

"You may address correspondence to the city's Opera House," Celwyn replied and watched the automat's face. He loved surprises. Kang just got grumpier and studied him with his brow up. "It is likely I will be at least near there or even live there. I cannot speak for the intentions of the Professor and his wife."

"I am quite happy to see you again, Jonas, and appreciate meeting Professor Kang also. A toast." Patrick got to his feet. They touched glasses. "To new friends and old ones, may our paths always walk in harmony."

Celwyn hoped so.

Chapter 14

WITH THE DAWN, THE FIRST LIGHT of day revealed meadows of golden grasses and fields as far as they could see. The *Royal Victoria* rattled along at a good clip, and she blew her horn but did not stop, as she slowed, rumbling through a village just greeting the day. Smoke trailed from chimneys into the clear air as villagers tethered oxen and loaded carts with sacks of grain.

"Where is Jax?" Celwyn asked Kang as they settled into their seats in the dining car.

"I do not know."

"Well, I think he may be concentrating on me instead of you," Celwyn said.

Kang's eyes lit up. "You don't say?"

"It happened yesterday." He verified no one was listening, noting the raucous drinkers had grown even happier. "I didn't get a chance to tell you privately, but after you and the others left my compartment yesterday, I became unusually sleepy and experienced an 'unscheduled' nap. I assume a sleeping draught would have no effect on you. Did Annabelle mention the same problem?"

"No. Do you really think someone dosed you?"

"Yes. In our whiskey. You will recall she had coffee, under protest. Regardless, whoever it was found that, asleep or awake, I was not vulnerable. I think it was Jax."

"But you don't know."

"No. We must be on guard."

Kang shook out his napkin and placed it in his lap as their waiter arrived with the coffee service. "Yes, please."

"Earl Grey, please," said Celwyn.

When the waiter had left again, Kang frowned. "Keeping Annabelle sequestered and out of sight of the police will probably not work much longer. Even when her hair darkens, we will need to be vigilant at every stop this train makes. There are at least twenty of them between here and Bangladesh."

"Thank you," Celwyn said as the waiter deposited his tea. "I would like a cooked English breakfast, please."

"And you, Sir?"

"The same, thank you."

Celwyn waited a moment, then asked Kang a question he'd been wondering about. "An off-topic question: if you have mechanical internal parts, how can you eat? I do not wish to be indelicate, but where does the food go?"

Kang blew on his coffee. "As either a form of torture, or to provide the experience of sensation and pleasure, we automats were built with the ability to taste and savor. To accommodate that, I have a small receptacle," he pointed to his middle, "that I empty as needed."

"Efficient. Let us talk about Jax."

Kang sighed. "Have I any clue where he is on the train? No, but I am certain he is here. We have yet to confirm if he is interested in you or in me. It could be he just wanted to satisfy his curiosity about you."

"Agreed." Celwyn began to wish he was still on the ship.

"Nevertheless, was it Mrs. Karras, or Jax, who attacked Annabelle yesterday? Mrs. Karras is a large woman and could have disguised herself."

Talk of the variety and purpose of disguises continued until their breakfasts arrived. The chef had added just the right amount of salt, a sprinkling of spice, and served the bacon crisp. Celwyn hoped all of their meals would be as perfect. Little did he know what awaited them.

After he finished his last rasher, the magician said, "To install himself on the *Zelda* as Colonel Gilliam, Jax would have had to make plans at least a day or two before she sailed out of San Francisco. When did you decide that you would travel to Singapore?"

"Two days previously. We'd received the report about the danger to Elizabeth's mother and hurried to pack and depart. The *Zelda* was the only ship available heading to Singapore."

"And Talos made plans to recruit me at the same time and then reserved berths for us on the ship also."

Kang shrugged. "Who else knew of our plans? The university staff and our housekeeper." He forked his eggs a moment. "It has been a long time since I saw Talos, and we were separated for hundreds of years before that; I do not presume to know Talos' mind. Would he actually collaborate with someone as evil as himself, like Jax? I do not know."

"It is a mystery. But was it Talos who told Jax? Did they even know each other?

"It is possible." Kang kept an eye on the entrance as several more passengers arrived in the dining room.

"I agree. Evil attracts evil." As Celwyn thought about it, the logic began to fit together. "Do you remember how Talos initially insisted that I deliver you to Junstan Island?"

"Yes. I thought it odd when you told me about it. There's little there." Kang chewed a moment and said, "Think about it a bit more: that is the connection. Jax has an interest in what Talos wanted to do with you there. And I think it was not only for my power source, my essence and brain, but also the weapon I'd developed."

Celwyn spread a thick layer of marmalade on his toast. "It might help if I knew more about your weapon."

"It is mostly theory at this point," Kang said.

"Tell me anyway?"

He looked at the tables next to them before he answered. "There are minute particles that makeup everything. Much, much smaller that you can see.

Anything from a leaf to a drop of coffee have hundreds of thousands of them. If those particles—"

Behind them, an argument erupted between two of the waiters. He waited until the debaters had been escorted out by the maître'd. "To continue, if those particles are manipulated, under certain conditions, tremendous energy is created." The automat leaned back and sipped his coffee. "The uses could be for power generation instead of burning coal for steam, such as what this locomotive does. Or it could lead to a very large destructive bomb used during war. Whoever possesses it would win."

The waiters came back, slinging dishes onto a tray as they cleared tables. Celwyn gathered all of the dishes on the trays at one time. Instantly the waiters became quiet, wide-eyed, and looked at each other to determine which of them had loaded the tray.

"Please continue," the magician said.

Kang eyed them a moment. "If there was anything left after the bombing of a country or city, it would probably be unlivable for a long time."

"How much of an area are you describing?"

Kang lifted his hands. "It depends on the size of the bomb."

The magician noticed a few passengers had arrived for an early tea or luncheon, depending on where they hailed from. "What do you think Jax will do if he obtains the weapon plans?"

"Sell it to whoever gives him the most money..." Kang lowered his gaze and raised it again. "The very idea is frightening, and in retrospect, it is all my doing if someone is hurt."

Celwyn pointed a finger at him. "You cannot hold blame dear. Nothing has happened yet, and you aren't responsible for evil intentions. If Talos expected to sell it to Jax, then we have an advantage: we know he wants it and can stop him."

"Also, my discovery works on too grand a scale to be a personal display of mayhem. I agree. Most likely, he expects to sell it."

"At least we understand more."

"If we're correct, you are in his way, Jonas. At the very least, you've challenged and irritated him."

Outside their car, the terrain became hilly, the farms fewer, and in the distance, clusters of buildings heralded another hamlet, this time set away from the tracks. The magician would make a point of traveling here again one of these days and exploring the countryside. From the automat's expression, he wished he could hide there now.

"Pay attention, Xiau. There could be another attraction we represent to Jax." Celwyn signaled for more tea. He could do it himself with magic but doubted Kang would approve.

"Oh?"

"I am by nature modest—"

"I disagree."

"Either way, do you think he might covet me as the ultimate body to host himself? So that he could use my immortality and magic forever?"

Kang put his head in his hands. "Until now, I didn't think this situation could become worse."

"Exactly." Celwyn sat back and thought more about what the last supposition could mean.

"It is just as likely that he thinks of you as my talented guard dog," Kang said.

The magician rather fancied that idea. He smoothed his hair back. "A well-dressed and handsome one."

"Pfft. This is a fine mess," the automat complained.

"He may try to neutralize me before he obtains the weapon. Remember, the blame for the Gilliam murder was his first subtle attempt. His next try may be more direct: threaten Annabelle to get your cooperation or similar."

Kang nodded. "Dangerous, but it makes sense. All the more reason to protect her and keep the police from snatching you."

"I wouldn't go into custody quietly. Welcome, my friend," Celwyn said as Bartholomew joined them. His tea arrived, and they requested more coffee for their companion.

This morning the big man wore a new suit and a somber expression across his broad face. The suit seemed a bit tight around his muscled shoulders, so the magician gave him more room there and also lengthened the sleeves a touch. Bartholomew tugged on his sleeve and frowned in puzzlement.

"I'll order in a few moments," Bartholomew told the waiter, who bowed and departed.

"We were discussing our situation and enemies." Celwyn had perused Bartholomew's thoughts in their previous encounters and noted a fine mind with a distinct desire to repay the magician for his small gesture when they met. "I'm sorry you had to witness that incident last night."

"It is me who regrets not to have been of more assistance. That was my first encounter with a vampire. I should not have hesitated just because she was a woman."

"It was my first close happenstance with one also, at least close-up," Kang said. "However, we do not believe we'll have any more problems with vampires, at least for several weeks, even after we reach Paris."

As the automat spoke, Celwyn wondered: *what if Delgado is still alive?* The magician didn't worry for himself: he could and would enjoy fighting the vampire a dozen times over. But the monster could easily hurt his friends and would enjoy doing so.

"Pardon me. Is there a problem?" Bartholomew asked.

Kang looked at the magician, and he nodded.

"Yes," the Professor said. "We do not wish to alarm you or have harm come to you. But you should be aware that we have, and will again, attract danger."

"Not just vampires?"

Bartholomew appeared to be as astute as he was large.

"There are others." Kang added, "Please be sure you are on alert. Our enemy could be anyone: it is like what your language would call a 'roho,' a ghost, who is inside of someone, someone who hosts them without consent. This enemy could be inside a policeman, a passenger, or even a woman."

What if Jax managed to get inside one of the vampires... Celwyn shuddered. That would be interesting.

"What is his name?" Bartholomew asked.

"I knew him as Jax ... years ago."

Bartholomew slapped his thigh and roared with laughter that rattled the windows. A few of the passengers pretended they didn't see anything. A few others leaned a bit closer to them. "It is doubtful that he could hurt me. In my village in Juba, I was taught about rohos and other evil things. I can usually recognize them, or at least avoid them."

A thought occurred to Celwyn. "How far does your current journey take you?" he asked.

"Initially, Constantinople. Now, I would be honored to accompany you to Paris and offer my help."

Celwyn's idea had wings. He smiled. "Please excuse us for a moment; I'd like to confer with the Professor."

They left Bartholomew in the dining car long enough for a short discussion outside the door. Kang liked the idea.

When they returned, the automat addressed Bartholomew, "We would like to propose a venture to you."

"I am listening."

"Would you care to join our party? We would pay you for your time."

Bartholomew fidgeted with his tie. "You do not owe me money. It is I who owe you, Mr. Celwyn."

The magician shook his head, dismissing the idea. Kang continued, "We need someone to help protect both Miss Edmunds and me. Mr. Celwyn can take care of himself but can't be with us all the time. It will most likely be dangerous, and for that, we wish to compensate you."

"Do you accept our offer?" Celwyn asked.

"I do, Mr. Celwyn." He grinned at them. "As long as you do not pay me. It is an honor to be asked to help."

"Can you call me Jonas?" the magician asked. It wouldn't take too much effort to provide compensation without the big man noticing.

Bartholomew looked him in the eye and in his deep, sonorous voice, said, "Of course, Jonas. On the condition that you do not pay me. I saw you thinking of it."

"There are various methods of payment." Celwyn sighed. "I feel better already, knowing you stand with us. You'll need background. Our story began with an irritating visit from a priest, who wasn't really a priest, in San Francisco."

"He was my brother," Kang said. "A very bad person. We are wondering if Jax was his partner."

Chapter 15

K ANG KNOCKED ON ANNABELLE'S door. She jerked it open with an irritated look that didn't go well with her otherwise becoming afternoon frock of sky blue.

"I thought you would be here hours ago," she complained and allowed them entry. Cigarette smoke billowed into the hallway as the automat closed the door. Celwyn crossed the room and opened the window letting in a rush of fresh cold air.

Annabelle tapped her foot. "Could you close that now?"

Kang did so and sat down across from her. As ever, he was a diplomat. "We bring good news to make up for our tardiness."

"Oh?" She lit a new cigarette and fitted it into a long holder.

"We must explain so that you can understand a situation that has arisen." Celwyn joined him on the sofa. "Foremost, we must know: do you still wish to travel with us to Paris? Or do you prefer that we hire a traveling companion for you? Please keep in mind that Patrick will exit the train in Kanpur to rejoin his army unit." Her expression turned melancholy before he added, "He has already asked if he may pay his attentions to you when he reaches Paris later this year."

Like a cat who had just licked a bowl of cream, a satisfied smile lit up her face.

"May we assume that this meets with your approval?" the automat asked. "And that you still wish to travel with us?"

Annabelle looked at Kang, then the magician, before inhaling from her cigarette. "Yes, at least until we reach Paris."

"Then there is something you need to know." The Professor regarded her. "You are in danger. Not from a forced marriage, although that is inherently dangerous by definition, but we have enemies who would harm you."

Annabelle studied Celwyn, not with sympathy. "What did you do?"

Kang snickered and the magician elbowed him.

"We have attracted the attention of someone who wishes to steal a scientific discovery the Professor has made." The magician waved the cigarette smoke out of his face. "This person would kill you or use you to obtain the discovery."

"That is ridiculous." She tapped out a new cigarette, and her hand shook when she tried to light it. The automat obliged her.

"This person fears your Uncle Celwyn," Kang said. "That is why he was set up as the murderer of Colonel Gilliam when the *Zelda* docked."

"I remember." She squinted at them through the smoke.

"Your Uncle Celwyn protects me and my discovery."

"I see." She yawned and covered it with a hand.

"We want to make it clear that you could be harmed," Celwyn said. "We would appreciate it if you took this seriously."

She shrugged lace-covered shoulders. "I suppose it is possible."

"At the least, your aunt is probably still looking for you," Kang said.

"I imagine she is. I inherited most of the family money."

The cynicism fit her well, but to her credit, she did not appear to take her aunt's avarice personally.

Celwyn said, "As expected, your hair has darkened nicely with the dye. With moderate application of face makeup and an accent, I believe you can leave your room. Perhaps to meet Patrick in the dining car for dinner tonight?"

She clapped her hands in delight.

"Precautions have been made for your protection," Kang said.

The clapping stopped and she narrowed her eyes. "Such as?"

"You are not to leave the train unless accompanied by one of us or the very large man named Bartholomew whom you met last night. We have hired him to accompany you, and he will be stationed in your uncle's suite next door during the day—with the door open—in case someone wanders by," Kang said.

"Or someone wanders in." Celwyn flipped a hand. "Or you wander out."

"Is this really necessary?" She took a long drag off her cigarette.

"It is our duty to keep you safe." Celwyn said, "Introduce Bartholomew as a companion that I hired for you. He will be discreet. Do not try to evade him."

From her glance out the window and irritated expression, she probably regretted her choice to stay with them. "Oh, all right. I suppose I can make do for a few days."

Kang and Celwyn spent a companionable afternoon drinking tea and playing poker with Bartholomew in Celwyn's compartment until Annabelle arrived in a cloud of ruffles and determination. She wanted to have tea in the dining car. Bartholomew stood and bowed. "I am at your service, Miss."

After they left, Kang and the magician elected to adjourn to the club car. It had wonderful views and the abundant miasma of books, cigars, and whiskey. What more could one want? Kang brought along a book on the history of the Templars. Celwyn settled in with the *Calcutta Gazette* from the previous week. The train would stop there this evening just before dinner.

"What are you reading?"

"I'm wondering what Boucicault's play *Grimaldi* is about. It opened a few months ago, according to this advertisement," the magician said.

"Knowing would just give us unseemly and unfulfilled dreams."

"Perhaps." Celwyn turned a page and laughed as he read an article about Ludwig Leopold Doebler, the magician. Next came a report on gout. He eventually located the train schedules.

"If Mrs. Pearse were to follow us, the best she could expect would be the *China Star,* which departs Singapore tomorrow. She would arrive in Paris a week after we do. Or, if we were fortunate, she would have been diverted by rumors about us heading to Venice instead."

"Wishful thinking on your part." Kang lowered his book. "What if she just alerted the authorities anywhere along the way? They could telegraph ahead of us."

"Each stop will be a test of our subterfuge," Celwyn said. "Either the police, or Mrs. Pearse, could be a factor. But, unless she lies about us, all she can say is that we're keeping Annabelle from enduring a bad marriage. After hearing Annabelle's statement about money, I had to revise my estimate of Mrs. Pearse's tenacity."

Kang raised his book again and pursed his lips. "I did also and advised Bartholomew regarding the same."

"Should we advise Annabelle?"

The book came down again. "A good question. You decide."

With care, and a bit of impishness, Celwyn said, "Or we could depart the train in Constantinople and travel to Prague instead of Paris."

"Oh?" Kang asked. His eyes lit up like a cluster of stars. "The pastries and the books!"

"I also just read of Ferdinand von Zeppelin's patent on his 'Navigable Balloon.' The photograph probably didn't come close to the majesty of it." Celwyn showed Kang the picture and then eyed him with a healthy dose of speculation. "I'm betting you know quite a bit about flying."

Kang just smiled and raised his book.

Chapter 16

AS THE *ROYAL VICTORIA* CHUGGED into Mandalay, everyone on the train anticipated a chance, even for a few hours, to stretch their legs, sharpen their senses, and inhale the spicy perfume of the city. The magician listened to unspoken comments from passengers about purchasing tapestries, artwork, tobacco, and the favors of the local harlots. Trivial matters all: Celwyn wanted to renew his personal supply of tea.

According to their travel guide, the shopping district lay only a few blocks from the train station. Kang and Patrick stood at the magician's elbow as they viewed the crowd in the train yard with skeptical eyes. Already they could hear the noise of a big city, the arguing taxi drivers, and the rattle and clanking of the carriages. Bartholomew did the same from the windows in the magician's suite. Annabelle had somewhat graciously—in other words she didn't throw anything—consented to wait in her compartment until they had verified that no one threatened or would be able to recognize her. Her hair appeared much darker now. Because she would be on Patrick's arm as they strolled into the city, and because Bartholomew would trail them at an appropriate distance, Celwyn felt a modicum of relief. The big man would also be close enough to be mistaken for a servant, which she didn't have when she left Singapore. That should derail some of their enemies. By extension, the logic made her disguise stronger.

Celwyn and Kang planned to exit the train separately. The magician couldn't see any unusual police activity, just train officials wearing worried expressions as their chicks scattered in different directions in their quest for adventure and a good deal.

"Anything?" Kang asked as the last of the passengers prepared to disembark.

"No."

Kang waved to Bartholomew. Moments later, they watched as Patrick, Annabelle, and Bartholomew headed across the terminal grounds and out the gates. They turned left toward the Kalama shopping district. Kang and Celwyn followed at a distance.

"I told Patrick to concentrate on the shops near the tea sellers first so that if something happens, I will at least be able to purchase my tea."

"Tea is important," Kang agreed with a fond and tolerant glance. After another moment, he said, "But I am again nervous that something will happen."

The crowd from the train moved onto the avenue, and Patrick made another left down the next street and past cafés with straw-roofed tables. Three women trailed them, all of Chinese descent and chattering faster than a gaggle of chickens. Behind them strolled a spindly, solitary man in a black suit carrying a walking stick. His silver hair shone in the filtered sunlight. From a distance, Celwyn watched the man as he continued walking, stopping only at the flower sellers. Everything appeared normal.

"I'll be right back," Celwyn told Kang as he ducked into a tea shop. It didn't take long to find both Earl Grey and Ceylon tea and purchase a respectable quantity of it. With the aroma of tea in his nose and grasping his package, the magician exited the shop only to find the automat gone. The situation deserved some profanity, and he used some.

In seconds, he had spotted Kang half a block ahead and walking fast. Celwyn broke into a trot, passing Bartholomew, who hovered near the love birds and roses. "Stay with them. I'll be back," he called.

Kang should know better, Celwyn fumed as he shoved through the shoppers and vendors, keeping an eye on the top of Kang's bowler hat. Further along, in front of a spice shop, the silver-haired man approached an elderly gentleman leaning against a post and smoking a pipe. As the magician neared them, he noticed fewer tourists and no one that he recognized from the train. Several local men in traditional dress sitting on the ground looked up as the silver-haired man addressed them.

So quick it must have been carefully rehearsed, four heavy-set men in thick coats came at Kang, two from each side of the avenue. He spun around, kicking one of them back with force, reminding Celwyn of Talos's strength.

As Kang turned, the other two pinned his arms while the remaining man raised a cudgel above his head. Kang flung one of the men away from him just as Celwyn removed the cudgel and turned it on his attacker. At the same time, the magician propelled the remaining attacker skyward across several rooftops before slamming him into a wall.

Celwyn grabbed Kang's arm. "Come—this could be a diversion while they attack Annabelle."

They ran back to the flower seller arriving in time to behold Annabelle on tiptoe as she pinned a carnation on Bartholomew's lapel. Beside him, Patrick already sported a red one.

"And here I had worried that a mild-mannered love-struck vampire," Celwyn panted, "wouldn't be up to protecting her." Celwyn bent over, catching his breath.

Kang wasn't even breathing hard from their sprint up the street. None of the attackers followed them. Neither had the silver-haired man. Patrick and Annabelle touched elbows as they talked between the tubs of flowers. Celwyn put the idea in Bartholomew's mind to take them to the café next door and to sit them in the back where they would not be as easily spotted. Bartholomew made a face, and his brows drew together in consternation. He looked at the magician, and Celwyn nodded. That caused more bewilderment as his mouth opened and closed several times before he escorted his charges toward the café. Celwyn realized that he probably should have informed the big man of his talents regarding suggestibility.

Again the magician checked the street, then turned to Kang.

"What the *hell*?" he growled. "Why did you take off like that? You could have been killed!"

Kang studied Celwyn and nodded. "Your concern is borne of your affection, my friend, which is appreciated. I understand, but I did not have time to wait for you."

Celwyn could admit that he liked the little bugger, worried about him, and would kill to protect him, but there was also common sense. He took a deep breath and asked, "Why?"

"You noticed that man's walking stick? While you were in the tea shop, the man doubled back, passing close to me. Purposely. Then he turned the stick outward so that I could see it clearly. He even pretended to drop it so I would observe the head of the cane."

This was not what Celwyn wanted to hear. "And?"

"Refreshment first." The Professor led him to one of the café's empty tables as a man hawking mangos sidestepped them. "Anyone entering this establishment will pass by us, and we'll be able to follow Patrick and company when they leave." They took seats under a striped umbrella, and Kang signaled the waiter. He regarded the magician. "In 1807 in Constantinople, I saw a lion head on a cane just like the one the man dropped. It had been in the hand of someone who I found out later had been occupied by Jax."

The magician fell silent, cursing up a colorful storm internally and thinking of their next move.

The next hour at the café passed peacefully with cups of the local coffee, tea, and bites of baklava sent from heaven. Kang appeared ravenous from his exertions. He ate his sweet and most of Celwyn's when the magician wasn't quick enough.

Celwyn's thoughts, meanwhile, had continued to the logical conclusion that Jax had simply stood a distance away and observed how Kang deported himself and studied how the magician resolved the rest of the attack. Jax had received much more information from the encounter than they did. By now, the bastard would no doubt occupy someone else as well. Damn.

"Did you draw any conclusions from the attack?" he asked. "Jax may be studying us to figure out a way of inhabiting us."

The automat shrugged and licked honey from his fingers. "Other than my trousers being a mite too tight for the higher kicks I delivered, no. Why?" He signaled the waiter for more baklava and studied the pedestrians walking by.

"It appears he is careful, he plans, but he doesn't carry out the attack himself, unless he is changing hosts or is threatened." Celwyn sipped his tea and stewed about their position of being on defense, not offense, with this enemy.

"True. A plan by Jax to isolate me and then attack confirms that he isn't particularly strong or doesn't wish to dirty his hands." Kang chewed on his lip while he thought. "In Constantinople, I saw him stab a man to death, but it was only to escape, not for another purpose."

Celwyn stood and threw coins on the table. "I'd like to think we're right, but we should return to the train before something else happens." The magician leaned far enough inside the café to catch Patrick and Bartholomew's attention. Annabelle chattered on, oblivious to those around her, and Patrick was soon gazing at her again. The magician pointed in the direction of the train and withdrew.

When they began to walk to the next shop, Celwyn said, "If you can resist chasing anyone down the street, here is a seller of silk ties you might be interested in. It will be several minutes before Annabelle will be ready to go."

As Kang entered the shop, he smiled and said, "I'm happy you were able to purchase your tea, Jonas."

An hour later, Annabelle had been escorted back to her cabin. She had no complaints, only stars in her eyes. Bartholomew sat next door with Celwyn's compartment door open, a deck of cards for solitaire, and Qing perched on his knee as they watched the hallway. When the magician remarked how cozy he and the bird appeared to be, the big man rolled his eyes. Between them, no one could sneak in or sneak out.

Patrick had left them to freshen up before dinner. This was to be the first time Annabelle graced the dining car, and he would be her escort.

Just as their porter appeared at the cabin door, the magician handed Bartholomew one of the fresh newspapers they had obtained.

Kang suggested, "We should try something besides whiskey."

"All right." Celwyn nodded. "If it is of quality, it will be a pleasant change." They ordered brandy liquors.

This afternoon, Kang read the Hindustan newspaper. His fingers had nearly as much ink on them as the pages. After a few moments, he remarked, "There are no further stories about either Annabelle, or you, and Singapore. In fact, the news concerns Friedrich Nietzsche, the philosopher."

"Your talons are sharp." Bartholomew put Qing on the table between them and raised a brow at the automat. "Because?"

"It seems the philosopher left the rails, as the Americans say. Supposedly he saw a horse flogged and went crazy."

"Anything else?"

"Let's see. This is old news from February: The Devil's Footprints, 'hoof-like marks' mysteriously appeared in southern Devon, England, after a snowfall," Kang said. "Interesting. You know, a few pages back, I read that this train will be in Bangladesh by Sunday and in Paris by another fortnight."

The magician listened but distractedly. On a very primeval level, he felt that something was about to happen. He could feel it, and it wouldn't be a pleasant situation when it occurred.

He glanced outside. The train traveled at moderate speed through hilly terrain as the sunset under a heavy bank of clouds that blurred the landscape. Celwyn's thoughts seemed to blur also. As he watched row after row of houses and churches go by, he felt the sense of foreboding crystalizing.

"Bloody hell." The magician couldn't ignore it anymore. The feeling wasn't about Annabelle's safety: that had been controlled. Nor was it Kang, who sat so close the magician could have knocked the newspaper out of his hand. One look at Bartholomew and an intruder would see he was dedicated and alert. Celwyn couldn't picture anyone getting the better of Patrick except another vampire, and unless Mrs. Karras could fly hundreds of miles, she was a long distance behind them. That only left Jax.

"It's another hour until dinner. Do either of you care to walk the train with me?" Celwyn asked.

Kang regarded him with a brow up. "For what purpose?"

"I'm not sure."

Kang folded the paper and stood. "After you."

"We will be right here," Bartholomew assured them. Qing twisted his head, watching them leave.

⁓

They stopped first at the observation car. Celwyn stuck his head inside and saw what he expected to see: a smattering of female passengers staring out the windows and wishing they were somewhere else, such as the club car, where they were not allowed. Next came the dining car, and with the automat in the lead, they marched through it— finding a few stragglers from the coach sitting— and stepped around waiters setting out flower arrangements and cutlery. Kang nodded at the head waiter and kept walking. Celwyn had never been in the dining car when it was so quiet and said so to Kang.

Soon they entered the kitchen. After excuses for interrupting, a few minutes more brought them to the passenger coach cars. Evidence of dirty clothes, unfolded blankets, and the odor of humans too long without the opportunity for a proper toilette greeted them. As they trooped up the aisle between the coach seats, Celwyn noted that a few of the passengers had skipped dinner. Was it funds or the food? He scattered coins into their pockets and the idea that the food was edible.

When they reached the staff dining car, they found diners filling most of the seats, so they increased their pace to limit the intrusion. Celwyn kept an eye out but did not see the man with the silver hair or anyone else out of place. As they went, the magician's sense of foreboding did not diminish, instead increasing the further they walked. Around them, he gathered unvoiced thoughts ranging from irritation to lusty curiosity as they passed by.

The final car before the locomotive housed the train staff. A sizable porter who appeared as clean-shaven as a newborn blocked their path.

"I'm sorry, Sirs, this is the staff car. No passengers beyond this point." He sounded stern and had no intention of moving out of their way.

"We would like to pass through to see the engines," Kang said.

The porter shook his head. "I'm sorry, Sir."

Celwyn stepped up. "Could you possibly open the door and allow us a look down the hallway?" Kang glanced at the magician, but with the porter inches away, Celwyn couldn't tell him that his sense of unease had grown ten-fold as soon as they had reached this car.

The Professor fished in his pocket and handed some coins to the porter.

"We'd just like a quick look, and you will be with us."

As he spoke, the door behind the porter burst open, and a man dressed only in his trousers and an undershirt pushed by, yelling, "It's James! Get a doctor!" The baby-face porter whirled and ran inside with Kang at his heels. Celwyn shut the door behind them and followed.

Immediately the heat from the engines covered them like an airless blanket. With fewer wall sconces, the shadows seemed more pronounced here, and the smell of the coal and steam much stronger. The porter must have been part greyhound as he bounded forward to the last cabin before the loco-motive. The noise from the engine made it impos-sible to speak. The porter rapped on the door and then pushed it open.

Over the top of his head, Celwyn could see another dead body. With a flick of a finger, he immo-bilized their new friend and sidled around him. Kang trailed behind him.

One glance revealed that strangulation had been used this time, even with a kitchen full of knives nearby. Interesting. Then Celwyn knew why.

"Isn't that your tie—the red one—around his neck?" he asked.

"Yes." Kang stared. "Jonas, I am beginning to sincerely regret accompanying you here."

Celwyn removed the tie, opened the window, and tossed it out. After closing the window again he said, "We need to get out of here: the man who discovered this mess will be returning, probably with the head porter."

The automat didn't need to be urged further. He dived out the door, and they hurried back the way they'd come. "It appears we're being framed for murder."

"Again."

As they entered the staff dining car, Celwyn saw the head porter and the shirtless man heading toward them. "Sit down, quickly."

By the time the two men reached the exit to the next car, both Kang and the magician were studying newspapers and too busy to look up. After the head porter passed by, they wasted no time reaching the first-class dining car again, where they could slow down and breathe normally.

Loud enough for the waiters to hear, Celwyn asked Kang, "Do you smell that? Roast pork. I am famished." He sniffed the air appreciatively. It wasn't an act: Celwyn was hungry, and it smelled good.

"Garnished with parsley and rosemary, I believe. It is still at least an hour until we dine," the automat said. "I hope the love birds appreciate the chef's efforts."

Chapter 17

BY THE TIME CELWYN HAD FINISHED his toilette and donned one of his favorite velvet dinner jackets, he could clearly hear his stomach romancing the tantalizing whiff of the pork roast. Although wonderful, as a distraction it couldn't displace their porter's death in his thoughts. The magician hadn't known James well, but a direct line of guilt could be drawn between his death and their arrival on this train: Celwyn vowed Jax would not fare well once he found him.

Kang awaited him in the hall, gazing out the window into the darkness they sailed through. Sporadic moonlight sliced through the clouds to paint the landscape across white rocks and hints of snow under the trees. Kang's reflection in the window glass revealed a furrowed brow.

"Care to share your worry?" Celwyn asked.

Kang made an effort to relax with several deep breaths. "Another death. Do you wonder why we are similar to human lightning rods? Why we attract evil like we're smeared in morbid honey? It is as if we represent a prize to them: as if ultimate revenge, chaos, and greed can be satisfied by conquering us."

Celwyn clapped him on the shoulder. "Let's go to dinner. You'll feel better."

"I doubt it."

They began walking toward the front of the train. In the adjoining car, the aroma of the roasted pork grew stronger along with the rumblings of his stomach. "Yours is a good description, however. Alone, we're tempting to nefarious forces, but together we're irresistible," the magician said.

"Have you tried to probe the minds of those around us to find Jax?"

Celwyn sighed. "I have not been successful."

The automat held the door, and they entered the dining car. As they sat at one of the rear tables, he said, "Annabelle will be here any moment. Quickly, tell me about the last few hours of Charles Delgado and how likely it is he will be waiting for us in Paris."

"You think so, eh?" Celwyn flicked open his napkin and said, "It is a good thing I'm ravenous, or your request would kill my appetite."

They ordered several bottles of wine, including a rosé, and the magician kept an eye on the door. "Like I said before, it was a difficult time. I was heartbroken, angry, out of control. Everyone avoided me. I burned with the desire for revenge and knew enough about

Delgado to know he'd want to gloat." Celwyn's gaze turned inward. "So, I gave him an opportunity."

Their first bottle of wine arrived. The waiter poured it with the pomp and circumstance it deserved. "A bit dry," Kang commented, but he savored it a bit too long to reject it.

"Delgado enjoyed holding court at the Hotel Corbeau with innocents and other vampires. One by one, I caused them to disappear."

"How?"

"By stuffing them into a downstairs closet. When I allowed Delgado to discover me, he was confident enough to be reckless." Celwyn sipped and enjoyed the memory. "We had a merry chase across a dozen rooftops. For every leap he made toward me, I only elevated my humble personage higher. I wasn't faster, but I could anticipate his anger and actions. Eventually, he tired, and it was a matter of enticing him off a roof into a net. Then I trussed him like a rotting sausage."

"And then?"

"I kept him in the Black Tower before moving him to the roof."

"Did he confess to killing Suzanne?" Kang asked.

Celwyn's jaw tightened, and he tried to control his anger. "He bragged about how he'd nearly seduced her, and when he could not finish the act, he destroyed her." With the sad memory, the magician closed his eyes and held onto the image of her laughing on the beach in Brighton and the day they rode their bicycles with the silly picnic baskets. For a long moment Celwyn, relived her smile until he could continue.

The dining car door opened, and Annabelle started down the aisle with Patrick at her heels.

"As you know, most vampires cannot survive in direct sunlight. At high noon, I pinned Delgado's net to the tower's precipice so that he'd be exposed to the sun. I watched the net catch fire."

Patrick arrived at their table in full dress uniform wearing a broad smile and Annabelle on his arm. He pulled out her chair and saw her settled in. As he sat beside the magician, he asked, "What are we discussing this evening? The sights of Paris?"

Kang nearly choked on his wine. "Err, no. Finance, we were discussing finance."

Patrick observed his expression and said, "Of course."

Tonight, Annabelle represented an artist's vision in white lace, heavy eye paint, and exotic brass jewelry with brilliant-colored stones. She fluttered a decorated fan as she inspected the other occupants of the car. Some of the other diners stared back, either because this was the first time they'd seen her or because of her youth and exotic beauty. As Celwyn wished he'd asked her to be less memorable, Kang said, "I understand we will arrive in Chittagong tomorrow, Captain Swayne. Do you plan to depart the train at that point?"

The corners of Annabelle's mouth turned down. Patrick's glance at her held concern. "No, not until Kanpur. We still have a few days yet."

As Patrick spoke, Celwyn inhaled the steam from his soup and listened to the conversation float around the dining car like playful clouds in a mountain sky. Nearby thoughts included:

"...that isn't her father. He is too young. The other man is half Chinese or something... he isn't related to her."

"...the tall one in the velvet coat has the most beautiful green eyes. And his lips! I wonder how they all know each other... he isn't married to that girl..."

"...I liked James... how did he die? Will someone kill me in my bed?"

"...the roast is fatty. I like fat."

"My fork is dirty!"

"The black man who chaperones that girl ate his luncheon here, in first class. My, my..."

Celwyn couldn't resist that last one. The magician dumped a glass of wine on the woman's lap. Heavens! The train must have hit a bump. The woman sopped wine instead of judging people.

"...they reopened the Opera House in Prague last year," Patrick was saying as he perused the embossed card announcing their menu. He nodded and replaced it in the middle of the table. "The reconstruction is not yet complete."

"The original Opera House had been bombarded during Napoleon's campaign." Kang's attention centered on Celwyn with a look full of suspicion. The magician thought it nice to know that their thoughts harmonized, at least in anticipating his thoughts.

Annabelle asked, "How much of it is still under construction?"

"The auditorium is nearly finished according to the papers. The basement will be completed last. There are new viewing boxes in the balcony." Patrick paused to sample the wine. "The orchestra pit was not damaged and will be cleaned up. I say, this is a fine wine."

Interesting. Celwyn caught Kang's glance and ignored him while he thought some more. What he'd planned to do in Paris could be done in Prague. Museums, galleries, gardens, and other inspirations littered the city. He stopped his internal discussion when he found Kang staring with a knowing look. Was it *he* who could read thoughts now?

"The city has some fanciful legends." Kang poured the rest of the wine and signaled for another bottle.

Patrick said, "You know, there is also the story of the monster of Prague that has been substantiated by several well-known men. The Pope and Disraeli both say that it is true."

"Explain, please?" Annabelle asked and placed dainty fingertips on top of Patrick's hand. He started to speak and couldn't.

"It is an interesting story." Celwyn searched his memory. "The legend says Rabbi Loew's golem was called Yossele, and it summoned spirits from the dead." He happened to know the story was true.

Patrick recovered enough to answer his beloved, "The golem was a large and strong mud figure brought to life. The golem saved many of the Prague Jews from harm. It was never a monster. Some even say the golem was a beautiful woman."

My, my, Celwyn mused, *this legend could also be a good distraction, or explanation, for the unexplained antics of a bored and handsome magician.*

As he considered the possibilities, Bartholomew entered the car. Celwyn waved him over. Part of their arrangements included the big man's vigilance over their sleeping quarters during the dinner hours. As he drew closer, Celwyn could see that his jacket had a fresh rip in the pocket, and his shirt collar wasn't straight. The magician fixed both before he reached them; there was no sense in having to explain something to Annabelle that she didn't need to worry about. Celwyn also placed a filter on what she and Patrick could hear.

"Trouble?" he asked, already knowing the answer as he pulled out the remaining chair.

Bartholomew sank into the seat.

"You could say that, Mr. Celwyn."

"Please call me Jonas."

Annabelle smiled blissfully and poured Bartholomew a glass of wine.

"Thank you, Miss." He turned to the magician with a brow up.

"She can't hear us. What happened?"

"I ripped my jacket while fighting—" He looked down and saw that his jacket had been repaired. Several seconds elapsed before he raised his eyes to Celwyn.

The magician waved it off. "It is nothing. Please go ahead."

"Not much to say." The big man fingered the material of his jacket before continuing. "As per your request, I stayed in your cabin with the lights off. With that damned bird." He pointed to a spot on his wrist. "It likes to sit on me with its claws out. Well, anyhow, I heard a noise in the Professor's cabin next door and went over there. Before I got the light on, someone hit me hard with something. We fought, and he ran out."

"You have any idea who it was?" Kang asked.

"None."

That pretty much settled things for Celwyn. The magician removed Patrick and Annabelle's filter and said, "We need to get off this train. I will not put you in danger any longer."

"From who? From what?" she sputtered.

"Keep your voice down, please. We're no longer going to Paris. I fear more danger there. Do you want to stay with us and endure our possible adventures and hardships along with more danger? Or do you wish for us to engage a chaperone for you so that you may continue to Paris? The danger will follow us, not you."

When her eyes widened, Kang explained. "If we are not near you, you'll be safe."

Celwyn's estimation of Annabelle's motivations and temperament meant that she needed to voluntarily commit to staying with them. Forcing either choice would not be a good idea.

"My word," Annabelle fanned herself and said with a strong southern drawl, "I *do* declare that I need a cigarette."

"Dinner first," Kang said. "We're offering you a difficult choice, but you should know that we'll honor whichever decision you make."

"Could I go to Agra with Patrick?"

Celwyn nearly spat out his wine, and Patrick's eyes widened more than he thought possible.

The automat said, "No. It is a frontier and battleground without any comforts or the security that an unmarried woman would require. I'm sure that the Captain will join you as soon as he is able."

Patrick reached for her hand. "The Professor is correct. I do not wish for you to be in an untenable position. I will come to you as soon as possible." He nodded to the others. "If you choose to stay with your friends, I have complete confidence in them."

She looked at the magician. "Where are you going?"

"Prague."

A moment of complete silence, and then Kang said, "Ah."

"It would be best if we do not discuss this openly here. But we do need to know your decision."

Annabelle favored them with an inscrutable look. "I will go with you to Prague."

Patrick hadn't released her hand. "And I will join you there." His tone sounded as moist as a wet dishrag as they gazed at each other.

The waiter interrupted the scene, arriving with their soup. Celwyn displayed a deep appreciation for the bisque, more than the soup itself deserved. Enduring bumps in a courtship was much too maudlin for the magician.

"After dinner, we'll all adjourn to my compartment. It is time we took Annabelle into our confidence."

"It is about damn time," she responded in a sweet and dainty voice.

———

When the last bite of iced cake had been savored, they did not tarry. The automat stopped along the way to order more coffee and whiskey from their new porter, Andrew.

Both the automat and Celwyn gave him a good look and exchanged a nod before they trouped to the sleeper car. Celwyn noted some interest in their party as they passed by the other passengers and monitored a few thoughts. The unspoken comments centered on Bartholomew, usually on the color of his skin. He seemed to be a walking distraction. This could be favorable to them because it could be less likely someone would recognize Kang, himself, or Annabelle. However, the combination of their disparity would be memorable to anyone who might talk. The gossip could eventually reach Mrs. Pearse—or one of the vampires.

Bartholomew stood aside as they entered the magician's cabin, then backed up against the hallway wall, prepared to guard the compartment.

"When I'm here, I'm able to guard us. Please," Celwyn held the door open and gestured for him to come inside. "You are our brother in arms."

Patrick perched on one of the magician's trunks. The others took seats on the bed and divan. Kang was the last to arrive with the porter Andrew and the refreshments. None of them mentioned that propriety no longer seemed as important as their safety.

Once everything had been arranged on the coffee table, and Andrew adequately tipped, Kang asked him to not worry about them for the rest of the evening. Celwyn noted he had brought two bottles of wine in addition to the whiskey and coffee. He agreed: they wouldn't need anything else.

As the door closed behind the porter, Celwyn let Qing out of the lavatory. The bird spied Annabelle and flew over to roost on the cushions behind her. The magician looked at Qing and shook his head. The bird eyed her earrings and moved a scant foot away.

"The Professor and I have a story to tell you, and then we need to make plans." As Celwyn spoke, Kang poured and passed glasses around. The magician had decided not to tell Annabelle about some of the details, but enough to be sure she felt safe. "Bartholomew, before we begin, we must also offer you the same choice. Without regard to our needs, you may proceed to Paris as planned. We'd hate to see you go but understand if you should choose to."

Bartholomew stirred his coffee and dumped in more sugar. "I wouldn't miss your adventures for anything, Jonas," he stopped and looked at Annabelle, "except, if Miss Annabelle needed me."

"That is greatly appreciated," she said.

"Some of you know what I'm about to tell you, some do not. After we docked in Singapore, someone attempted to kill the Professor. Then one of the passengers was murdered and left in my cabin. It could have been done by another passenger, but we suspect it was one of our enemies."

Bartholomew's attention stayed with Celwyn as if he suspected something would happen if he didn't. Annabelle's lay with the whiskey bottle, while Patrick couldn't stop wetting his lips and staring at the object of his affection as if she would dissolve any moment.

"Between the Professor and I, we have attracted the attention of an evil entity. Not a man, but one who can masquerade as one." That reminded the magician; he wiggled a finger placing a wall of silence between them and the hallway before continuing. "This isn't easily explained, but our enemy could be anyone."

"How?" Annabelle asked.

"He takes over the body of the person he chooses to be. Do you recall the death of Mr. McAlistair, the Lloyd's investigator, in Skudai?"

Annabelle made a face. "Yes."

Kang said, "That was Jax, the evil that Jonas has described. Earlier today, he strangled our porter, James."

Annabelle's mouth opened, and nothing came out for several seconds.

"James is *dead*?"

"It happened this afternoon," Kang said. "As he leaves the person who has hosted him Jax murders them before he assumes a new host."

"That is monstrous." Bartholomew gulped and breathed deep, perhaps wondering what he'd stepped into.

As he should. Celwyn watched the lights of a town reflected through his window as their train passed by. Beyond that, a thin line of light remained on the horizon. It grew late, and the *Royal Victoria* would stop for the night soon. "To continue, we believe Jax wants something from either the Professor or myself, and he will hurt anyone who is near us." He turned to Annabelle. "We won't hold it against you if you change your mind about staying with us, my dear."

Annabelle looked at each of them and demanded, "Do you know how utterly boring it is to be rich and not have a purpose or anything to do besides buy hats?"

Kang smiled. "No, I don't."

For himself, the magician sometimes tired of teasing priests, but that was another story. "I'll assume by your remark that you're still with us," Celwyn said. Bystanders waved greetings as they chugged by another well-illuminated town with clusters of shoppers and revelers. "What I've described is serious enough, but the other evening it became even more complicated. You remember Mrs. Karras?"

Annabelle frowned, half in fear, half in distaste. "Yes."

"The night you met her; your uncle tossed her off the train." Kang moderated his voice but did not hold back things one would normally not alarm a lady about. "She intended you harm, and Patrick also. She is a vampire."

"Holy hell!" Annabelle exclaimed as no well-bred society girl would. "Vampires?"

Patrick had the grace to look a bit ashamed. It appeared he hadn't brought the subject up yet. Celwyn would leave it to him. Romantic revelations weren't part of his duties.

"To continue: Mrs. Karras is affiliated with a vampire called Charles Delgado." Kang patted his pocket, possibly looking for a cigar.

"I have no idea who that is," Annabelle said.

"He is someone who wishes your Uncle Celwyn harm," Kang said. "But he is in Paris—or we hope he is. That is why diverting to Prague is a good plan."

"I thought he was supposed to be disposed of." Patrick frowned.

Celwyn agreed with Patrick, but his doubts grew the more he thought about it. He'd heard a long time ago that in rare instances, some vampires did not react badly to the sun. Even more evidence: the most logical Professor Xiau Kang spoke as if Delgado was alive and well.

"Mrs. Karras will soon be on our trail. Although not harmed when I removed her from the train, she will be very angry." Celwyn sighed, but there was nothing to do about it.

Annabelle turned a horrified look on the magician. "How can you say she wasn't harmed?"

"Because she is a vampire. A little tumble down a ravine will just muss her up a bit."

Annabelle stopped fussing with her coffee cup and poured a measure of whiskey. "This is becoming complicated." She gulped her drink and studied each of them in turn. "So, the plan is to run away."

"Yes," the Professor replied.

She examined him over her glass. "How do we elude this Jax person? Especially since we do not know what he looks like at the moment."

"I have a suggestion." Kang stood and walked to the door and back in quick, short steps. Celwyn would later see him do this every time they faced adversity, like an annoyed marionette. "This also solves our issue of leaving the train without being detected."

"That would be very useful." Bartholomew nodded.

One by one, Kang regarded them as closely as if he were a tailor or dressmaker fitting them for new clothes. Which of them would panic? Which could improvise if the occasion called for it?

"I doubt my idea will apply to all of us, but even if only a few of us can utilize it, trying this becomes attractive: when we stop in Kanpur tomorrow, we should concentrate on the international section of the city and look for someone who resembles each of us. We'll check for individuals who would take our places on the train for a substantial fee and free passage to Paris."

"And allow us to leave the train undetected," Bartholomew surmised.

Collectively, they pondered what Kang had suggested. The more Celwyn thought about it; he liked the possibilities. "Excellent." The magician considered Annabelle. "When we arrive tomorrow, Bartholomew will again guard you. Patrick will stay with you until his train for Agra departs." The magician turned to Kang. "We will find our doubles also."

For the first time in days, Celwyn felt like they might escape the dark cloud of harm over them. There was hope.

"Then that is settled. We will establish a temporary base outside the terminal for supplies and what parts of our personal property that we can smuggle off the train without being seen. Some things will have to be left behind," the magician said.

"Including some clothing so that our doppelgängers can dress like us." Kang pointedly didn't look at their ward.

Annabelle's bottom lip protruded.

"Do I need to explain how the wonderful things I have just bought cannot be left behind?"

"I will see what I can do," Celwyn promised. "Now, I must arrange our new transportation. Say nothing of our plans to anyone. Agreed?"

Everyone raised their glasses in a toast. Qing walked up Bartholomew's leg. He stood there squawking before settling on his lap to watch the room. Bartholomew pretended the mechanical bird wasn't there.

"We arrive in Kanpur before noon. Then we'll begin our foray into the city if that is acceptable," Kang said.

After Bartholomew and the love birds departed, Kang relaxed and watched Qing fly loops around the room.

"He really enjoys the company," Celwyn said.

"Yes, he does." Qing swooped by so low he fluttered the hair on top of Kang's head. "I think our new plan will work. Or at least confuse Jax to the point he won't know who to follow."

Celwyn agreed. "We'll find our temporary base while the others are waiting for their luncheon. Most likely, it will be an expensive bolt hole."

"For how long?"

"A day, maybe two. Don't worry about our luggage, I'll arrange for it. Despite initially thinking we'd be limited in what we could take with us, I have figured out a way of smuggling most of our things off the train."

"Does it involve violence?" Kang asked.

Celwyn smiled. "Not this time. Just something distasteful."

Chapter 18

THE NEXT MORNING KANG AND THE magician went looking for the individual always common to train terminals, ports, and hotels—anywhere that required the special talents of a person who can obtain whatever is needed, legal or not. The search didn't take long.

Their quarry stood off to the side of the terminal, out of the sun and under a leafy tree. His plumage befitted a colorful parrot: a suit of bright pink, orange, and blue that completed the image: like an aviary, he also had a prominent chest and small rear.

As they walked closer, Celwyn verified that they had indeed found the rascal who could help them. The man's interior monologue centered on the beautiful cut of Celwyn's coat and how much he could charge for a similar one. He scrutinized Kang's nationality and speculated upon how much money they would spend on whatever he could sell them.

The man's conclusion seemed to be that they were a "nice set of fishes."

Kang addressed him with confidence. "Good morning."

"Kumar Tiwari. At your service." He bowed. "Could I interest you in anything?" He studied them a second more and asked, "Or help you with a service?"

"Yes. We would like for you to obtain, discreetly, a very clean set of rooms for tonight. They must be located within a few blocks of this train station." The automat gestured around them. "We require luxury and will pay handsomely for good quality accommodations."

Celwyn had been against dangling a large amount of money in front of whoever they met, but Kang had talked him out of it.

Although his eyes looked so full of curiosity Celwyn thought they'd pop out of his round face, Mr. Tiwari only said, "It will be arranged. I will be at this spot at five this afternoon with keys for you." His wide smile could have sold derelict warships to Napoleon. "Will that do, Sir?"

With a handshake, the magician handed him enough money to begin the transaction, and with a doffing of their hats, they retraced their steps to return to the train.

"Do you think we can still catch a spot of the late breakfast session if we hurry?" Kang asked as he broke into a jog.

Celwyn caught up with him and consulted his pocket watch.

"Certainly. Annabelle will be late. She is female. I assure you they will hold our table."

⌣

Over breakfast, their discussion centered on the probability that finding someone similar to oneself could take from seconds to days, even in the cauldron of cultures that made up Kanpur. Patrick's train was due to leave by mid-afternoon, and they wanted to find a substitute for Annabelle before he left. When Patrick departed, half of her security detail would also. Locating a person who also desperately wanted to go to Paris made their quest a mite complicated.

Over the next few hours, Annabelle did her best to help, focusing her attention on the young women they encountered in dress shops, haberdasheries, goldsmiths, confectioners, and other establishments, but each time she thought she saw someone suitable; it took only a few questions to determine that they did not want to travel to Paris.

Kang frowned and rubbed his chin as they stood in a huddle outside of the third dress shop they'd searched unsuccessfully. His nose twitched. "I did not like the perfume in that shop." He eyed Annabelle thoughtfully. "I believe we need a different approach."

As he surveyed the street, Celwyn agreed, seeing many citizens, some tourists, and a few criminals who kept their distance from them. Because of Bartholomew's presence, most criminals would think twice about approaching them with the big man nearby. In this section of the market, the shops appealed almost exclusively to women: not a tobacconist in sight. Celwyn couldn't spy anyone acceptable to impersonate a privileged young woman, and now that she had rinsed the dye out, someone with Annabelle's exact color of golden hair. Or her pout. "Please explain," he asked Kang.

"Our first question should be: who would want to travel to Paris? Finding a close physical match to Annabelle is the second consideration. We could buy a blond wig if we had to." He snapped his fingers. "It is simple; we inquire at the nearest mission or church. They will know of someone who requires transportation and who does not have the funds."

Patrick asked, "What if there isn't anyone?"

"Then we'll try the schools that cater to English or French students. There could be a homesick teacher ready to go at least as far as Paris."

"We passed a church about three blocks back. Shall we?" Celwyn bowed them ahead, once again thankful for Kang's logical mind.

To Celwyn, success felt good, especially after their initial search. At the first church they entered, they'd found a passable substitute for Annabelle. The only difficulty had been convincing the office staff that all they wanted to do was offer passage to a deserving young lady, and could they meet someone who would like to make the journey? Yes, Annabelle wanted to remain in Kanpur for an extended time, and they wanted to donate the train ticket. After interviewing the candidates, they offered the passage to one of the women who would do.

As they closed the church doors behind them, Annabelle said, "I told her to eat dinner early enough to be at the terminal by nine tonight."

"What is her name again, please?" Bartholomew asked.

"Henrietta Bryer. She is twenty-two years old and a missionary from Boston. She knows to be discreet when she arrives at the terminal."

"And not to speak unless necessary until the train leaves tomorrow. We only need the deception to last until then." Kang rubbed his hands together in satisfaction.

Chapter 19

Hours later, they gave up on the remainder of their quest: it had been impossible to find a seven-foot-tall Negro who spoke English fluently, had a high degree of education, and walked with Bartholomew's bearing. Since the big man wasn't Jax's main focus, their search shifted: Patrick would leave them soon, and Kang and the magician still needed their own substitutes. Celwyn checked his watch and saw that it neared three o'clock. A dramatic scene of professed love—that the magician could do without—was about to commence at the train terminal.

When he and Kang joined the others, Patrick's trunks had already been stowed on the scheduled train to Agra. The captain wore his uniform proudly, but more noticeable was the kind of misery painting his face that only the love-struck could understand. He couldn't help but glance at the man-sized clock on the terminal wall above them. The all-aboard would soon be called.

Celwyn shook Patrick's hand and then gave him what the Americans call a bear-hug. "Be well. We will be very close to the Prague Opera House, and circumspect messages can be left for us there. I would suggest other, more obvious, messages also be sent to Paris and Venice."

Celwyn whirled. Kang did also. The same prickling scrutiny that the magician had experienced on the *Zelda* had just crawled up his legs and onto his back again. It felt like a tiny animal with claws. Behind them, most of the crew of the *Royal Victoria* stood there smoking, talking, or both. Porters, cooks, and officials watched them, along with many of the other passengers. Kang cursed. It was the first time Celwyn had heard his friend do so, and if anything, it made the situation grimmer.

"Did you feel it too?" Celwyn asked.

"Yes, and I am beginning to think Jax does this just to intimidate us. You notice it doesn't happen all the time."

"Yes." Celwyn turned back in time to see Patrick and Annabelle in an embrace that would have made a courtesan blush. As he looked away, his eyes widened as he scanned the area. He stopped and cursed, but for a different reason. Just when they might find out something about Jax, Celwyn had finally found what they'd been looking for.

"Stay with them," he told Bartholomew. "You too," to Kang and made sure he acknowledged the request. Just to be sure, he put a protective field around them.

The field would last a few minutes. If something did happen, it could provide Bartholomew with the opportunity to defend their party that he'd been hoping for.

Celwyn darted out of the terminal and around the side of the building. After waiting a moment to ascertain no one from the train followed, he sprinted to the rear and approached the line of carriages. His quarry smoked a cigarette and leaned on a rake. Here was the man he'd spied through the window in the terminal, someone tall, muscular, in his 40's, strong of face, and with a full head of dark hair. As the stranger began to rake leaves, Celwyn ran up to him and caught his breath.

"May I help you?" The man's voice sounded deep, near a baritone in range with an undetermined accent, which would do very well. Up close, he appeared to be of mixed race, clean-shaven, with dark grey eyes. Not exactly the same, but for a few hours, he would do. At the moment, his expression held only curiosity, no fear, which might indicate an adventurous nature.

"I have a proposition for you, Sir," Celwyn said.

By the time the magician returned to the terminal, Patrick had boarded his train. He hung out the window, bravely waving his hat. Annabelle waved back with tears streaming down her face. Beside her, even Bartholomew wiped away a tear.

"He loves you, Miss Annabelle," the big man said.

As the train's whistle sounded and the wheels began to move, Annabelle's cries became wails attracting all kinds of attention from various passengers and railway personnel.

"Oh, for pity's sake." Celwyn pulled Kang aside. "Please take her back to our train and remind her of the dangers we face. Mention again the need for discretion because of her aunt—that seems to put the most fear in her about the situation. Perhaps, she could write a nice thank you note to the church here?"

"She also needs to sort through the things she should leave behind for Henrietta to wear, too." Kang said, "I doubt a missionary owns evening clothes. Where will you be?"

The magician tapped out his pipe against the wall of the terminal. "Arranging our new transportation and finding a substitute for you for when we decamp from the train." He pocketed the pipe. "Please ask Bartholomew to meet me here in an hour?"

Celwyn wasted no time leaving the terminal behind and walking around the corner of the adjacent building. He ducked into an alcove for what seemed an eternity, but no one followed or even looked in his direction. The magician hurried down a rather aromatic alley and north across a pot-marked field of yellowed weeds. A few strides more and he hopped over a fence and into an older train yard: no fancy buildings here, no vendors, vagabonds, or passengers could be seen.

Instead, he found sets of train wheels as big as a small carriage and discarded engines bigger than a small house, and empty passenger cars with, and without, window glass. He inspected several locomotives of varying conditions and countries of origin. At the rear of the yard, he spied a semi-roofed ten-by-ten-foot shack with a tiny porch, and on the porch, a man sat in a wicker rocking chair. He appeared to be a specimen from early in the century. He sported coveralls that may have once been blue, but the grease and dirt from the trains had turned them darker. A visor shaded the old man's eyes, but not his full face of whiskers.

As Celwyn approached, the man didn't say anything but brought up a rifle from his side and laid it across his lap. The magician smelled the telltale wisp of tobacco on him and could see the long stem of an old-fashioned pipe poking up from the coverall pocket. Where it hadn't been before, the magician extracted a velvet pouch from inside his own pocket and tossed it to the old-timer. He caught it, sniffed, and regarded the magician for several seconds. Celwyn waited. With a wary eye on his visitor, the old man opened the pouch.

Minutes later, he took the first puff on the pipe, held it for a moment, and then closed his eyes in a state of bliss.

"Whatever you want, boyo, you can have." One devious blue eye opened and winked at him.

Celwyn turned and pointed at one of the older locomotives that must have been part of a military conflict or had gone off the top of a mountain. Even from here, the dented wheels, pitted sides, and evidence of an engine fire gave it the distinct air of neglect.

The old-timer puffed. "Done. What else?"

"Eight cars, three of which are sleeper cars. No need to furnish them. Kitchen and dining car, crew quarters. The remainder is for extra storage and coal. As long as the cars are sound and have wheels, those are my only requirements. It doesn't matter what they look like inside or out."

"This is fine tobacco, but what you want will cost you, boyo."

Celwyn named an amount, and then added, "There will also be more compensation if you'll have everything delivered to that unused track." He pointed to the other side of the field beyond the locomotives, "By ten this evening. Is this acceptable?"

The old timer regarded the magician without a word for several moments.

"I will also provide more of what is in that pouch," Celwyn said.

"Do I know you?" He squinted at the magician. "From London, p'rhaps in '35?"

Possibly. Celwyn had been there for a very colorful performance of sorts and quick departure. "No."

"If you say so. We have a deal, boyo." The old man shrugged. "It may not be by ten, but real close to it."

"Excellent. I have a few other requests, too, if you'd be so kind."

Chapter 20

WHEN CELWYN RETURNED TO THE terminal, Bartholomew stood on the shady side of the building waiting. He smiled wide at the sight of the magician.

"Are you pleased to see me, or do you simply find a break from Miss Annabelle's tears agreeable?"

"Both!" Bartholomew rumbled and waved a hand at the yard. "I am also anxious to begin the next leg of our journey."

"Good. We have a great deal to do. We will be traveling by train. By the end of today, we must lay in initial supplies." Celwyn handed him a list. "And we depart before dawn tomorrow. There is a gentleman in that train yard across the field who is expecting you and the supplies." The magician pointed to the derelict yard. "Please be sure you aren't followed when you make the arrangements. The gentleman has also agreed to provide us with a few crewmen for our entourage."

Bartholomew studied the list. "That is a great amount of coal, Jonas."

"We will have extra bins to store it, and it is desirable to not have to stop for fuel unless we want to. Do you happen to know of Bowden Street?"

"About three blocks south." The big man read the list and asked, "Where should I obtain the fresh fish and other things you list?"

"The gentleman at the train yard will assist you, and please do not forget the ice." Celwyn handed over funds. "Mr. Tiwari should be here any moment with keys to our hide-out for tonight. He will also provide assistance to fill our list ... for a price." He handed over another fat purse.

"Nice to hear." The big man nodded.

"I have several more errands before dinner. Good luck on your quest." They shook hands.

Most of his errands would be termed uninteresting, or even dangerous, by Annabelle, Kang and the big man, but one of them had an artistic foundation Celwyn looked forward to. The magician enjoyed thinking about Kang's reaction all the way to his next stop. Teasing the automat could become an enjoyable pastime.

By the time they returned to the *Royal Victoria*, they had just enough time to dress for dinner. Qing greeted Celwyn at the cabin door, and the magician sat him on top of the lavatory mirror so they could enjoy each other's company while he washed up.

"Which do you prefer? This one?" Celwyn asked and held up a brown tie. Qing peered at it, twisting his head side to side like he had when they first met, then took the tie from the magician's hand before dropping it back into his trunk.

"Blue it must be, then." Celwyn finished dressing and had paused in front of the mirror to admire his profile when Kang knocked. Annabelle stood behind him. She didn't appear as miserable as he expected, even managing a wan smile.

"Shall we?" The magician ushered them down the hall.

They found Bartholomew already seated at the dining table. As they approached, Celwyn's glance revealed that the woman who had a problem with Bartholomew associating with them last night, and who ended up with a glass of wine in her lap, sat behind him. Tonight she watched them go by without a word spoken or thought, but she did reach for her glass.

The dining car seemed quite full and abuzz with good spirits. Refilling the train's provisions in a large, multicultural metropolis affected what the dining car offered, even if only the wine list needed replenishing.

As the magician opened his napkin, he remarked, "I smell cinnamon, garlic, and chicken. And not Mrs. Karras' perfume, thankfully."

Kang rolled his eyes while Annabelle continued to read from the card on the table. "Chicken tandoori with aromatic rice. Salad greens, cheese, and lemon tart."

"The wine had better not be too dry," Kang warned as he regarded the bottle.

After ascertaining that they were alone, Celwyn still kept his voice down. "Bartholomew and I will take everyone to our new accommodations at midnight. Our stand-ins should arrive before then, and we'll finish coaching them and answering their questions. Annabelle, be sure to have Henrietta watch you walk and then verify that she can walk like you. Practice with her. This train departs at ten tomorrow morning, so the stand-ins only have to appear as us at breakfast to establish we're still on the train. Perhaps have her wear one of your hats with a veil?"

Annabelle nodded and made a face. "Where will we eventually sleep? Is it clean?"

"Yes, and privacy assured. I have a few things to finish this evening, but like I said, we should be in our temporary quarters after midnight.

Bartholomew asked, "Do you think our imposters will be safe after we leave the train?"

"I do." Celwyn made sure they were not being listened to and continued, "I have instructed them to stay in their rooms until breakfast. Our pursuers are interested in us, not them, and when they can't find us, they will exit the train as soon as possible. There would be nothing here for them."

Kang watched Celwyn with a furrowed brow. "I was not able to find a stand-in."

"I have a temporary solution."

The automaton stopped sipping his wine and regarded the magician. "You seem rather proud of yourself."

"Of course." Celwyn thought he should be. It had taken several tries until he was satisfied with the results.

Their soup arrived, once more reminding Celwyn of the quality of this train. Potato leek with ham, and the aroma smelled divine. He desperately hoped their new chef would be of the same caliber.

Annabelle finished her soup and put her spoon down. "What about my trunks? I've separated clothing for Henrietta's use. But what about the things I wish to keep?"

"Before midnight, everyone's trunks will be taken care of. Bartholomew and the Professor will also assist. Is that acceptable?"

She flashed a relieved smile at them. "Of course. Thank you."

While they awaited Henrietta and Celwyn's replacements, the magician made sure their new porter became thoroughly occupied in the other first-class car. It seemed that a colorful snake had been found in the back of one of the compartments, and it took several sets of hands to capture it as it moved from one cabin to the next, all the while accompanied by hysterics from the passengers.

Certain that the porters and nearby passengers were occupied, Bartholomew and Celwyn loaded a cart with their trunks. Conveniently, no one outside the train car could move, or remember anything occurring, until Bartholomew drove the cart away.

When the big man returned, the magician led him to Kang's compartment.

They stood in the open doorway. Celwyn gestured. "Assume that you are an inquisitive porter, or Jax, and you have knocked on the Professor's door. You decide to come in and look for him."

Celwyn motioned Bartholomew into the room. A single lamp bathed the cabin in a soft glow. As they stood there, Kang entered behind them and stopped dead, staring at the bed. He swallowed and approached it slowly.

"I'm well aware of your talents, Jonas, but this is extraordinary."

With covers up to its chin, an effigy of Kang lay on its back on the bed. Every feature had been reproduced; the slightly too long black hair, the elfin ears, and the pale, leathery skin painted in the weak light.

Kang leaned over and, with a fingertip, touched the effigy's cheek.

"What is he made of?"

"Clay. Would you like to see him breathe?"

"No!" Kang backed into a table. "I believe I will await our departure in your suite."

Bartholomew approached the bed, his face void of expression, but Celwyn could see the whites around his eyes clearly. He stopped a foot away, and for a moment, didn't speak or move, then turned and murmured an imprecation under his breath before walking out the door.

"A bit superstitious, I fear," the magician said.

Kang opened his eyes at Celwyn. "Do you blame him? Good grief, Jonas!" He nodded at the bed. "That is too much to accept as normal. Let me go talk with him." Kang scurried out and down the hall.

Celwyn shrugged. *Artistry is never fully appreciated.* He rejoined Qing in his own suite to finish packing a small bag. A few minutes more, Bartholomew and Kang knocked and entered.

Bartholomew kept a wary eye on Celwyn as he sat down. Kang picked up Qing and closed the window drapes before saying, "I thought an explanation should come from you. Bartholomew suspected you have unusual abilities and has seen some of them. But he would like to know more."

From the fear in his eyes, Celwyn doubted Bartholomew really wanted to know more but he would need to. He sighed. The first time he'd had to explain a magical occurrence he had been in short pants. The fear in Bartholomew's eyes could change to acceptance.

"What is the word for 'magic' in your language?"

"*Uchawi.*"

"May I assume that you've encountered, or know of, good and bad magicians or priests?"

Bartholomew nodded.

"I try to be a good magician, but as the Professor can attest, I sometimes become impatient."

To demonstrate something innocent, the magician caused the glass of water beside the bed to elevate a few feet and then slowly descend again. Bartholomew appeared interested but not more anxious than when they walked in. The water in the glass turned sea green. Tiny waves rolled across the surface, and minute dolphins dove to the bottom of the glass. Bartholomew watched it and licked his lips. When he looked at Celwyn again, a small hint of bravery shone in his eyes.

"My magic is beautiful, playful, but sometimes becomes violent. I do not terrorize innocent people, but there are occasions when I intervene in situations that I do not approve of."

Kang said, "And I've pointed out how ill-advised that can be sometimes."

"Humph. To go on, my abilities are great, as I've been honing my skills for hundreds of years. I hope that does not frighten you?"

The big man stared at the dolphins in the glass and said, "No, in my village, we had men who caused strange things to occur."

Celwyn nodded. "During those years, I've engineered spectacular displays all over the world, settled wars, and ended the reign of petulant kings. These were all things that needed to be done."

With a languid hand, he swirled the air between them. A cerulean blue mist arose, moving in a river of air and forming a swirling vortex. As the mist spun, the music of a harp began, the notes tinkling and falling like a waterfall. The mist thickened and flew out of the vortex, enveloping them with the scent of fresh oranges and the sea. Above the vortex, silvery birds flew within the mist as if it was a cloud. Then the mist thickened and from inside it, a swath of bright-colored cloth faded in and out. Inside the vortex, a maternal voice spoke to Bartholomew in his language.

The big man's eyes watered in memory, and his tears fell freely. He reached out to touch the cloth.

Celwyn said, "You loved your mother very much, and I thought you would want to hear her voice telling you she loves you and misses you also." The magician had no trouble hearing her voice in the big man's thoughts and his sorrow at not seeing her.

The silence became as complete as Bartholomew's memory and sad smile. "Thank you."

As he spoke, the mist faded to nothing, and the faint noises from the train once again reached them. Bartholomew regarded Celwyn, hardly blinking.

The automat said, "Jonas saved my life, and that of my wife, during our voyage to Singapore. He probably saved the crew and passengers in doing so."

"What happened?"

The automat looked at the magician, and he nodded. Celwyn observed that Bartholomew had crossed over from fear to accepting what he'd previously found frightening. Yet Kang wasn't completely sure. He asked Bartholomew, "Do you fear Jonas ... or me?"

Bartholomew thought a moment and smiled. "No. But I cannot deny that there are evil spirits in the world, and there are things a wise man does not cross." He watched Qing. "Such as that."

The Professor nodded. "He is mechanical and also very spoiled because of Jonas." Qing hopped onto Bartholomew's knee and examined the heavy gold necklace he wore with a bright acquiring eye. "It is not only Qing who is mechanical. I am also." When Kang saw Bartholomew's brows drawn together and his breathing increased, he said, "I am not a magician, and I can be hurt. However, I am very strong and believe I contribute to the world's scientific knowledge."

Bartholomew relaxed a bit. "But you look and sound very real."

"Thank you. To answer your question, it was my brother who attacked us on the ship in an effort to capture me. Jonas destroyed him, and hundreds like him, in a spectacular way. His loyalty to me is very much appreciated."

"As mine is to the Professor," the magician said. "Although he has yet to rescue me, except from myself." After they traded a tolerant and fond glance, Celwyn continued to Bartholomew, "Our path forward will be dangerous. You are also someone I respect and will protect."

Bartholomew looked at both and said, "There is strength in each of us, and we will prevail."

"You should also know that we suspect it is the Professor's work that motivated the attacks, and it could be that is what Jax is seeking. By tomorrow, we'll be gone from this train and, we hope, away from the danger to all of us," Celwyn said.

"Does Miss Annabelle know about this... unusual...?"

Kang sighed and said, "Not yet. We're fairly certain she wouldn't take the news calmly. But it can't be put off too much longer."

Bartholomew rubbed his chin, thinking. "There are several threats. What about that woman with the large bosoms you threw off the train? She was a *pishash*."

Celwyn thought it amusing how sometimes descriptions are sparse but get the point across. "That was unfortunate but necessary."

"In the next few weeks, there is only one other train coming west on the path we have traveled. The *China Star*. It is three days behind this train, and we'll be gone before the vampire arrives, even assuming she boarded it after her, uh," the automat looked at the magician and shook his head, "tumble the other night."

"She also thinks we're traveling to Paris or Venice." Celwyn enjoyed the misdirection. He wondered if it would also work on Mrs. Pearse.

Bartholomew asked, "But why does she pursue you? It appeared that her anger was for Mr. Patrick."

Celwyn clapped him on the shoulder. "Tonight, you will hear the story. I can assure you my talents are greater than any vampire I have encountered, and I am able to protect all of those I care about." Suzanne's face briefly crossed his thoughts as a somber reminder of the time he hadn't done so. "However, I must be near enough when there is danger."

"We need to stay close," Kang said.

Celwyn hoped he included himself in that statement and would not go haring off in pursuit of their enemies. One of his unvoiced worries concerned Jax and the vampires either purposely, or inadvertently, joining forces.

PART II
More Tea

Chapter 21

JUST AFTER MIDNIGHT, THEY ENTERED a smoky hookah lounge, and, one by one, ducked behind a tapestry of beads before climbing a clean unadorned staircase. At the top of the stairs, Bartholomew unlocked a door and ushered them forward.

Annabelle dropped her purse and stared. "What *is* this place?"

Granted, the rooms did not look new, but Celwyn thought they appeared sanitary and would do for a night. Annabelle would have one room, and the rest of their party would take the second bedroom and sofas covered in red velvet in the main room. Red satin lined the walls.

"Is this ... a ... brothel?" she stammered.

"No," Bartholomew said quickly. "Mr. Tiwari says it is the private quarters of a government official."

Annabelle examined a wall of gilded mirrors and tapestries. "I imagine these tapestries are considered tasteful," she studied one that displayed frolicking deer and nudes, "for scientific purposes." The soldiers next to the nudes wore Eastern dress and hooded visors. She moved to another tapestry and exclaimed, "What *are* they doing?"

Although amusing, time was wasting. Celwyn waved a hand, turning the room into a stately elegant example of an English hotel. Crystal sconces replaced the red gas lamps and, cream-colored draperies supplanted tapestries of frolicking nudes. Antique armoires stood by the windows. Through other doors lay two similarly appointed rooms.

"Will this do?" he asked Annabelle.

If her earlier outburst originated in moral outrage, now she didn't know what to do. Annabelle stared and ventured to touch the nearest drape, letting it fall from her fingers. She blinked at the magician with wide eyes and demurely took a seat on a nearby couch. As she gazed at Celwyn, she stroked the brocade with her nails loud enough for everyone to hear.

If the magician knew her temperament, and he did, she wasn't rethinking her decision to stay with them but analyzing the situation with a hefty consideration for her goals and comfort.

In contrast, Bartholomew smiled broadly, displaying a fine set of white teeth. This demonstration he could approve of: tangible changes wrought by pure magic. He examined a rug at his feet and then peered at the room's reflection in the mirror of the armoire.

"I hope you provided lavatory facilities," Kang said with skepticism.

"But of course," Celwyn said. "With gold fixtures."

Qing popped out of his coat and flew to the top of the armoire. He peered out the window.

"I am hungry," Annabelle said. "And I want something to drink. Not coffee." Her hand shook as she removed her hat and smoothed back her hair. When no one moved, she blurted, "*What happened to this room?*"

From a cupboard beside the windows, Celwyn removed a tray of meats and cheeses that hadn't been there before. Kang joined him, grabbing a bottle of whiskey and glasses. Bartholomew pushed up chairs until they sat in a circle around the couch.

Annabelle made several selections from the tray as Celwyn asked her, "Have you heard of Nevil Maskelyne or Harry Kellar? They are magicians of note in London and America."

At the question, she eyed him, hesitated, and went back to chewing. She nodded and picked up a piece of cheese. Whether the nod was for the question or approval of the cheese, he couldn't tell.

"Have you ever attended a magic show?" Celwyn asked.

Annabelle gestured at the room. "I have now, apparently." She reached for her glass, but it met her hand halfway, suspended in mid-air. She gawked at the magician and then slowly wrapped her fingers around it.

"My intentions are good, I assure you."

The magician added a faint chorus of flutes to their party.

Annabelle jumped, and her gaze scoured the room. She regarded Bartholomew, who nodded back and said, "It took a certain amount of bravery for me to accept that these things are possible, but I have total faith in Jonas' heart and his intent."

Without taking her eyes off Celwyn, she sniffed the whiskey and took a tentative sip. In one gulp, she drained the glass and set it down. When she caught her breath again, she considered them all without speaking.

Kang saw her indecision and stepped in.

"As a group, we face dangers. Bartholomew will protect us, and as you've seen, your Uncle Celwyn will also." Kang watched as she took a deep breath before saying, "If you prefer, I will take you back to the train and ask Miss Henrietta to be your companion. Or," he poured her another glass of whiskey and handed it to her before asking, "an adventure awaits you as we travel to Prague. Do you wish to continue?"

Qing chose that moment to fly off the top of the armoire, circle the room at great speed, and then land on the table between them. He waddled to the whiskey decanter and scraped his beak across the crystal in a highly annoying manner.

"Stop that," the magician told him, albeit without great heat. The bird turned a glittering eye on the decanter and scraped it again. Kang laughed, effectively breaking the tension in the room. Qing hopped around the bottle and pecked at it.

"And you say it is I who spoil him?" Celwyn asked Kang, who shrugged it off. The magician looked at Qing and said, "Guard me."

Qing stopped pecking and landed on the magician's shoulder. He hissed at everyone and tried to make himself bigger. Kang applauded. "I see you've been working with him."

Celwyn stroked his feathers. "Yes. But it is a slow process. It isn't as if I can offer him an edible treat as a reward. I have to find shiny toys he likes." Qing nuzzled his chin as he stroked the bird's feathers. "One thing he has learned is to screech if anyone he doesn't know comes into the room. I will also have a protection layer over the rooms tonight."

Annabelle listened and fingered the fringe on the pillow beside her. The magician monitored her thoughts, finding a high level of confusion layered with a sense of excitement. Her peace of mind required a non-threatening distraction. Celwyn waved a hand, and a sweet violin began to play, announcing clouds of dancing bubbles that filled the ceiling. As they fell, Annabelle held out her hands, clearly delighted.

"Again, my intentions are good." The magician stood. "Bartholomew and I have further preparations to make before our departure tomorrow."

They left, closing the door behind them as Annabelle fluttered around the room, giggling and catching the bubbles.

A little after four in the morning, they walked through darkened streets, yawning, as they passed by several mosques, a greengrocer, and a basket shop. The only thing that seemed to be alive this early were the rats. Red eyes watched them from behind piles of debris and jagged holes in block walls.

In a low voice, the Professor kept up a running dialog as they neared the railyards. It could be Kang did so to prevent Annabelle from repeating her caustic comments about the early hour. If pressed, Celwyn doubted she would be able to name another morning when she had been compelled to arise and greet the world this early. Dawn in March would be just after 6 a.m., and the magician wanted to be well away from Kanpur by then.

"Do you know how long the Chinese have been in Baghdad?" Kang asked.

Annabelle growled, "No, I do not." She stopped in front of a pile of aromatic rags. "What is *that?*"

The automat urged her forward. "You do not wish to know." He continued, "As I was saying, Baghdad's first Buddhist temple was established by..."

Only a few steps behind them, Bartholomew and Celwyn kept pace, both on alert. If they'd been followed from the train last night, and Celwyn doubted they were, this would be a vulnerable point in their plans.

He did not see anything in the murky darkness except a well-lit bakery. As they approached, he noticed the *bekari* had a wide, glass front and a view of the bakers rolling, punching, measuring, and shaping the loaves. It smelled divine. Annabelle's steps slowed, but with great personal restraint, Kang kept both his pace and grip on her arm firm. Soon they entered another block of unlit storefronts where the only light came from the lanterns Bartholomew and the automat held aloft. The magician reflected that he could have transported them by his talents, but both he and Bartholomew had decided they needed to know if they were followed last night and not be surprised later.

The air seemed both foggy and misty, trapping the acrid stench of burned coal that the residents used for heat. Instead of turning right onto a street that dead-ended at the railyard, they continued for another block. On the other side of the field, Celwyn spotted the brilliantly lit smokestacks of the *Royal Victoria*. The magician sighed in satisfaction: their journey had reached the point where their party left behind the expected for the unexpected.

As they entered an alley between two derelict buildings, a chorus of squeaking arose, and the rats protested the intrusion.

When they emerged from the alley, the vibration of a rumbling locomotive greeted them.

Brilliant flames of gold flared starkly against the night, accompanied by the screeching of metal against metal as a train moved forward toward them. Beautifully painted jet-black, with gilded lettering and decoration, her brass shone in the meager light. Although older, she appeared as big as the locomotive of the *Royal Victoria*. Seven cars had been hooked to her, and even at a distance, the windows sparkled. From within them, stained-glass lamps glowed a warm welcome.

Through the clouds of steam, the lettering over the nose of the locomotive read: "*The Elizabeth.*"

Kang stopped dead still. "Oh, my." He looked at Celwyn. "Thank you, my friend." He stepped closer. In a near whisper, "Where did you get her?"

Modesty was something the magician tried to cultivate.

"It was a small project. I made her from a derelict. She will run faster than most trains ... if we require it."

When the big man left them to inspect one of the wheels, Kang said, "I would advise not telling Bartholomew that you made this. It will only upset him." He rubbed a hand on the painted side of the train.

As they spoke, Annabelle cautiously moved forward. Her expression appeared more confused than awed. "This is for us? Where did you get a train?"

"Yes, it is for us: engine, storage, kitchen, club and dining car, crew car, and our quarters," Celwyn said as she approached the tracks, stopped, and turned.

"Is it real?" Annabelle's voice sounded nearly as confident as usual. "Will it be safe?"

"It is safe, and it is based upon something real. I just cleaned it up and restored its beauty." Celwyn bowed before the steps. "Come aboard."

"All right, I will." Chin up, she lifted her skirts and ascended the short stairs with Kang steadying her arm. Once inside, she exclaimed, "It is beautiful! Look at the flowers!"

Celwyn thanked her and pointed out the glass ceiling over the dining table and bar. "You'll be able to watch the stars."

Inch by inch, the automat took in what he saw. "You have outdone yourself, Jonas. But I would feel better if we could get moving. And I suggest we do so with all haste. It will be dawn soon."

As Bartholomew exited to pass along the request to the conductor, the magician introduced the two men waiting at attention in front of the bar. Ricardo and Selkirk would be their porters and waiters. Ricardo stood slim, neat, and dark-haired with lively eyes. In contrast, Selkirk had the pallor of someone who had recently been ill. Although nearly as tall as Celwyn, he weighed much less.

The ornate and well-stocked bar took up the left side of the car, and the crystal glasses gleamed. A formal dining room table and sofas made up the space, while broad windows framed both sides of the car. Celwyn thought that between Bartholomew and the old codger at the train yard, everything had been organized very well.

The train shuddered violently, and the wheels again began to throw sparks as they rolled forward. Steam billowed on each side of the *Elizabeth,* and they picked up speed, bumping over trestles and disused rails. The magician stood at the windows, noticing that the smoke from their stacks hung in the air long after they passed nearby shacks and out-buildings. As they left the yard, the magician could see the tail end of the *Royal Victoria* across the field. *Au revoir, Jax*, he waved.

Celwyn felt a certain amount of pride as they toured the rest of the dining car and club area, especially noting the deep leather seating facing the windows. Petite tables nestled against each chair for resting a refreshment, a cup of tea, for instance, or a glass of whiskey. A full and varied library took up another wall.

Kang nodded his approval. "Excellent. I love the map table. Most useful."

Bartholomew's expression appeared blissful. "I will enjoy this journey very much. Even if we do encounter problems."

"You can thank Bartholomew, a Mr. Tiwari, our new porters, and the yard man for all of their work getting us ready to go," the magician told Annabelle and the automat.

"It was a group effort." The big man held up his hands to fend off their thanks.

Annabelle told him, "It is marvelous."

"Let me introduce you to your quarters." Celwyn smiled. Bartholomew hadn't seen the changes he had made.

As if he thought as the magician did, Bartholomew said, "I know nothing about our sleeping quarters. Jonas insisted he would take care of them."

In the cabins, the magician had taken even more care to arrange everything to match their personalities. Minutes later, as Bartholomew surveyed his compartment, he said, "I have never seen anything finer. The tub! It is big enough for even me." He pointed to a collection of three tribal masks decorating the wall. "Where did you find those masks?"

"You do not wish to know," Celwyn said and winked. Actually, they'd been borrowed from a nearby museum's storage closet. He hoped and expected that it would be months before they were missed.

They moved down the hall and waited for Annabelle's reaction. From inside her cabin they heard cupboards opening and closing, then she stuck her head out of the door. "How did you know my favorite color was green?"

"Don't answer that," Kang warned in an aside.

"I'll explain later. Does the room meet your approval?"

"Oh, yes!" Annabelle hopped forward and hugged the magician. "It even has my favorite bath salts!"

The refurbished train clearly tickled their fancy. The magician followed Kang further down the paneled hall. Inside the automat's room, not only had Celwyn reproduced a gentleman's study with a heavy oak desk, but he had added a hand-cranked microscope. It had taken him two visits to the curiosity shop in town until he was satisfied with the various measuring tools, both from the east and west, that he had found. Along the south wall, a full-size chalkboard stood ready for calculations and theories. Kang walked the length of the room, rubbing his hands together. "Perfect. Simply perfect."

Muttering about needing a maid, Annabelle excused herself to go unpack, and as Celwyn sat down in front of the chalkboard, Bartholomew joined them. The magician allowed that if he had that many clothes and hats, he would need a maid too. Kang took the desk chair, his brow up in inquiry.

"I wanted to keep you in my confidence so that we can provide assistance to each other." Celwyn had installed something here, and in the other's rooms, they wouldn't have expected. The rooms sported shutters instead of curtains, which helped with the clanging noise from the rails. And now, through slits in the wood, enough light shone through to announce the arrival of dawn.

"That is appreciated," said Bartholomew. The automat's sarcastic appraisal of the magician's motives showed in his raised brows.

"My magic has evolved and progressed over the centuries. This train can travel very well without my assistance as long as we have coal and the conductor's assistants to shovel it into the ovens. You will meet them all soon." He waved toward the front of the train. "Much of what you see, from the chairs to the globe over there, I made. I do not need to maintain them. However," he paused, partly to decide how to explain his next topic, and because his stomach announced it was nearly time for breakfast. "First things first."

Celwyn gestured to the table, and when he removed his hand, a platter of toast, marmalade, and pots of coffee and tea appeared. "Just something to hold us until our chef has breakfast ready."

"This, and other impromptu creations, is temporary. It takes little effort to produce them."

Celwyn waved a finger, and they heard a whoop of delight from Annabelle's room. "The kitten Annabelle just received is not particularly hard to produce, but, if it stays, it takes a bit of my energy. Later on, if we encounter a dangerous situation that needs all of my attention, the kitten might fade away temporarily."

"What you performed on the *Zelda* when we encountered the other ship would have been exhausting," Kang said.

"It was."

Bartholomew had listened intently, and a deep frown crossed his brow. "The animal would fade away? You would kill it? It is possessed?" He stood, ready to bolt out the room.

"Please," Celwyn put a hand on his arm. "Nothing will harm the kitten. It would just not be visible until I could be fully myself again." He encouraged the big man back into his chair. "I can't be in two places at the same time and be effective with my magic."

"Our priority should be in keeping our enemies at bay." The Professor turned to Celwyn and asked, "Do you anticipate you will be able to answer any trouble that we happen upon? The effort to manage the train will not interfere?"

"No. Like I said, the train would still run. Ordinary issues will not be a problem. For extraordinary issues, I will need your and Bartholomew's assistance." He pointed outside. "We will travel through rough territory that has not known private rail traffic since the British problems in Adwah."

"Together, we will guard the train. I am an expert shot," Bartholomew said, his superstitions forgotten.

Kang sat up straighter. "I will do my best. Do we have firearms?"

"Rifles. Under your beds. I hesitate to put one in Annabelle's cabin, but we may have to teach her to shoot."

"Consider it done," Bartholomew said. "Please excuse my failure to trust you earlier."

"It isn't a matter of trust," Celwyn told the big man. "You would be a very unusual man not to be apprehensive." He offered the plate to them. "Toast? You must try the marmalade."

A few pleasant minutes later, the magician included them both in a frown. "Now, if presented with danger, our first choice is subterfuge, perhaps with a dose of violence before any shots are fired. Do you agree?

"Yes," Kang said as Bartholomew nodded.

What Celwyn didn't say was that his subterfuge would be artful and enjoyable and accompanied by music. If only they were at sea!

Chapter 22

THE TERRAIN REVEALED BY THE dawn should have been left in darkness: Celwyn did not like sand and desolation. He could never have led the Arabian princes to victory as Lawrence did unless they relocated their war.

Nonetheless, after a while, the magician tolerated the view better. He saw a suggestion of mountains in the distance beyond the scrub and sand and the occasional block buildings and water wells under arched overhangs. They passed pens of donkeys and infrequently the smoke from occupied shacks. The magician sipped tea and enjoyed the warmth of the dining car.

Next to the dining table, Kang had posted a large map with a red line denoting their journey to Prague. The map's cartographer had meticulously drawn tiny castles, designating past kingdoms. He had also drawn a set of skulls in the plains of Rumar.

Emperors and princes had long fought over this land, and Celwyn remembered Napoleon's efforts vividly; it hadn't been a pretty sight.

In the next few weeks, the *Elizabeth* would steam across forests and mountains and eventually chug her way into Prague. Most rail traffic originated in Vienna and Constantinople, but Celwyn preferred to come in from the east, less conspicuously. However, they had no guarantees the tracks remained in working order, and therefore traveled at a sedate speed in the hope of spotting obstructions in time to avoid them. When the train began the journey through the high mountains, Celwyn planned to enhance the engines so that they would climb slowly, and still be able to stop if needed.

Kang had plotted where the *Elizabeth* would stop for coal, provisions, and the places of interest where they could get exercise and Annabelle could buy hats. As the Professor worked, Bartholomew arrived in the dining room, along with the porter and a second pot of coffee. When Ricardo had closed the door to the kitchen again, Bartholomew spoke.

"I must thank you for everything, Jonas. I will sleep very well tonight."

"No need for thanks, my friend. Sugar?" Celwyn asked. He nodded, and the magician passed the bowl to him.

"Tell me, if you do not mind, what were your original plans after you reached Paris?"

The big man said, "I'd decided to make a new life there. It would have been interesting: I knew no one in that city."

"Will you still go there, eventually?"

"In the future, perhaps. I have a nest egg I plan to invest."

Celwyn watched him dump in several spoons of sugar, taste the coffee, and add more as they rolled by a stone orthodox church that appeared very old. Its open door revealed complete darkness and the faint glow of candles. A quarter mile more and a lone dog stood beside the rails, and its howl reached them over the noise of the locomotive.

Celwyn asked, "Would you agree that we are a rather unique group?"

The big man's eyes crinkled with a smile. "Yes. A very unlikely group also."

"When we reach Prague, our danger increases. The authorities could become interested in us, either because of my notoriety or the perceived welfare of Annabelle. By that time, I wouldn't be surprised if the Professor isn't suspected of killing the porter on our previous train: his tie had been used in the strangulation."

"I didn't know that." The big man's frown deepened.

"I removed it before the body was examined, but whoever framed the Professor will probably do something else to ensure suspicion follows us." As a welcome distraction, Celwyn began to think about a formal breakfast. The faint odor of bacon had reached him and, like a beautiful woman, could not be ignored.

While the magician spoke, Kang entered the car, poured coffee, and sat down. "That tie was one of my favorites. Yes, if the intent was to compromise me, the efforts will continue."

"Once we reach Prague, my plans place us in the public eye. If you wish to remain with us, and we hope you do, the dangers we've talked about will remain a problem," Celwyn told Bartholomew.

He regarded the magician over the brim of his cup. "You suggest that I grow a beard or use a disguise?"

"No." Celwyn opened a hand and produced a slim white collar. "If needed, you would make an excellent priest."

Bartholomew took the collar and fitted it around his ham-sized neck. He studied his reflection in the window glass for a moment. "Father Bartholomew, at your service."

Kang asked, "What was your occupation before we met?"

The big man's smile faded, and he lowered his head.

"Perhaps you will tell us another time," Kang said.

"It won't change the facts." With a sigh that strained the buttons on his shirt, Bartholomew told his story, "I have a degree in engineering. After university, I was a successful trader in our city. Soldiers attacked and killed my wife and baby." His hand trembled hard at the memory, and he knocked over his cup. He carefully wiped up the spill. "I killed the soldiers, all of them, and then packed my memories into a bag and left."

"You have my condolences." Celwyn felt a rising tide of anger. "If I had been there, I would have assisted you."

"I also, my friend," Kang said. After a moment, he turned to the magician with a brow up. "Could you explain your remark about becoming visible in the public eye in Prague?"

Celwyn stood and shook his trouser legs down. "I intend to become a part of the Emperor's Opera House. My music will ring from the rafters." He sniffed. "Can you smell that? Breakfast is afoot!"

Their porter Selkirk served their repast with a flourish. Celwyn doubted the attention was for his benefit, Kang's, or Bartholomew's. After Annabelle had arrived in a beautiful dress of gold and lace, the porter couldn't help his stare. For her part, Annabelle announced she needed a cigarette and hoped they could get breakfast over with quickly.

Selkirk didn't appear to be much older than Annabelle, and the magician knew little about him. In their hurry to get underway and out of Kanpur, Celwyn hadn't vetted him or the other crew. Yet, he didn't consider it a problem. The magician could gently put them off the train in any town they passed through if need be. If Kang wasn't watching, it would not necessarily be a gentle parting, perhaps a toss off the last railcar.

"Where do you hail from, Mr. Selkirk?" Celwyn asked. Some American expressions made no sense, but he liked that one.

The porter had deposited plates of eggs, rashers, bacon, and toast in front of them. The rashers did not appear to be browned, and the toast slightly burned. From Kang's expression, as he poked a finger at his toast, the fare did not seem to be to his liking.

"I left Her Majesty's service recently, Sir." Selkirk poured water into their glasses. "I had an injury."

"I'm sorry to hear that."

Kang picked up his knife and began cutting his rasher. He sawed harder, without result.

Annabelle patted a yawn and said, "My room is wonderful, Uncle Celwyn. And it came with a kitten!"

Celwyn had forgotten about the kitten.

Selkirk asked, "Will there be anything else, Sir?"

The complications of responsibility. "Yes, please arrange for a box of dirt or shredded newspaper to be delivered to Miss Annabelle's room. She has a pet which will also require a bowl for water and kitchen scraps." Qing peeked out from Celwyn's collar and stared at Annabelle. The magician tapped him on the shoulder. "Be nice."

The porter blinked several times at Qing and took up his post nearby with a last wistful glance at the top of Annabelle's head.

Celwyn tasted his first bite of eggs and nearly coughed them all over the table. He couldn't decide if it was the abundance of salt, addition of curry powder, or wetness of the eggs. Kang continued sawing at his rasher. Bartholomew had drawn the marmalade close and sniffed it with a wrinkled nose.

"Where is our chef?" Celwyn demanded.

Selkirk darted inside the door leading to the kitchen. A moment later, the door opened again. It isn't often Celwyn was surprised, but that morning he was astounded.

"Here I am, boyo!"

The old man from the derelict train yard walked up to their table, pulled out a chair, and sat down. He had washed and no longer sported the soot-covered overalls. Instead, he wore a chef's tall hat that almost covered his bald dome, and his new apron displayed a broad swath of grease across the middle of his large paunch.

Bartholomew said, "Mr. Celwyn did not find his eggs edible."

The old man regarded Bartholomew down the end of a bulbous nose and then turned to the magician. "So that is yer name." He winked. "Pleased to meet you. You didn't ask before, but you can call me Sully. Chef Sully!" He laughed hard enough to bring tears to his eyes. Celwyn did not find the situation funny or his look of contempt at Bartholomew tolerable.

Kang put a finger on his wrist. "Allow me." He turned to Sully and said, "This is our initial dining experience. Perhaps you are not familiar with a new kitchen."

Celwyn hadn't exchanged pleasantries with the old-timer, just quickly made the transaction for the locomotive, coal, and supplies. "Why are you here?" Celwyn demanded.

Sully shrugged. "I couldn't find you a cook in time, and I was tired of the train yard." He peered at the eggs. "What is wrong with 'em?"

Celwyn pushed the plate aside. "Too much salt, and I think they contain curry paste."

Kang tasted the eggs and put the offending bite into his napkin. "What possessed you to add curry to eggs?"

Sully pulled out his pipe and began packing in tobacco. "We're in the Queen's India. Everyone here likes curry." He chuckled and coughed as he added, "Spices are wonderful, ain't they?"

Annabelle drank coffee and said, "This is going to be an interesting trip."

As soon as Sully had retreated back to the kitchen, Celwyn replaced their breakfast with a succulent feast, including mushrooms bathed in a cream sauce over oysters. "Let us partake before he gets back."

Chapter 23

Two days passed. Clouds of steam arose over the verdant foothills of the Poltava Range. The steam increased, keeping time with the chugging of the locomotive as the tall stacks of the engine appeared. The train sounded its whistle as it rolled downhill and into the village of Pushkari.

The noonday sun brightened the town square chasing the shadows from the medieval church and the graveyard beyond. Most of the buildings had been built of white stone with blue tile roofs. There seemed to be less of the usual flower boxes indicative of a cherry village. It seemed as if a pall hung over the town. According to Kang, a majority of the city dated from the dark ages, with some of the newer two-story buildings erected during the prosperous time of Napoleon.

The conductor applied the brakes, and the screech of metal on metal began as the train coasted to a stop behind the stables. The rumble of the engine vibrated the ground as if a giant had stomped his feet, rattling nearby windows. Children and their mothers emerged from the small houses, and various shopkeepers followed them toward the train.

In front of the dining car, Celwyn removed the tasseled gold rope at the top of the stairs leading to the ground. Bartholomew descended first. Several of the curious children backed away, hiding behind their mothers' skirts. Off to the side, groups of men puffed on long-stemmed pipes and pointed at the train.

As Celwyn escorted Annabelle down the steps, he listened to the villagers' unvoiced concerns, fears, and prejudice. Bartholomew seemed to be the first black man many of them had ever seen.

Kang joined them in front of the train, and together they strolled toward the town square. According to the automat's research, the commerce of Pushkari depended on a nearby coal mine. The magician considered this stop a welcome respite before the *Elizabeth* began the more dangerous stretch of her journey through the mountains. It was here that Charlemagne had wintered over, lending background to many myths and stories.

They approached a greengrocer selling cartons of limes, pomegranates, and oranges. Annabelle made selections while the others studied the town.

"I do not see telegraph wires, do you?" Kang said.

Bartholomew stretched to his full height, and his head swiveled on his muscular neck. "No, I do not.

This is helpful. It would be unlikely the authorities have been alerted to our arrival."

"If we needed hay, I believe we'd get a good price." Kang pointed to the east end of the square, "The barn there is overloaded with it. Here, let me carry those for you," he took one of the bags of oranges from Annabelle. Celwyn took the other.

A black carriage stopped in the street beside them, the whiskered driver careful to keep his hat low and avert his face. From inside, skeletal fingers pulled aside the curtain, and the shadowy occupant appeared to study Celwyn, the train, and the rest of their party. After another moment, the driver shook the reins, and the carriage rolled away down the street and turned left, picking up speed.

"Stay here." The magician tossed the bag of fruit to Kang and sprinted after the carriage. He arrived at the corner just as the coach reached the end of the road and sped up a driveway leading to a tall house at the top of a hill. Celwyn didn't often have premonitions, but as he gazed at the high turrets and ivy-covered walls of the house, he felt a distinct foreboding in the pit of his stomach. The windows reminded him of large dead eyes. He squinted and spotted the flurry of a red cape as someone slipped inside the side door of the house.

Little by little, Celwyn became aware of a foul odor next to him, part manure, part unwashed body. He looked down.

A small boy, dirty from the top of his unshorn head to his bare feet, stood a yard away wearing a glare of defiance and the unmistakable look of hunger. In Roma he croaked, "Van Maskolc lives there."

Celwyn turned aside and produced a flask of milk and small package of ham. He handed them to the boy.

"Eat, then we talk."

The boy didn't ask why but drank so fast some of the milk ran off his face and down his threadbare shirt. As he unwrapped the ham, he watched the magician. "Van Maskolc is a bad man," he said and licked his fingers.

Celwyn peered down the street and spied what his nose had already detected. "I see a bakery. Let us sit down and have refreshments." He nodded the boy ahead, already hearing the child's unspoken worries bubbling out of his thoughts like an overflowing fountain. *Jacques cried. He cried. Telly, where are you? Van Maskolc … he watches them.*

When they reached the entrance of the bakery, the yeasty smells became intoxicating, but the boy halted in his tracks.

"My name is Jonas. There is no need to worry."

"I cannot go inside. The *soţia* will chase me because I am too dirty."

"That won't be a problem," Celwyn said. As he ushered the boy inside the painted door, he made sure the urchin smelled and looked as pristine as himself. When the child saw his feet in shoes and then touched his clean trousers, he had to be propelled ahead to a table. The magician said, "I'll explain later. What should we order? Some pastry. And tea!"

The boy's hunger overrode his caution. "Yes, please."

Celwyn asked, "How old are you?" and wanted to ask, *who would let you wander the streets and let you starve?*

"Ten."

That means eight, most likely, the magician thought. The waitress arrived, and he said, "Two pastries, tea, and milk, please." Over her shoulder, he saw Kang enter the bakery and added, "And another pastry and coffee please."

The automat reached their table and waited for the boy to notice him. When he did, he tensed, ready to run. Celwyn said, "This is my esteemed friend Professor Xiau Kang." He gestured to the boy, "And our new friend was about to introduce himself."

Keeping an eye on Kang, he said, "My name is Zander."

As the waitress deposited their pastries on the table, the boy's attention gained intensity, but he waited until she had left again to ask Kang, "Are you going to sit with us?"

"What did he say?"

Celwyn replied, "He asked you to sit."

"I would love to," Kang said as he sat down. "My languages do not extend to yours. *Sprichst der Deutsch?* Do you speak Deutsch?" he asked the boy.

Zander nodded, but his eyes remained on the pastry frosting. He licked a bit of frosting as the tea arrived, and when the buxom waitress who'd brought it left, she trailed a suspicious look at the boy.

"Please eat, Zander. These are very good," Celwyn said. "When you are ready, tell me about that house on the hill."

Between wolf-size bites, the boy told him, "Van Maskolc lives there. He stole two of my friends and keeps them there." Tears formed in his dark eyes, but he batted them away. "At night, I hide outside. I can hear them crying." He looked at Kang. "I heard Jacques scream a few days ago, and now I do not hear him anymore."

The automat eyed the magician and said in English, "I suppose we will intervene?"

"Certainly. To that end, we will be blamed for whatever befalls Van Maskolc." He gestured outside. "It will be dark soon, so we'll leave town later tonight instead of tomorrow." In German, he asked Zander, "Do you have family here we can take you to? Friends?"

The boy shook his head.

"Does Telly or Jacques have family?" Celwyn assumed not but asked.

"No, we live," he pointed to the street, "outside." Then his eyes widened, and he jumped to his feet. "How do you know their names?"

"Sit, please. If we are to help your friends, I must know more." Celwyn waited for him to sit down before asking more questions. Over the next quarter hour, Kang's knowledge of the German language improved as they listened to Zander's story.

It had been three years since the boy's father died and his mother directly afterward. Soon Jacques and Telly had joined him as he slept in the stable and begged for food. Many of the villagers had sympathy for them, but the mayor, Van Maskolc, had jailed anyone he caught feeding them. Everyone knew the old man hated children, yet he watched them with an unsettling intensity.

Kang said, "This town isn't big enough to support an orphanage."

"They send children like us to the missionaries in Riffela."

"Would you like us to take you there?" Celwyn asked. He signaled for another round of tea, milk, and pastries.

Zander asked, "On the big black train?"

"Yes," Kang said.

Zander looked at his plate and chewed on his lip.

The magician said, "You can decide later. Does Van Maskolc have servants in his house? Does his coachman sleep at the house?"

"I think he sleeps with the horses," Zander said, then watched as a plate of pastries arrived along with a question.

"Is that you, Zander?" The waitress had stopped right next to him.

He nodded.

She regarded him with a frown. "You are very clean. Where did you get those clothes?"

The magician caused a tray of glasses to inch off the counter and fall. Their questioner whirled and ran to clean up the mess.

Celwyn turned back to Zander. "We will meet you outside of Van Maskolc's mansion after dark. Your friends will not spend another night in that house."

As he reached for a pastry, Zander said, "Will you tell me why I have shoes now? Where did they come from?"

Kang looked at the new shoes, then at Celwyn, and bestowed a cynical look on the magician.

Celwyn shrugged and added a warm scarf to the boy's neck and apples in his coat pockets.

Because there didn't appear to be any pubs or alehouses, the town seemed to settle down for the night early. As Celwyn scanned the street, he saw several townspeople entering the church.

Kang walked beside him. They'd decided Bartholomew would stay on the train to protect Annabelle. What settled it was Kang's remark that it would be a difficult conversation if she found out the three of them had enjoyed an adventure without her. From what Zander had described, Celwyn suspected a dangerous and distasteful encounter awaited them that Annabelle should not see or participate in.

Darkness became complete the further Celwyn and Kang walked from the train. No gas lights decorated the storefronts, and it became difficult to see the boards of the sidewalk. When they reached the corner and stepped out from under the awnings of the shops, moonlight bathed them with a silvery hand. Kang's skin seemed to glow under the light.

"Do you have a plan? Other than a rescue mission?"

Celwyn replied, "Not really. I wish Zander had dined with us."

"I know, but little steps are best. You saw how easily frightened he is. He will meet us there."

They passed the town square where the shadows around the central fountain seemed to float, and the sound of cascading water reached out to them. Warm light emanated from nearby houses as they continued by. Celwyn tried not to think of a small boy out in the cold and looking through those windows. "Do you know if the train's coal bins were filled this afternoon?" The magician asked as if it didn't matter.

Kang eyed him with a frown. "This makes me nervous, Jonas. Yes, they were. Plus, our provisions were laid in. We will once again have fresh fruit and meat, although I'm not sure what Chef Sully will do with it. Tonight's dinner tasted awful." They stopped walking and listened. A strong wind blew through the surrounding trees, and they heard the plaintive howl of wolves in the distance. "Why do you ask?"

Celwyn studied the street, noticing fewer and fewer people strolled the boards. At the top of the hill, Van Maskolc's mansion stood in stark silhouette against the moonlight.

Kang said, "Let me answer my own question: you anticipate that we may want to depart in a hurry."

"Yes."

"I told the conductor to have the engines stoked by nine tonight and that we would leave shortly afterward."

They'd reached the end of the street and waited in the shadows of the driveway leading up to the house. "I should inform you that it is highly disconcerting to have my intentions so easily anticipated." The magician didn't sound pleased.

Kang chuckled. "I'm sure there are those you've encountered that have had the same reaction." Moments ticked by. "What are we waiting for?"

Celwyn gazed through the darkness beyond the overgrown shrubbery to the dense trees lining the driveway on both sides. "I'm listening for others' thoughts."

"We appear to be alone."

"Perhaps." Celwyn started up the driveway on the far right, walking in the shadows of the trees. The moon floodlit the road and front of the darkened house. "When we reach the house, I will go in alone while you keep watch and disable the carriage driver if he should try to participate."

"Why are you going in alone?"

Celwyn regarded the automat. "I do not want you to object to what I might have to do. You will also want to keep Zander from harm or from interfering."

Kang tripped over a bump in the driveway. When he got to his feet again, he said, "Please refrain from your more flamboyant urges. The notoriety will follow us, even after we reach Prague."

The magician sighed. Sometimes he wished Kang wasn't so logical.

From inside the mansion came a short cry followed by a guttural laugh.

"We can't wait any longer for Zander." Celwyn produced a whistle and handed it to Kang. "Use this if things go badly out here."

The magician dashed to the far side of the mansion and around the corner. All of the downstairs windows appeared dark. In seconds he had broken one of them and stepped through.

He froze. The moonlight illuminated a horrific room of boars, bears, and lions mounted on the walls. He had no trouble seeing the open mouths and bared teeth. Celwyn waited, listening for footsteps or thoughts, and then crossed to the adjoining hallway.

Cold air blew by, bringing the smell of something burning, yet he saw no smoke. To his right, light seeped from under a closed door. The cold air had come from above. He went left, floating up a sweeping staircase leading to the second floor. Softly, so quiet he almost missed it, came an unspoken plea that went straight to his heart.

...Help me...

The magician raced up the rest of the darkened stairs, hearing the plea again, but much weaker. Once he made the landing, he opened the nearest door and saw white tables and beakers of mysterious liquids along with dozens of boxes. The smell of rotting meat thickened the room, along with the sharp tang of chemicals and burned hair. He produced a lantern and held it high. With a fingertip, Celwyn lifted the flap of the first box. When he saw what it contained, the magician felt bile rise in his throat.

Help me.

Then came the most pitiful weeping he'd ever heard.

The magician ran out of the room, following the sound. By the time he reached the far end of the hall, it had become an audible cry, followed by a scream. He reared back and blew open the door.

As the debris settled, he threw illumination into the room, seeing another long table and a child on top of it bound in chains. Gas lamps smoked, mixing with the stench of burned skin. Celwyn whirled and sent a heavy man nearly as large as himself flying hard to the ceiling and then falling to the floor. He turned his attention to the gnome-like man, with wild eyes, holding a knife under the child's chin. When he started to speak, Celwyn removed the gnome's hands and in a rainbow of spurting blood, the knife clattered to the floor.

The magician turned to the child, holding a hand over her eyes and suspending her consciousness. For now, he relieved her pain, but he needed to get her out of this hell. The chains fell to the floor as he lifted her into his arms. He nearly dropped her when he saw the dead body of a small boy laid across another table with a collection of knives next to him. Celwyn growled deep, and a chorus of angry violins rose up, keening high like a gathering of banshees.

The wizard-like man cackled, holding the bloody stumps of his forearms high. "I know what you are! You think you can—"

The magician sliced a hand through the air, sealing the windows and igniting the corners of the room. Cradling the child in his arms, he backed into the hallway, seeing for the first time the horrific taxidermy lining it. Van Maskolc had been torturing children for a very long time. The magician pivoted, and the music soared as he covered the room in fire.

Both Van Maskolc's screams, and the flames followed Celwyn as he streaked down the steps setting the staircase on fire. As he burst through the front door, the air rushed in. With a reverberating boom, the fire imploded. He raced down the driveway. Kang ran with him holding Zander's hand.

"Hurry!" Celwyn yelled.

Behind them, the burning mansion lit up the sky and dark forest behind it. As they ran up the street toward the train, the magician covered them in darkness and propelled them with magic. Bartholomew paced in front of the train car, and behind him, clouds of steam rose from the *Elizabeth's* engine. As they reached the steps leading up to the train, Celwyn lifted the darkness. The conductor had been hanging out the window of the engine and saw him. Bartholomew whirled and held out his arms for the child.

Zander climbed up the steps with Kang right behind him. "Inside, quickly!" The grinding and flames from the wheels began as Celwyn swung aboard behind the others and slammed the door behind him.

Townspeople flooded the square, some staring at the train and others running with buckets of water. The train gained speed, blowing her whistle.

Bartholomew laid the child on the sofa as gently as if she was made of glass. Kang pulled a trembling Zander aside and covered him with his coat. "I hope your answer was that you wanted to come with us?" The boy nodded and hugged Kang.

Celwyn saw the door leading to the kitchen begin to open, and, with a flick of his finger, closed and locked it.

Zander peeked around Kang and whispered, "Is she dead?"

Celwyn shook his head. "I need quiet, please." He knelt beside the sofa. Behind him, through the windows, the flaming mansion on the hill lit up the sky against the sky, just before the train entered a forest of trees so thick, they blocked out the moonlight.

"Come, we must find your friend some clean clothes and let Jonas help her." Kang tugged on the boy's hand. "I must also introduce you to Miss Annabelle and our other friend."

As he spoke, Bartholomew entered the room again, holding a pile of blankets. Zander stopped and looked up. His lip trembled. The big man squatted beside him, removed Kang's coat, and gently wrapped a blanket around the boy's shoulders.

"Welcome, I am Bartholomew," he told the boy as he handed Kang's coat back to him.

Zander's eyes widened further. He touched Bartholomew's face. They both smiled at the same time. "We will be friends," the big man said.

The boy's smile grew until he said, "Call me Zander."

With a pat on his head, Bartholomew said, "I must get these blankets to your friend, and you must go with the Professor."

Across the room, Celwyn examined the girl's injuries. His anger grew. He wished he had done much worse to Van Maskolc. Inch by inch, Celwyn repaired the damage, healing unspeakable wounds.

Bartholomew placed the blankets around her, and his voice wobbled as he hummed a lullaby in Cushitic. He tried not to let the fear show in his eyes as he watched her burns fade and cuts and tears in her flesh heal as if they'd never been there.

When the bruises around her wrists dissolved, Celwyn pulled the blanket up to her chin and sat back to study her mind. She lay as quiet as the dead in the profound sleep he'd induced. As he went deeper, he encountered a maelstrom of terror and visions he couldn't tolerate. In moments, he'd stilled her thoughts and replaced them with images of toys, flowers, and song. Every time a terror threatened, she would find herself in a field of white flowers under a warm blue sky.

The magician brushed back the matted, red curls from her forehead. "Let's not hover over her when she wakes up," he suggested. As they moved to nearby chairs, Annabelle burst through the door from the sleeping car with Zander and Kang in her wake.

"Where is she?" Annabelle demanded as she rushed forward.

Zander darted around her and stood beside the other child. "Telly!" The boy bit his lip.

As Zander gazed at the girl, Celwyn felt relieved he had not seen her in the darkness as they escaped the mansion, only now in good repair.

"Her name is Telly." Tears seeped from Zander's eyes. Annabelle reached for his hand and held on.

Kang cleared his throat. "She is safe now, as are you." He looked at the magician with a resigned expression. "Our party has grown tonight, as has our notoriety."

Celwyn nodded. "The town will find it curious that we departed as the mansion burned, but nothing more."

Telly coughed, and her eyes opened. She saw Zander, and her face lit up. Then she spied Annabelle and Kang standing behind him. When she got to Bartholomew and Celwyn, she started to tremble. Zander blurted, "They are our friends! They are all our new friends!"

Bartholomew's lullaby reached her, and the hypnotic chant seemed to calm everyone. Celwyn said. "Welcome, Miss Telly. Would you like some milk? I believe we have a supply of pastries also." She watched him walk to the kitchen door and make the request.

"Add a tray of meats too. They both could use protein," Kang called.

Telly held the blanket around her shoulders and sat up, absorbing the details of the brightly lit room, the dining table, sofa, chairs, and wall of windows before the moonlit trees they sailed through. The train bounced along a trestle, and before she could become afraid, Kang said, "We are on a train. It is very safe." He bowed. "Please, call me Professor."

Annabelle stepped forward and sat beside Telly. "I am Miss Annabelle. May I hug you?"

Telly's mouth opened in wonder. "You are so pretty!"

Annabelle hugged her and stood. "Let's go wash up and have some cake." As they left, Zander followed, either because he also wanted to wash up or to be certain his friend was not afraid.

Chapter 24

CELWYN RELAXED, EXTENDING HIS legs and slouching in a club chair. Long ago, he'd concluded that while the expelling of magic tired him, he also felt the aftermath of the excitement. At the moment, he was dead tired, mostly a reaction to the horrors he'd seen in the Van Maskolc mansion, Telly's mind and imagining the pain and fear she'd endured. Perhaps he should immerse his soul in fields of white flowers.

The girl appeared to be about Zander's age but frailer and much smaller. That reminded him that he needed to add clothes for both children to Annabelle's room. When he'd done so, he poured another cup of tea and waited for Kang to speak.

When he didn't, Celwyn said, "We've slowed down so that we can see obstacles, and we will reach Dagge in another hour. The conductor said we will stop there for the night."

Kang said nothing. He seemed deep in thought: for the last several minutes the mechanical man had paced the train car like an expectant father. Across from Celwyn, Bartholomew stewed in his own thoughts while he studied, but didn't really see, the colorful map on the wall. He still hummed the lullaby.

"They'll stay in Annabelle's compartment. I had doubled the size of the cabin initially to accommodate her future wardrobe," the magician said.

"You are suggesting that we won't entrust them to the first adequate church that we encounter?" Kang asked. He'd stopped behind Bartholomew and tapped the map on the wall. "Uman is about a day away. It would have several churches."

Celwyn regarded him. "Is that what you recommend?"

Kang frowned and paced again to the door leading to the kitchen and back. Repeat. Finally: "Yes."

"Why?" Bartholomew asked.

"It is obvious," Kang responded. "If they are anywhere near us, it is dangerous. Our enemies haven't changed. It is highly illogical to keep the children with us."

The big man frowned. "But we would take care of them. We would protect them."

Celwyn looked between the emotional and the practical partners. Could he be the balance that guaranteed the orphans' safety?

The door leading to the sleeping cars opened just as the train sounded its whistle. At the noise, Telly jumped and buried her face in Annabelle's skirts.

Zander ran to Bartholomew, who gathered him into his massive arms.

Just as if they'd planned it, Ricardo saved the moment as he arrived with a cart piled high with plates of meats, cheeses, bread, and cake. His quick black eyes observed the mood of the room, and he squatted at their level to greet the children with respectful reverence. "Good evening, my lambs," he told them in a singsong voice. "I am Ricardo, and you are Telly and Zander."

Zander watched him with big eyes before returning his welcome. Telly managed a shy smile.

Annabelle led Telly to the table, and the others gathered. Kang observed the scene and said, "Why fight the inevitable?" He looked at the children who needed no encouragement to start eating.

Celwyn frowned. Kang's primary observations were correct, and they all would need to be vigilant. Putting cheer into his voice, he said, "What a beautiful blue dress you are wearing, Miss Telly." And to Zander, "That is a very grown-up jacket you have."

Aiming a pointed look at the magician, Annabelle drawled, "I *do* declare. The clothes just appeared in my room." She pointed to the girl's feet. "However, the shoes are a touch too small."

"That can be fixed," Celwyn said and did so. "Anything else?"

"Ribbons to match the dresses. Socks and undergarments for both. And," she eyed Celwyn, "if you don't mind, please keep it to a minimal amount so that I can select the rest myself when we reach Satu Mare."

"As you wish," Celwyn replied as he spun the globe beside the bar. "Would you also purchase some primers and books? I believe we will have time to begin their education."

"Excellent," Bartholomew said and held the meat platter for Telly. Several minutes went by as the children ate. Telly finished half of her plate and yawned.

"I've never taught before, but," Annabelle hesitated, then hugged Zander, "it will be fun." She turned to the children. "Would you like to play with a kitten? His name is Herriot, and he is probably under my bed."

Both Zander and Telly were on their feet at the word "kitten."

"You may be excused from the table," Annabelle said. "I'll be along in a moment and get you ready for bed." As the door to the sleeping car closed behind them, she said without a trace of an accent or humor, "Where did those new beds come from? There will be none—you hear me? —no magic performed in front of them. Do you understand?"

The magician held out his hands, palms up. "I wouldn't dream of it."

Annabelle's eyebrows went up. "Yes, you would. You can't help yourself." She implored Kang, "You understand how difficult it is to accept that there is magic at all."

Like she said, I can't help myself, Celwyn thought as he caused her empty teacup to lift off its saucer and dance across the table and back. The flower on it unfolded, and a tiny voice trilled, "Magic!" Little displays pleased him.

"You aren't taking this seriously!" Annabelle exclaimed, but she watched the dancing cup with half a smile. "Oh, hell. Just be careful, please?"

When everyone arose the next morning, the *Elizabeth* had been chugging her way across the countryside for several hours. Fields of tall grasses gave way to forests before snow-covered mountains. The air had lost its warmth, turning frosty as a cold wind whipped around the dining room. Celwyn closed the window.

Behind him, the breakfast table had been set, and the magician had already had a conversation with the conductor confirming that the train would reach Satu Mare by mid-afternoon. More coal and produce would be loaded aboard while Annabelle shopped, and they explored the city. It should be enjoyable. According to Kang, the city had been settled by the Ottomans around an extensive bazaar. Modern culture had brought several museums representing many countries.

Celwyn rubbed his hands together, anticipating a broad selection of tobacco and tea. He hadn't tasted a worthy Earl Grey since leaving Singapore. As he watched the countryside glide by, he became aware of a small presence nearby. Zander had joined him at the window, smelling much better this morning than he did at their initial meeting.

"Sir," the boy said solemnly as if he stood in a graveyard. "I am afraid."

"Why are you afraid?"

It was then the magician noticed the boy's hand shaking just visibly as he touched the glass.

"Because I've never been on a train. I've never been outside our city." He hesitated and added, "And most of all, I do not know where we are going."

"Follow me, please." Celwyn took his trembling hand and led the way to the map on the far wall. Colorful pins showed their route. "Your town...was here." The magician pointed. "We're going to be in Satu Mare this afternoon," and pointed again.

The boy studied the map and glanced out the window and back. "We are here, now?" He tapped the beginning of Carpathian forests.

Celwyn ruffled his hair. "You have a sharp mind, young man." He sniffed. "I smell bacon, do you?"

Zander obediently sniffed the air. "Yes, Sir."

"Would you like to call me Uncle Jonas?"

"Yes!" The boy gave Celwyn's hand a squeeze, and the magician lifted him up so they could study the map together.

"We will have an enjoyable journey, but I must warn you that our chef produces somewhat ... unique meals. Do your best with them."

Bartholomew entered the car from the kitchen and greeted Zander. The boy ran to him and hugged him around the knees. "Does he know of our adventure for this afternoon?" he asked Celwyn.

"Not yet."

The big man squatted beside the boy. "This afternoon we will visit a big city. If you are good, we will go to the zoo. I hear they have kangaroos and monkeys."

As he spoke, Annabelle and Telly arrived, and the girl heard the last of what was said. She bounced on her heels and clapped her hands. Now Celwyn knew what her smile looked like.

"Where is the Professor?" Bartholomew asked.

"In his room." Annabelle lowered her voice, "He is making something for the children."

As they settled at the dining table, Kang joined them, carrying two tissue-wrapped packages. He handed one to each child and sat down.

"This is for me?" Telly wondered aloud. Celwyn winced, realizing the child had probably never had a present.

From the automat's pained expression of sympathy, he wondered the same. "Yes. They are both alike. Please, open them."

Zander didn't need further encouragement and sent the tissue paper flying.

"Intricate. Beautifully done," Celwyn told Kang. "I did not know you carved."

"Just a hobby."

"It is so wonderful," Bartholomew said as he leaned closer to the object in Telly's hand. "What is it?"

"Yes," Celwyn agreed with a mischievous grin. "What are they?"

Telly held her toy in the air for all to see. It measured as big as a man's hand in an oblong shape and a point at one end. Wings like a bird sprouted from the sides. On top, a small box had been carved out of the body. The magician's grin broadened: a little man sat inside. He had elfin ears and waved a tiny hand.

"What is it? I love it!" Zander said.

Kang asked the children, "Have you seen the birds in the trees, how they flap their wings and fly?"

"Yes!"

Kang said slowly, "This toy is like a bird, and the man is riding on its back. Notice how you can move the wings a bit." The automat stopped when Selkirk arrived with a tray of food. As he set out the plates, Kang told them, "We will play with them later."

Celwyn leaned close to Kang to whisper, "You must tell me more about these birds. It is almost as if you have ridden in one yourself. They are so real and detailed."

"I'm sure I do not know what you mean," Kang murmured back with a smile playing at his lips.

Celwyn elbowed him. "When you prevaricate, your ears twitch. You may want to remember that if we're ever in a position of necessary subterfuge."

"Noted."

"What gives the birds power?" Celwyn whispered.

"Not now," Kang hissed.

Annabelle said, "What are you two whispering about?"

"We were discussing whether or not to stop for toys before or after the zoo this afternoon." Celwyn turned to the children, "What do you think?"

As expected, both orphans squealed in delight, effectively distracting Annabelle. She eyed Celwyn like she would an errant puppy. "Really. You two are not subtle at all. Anyhow, we will need to stay in Satu Mare a few days. I have a mountain of laundry to send out, and it will take that long to have new clothes for the children tailored."

Celwyn agreed. "I plan to move my things to the salon at the rear compartment of the train. The pianoforte is already there. That will free up space for your classroom and playroom."

"Thank you." Annabelle sighed with relief. "I'd worried how we would do this."

"Can I learn to carve wood, too?" Zander asked the Professor.

"Of course. We will get more tools and wood. Perhaps you can make a flute for Telly."

Telly had tears in her eyes. "I can't believe all of this."

"I...I," Celwyn tried to find the words. He wanted to offer the little girl comfort but didn't know what to say. It made him realize that hundreds of years had gone by without him talking with a child about something so elementary.

Annabelle patted the girl's hand. "What Uncle Jonas wants to say is that you are safe with us." She switched to English, "And you will learn many languages too."

"Thank you," Bartholomew said. "I do not understand Deutsch that well ... or Roma."

Celwyn said, "I doubt that Ricardo or Selkirk do either." To the children, he said, "We will translate as we go. Please listen carefully."

A short lesson ensued with the translation of the word 'salty' with the word for salty in Deutsch and English used to describe the eggs placed before them. Both of the children ate fast, covering their plates with their arms to protect their food. Kang watched them with pity written across his face.

"Here." Annabelle demonstrated how to hold forks and other general table manners. Both orphans obediently imitated her, giggling and enjoying themselves until Qing squeaked from atop the bar.

The children froze, watching the bird circle the room, coming to rest next to Kang's hand. He pecked at a spoon and turned a glittering eye on Bartholomew's ring.

Celwyn said, "This is Qing. He will be your friend, too, and protect you."

Zander watched Qing, and the bird returned the regard. He waddled closer to Telly and sat down.

"He likes to have the back of his neck scratched," the magician told her. Telly backed away to stand behind Annabelle.

"You'll get used to him." Annabelle nodded at them.

After breakfast, the *Elizabeth* skirted a serene lake that looked bluer than the sky. Swans glided across the water, and a crane soared overhead. No longer in the far distance, the snow-covered mountains seemed much closer. As the train began to climb, Celwyn excused himself, saying that he and Ricardo would see to moving his belongings to the salon. Bartholomew joined him, leaving the children standing at the window watching the countryside and clutching their toys.

From the chairs by the bar, Kang and Annabelle exchanged a glance. "It was kind of you to make the toys," she said.

"Thank you." Kang bowed. "We'll need a chalkboard and many other things to educate them." He smiled as Zander tugged on Telly's curls, and she stuck her tongue out at him. Kang switched to English. "They need a family most of all. We are probably not what most people would consider a proper family, but we mean well and will love them." He studied the children a moment. "I doubt they have had any schooling at all. Both are about eight and have been orphans for three or more years."

Annabelle sighed. "I tried to talk to them last night about their past."

"Do they know how their parents died?"

"Their fathers perished in a cave-in at the coal mine. Then their mothers just ... died."

"Do you find that odd?" Kang asked.

Annabelle frowned as she played with one of her ribbons. "Yes. What exactly *happened* to these children?"

Keeping his voice low, Kang related a sanitized version of what Celwyn found in the Van Maskolc mansion, but enough to describe the horrors Telly had endured. "And the boy had the wits to escape a madman. Living on the streets has made him wise."

"There were other dead children in the house?"

"Yes." Kang thought for a moment. "I suspect Van Maskolc may have had Telly and Zander's mothers killed to get to the children."

Annabelle's mouth opened and closed several times. "That's monstrous!"

"It is."

Telly grabbed Zander's toy. He tried to retrieve it while she giggled.

"You don't want to know the details. Jonas rescued Telly just in time. If Zander hadn't told him she was in the house, she would already be dead."

"I must thank Uncle Celwyn for saving them," she said. "What happened to Van Maskolc?"

Kang shook his head.

"I'm sure neither of us wants to know what your uncle did to him."

Chapter 25

SHROUDED IN CLOUDS OF STEAM, the *Elizabeth* pulled into the train station of Satu Mare at two that afternoon. As expected, the town was large. Rows of brick buildings were sandwiched between churches and warehouses. Quaint houses lined the streets to the east. Before the train stopped, the passengers glimpsed flags fluttering above the bazaar in the distance. The orphans squealed in excitement as they saw all the people talking and laughing. Several other trains had arrived that day as well, and the yardman directed them to a side trestle.

As they shuddered to a stop, Celwyn verified that no one seemed to be paying the *Elizabeth* any undue attention: in particular, no voluptuous vampires who'd recently taken a tumble off a train, nor any disgruntled aunts or corpulent police lieutenants.

Celwyn volunteered to stay by the bar and watch outside while workers loaded coal aboard, and the conductor and his assistant took a well-deserved break. Ricardo and Sully won the coin toss to go first into the city and fairly skipped down the path toward the street. He watched Annabelle and the children's preparations for their outing and remembered how uncomplicated his life had been only a few months ago.

"I have a list of the things we need." Annabelle turned to the children. "What are the rules?"

"I hold either Bartholomew's hand or yours." Telly grasped her hand with a smile.

Zander piped up, "I will hold either the Professor's hand or yours." He turned to Celwyn. "You come with us?"

The magician ruffled his hair. "I have to stay here and will be waiting to hear about everything you saw when you return."

Hours later, the magician lounged in front of the club car windows with a cup of tea and an alert eye on the train yard. A few moments ago, the remaining porter, Selkirk, had left for his evening out as Sully and Ricardo returned. From the level of jocularity, Sully appeared to have enjoyed himself and his libations immensely. Ricardo hefted him up the stairs. The condition of their chef would make the quality of their dinner most interesting.

Celwyn sipped and watched sundown approach. On the sidewalk thirty feet away, a family of twelve navigated through the vendors in the street. Each of the girls wore white aprons over their blue skirts, and the boys wore matching short jackets. Beyond the vendors, a familiar feathered hat appeared, then the top of Bartholomew's hat. A cart piled high with packages came next with two tired-looking shopkeepers steering more carts. Both children held dripping fruit ices and clung to Annabelle.

A half-hour later, everything had been transported inside the train, and the shopkeepers departed, counting their tips. Annabelle announced she needed to freshen up and that the children did, also. Zander informed everyone that one of the packages contained new underwear that he wouldn't need to wear.

Bartholomew collapsed next to the automat on the sofa as the magician ferried whiskies to them. "How much of the shopping did you complete?" he asked.

Kang groaned. "Not enough. We'll have to finish more tomorrow before we see the zoo." He eyed Bartholomew speculatively. "I may beg off and stay behind tomorrow."

"I will recover by then." The big man wiggled his feet. His face grew dark. "I hear that at the zoo, there are animals that were captured from my homeland and put in cages."

Kang inhaled. "I would agree we need to preserve all species and educate everyone about animals. But, on a basic level, I do not approve of the conditions in many zoos. We'll limit the children's exposure to the enclosures if it isn't a well-run establishment."

They all thought about what he said for a moment. Then Celwyn stood and patted his stomach. "I wonder what is for dinner. Excuse me."

Before he reached the kitchen door, Kang called, "Please do what you can to make it edible."

The magician chuckled and entered the kitchen. Steam fragrant with garlic and thyme met him, and he spied Sully in the corner by the icebox, chopping a pile of mushrooms.

"What is on the menu?"

"Beef Boulogne. Have a taste." He handed Celwyn a spoon.

As he accepted the spoon, the magician wondered why he felt like the innocent bird sent into a coal mine to see if it survives poisonous gasses. He took the lid off the pot. It smelled much better than it should, considering the source of inspiration. The contents appeared as expected: a deep red wine sauce simmered with beef and carrots. Celwyn dipped the spoon in the sauce, let it cool, and touched it with his tongue.

The sauce tasted ... very good. Not too salty or heavily laced with cumin or other spices.

"Like it?" Sully poured vinegar into a bowl, added herbs, and began to whisk the contents.

"Yes. You have my compliments." Celwyn bowed. "I'll let the others know that dinner is imminent." As he headed back to the dining car, he wondered if inebriating Sully could be the key to culinary bliss.

Midafternoon the next day brought a soft spring rain as the children returned with tales of giraffes taller than the train and baby pigs that sniffed their fingers. When they gathered around the dining room table, stories of monkeys dominated the conversation.

"The walrus has a whole pool to himself," Telly announced in halting Deutch.

"I think we can declare the visit to the zoo has been a success." Kang watched Telly yawn and curl up next to Bartholomew. "If you're still awake after dinner, we'll have a wood carving lesson," Kang told the children.

"Perhaps they will have an early night?" Annabelle suggested. "We must get on a schedule because our schoolwork begins right after breakfast tomorrow."

"I look forward to teaching." The big man refilled milk glasses. "When do we depart this city?" he asked Celwyn.

"After the last of their new clothes have been delivered to the train tomorrow. I'm not in a hurry to reach Prague."

The Professor raised a brow. "I'm not either. Why do you wish for a more leisurely trip?" The children had moved to the other side of the room to play dominoes.

"The children have been through more than any child should endure, and I'd like a few weeks of stability for them. They need to have confidence in their security with us." Celwyn bobbed his head at them as they played. "They should be doing that instead of scrounging in a barnyard for food."

"There is more too," Kang surmised. "You want to decide if anyone is following us or know what to expect in Prague."

The magician nodded. The silence continued except for a squeal from Telly when Zander jumped her tiles.

"For their safety, we need to train the little kinders to obey us during an attack and not run away in a panic," Bartholomew said.

Annabelle cast a worried smile at the children. "Telly sleeps restlessly. She wakes up from nightmares and talks about flowers."

"I made the suggestion to her that the flowers were safe and to concentrate on them if she was afraid," Celwyn said.

"Poor little one." Annabelle sent her a worried look. "Zander is adapting, and he fell asleep instantly."

"We will help them heal." Bartholomew's frown contained more than sadness.

"Another thing." Kang gazed at each of them. "It would be helpful if we all speak the same language, especially during stressful times."

"I agree. We will concentrate on language skills first in our classes." Annabelle nodded. "All of their new books are in English, which will help."

"They also need to learn how to interact with others they meet." Kang watched as Zander shoved Telly after a particularly clever domino move. She pushed him back, laughing. "They will need to learn about other children and cultures, too."

"I also must begin Telly's embroidery lessons." Annabelle added a note to the list she kept at her elbow.

"Why?" Celwyn asked.

"All young ladies should know how." She raised her brows at him. "I'll teach Zander too if he will sit still for it."

"Ha!" Bartholomew joined in the teasing.

As they listened to the giggles coming from the domino board, the automat said, "I have another concern that must be settled and then practiced before Prague. We need to explain the children's relationship to us, and they must also be able to articulate it, if asked." He nodded at them. "This is something that their reactions and speech should account for also. Calmly and without hesitation."

Annabelle's frown wrinkled her smooth forehead like tiny ripples on a tennis ball. "Do you mean to have them call us 'Mother' and 'Father'?" She looked at the children. "That would be too soon."

"I agree." Kang sipped whiskey as they studied the children as they played. It appeared Zander was winning at the moment. "May I suggest that the children are your niece and nephew, and you took charge of them in Baghdad after their parents perished there?" Annabelle listened, and the frown lessened. Kang added, "If so, the story is helpful because we wouldn't be associated with the city where we found them, which could prompt questions."

"I can remain Uncle Celwyn or Uncle Jonas ... since we're not related." The magician celebrated by showering the air above them with a cluster of tiny exploding stars. The children were too engrossed in their game to notice. "Purely an honorary title, which I bear with pride."

"I like it," Annabelle said, oblivious to the stars that dissolved above her head.

"It accounts for their background without being too complicated to explain or maintain details for," Kang said. "And you, Sir, what do you think?" he asked Bartholomew. As he spoke, the big man spied the last of the stars and pretended he didn't, except for a quick glance at the magician.

Bartholomew regarded the children for a long moment. "I like the Professor's workable explanation. We are far from the United States—where Annabelle is from originally—and our story would have to be verified there by the authorities in order to contradict us."

"Fortunately, Prague is a mix of nationalities: we will blend in beautifully." Celwyn turned. "Zander and Telly, could you rejoin us for a moment, please?" When they were again seated on each side of Bartholomew, he continued, "We would like to ask you some questions and talk. Is that all right?" Both of them stopped smiling and nodded. Zander started kicking the table leg. Celwyn said, "No, no. You have not done anything wrong. On the contrary, we're very happy you're here."

Telly climbed onto the magician's lap and blinked at him with unshed tears. Celwyn blinked back with unshed tears also, emotion making his voice more gruff than usual.

"We want to be sure you are safe and keep you with us. It will help if we show anyone who asks that you are part of our family." Celwyn watched the children and noted Telly's quick glances at Bartholomew, Kang, and Annabelle. Zander's bright eyes shone with relief. "We plan to tell anyone who asks that you are the niece and nephew of Miss Annabelle. Do you think that is a good idea?"

Telly's smile spread like a rising sun across her small face. "Yes."

"I think it is a grand idea!" Zander said and also climbed into the magician's lap. As he did so, Celwyn admonished himself. Next time he would first announce that their talks were about good things instead of scaring them.

Kang said, "Excellent. So immediately, you must begin calling her Aunt Annabelle. Could you practice that, please?" They both demonstrated loudly with giggles.

"Thank you," Celwyn said. "If you are asked, or hear anyone talking about you, tell them you joined us in a city called Baghdad after your parents passed away." He patted Zander's shoulder. "I know it is sad, but we must be prepared in case it comes up."

He looked at Telly, whose eyes had taken on a far-away look. When her gaze reached him, he said, "It could be anyone who asks, such as a porter, a waiter, a little friend, or a policeman: they must all be told what we've said if you are asked. Do you understand?" As he spoke, he entered each of their thoughts and embedded the explanation.

The door to the kitchen opened, and Ricardo announced that dinner was ready to be served. "This will be interesting," Kang murmured.

Chapter 26

B Y THE TIME THE COMMISSIONED clothing for the children arrived the next day, steam billowed from the *Elizabeth's* engine, and the magician paced from side to side of the dining car. He followed the delivery into the dining room.

Telly held up a lacy dress with a squeal of delight, and Annabelle examined a winter coat for Zander with a critical eye. Celwyn sent the courier on his way with a fist full of notes.

Today had been a special occasion: the first day of class. Kang and Celwyn followed Annabelle and the children to the classroom next to the compartments where they all slept. Small chairs, tables, art stands, and chalkboards had been set up during the night by Bartholomew. He'd stacked dozens of books on shelves all around the room. On the chalkboard, "Water, sister, brother, friend" appeared in block letters with the alphabet below.

As solemn as only a child can be, Telly said to Bartholomew, "Thank you."

The big man knelt down beside her and just as gravely said, "You are most welcome."

Zander walked the room with the kind of childhood delight that they would all remember for a long time. "I will be a professor like you!" he told Kang.

In the dining car a few minutes later, Celwyn said, "You noticed that Zander didn't want to be a gruff ruffian like me?"

"Give him more time." Kang relaxed by the globe. "You know, we will be stopping tonight in Hunedoara."

They watched the terrain outside the windows. Picturesque villages of thatched-roofed houses went by along with small white churches, most of them of Greek Orthodox extraction. Carts of hay lined the road, and women hung washing outside to dry, turning to watch the *Elizabeth* rumbling by.

Kang crossed to the wall map. "Hunedoara is next to Lake Stephan. We might consider a fishing trip the next morning before we depart." He caught Celwyn's skeptical glance and added, "For the children's education, of course."

"Of course."

Kang licked his lips deep in thought. "I know an excellent recipe for baked trout." He sighed. "Last night's dinner may never occur again. Who knows what Sully would do to a trout? Slather it in cake frosting, most likely." He shuddered.

Celwyn pointed at a glimmer off the surface of a lake in the distance. "It could be that we will have an opportunity for a fishing trip before tomorrow."

"Perhaps. For now, I must leave you to your pursuits and work at my desk. Let me know if there's something you need." The Professor hitched up his trousers and headed to the sleeping compartments.

Celwyn spent a pleasant few hours with the teapot, his pipe, and the maps. Occasionally he poked his head into the hallway and heard giggles, or a lecture, coming from the classroom.

From their many purchases at their last stop, Kang had added several topographical maps to their collection. Maps presented decisions.

Celwyn poured another cup of tea and tapped a pencil on one of them. Mountains surrounded Fara, and he debated whether they should skirt around the area or confront it in a straight line. Going around would add several weeks to their trip. There was taking their time, and then there was wasting time.

The magician picked up the teapot and received half a cup. *Rats.* He arose and went to the kitchen to request a fresh pot. When he returned to the dining room, class was in recess, and his quiet time with the maps was over. The automat enjoyed maps more than he did anyhow. Telly played jacks in the middle of the floor between the sofa and dining room table. Every time she tossed the ball into the air, the kitten Herriot chased it under the sofa. Meanwhile, Zander threw his larger ball across the room, where it hit the wall and rolled back again. Celwyn resisted the urge to use magic to contribute to the fun. That reminded him.

"Where is Annabelle?" he asked.

From his reclining position on the sofa, Bartholomew said, "She is lying down for a moment with a headache."

Celwyn had arranged for midafternoon sustenance for the children, and as expected Selkirk arrived with large glasses of milk. As he turned to ask Zander to join Telly at the table, Celwyn stopped still. Kang halted on his way to the sofa. A few feet in front of the bar, Zander rolled a walnut to the kitten, and the kitten batted it back to him.

Celwyn made his voice as casual as possible and pointed at the walnut. "Where did you get that?"

Zander held it in the air. "In the classroom."

"Oh my," Kang said and collapsed into a chair.

As if it didn't matter, Celwyn asked, "Was that before or after your new clothes arrived this morning?"

Zander shrugged and drank milk.

Bartholomew had crossed to join them at the table. He asked Zander, "Could I have the walnut for a moment, please?"

In careful and accented English, Zander handed him the walnut and said, "Yes, you may."

"Very nice, Master Zander," Kang said.

After examining the walnut, the big man handed it to Celwyn. "There is nothing distinctive about it."

The children resumed playing and not listening. Bartholomew chose his next words carefully. "The first instance of the walnut could be a challenge from Jax just to begin his game. But now? He is taunting us."

"Or he was inside one of the townspeople who made deliveries to the *Elizabeth* and is following us on his own," Kang pointed out. From the door leading to the cabins and classroom, Annabelle stuck her head inside the room and announced that class was resuming. Without being urged, the children ran to her.

"I will be there shortly, Miss Annabelle," Bartholomew called.

Kang waited until the door shut again before saying to both of them, "Again, I am concerned. It is one thing for us to endanger ourselves. It is another to expose the children to Jax."

The train slowed, rumbling over a bridge above a fast-moving river. Celwyn crossed to the windows, deep in thought. Thick forests surrounded the tracks as a light rain fell, obscuring everything beyond the trees. Moments passed before he said, "I agree. But could we really give them up to an unknown fate?"

"I could take them away and find them good homes far from Jax," Bartholomew said.

Celwyn made a face like he had swallowed a lemon. "I don't like that either."

"Answer this: why did Jax want to scare us by announcing his presence?" Kang tapped his lips and thought. "Why do that instead of just attack?"

The train began a climb, and Celwyn sat down again. The kitten jumped into his lap and turned a green-eyed stare upon him. Celwyn stared back and scratched its ears. "We do not know if Jax is on the train. Or if he just boarded it for a few minutes this morning."

"We are not certain if he intends to follow us: for all his nefarious actions, Jax does not appear to be overly clever, just persistent and evil," Kang murmured.

Bartholomew shrugged. "He may wish us harm, or he may be waiting for something."

"Such as a confederate in Prague?" Kang speculated.

"Damnation!" The magician growled, "If we split up now, we wouldn't know if Jax decided to follow us…. Or worse if he followed Bartholomew and the children. If we stay together, we're stronger against him." Herriot began kneading his claws on Celwyn's knee. The magician brought the kitten close to his face and enjoyed the tickle of its whiskers. "That isn't a nice thing to do to my trousers." He rolled the walnut across the floor, and the kitten chased it. "The same logic would apply if we left the children with a church: we do not know they'll be safe."

The Professor rubbed his forehead. "A horrible conundrum."

"What if we set a trap to identify who Jax is inhabiting?" Bartholomew asked.

The magician's smile was not from humor. "I like that proposal: we attack instead of waiting for him to do so." Celwyn rolled the walnut again. Every time the kitten pounced, the walnut rolled away.

Kang sighed. "I hate to say so, but I agree."

"Also, Jax won't be expecting us to take an offensive stance." The magician scattered dozens of walnuts across the floor.

As the *Elizabeth* entered the mountain town of Hunedoara, the sun set in a blaze of pinks, oranges, and golds below layers of storm clouds. Little stone houses perched on steep hills, surrounding the town like children's blocks, and donkeys drew carts along the winding streets. Several larger buildings framed the main church.

"Hunedoara sits at the foot of the Carpathian Mountains. It has existed since the early fourth century, with the Bavarians ruling over them most of the time." Kang lectured the children. "Only eighty-five years ago, they repelled Napoleon's invasion."

Zander asked, "Who is Napoleon?"

Telly ran across the classroom to the stacks of books. In halting English, she said, "Please, wait a moment." She opened a book, then another, and her lips moved as she tried to read the text. "I cannot read it yet, but Napoleon holds his stomach in the picture. He also has elephants."

"Very good," Annabelle said from behind her desk. "We need to know more about Napoleon. Could you both start a list of any other books we will need, please?"

"We saw an elephant at the zoo." Zander pointed out the window to the buildings. "Is there a zoo here?"

From the desk opposite Annabelle's, Bartholomew said, "I do not think so. But there is an excellent park. There is also an inn where we will have our dinner."

He pursed his lips, pretending to remember. "I think they have wonderful cakes there!"

Zander jumped to his feet and started for the door. Annabelle intercepted him.

"Not until you have washed and dressed for dinner, please."

Telly held Herriot up to the window glass. "I see snow."

"There is snow. We will have to wear our coats and mittens too," Annabelle said. She spied a shredded shoelace from one of her boots in the corner. "And purchase toys for the kitten."

———

As they filed off the *Elizabeth* one by one, Celwyn asked Kang, "How impatient is the crew to go into town?"

"Moderate." He offered his hand to Telly as they stepped onto the sidewalk. "But they will wait and guard the train until we return from the inn."

"Where is it?" Zander asked.

Celwyn bent down until he was on Zander's level and pointed. "Do you see that gold light at the other end of the square?"

"Yes. There is a picture of an animal next to the light."

Bartholomew and Annabelle trailed behind Kang and Telly as they walked across the plaza. From their position at the rear of their little parade, the magician told Zander, "It might be a picture of a boar on the sign you saw. Our travel guide indicates the name of the establishment is the *Ebers Pfote*, the Boar's Paw."

The boy walked in silence for several minutes. As they neared the inn, he said, "It is very cold. Thank you for my coat, Uncle Jonas."

Celwyn blinked away an emotion that threatened. Such a basic thing: how many other children around the world are cold right now? "It is my pleasure, Master Zander." He patted the boy's head and said, "You deserve many things. Come on, we'll hold the door for everyone." They trotted ahead and held open the heavy wooden doors.

Telly giggled as they passed inside. The magician studied her eyes as he had been since they brought her aboard the train. He saw less anxiety tonight. But she remained as nervous as a cat, jumping when the train's whistle blew, or they hit a particularly rough section of track. Celwyn made a tour of her mind, hearing only girlish opinions of how her dolls were dressed and how the kitten liked to bite her finger. The news that the kitten had made a mess under her bed stayed foremost in her thoughts because she hadn't told anyone. The magician found evidence that she might recover from her ordeal: she seemed pleased because she had hidden Zander's airplane behind the sofa. For now, Celwyn relaxed; her thoughts seemed to be benign, not filled with terrors.

The wood-paneled dining room of the *Ebers Pfote* contained more than charm and warmth. Historical relics of multiple wars that had stormed through the mountains decorated every corner of the room. A musket hung above their table, and a scythe decked the wall above the roaring fireplace. Upon closer inspection, Celwyn felt fairly sure that dried blood still encrusted the blade.

They had just ordered their dinner when the maître'd returned to their table with a bucket of ice and bottle of Pommery champagne. Celwyn raised a brow at Kang and Bartholomew, who both shook their heads.

"Excuse me, please, but this was not ordered."

The maître'd uncorked the bottle and said, "The bottle is courtesy of the gentleman in the booth," he nodded to the far corner of the dining room. "He said you would remember drinking the same at the carnival in Piccadilly Circus."

The magician clenched his jaw—he did remember, and his anger grew by the second. It took a great deal of control as he carefully put his water glass down without crushing it. His hand remained steady. "You may leave the bottle, thank you." Beside him, Zander started to speak, but Bartholomew put a finger to his lips.

Celwyn had no problem recalling Piccadilly Circus and the Carnival of Lions, nor remembering Prince Leo's twisted smile, shining bald dome, and a voice that croaked like a fat constipated frog—of all things, a voice like that coming from a dwarf. What was the man doing in a remote inn in the Carpathian Mountains?

With a sigh, Celwyn threw down his napkin and prepared to go find out. Only he was too late. Prince Leo arrived at their table in a red shirt, fluffy scarf, and cloud of cologne. In all his dealings with the man, the magician had never asked why he dressed like a court jester in a Shakespearean play.

The dwarf bowed and said, "Good evening, my darlings. It is Prince Leo!"

The children stared with childish wonder, and Annabelle sneezed and scrutinized the heavy gold chains around his neck. Bartholomew managed a neutral, "Our pleasure."

Celwyn itched to remove the Prince—with violence—but he had already observed the children's fascination. Telly tentatively touched his glittery scarf with a fingertip.

"Excuse me, please. Prince Leo and I need to speak privately for a moment." Celwyn got to his feet. "We'll be right back." The dwarf hesitated, and the magician gave him a discreet shove toward the door.

Once outside, the man lit a cigarette and made sure he was well within sight of the maître'd through the doorway.

"Afraid I might harm you?" Celwyn tapped him on the shoulder. The magician had no trouble recalling the urge to put Prince Leo in a cage with his lions and would do so with little provocation. "It has been more than twenty years, but you should still remember that I could toss you so far into that forest ... and so swiftly ... that no one would see you disappear. In fact, maybe a lake would be better. Do you—"

"Please. I mean no harm."

"You mean no goodwill either."

Puffs of cigarette smoke rose around Leo's pockmarked face. His facial topography looked like someone had taken a tiny spoon and scooped out a hole every inch or so. "I am an honest businessman, Jonas." He gestured with the cigarette and fiery ashes scattered between them. "There is no proof. Otherwise, I would be in jail." When the magician said nothing, he socked the magician's arm playfully. "You know I would not do very well in the 'hoosegow,' as the Americans say."

With as much patience as he could muster, the magician said, "What are you doing here?"

The dwarf puffed furiously, which Celwyn considered a sign of an impending prevarication. "I could ask you the same, but ... we shall say that I am taking a short recess from my normal activities." Prince Leo blinked at him.

"Who are you hiding from?"

A shrug. "The Vienna guards."

Knowing Prince Leo, the magician surmised it most likely was someone as much unlike the Vienna police as possible. The man had no scruples or allegiance at all.

"How long have you been here?" he asked.

The dwarf thought a second and found no reason not to answer truthfully. "Almost a month. I love the food, but the scenery is extraordinarily boring." He ground out his cigarette under a well-made boot and gazed back inside the Inn. "Why are you here? Who are those people you are seated with?"

Celwyn regarded him without favor. Prince Leo gossiped as much as any housefrau, and he did not need to know about the children or anything at all about Kang and Annabelle. Only Bartholomew was not in danger, not sought by the police and money-hungry elderly aunts. Without a word, the magician pivoted and went inside, with Prince Leo hurrying to keep up.

When they reached their table, the magician took his seat and said, "This is Miss Dolly, her niece Miss Telly, and nephew Master Zander." With a bit of urging from Kang, the children stopped staring and greeted Prince Leo.

The dwarf performed a little bow and with an obvious effort to know more, said, "My, what a little beauty you are, Miss Telly. And such an upstanding young man, Master Zander." He turned to Annabelle. "I am honored to meet you. Where did you meet Mr. Celwyn?"

Before she could answer, Celwyn said, "And this is Professor Randolph and his colleague Doctor Bartholomew."

Prince Leo stared at the big man. "You are colored. How did you come to be with this group?"

The magician did not like the dwarf's tone and was through tolerating him. As he decided how to remove him, Kang interjected, "We are honored to have Doctor Bartholomew as our spiritual advisor. Are you fortunate enough to have such an advisor?"

Beside him, Zander's brows drew together: he wanted to ask questions. Celwyn sent him thoughts of riding an elephant through a jungle with monkeys and tigers.

Celwyn bowed to Kang's good sense. Again. There would be no benefit in calling attention to their little party. The idea of Prince Leo dangling off the scythe by his drawers above a roaring fireplace would have to wait.

"I am sorry to say that I do not. Moreover, I do not believe in religion," Prince Leo answered with a challenging glare at Bartholomew.

Zander blurted, "Neither do I!"

"Zander," Annabelle favored him with a serious look, "we'll discuss this in private."

Their soup arrived, and Prince Leo said, "I will leave you to your dinner. Are you staying in Hunedoara long?"

"No. We leave tomorrow for Paris," the magician said before anyone else could offer anything different. When Telly would have corrected him, Kang handed her the butter, asking that she pass it to Annabelle.

"Very well. It is delightful making the acquaintance of all of you. Please, enjoy your evening." Prince Leo trailed a suspicious—and speculative—glance across each of them.

Chapter 27

AFTER THEIR PARTY WAS ONCE aboard the *Elizabeth* again, the crew left for their evening on the town. Having heard enough about the flamboyant interruption to their meal, Kang specifically warned the crew away from the Inn and Prince Leo. Sully tipped his hat to Celwyn and followed Selkirk and Ricardo off the train. Ricardo's tenor floated back to them, leaving no doubt about the exciting evening they had planned.

"Whiskey or bourbon?" Kang called over his shoulder as Celwyn settled into a club chair again. Bartholomew already had a glass of wine and a sleepy droop to his eyelids as he relaxed on the sofa.

The magician shook his head. "I'm still in the mood for Earl Grey."

"I'm surprised that teaching is hard work," the big man announced. "You should know, my degree is in engineering, not children's studies."

From the other club chair, Annabelle groaned and said, "It certainly is. Please just bring the bottle, Professor."

He did so and asked, "Where are the children?"

"Zander is in the tub. Telly is playing with the kitten on my bed."

The magician decided now wasn't the time to mention the mess under Telly's bed. He opened his coat and let Qing inch his way out. "Behave."

"Did you notice the rather corpulent man with the walrus mustaches in the far corner of the restaurant?" Celwyn asked.

Bartholomew yawned. "I did, and the pretty woman with him."

"I can assure you that was not his wife by the way they behaved," Annabelle said. "Why do you ask?" she asked the magician.

"From his thoughts, I learned he owns the bank in town." Celwyn sipped his tea. "I'd like to think we do more good than harm. So, I silently and strongly suggested that he spend his extra money in a continuing donation to the church here, specifically to house and feed people."

"Nice." Bartholomew nodded.

"I plan to do something similar at each of the cities we stop in."

Kang started to laugh. "The irony of it. You do realize that this *is* the type of notoriety that is good, but that we still probably shouldn't be noticed for."

"Because?" Celwyn drawled.

"Because then they'd discover what else you *have* done that you do not need notoriety for."

Dawn tinted the mountains as Celwyn left his compartment and walked up the hallway outside the cabins. He peeked in on the children. They had some obvious differences: it would be difficult, but not impossible, to claim Telly's red curls as a family trait along with Zander's raven locks. They looked so peaceful and slept quietly. Interesting: Annabelle's snoring made anyone else's snorting and snuffling seem like faint background noise.

He closed the door with care and continued to the dining car. The *Elizabeth's* engine rumbled like a pride of lions as it warmed up. Soon they would once more bounce along the rails while he tried not to spill tea on his trousers—

Celwyn stilled. Again, he had heard snoring, most delicate and unexpected. He lit a lamp and leaned over the slumbering form on the sofa. When he saw who it was, he nearly dropped the lamp.

"What the *hell* are you doing here?" he shouted.

The screech of metal on metal began as the train's wheels turned, and a long hiss of steam escaped from the engine as the train started to pick up speed.

Celwyn shook Prince Leo. "What are you doing here?" he demanded as he pulled him off the sofa. "Get off my train!"

"Now, now, Jonas. I can explain." He rubbed his eyes.

The train gained more speed, and buildings whipped by as Celwyn realized the futility of the situation, short of physically throwing the dwarf off the train.

"Are you going with us?" a small sleepy voice asked.

Zander approached them in his nightshirt, staring at Prince Leo.

"Why, yes I—"

"Master Zander, why are you out of bed?" Celwyn let go of the dwarf's collar and turned to see Sully coming through the kitchen door.

"Aunt Annabelle's snoring woke me up. I thought girls didn't snore."

Celwyn closed his eyes, and when he had control again, he looked at Sully. "I suppose it was you who brought this man aboard?"

"Sure was, boyo! Said he was an old friend of yours. Ricardo and I helped him with his trunks." He looked at Prince Leo. "Poor bugger wasn't sure he could get packed in time to get here."

Celwyn told Zander, "Please go and get dressed. When you return, we'll have a game of checkers."

Zander ran out of the room, and the magician turned to Sully. "I want my tea, and help him," he pointed at the dwarf, "to store his trunks in the storage room. He can sleep there, too, until we get to our next stop."

"But there isn't a bed in there, gov'ner."

"You will see that there is. My tea, please?"

As Sully left, Celwyn added a bed and a basin to the storage room. If this continued, he'd have to add another water closet and train car. Prince Leo waddled by him, pulling his other trunk. "Thank you, Jonas."

The magician looked again: Prince Leo wore a fur-trimmed woman's dressing gown and fluffy slippers.

Celwyn cursed—it was too early for something like this. He needed his tea.

⌣

Hours later, the magician's mood hadn't improved. If it weren't for Zander, he would have stopped the train and put the dwarf out in the snow, looking like a peculiar signpost.

Since leaving Hunedoara, the train had climbed steadily, and around them, the snow piled in drifts higher than their smokestacks. At the top of Mt. Peleaga, the *Elizabeth* came to a halt, belching steam and attracting the attention of a railroad official who waved the train's conductor down. They conferred for several minutes while a handful of villagers looked on, whispering deep interest.

Annabelle asked, "Are we going to be here long enough for the children to go out and play?"

"I believe our breakfast is nearly ready." As he spoke, Bartholomew stared at Prince Leo and, like Celwyn, did not appear happy about the intrusion. "We may want to eat it before starting down the mountain."

"I'll check," Kang said as he left the train and joined the conductor's conference with the railroad master. It didn't take long before Kang climbed back inside, stamping the snow off of his shoes. "We are delayed," he announced. "Several hours. They need to clear off the tracks about halfway down the other side of the mountain."

Zander ran to the window and back. "We can play in the snow!"

Telly stared out the window, unblinking and lost in her thoughts, but she nodded when Celwyn said, "You can play for a few minutes before breakfast."

While they watched Zander pelting Bartholomew with snowballs, Kang's brows drew lower. "Like the railroad official, I do not have an abundance of confidence in the tracks going down the mountain. There could be other avalanches we do not know of."

Standing beside the tracks, Telly leaned against Annabelle as they watched Bartholomew roll a snowball. Celwyn wondered if she had ever played in snow before. To Kang, he said, "I plan to join our conductor at the controls for the trip down the mountain. If necessary: I'll intervene."

"I can imagine what that will entail." Kang sent Celwyn a speculative glance. "However, I feel better knowing you'll control the situation." They watched Zander laughing and rolling in the snow. "If I was as carefree as Zander, I wouldn't be worried. The only thing I'd think about is making another snowball."

With a clink of pottery, Selkirk and Ricardo arrived carrying trays of food. Kang waved at the big man, who gathered everyone to come back inside. Prince Leo joined them at the table and demurely placed his napkin in his lap. The fluffy sleepwear had been replaced by a canary yellow suit. Celwyn eyed him and murmured, "You are on probation. Irritate me, and you'll be wearing that gaudy suit while sitting in the snow."

"Please," the dwarf said and straightened his tie. "I respect that I am a guest. I only require your patience and a few crumbs of food until we reach Prague."

The magician clenched his fists to keep from throwing him across the room. "Who told you about Prague?"

With his little finger in the air, Prince Leo sipped his tea. "Mr. Sully, of course. Why else would I have boarded this train?" He looked down his nose at the magician. "He was very helpful. He also clarified Miss Annabelle's and the others' names. You should really develop a bit of trust, Jonas."

Kang laid a restraining hand on Celwyn's arm. "The children are almost here."

⁘

Telly and Zander went outside, with Kang chaperoning this time. Annabelle laughed as she joined them, bundled in so many furs she could hardly move her arms. Celwyn regarded Prince Leo, who lounged beside him on the other club chair, at ease, as if he were a part of their party. the magician had attempted, without definitive success, to school Sully into not bringing any more stray charlatans home. The magician suspected Sully identified with them closely.

Bartholomew detoured to pour coffee and joined them in front of the windows. He said, "I have finished the children's lesson plans for the week. You are scheduled for mathematics tomorrow morning, Jonas. The Professor reports that you are a wonderful teacher, which I saw also."

"Butter, butter, butter." Celwyn rolled his eyes. But that reminded him. He turned to Prince Leo. "Just to be sure of where you stand, I have placed a block on the sleeping car and classroom. You won't be able to enter. The same applies to the cars beyond where you will sleep."

"But Jonas," the dwarf whined and turned toward the big man. "There is nothing to fear from me. I am innocent."

Celwyn snorted. "Perhaps Bartholomew isn't fully aware of your habits, but I am."

"I can explain."

"You tried to swindle me. Then throw me to the London bobbies so you could get away."

"But Jonas—"

"Call me Mr. Celwyn." The magician elevated him off his chair and turned him upside down. Coins fell like rain from his pockets. "You have probably endangered us further by your actions. Who are you running from?"

Bartholomew smiled broadly as the dwarf yelled, "Put me down!"

"Who are you running from?" Celwyn shook him like a piggy bank.

"Put me down!"

Celwyn yawned and wiggled his finger. The man began to swing side to side like a pendulum.

"I'm going to be sick!"

"Upon that disgusting tie you're wearing?"

"Jonas!"

Celwyn increased the swinging until Prince Leo was almost vertical before turning him upside down again. The dwarf yelled, "All right! It is the Russians."

"Why?"

Prince Leo's lips tightened. Celwyn swung him nearly out the window.

"Stop it! Stop! I have some rubies."

The magician dropped him on the floor. "Royal rubies?"

Prince Leo rubbed his rear end. "That wasn't necessary."

"Yes, it was," Bartholomew insisted, "if you imperil the children by your presence."

"Answer my question." Celwyn lifted him a foot off the floor.

"Yes! Royal rubies." He scrambled back into his chair.

"How close are they?" Bartholomew growled.

Prince Leo made a point of drinking tea before he answered and, even then, directed his response to Celwyn. "Not very. Yet."

Celwyn applied invisible pressure, and the little man winced and rubbed his hand.

"I'll not tolerate any bigotry if that is what your problem is. None. Bartholomew is held in high esteem by everyone he knows." He released Prince Leo's hand. "Now, would you recognize whoever is after you?"

The dwarf attempted a conciliatory smile in the big man's direction and said, "Of course. Normal louts. Nearly as big as Mr. Bartholomew here, with heavy faces and thick whiskers. Their leader has very bad teeth."

The magician leaned close enough to smell his breath. "If they endanger anyone on this train, I will hold you responsible."

Bartholomew glared. "If you see them, you will tell us immediately, so we may defend ourselves."

"Of course." The dwarf waved his hand. "What are we going to do in Prague?"

Celwyn eyed him. "It isn't a joint endeavor. Excuse me."

When the magician returned, Bartholomew still glowered at Prince Leo. Celwyn sat again, and Qing hopped off his shoulder. His eyes glittered at the dwarf. Celwyn said, "I told him to watch you." He stroked Qing's feathers. "He bites."

The little man watched Qing and licked his lips. "I suppose he isn't just a normal bird."

"You suppose correctly. I am also teaching him to speak; he understands much more than you'd expect."

Bartholomew gave up glaring at the dwarf to ask, "Jonas, how much longer do you think we'll be marooned here?"

"An hour? I do not know."

For several minutes, the three men gazed outside the windows. The snow had fallen until it was nearly up to the eaves of the quaint train station. Bartholomew squinted.

"Oh no—"

The big man bolted from his chair and out the door. Through the window, Celwyn saw what had caused his concern. He ran after him.

Kang struggled through waist-high snow toward the train, holding Telly in his arms. Annabelle and Zander were on his heels. Bartholomew took Telly from Kang and led the way back inside.

As he and Annabelle lay Telly on the floor, Zander rushed in behind Kang, crying. "Is she all right? *Is she?*"

The girl's face was blue, and she struggled to breathe. Celwyn knelt beside her and sent Bartholomew a look. With ease, he herded Zander and Annabelle to the side of the bar so they couldn't see the magician examine the girl.

"What happened?" he asked the automat in a quiet voice as he bent low to blow air into the girl's mouth. Her eyes remained closed.

Kang glanced at Annabelle, who interpreted his look and guided Zander even closer to the corner of the room, turning to block his view. "The farther we went from the train, the more upset Telly became. When I told her that the deep snow was dangerous, she purposely ran straight through the woods to it. She was crying."

Celwyn cursed himself and continued working on the girl. His magic diminished at certain distances. The protection against the horrors she'd endured must have failed the farther away she ran.

Moments more, and she began to breathe on her own. Celwyn sat back and smoothed her brow.

"What happened next?" he asked Kang.

"We told her that the snow wasn't safe. But she still ran into it. On purpose." Kang made sure he and Celwyn had eye contact. "She *knew* it was dangerous." Kang finished telling him the rest in a whisper, "Then she fell into a deep drift, and even more snow fell on top of her before we could dig her out."

"Oh, my." Celwyn wiped away tears. He felt so sorry for the little girl. She needed more than his magic, and he had missed that. His talents were only a temporary solution.

"You saved her life, my friend," Celwyn told Kang.

Telly opened her eyes. She focused on Celwyn and smiled. As the magician hugged her and silently suggested that everything was fine, he added field after field of white flowers and playful flute music to her thoughts.

Zander approached them, holding Annabelle's hand. When he saw she breathed and smiled at him, a big tear fell from his eye. Celwyn helped the girl to stand, and one by one, everyone clapped. Telly grabbed Annabelle's other hand and followed Bartholomew to the classroom. Kang stayed behind.

"We need to find someone for Telly to talk to. Someone that knows children. She needs to face what happened to her and learn how to live with it," Celwyn said.

"I've been thinking the same thing. Dr. Freud is in London, not Vienna, at the moment." Kang added, "He has well-qualified disciples in other cities, too."

Prince Leo ventured, "I do not know of what the young lady has endured, but I do know Dr. Ivanko resides in Prague. Or did so last year."

"Thank you," Celwyn said.

"We'll keep watch over her," Kang said. "It is all we can do until we reach Prague."

Chapter 28

THE MAGICIAN STOOD WITH KANG at the top of the steps leading off the train. Snow, so much snow as far as he could see. Snow is silent, too. Quieter than the sea and just as mysterious at times. Only the top of the trees could be seen. In the vastness of it, the echoing of the *Elizabeth's* engine grew louder.

The same villagers who'd watched the *Elizabeth* arrive at the mountaintop station waited, trading worried glances.

It was time.

"Is Telly showing any signs of distress?" the magician asked.

"From what I can tell, no," Kang said.

"Are the children sitting down and ready?" Celwyn asked as they went back inside.

Bartholomew jerked his chin at the hallway leading to the cabins. "Yes, we plan to sing all of our songs we've learned. Miss Annabelle has everything secured. They know the train may go fast, but that is all."

The engine noise grew louder, and the wheels began to turn and then stopped again.

"It is going to be a steep descent of at least 8%. We'll be in the cab with the conductor." Kang paced in a tight circle. "In a worst-case scenario, you are strong enough to lift everyone out of the train car."

"I will also lift heavy debris if it comes to that," the big man said as he walked toward the door leading to the classroom. "Jonas will keep us safe." His tone sounded confident, but the magician caught the worry clouding his eyes.

"Could you put Qing in Jonas' lavatory, please? Just to be sure he doesn't fly through an open door in a panic?" Kang asked Bartholomew. "If you give him one of my watches, he'll go willingly."

The big man nodded. "That bird can probably tell time too."

Without speaking, Kang and Celwyn moved to the front of the train and entered the engine cab. The magician shook the conductor's hand, noting it appeared steady and his manner professional. To Celwyn, the man's expertise was evident from the way he studied the gauges and flipped levers. Still, he suspected that his ability to accept evidence of magic would be limited.

"Jimmy and I checked every single one of the brakes. We'll be able to slow the train as needed." The conductor added, "Our only worry will be to stop in time if the tracks are blocked with rocks or snow."

Kang replied, "We understand."

Celwyn spied even more villagers hovering near the station. Many of the men smoked long-stemmed pipes as they cast worried glances down the mountain. A few women stood by, too, bundled in bright-colored shawls. They stamped their feet in the cold and stared at the *Elizabeth*. Few trains dared to go down the mountain in late winter.

"The sun is out," Kang observed.

"That isn't helpful, Sir. The glare off the ice and snow will make things more difficult. But still," the conductor said as he shaded his eyes and looked down the mountain, "we should make it through."

A minute later, the familiar screech of the wheels began, and the conductor pulled on the whistle. Hot steam billowed into the freezing air, shrouding the *Elizabeth* as she moved forward. Off to the side, the cluster of rail officials watched the train with what Celwyn thought of as graveyard faces.

"They have no faith in us," he remarked.

"Or they don't know much about you." The automat tilted his head to better see outside.

Their speed remained slow through the first few curves, but after the third bend, the train began to move much more quickly because of the increasing degree of descent. Kang and Celwyn both sat down abruptly in the jump seats to the side of the conductor. Blowing snow pelted the glass.

Heat from the engine filled the cab, and the conductor took off his jacket and rolled up his sleeves. Celwyn and Kang soon copied him. They watched the forest thicken on each side of the rails, and the mounds of snow grew higher. The wooshes of ice air slammed the train every time the *Elizabeth* rounded a curve, and the conductor applied the brakes, receiving a loud and shrill response in return.

Turn after turn of blind visibility caused them to hold their breath, expecting to find a wall of snow and certain death, until the train straightened, and they saw the tracks again. In the distance, as far as Celwyn could see, dozens of snow-capped mountains lined the horizon. Far below them, slivers of color dotted the snow: roofs from another village and a meandering river. The magician leaned out the window for a better view.

Then he saw it.

Farther down the mountain, little puffs of snow signaled an avalanche. Clouds of dirt and rocks seemed to explode as a wedge of the mountain moved, causing trees to fall and sending house-sized rocks tumbling downward. Celwyn held on to the bars above his head, straining to see the map the conductor had pinned above them and pinpoint the location of the avalanche.

It took several anxious seconds before he found the avalanche on the map: a stretch of straight track lay before and after the slide. Back and forth he studied the avalanche area against the map.

Celwyn stabbed a spot on the map and asked the conductor, "How fast will we be going here?"

The conductor frowned. "At this rate, perhaps 30-40 miles per hour. Why?" He looked at the magician. "Even at this point, there is no possibility I can stop before then with this much of an incline." His attention reverted to the tracks, with both arms flipping switches, and pulling levers. "Why?"

As usual, Kang understood. In a clear demonstration of his faith in Celwyn, he said, "I'll alert the rest of the crew to remain calm and then stay with Annabelle and the others." He clapped the magician's shoulder. "Good luck, my friend. I know what you intend to do."

"We will definitely need a whiskey when this is over," the magician said, still studying the terrain and then the map. As Kang left, Celwyn regarded the conductor: a solid and logical man. Logic wasn't an ideal response to magic, but he would need his cooperation ... or at least calmness.

The conductor stared straight ahead and asked, "Sir, what do you 'intend' as the Professor just mentioned? And what is it you see?"

Celwyn knew there wasn't time to explain, and the man would argue about something he didn't understand.

"When we come out of the next curve, do not brake. Accelerate."

"*Sir?*" The conductor reacted as if he'd offered him a snake to run the train. He continued to pull levers and stare out the glass.

"Accelerate," the magician repeated as the train swayed to the left.

"Sir, I—"

"Do it!"

When the conductor would have braked, he cursed, "...and God help us," as he increased their speed.

"Faster!" the magician demanded.

"For the love of—"

"NOW!" Celwyn roared as the towering avalanche of snow, rocks, and trees came into view.

"Are you daft, man?" the conductor yelled, but he signaled for his assistant to shovel coal faster into the fires that fed the engine.

Celwyn drew himself up, flexing his hands, concentrating, flexing his hands again and again as they hurtled downward. The conductor prayed at what he saw.

Building. The music from scores of violins rose up, growing stronger, increasing to a roaring crescendo all around them.

When the magician raised his hands, the nose of the locomotive lifted off the tracks, rising higher and higher, lifting the train with it. His open palms went even higher. The veins in Celwyn's forehead stood out as he held his hands above his head. The locomotive and cars sailed over the avalanche. Behind them, the caboose trailed through the top of the slide, sending clouds of snow and rocks flying.

When the train cleared the top of the avalanche, the conductor fell in a dead faint to the floor. The magician stepped over him and brought his hands down slowly. Below them, the straightaway loomed. Celwyn grabbed the controls, slowing the *Elizabeth* as the conductor had, as the nose lowered.

With a loud and tremendous screech sounding like hundreds of train wheels crashing, the locomotive landed, grinding and bouncing onto the tracks once more. The vibrations echoed again and again as each of the cars followed them back to earth. The magician slowed the train still further and kicked the shoulder of the conductor.

"Get up, please," Celwyn said, not taking his eyes off the tracks. They still traveled too fast, and he had to use magic to slow the train even more. He needed this man's help. The conductor stirred but didn't move until the magician scraped a handful of snow from the window ledge and flung it on his face. He yanked the conductor to his feet.

"Don't think about it! Just get us down this cursed mountain!" Celwyn yelled as he positioned the conductor in front of the controls. Sweat poured from under the man's hat, and when he began to manipulate the controls again, Celwyn finally breathed a sigh of relief. The conductor pointedly wouldn't meet his eyes, but the train noticeably slowed to a manageable speed.

As exhausted as he was, Celwyn covered the conductor and crew with no memory of the flight of the *Elizabeth*. He included Prince Leo, Annabelle, and the children in the blanket of not knowing what had transpired. By now, Kang had gotten used to what Celwyn did. Bartholomew hadn't reached that point but was learning to accept it. No doubt Annabelle would have a fit if she knew of the danger they'd just escaped.

Celwyn swayed with the train, slowly making his way past the dining car and sleeping compartments to his own quarters. The triumph of the trip down the mountain called for music. Beautiful, nebulous music.

He chewed on his last peyote button as he sat at the pianoforte and began to play. The notes blended into his soul as they reverberated through the canyons of trees and snow, and the *Elizabeth* surged downhill into the valley below.

The music still echoed as Celwyn crawled into bed to rest. As soon as he closed his eyes, an annoying tapping began. Without a word, he wiggled a finger to let Qing out of the lavatory and went back to sleep.

Hours later, Kang knocked on his door and stuck his head inside. "It will be dark soon, Jonas. We'll stop in the village ahead. According to the conductor, they have a separate trestle we can use."

Celwyn took Qing off his stomach and sat up.

"Come in. Has the conductor shown any signs of hysteria?"

Kang opened the door and strode in. Qing squeaked in delight and flew to his shoulder. "No, but he has a large bump on his forehead." He eyed Celwyn with a raised brow.

Celwyn nearly laughed. "It wasn't me. The man fainted and bumped his head while I was bringing the train back down again."

"You should have some sympathy for him." Kang gazed out the window and tried not to smile. "It scared the bejeebers out of Bartholomew too. He has decided to deal with it by figuring out how you did it."

"I couldn't explain it if I tried. What about our new unwanted guest?"

The automat said, "He doesn't remember a thing. Just grumbles about how you do not trust him." He put Qing on the windowsill. "You should have let him see the train in the air so he'd respect your wishes more readily."

"Perhaps. I have a feeling we'll have more opportunities for demonstrations."

<hr>

The dying light of the afternoon streamed through the club car windows, warming the room and reflecting off Kang's glass as he poured. The *Elizabeth* rolled languidly through farmland, disturbing sleepy cows and scattering chickens. They passed a tiny church no wider than a large bed but with windows so clean they sparkled.

"It has been a week since we left Hunedoara," Kang remarked. "The crew appreciates the nights we stop in towns and villages."

"I know."

Kang added, "Everything seems perfect."

Celwyn studied him. "Yet?" When Kang didn't respond, he added, "Your description sounds idyllic, yet you predict an imminent catastrophe."

"Exactly. It is too perfect. You know things don't seem to go very well for us."

"I do."

"Our plan to pretend that we are not afraid of Jax doesn't appear to be enticing him to confront us." Kang started pacing. "Either he is waiting for something, or he isn't on the *Elizabeth* at the moment."

"It does seem so." The magician yawned and watched Qing as he pecked the window every time they passed a cow. He tossed him a peanut and Qing caught it. "Regardless, we will take our time to journey to Prague. The children will benefit from the routine and the work that you, Annabelle, and Bartholomew are doing with them. Moreover, if anyone is still looking for us, we're not as easily found because we're taking the backroads, so to speak."

Qing cracked the nut, scattered the pieces, and went back to pecking at the cows through the glass.

Kang continued to pace and sent him a quick look. "I agree. What do you know of mathematics?"

Celwyn regarded him as if he were a spy for the Russians. "As little as possible. Are you trying to trick me into tutoring the children this afternoon?"

Chapter 29

WHEN THEY PULLED INTO KRIVOY Rog, Celwyn made a point of observing the crew and the conductor. The magician stationed himself near the engine and shook the hand of each one of them as he entered their thoughts, checking for fears or anxiety about flying trains. He congratulated the conductor and his assistant on the successful descent of the mountain and urged them to enjoy themselves in the village and not worry about inspecting the train until the next morning. He pressed a pouch of coins into the conductor's hand and said, "For everyone. Please enjoy a relaxing evening. I insist."

When Celwyn remounted the stairs and entered the dining car, he found Prince Leo wearing a garish maroon scarf over a motley fur coat, bilious green trousers, and preparing to depart for the evening.

His hat sported a matching green feather, and his expression did not look innocent at all.

The magician held up a hand. "Please. Remain as my guest for the evening, Leo."

The dwarf stopped his progress toward the door and faced Celwyn. "I must decline, Jonas. I need to stretch my legs and enjoy the city."

The magician stepped in front of the doorway. "No. You intend to visit the telegraph office and probably contact someone you wish to sell the rubies to. That will bring the Russians running." He looked down at the dwarf's shifting gaze. "I can't trust you."

Wide eyes regarded him. "What do you mean? My only intention is to order a fine cut of beef and bottle of wine."

"No."

Prince Leo's eyes flitted to the door and back to Celwyn.

"Don't try it."

Prince Leo feinted left and ran for the door. Celwyn removed the scarf from his neck, wrapped it around the dwarf's mouth and marched him toward the kitchen. As they passed through, Celwyn froze the activity inside and propelled Prince Leo into his cabin. When he was safely enthroned on his bed, the magician locked the door and returned to his whiskey and enjoyable view out the dining car windows.

As they sat down to dinner a few hours later, Celwyn announced, "Prince Leo is indisposed for the evening and sends his regards." At his left, Kang raised a sardonic brow and said nothing. On his right, Bartholomew shrugged with a smirk. Annabelle faced him from the other end of the table framed by both children.

"We'll make do without him," she said.

Telly appeared paler than usual. Celwyn entered her thoughts, fearing what he'd discover. He found worse.

In vivid color, Telly's mind had created the horrible room that the magician had found her in weeks ago. From the shining knives to the bright lights and the hulking carriage driver, she saw everything in clear detail. Every image looked oversized, grotesque. Van Maskolc loomed over her with glazed eyes and a knife. Celwyn wiped the image away and searched until he destroyed the other memories from that dreadful house. Then he bombarded Telly with images of the kitten playing, kisses from Annabelle, and games of dominoes with Zander. He added a memory of her perched on his lap while they read a book and memories of Bartholomew handing her bouquets of flowers and bestowing kisses. He showed Kang escorting her through a candy shop and Zander laughing as he rolled his ball to her. The magician would add more dolls to her playroom. In the end, Celwyn sighed: everything he did felt like a bandage that couldn't stop the bleeding.

"How long until we reach Prague?" Celwyn asked Kang and pointed at Telly with his eyes.

Kang glanced at the girl. "Three days, maybe four, depending on the weather." He nodded at Annabelle and Bartholomew. "I will be sure that the crew knows we leave at dawn."

"I understand," Annabelle said. She couldn't help casting a worried look at Telly.

With an innocent, fixed smile, Ricardo deposited soup bowls in front of them. After he left, Bartholomew said, "I believe it is my turn to sacrifice myself for the greater good." He gingerly dipped a spoon into the soup.

Annabelle told the children, "He is tasting it for us...to be sure it is edible." Bartholomew's face relaxed, and she said, "It is good. Please start eating."

As Zander sipped his soup, he asked Celwyn, "What does 'indisposed' mean? You said Prince Leo is indisposed."

Kang grinned into his soup.

"He has a stomachache," Celwyn said.

"Will I have that too?"

Celwyn said, "I doubt it. Shall we talk about Prague? There are riverboats and zoos."

⌣

Dawn pinked the top of the eastern mountains surrounding Krivoy Rog. Outside the *Elizabeth*, the conductor and his assistant examined the train's brakes by lantern light. Celwyn left them to it and continued his walk, enjoying the early morning air and serenity. A dozen shops, an inn, and a smattering of houses decorated the edges of the town square, and as always, a church stood as the centerpiece of everyday life. This one appeared to be Catholic. Some of the nearby chimneys emitted curls of smoke into the swirling mist, and a lone donkey brayed a greeting to the day as the magician's thoughts turned inward.

Am I changing? Such responsibilities: children. Celwyn surprised himself, even enjoying close friendships with Bartholomew and Kang. In hundreds of years, he hadn't had anyone he would term a friend, just enjoyable acquaintances that sometimes he would meet again. What was the point? Within a few years, disease, or wars, or duels usually took care of those relationships. Annabelle had become another ward of sorts, but he had grown to respect her for more than her ability to procure hats. She had the character of a caring person, and she demonstrated much more substance than the frills and feathers of most society women. The magician thought her fond disapproval of his magic was endearing. Here they were: the magician and his band of merry adventurers, with a collection of evildoers at their heels.

Celwyn puffed on his pipe and strolled toward the front of the train. They would have to make a decision soon about the children and their safety. Above all, Telly worried him: the experiences she continued to relive must have been much worse than he thought, and reinforcing the distracting images in her thoughts would need to be done with more frequency.

As the magician passed the storage car, he heard angry thumping. Celwyn listened. Ah, Prince Leo. He would let him out once they'd left town.

After breakfast, the *Elizabeth* puffed her way across the valley, trailing steam from her stacks and accompanied by the children's voices raised in song. They would continue through Sevan until they entered the deep forests of Ettene.

Kang studied the oversized map pinned to the wall next to the dining table. A few feet away, Celwyn sipped tea, read Robinson Crusoe, and watched fields of tall grasses swaying in the breezes. The land here lay completely flat, and he couldn't determine how far it was to the next range of mountains. In the distance, flashes of lightning flickered and danced like fireflies within the walls of dark, ominous clouds that obscured the horizon line.

The magician frowned. Although he thoroughly enjoyed an electrical show during a flamboyant storm at sea, it probably wouldn't be prudent to be inside an iron box on wheels when the lightning began. They needed shelter.

Celwyn put down his book and said, "Where are we now?"

"You would ask a question I can't properly answer," Kang complained. "From what I can tell—about here." He pointed on the map. "Perhaps three hours from Bratislava."

Celwyn stood at the windows. "There is a significant lightning storm to the north. It appears to be going to the south and west, following the natural path of the Summering River. Do you agree?"

Kang studied the map and scrutinized the terrain. "Yes. If the storm keeps south, it will intersect us here." He stabbed a spot on the map. "If it travels west between here," another tap on the map, "and here, we will likely encounter the storm full force."

"But if it moves east or further north, we won't care."

"For now."

"What do you suggest?" the magician asked. "Yesterday I talked with the conductor. He hasn't been this far north before. These tracks are only used for transporting crops in the summer."

Kang pulled out his pocket watch. "It is nearly noon. By approximately two o'clock, we could be in Gratalek and take shelter before the storm arrives." He crossed to the window and looked far ahead at the storm clouds piled high and black in the sky. "If I am wrong, we will be in a pickle."

"I agree. We should confer with the conductor."

At the end of their conference, the conductor called for full speed if they were going to "outrun the bloody storm." Celwyn took off his jacket and joined Jimmy in shoveling coal. Kang said he would inform Bartholomew and Annabelle. "Then, I'll send Ricardo back to relieve you, Jonas."

A half-hour later, when they had all gathered again in the dining car, Kang's voice had taken on an even graver tone. Working at full speed, the train's engines labored loudly, and they had to raise their voices. Everyone held onto something to keep from falling as the train swayed and bounced.

"Look to directly ahead. The clouds are denser and darker," the Professor said.

Bartholomew's eyebrows rose, and the whites of his eyes stood out as he gazed out the window. "If possible, we need to go even faster if we're going to outrun it," he said with a hinting glance at the magician.

Celwyn elbowed him and said, "My thoughts exactly, my friend."

"You'll notice Jonas enjoys this kind of excitement," Kang drawled.

The big man laughed, "I do, also." He looked outside again. "To a point."

The magician faced the locomotive and concentrated until the train increased speed, flying down the rails, perhaps slightly above the rails if one didn't look too closely. Behind him, Prince Leo approached the windows. The little man had been pouting all afternoon about his earlier confinement. He ignored the magician and addressed the automat.

"Why are we going so fast?" The motion of the train had become so exaggerated it was difficult to stand, and one by one they all took seats. The dwarf peered out the window at the storm.

"Should I get my affairs in order?"

"No!" Kang shouted over the roaring engine. "However, I'd put on a weatherproof jacket, galoshes, and be ready to exit the train."

Bartholomew stood and held on to the dining table. "I'll let the crew know while you tell Annabelle so she can get the children ready."

Kang nodded and trotted toward the sleeping cars. "Pick up Qing too, please," Celwyn called.

The rain began a few minutes later, and the magician slowed the train to its regular speed. As he did so, the lightning increased, traveling with them along the foothills striking randomly like tremendous gunshots. Impenetrable forests stretched from the foothills to the train tracks they rode on. Thunder shook the *Elizabeth* as Annabelle and the children joined them, and even Kang jumped when a bottle crashed off the bar to the floor. The orphans' eyes bounced nervously between the windows and Celwyn.

The magician squatted until he was on their level. He pointed outside. "This will be our stop today. It is our first adventure, and it will be noisy and wet." He watched Telly as she licked her lips and stared back at him. "Have either of you seen thunder or lightning before?"

Zander said, "Yes. When it came, my mother used to make me hide under my bed."

Telly grabbed Zander's hand and held on. "Yes. But I know it will stop."

"That it will. The mud will be too deep for you when we go outside. You would sink. Do you want the Professor to carry you?" A much closer boom of thunder reached them over the noise of the train and storm.

Telly looked at Kang. "Yes."

Celwyn added what he hoped were enough calming thoughts and images to get her through this ordeal as he handed her over to Kang. The automat's medical bag was strapped to his back, and he placed her atop his shoulders. "Hold on to my neck, please," he told her.

"You can carry me. But I am heavier now." Zander told the magician.

Lightning exploded a tree just as the train passed by, floodlighting the cabin with an eerie blue light. Telly screamed and buried her face in Kang's shoulder. The magician sent Bartholomew and Annabelle a silent message to remain calm. Kang nodded gravely.

To Zander, he said, "On up, then." Celwyn swung him onto his back. "We'll go faster this way. Duck down as we go through the door." As he spoke, the lightning touched down again, much closer. Ricardo and the rest of the crew had joined them, ready to go.

"Everyone!" The magician picked up a lantern and called over the booming of the thunder, "As soon as the wheels stop, follow me as quickly as you can."

The screeching of the brakes began, competing with the thunder as the *Elizabeth* rolled slower and slower until she came to a stop. The conductor swung out of the cab and hurried to them. Simultaneously, the magician hopped off the train and, with Zander on his back, sprinted into the forest. Directly ahead, the lightning touched down again, blowing apart a towering tree, the boom as deafening as cannon shot.

Celwyn jogged to the left, and the others followed. Zander hung over the magician's shoulder with a lantern, lighting their way. Kang covered Telly's face as he ran with them. Like they'd arranged, Bartholomew carried Annabelle, and Prince Leo and the crew followed.

The thundering reports tumbled closer and louder. Lightning floodlit the forest as clear as day, helping Celwyn find what Kang said would be nestled at the base of the foothills. He waited for the others to follow as he plunged into the thickest part of the forest.

Caves. Natural limestone caves hidden by the trees lined the base of the hills. Thunder rumbled low overhead, and he heard a shout as Bartholomew stumbled and went down. The big man held Annabelle high and got to his knees again. Soon, they again trailed Celwyn. As the magician reached the nearest cave, Zander started to yell in his excitement as the sky split open and the rain became a deluge.

The magician deposited Zander on the ground and crouched before the entrance. The light from the lantern revealed a very tall ceiling just inside. A few feet further inside and it opened into a large room. This would do nicely. He waved everyone closer.

He stood aside as Bartholomew, Kang, and the conductor rushed inside along with the others. Several of them had lanterns, but even that much illumination couldn't reach the full extent of the interior. As they huddled and shivered, the thunder seemed to hover directly overhead, and angry, as if Zeus himself were pounding on top of the mountain to reach them. The lightning illuminated the forest once more, and the crackle of electricity came to them clearly along with the acrid stench of burning wood. Water ran inside the entrance and trickled into a pool in the center of the cave.

"Is there a back way out of here?" Celwyn asked Bartholomew.

Bartholomew had been touring the cave perimeter and stopped still in the furthest corner. He tapped on the wall, and chunks of rock trickled down. Annabelle hugged the children close and shivered.

"No. One way in and out." The big man waited until he had everyone's attention. "I believe others have used this cave. Recently." He held up a shoe that looked like it had been one of the rats' dinners. While everyone thought about the implications of what Bartholomew had said, the big man kicked a stack of wood and a rat scooted past a squealing Prince Leo and out into the storm. The big man arranged the wood, and Selkirk began searching for dry kindling.

Bartholomew checked what he had found and said, "We will need more kindling to start a fire."

Kang released Telly's hand long enough to pluck some papers out of his coat pocket and hand them over. The big man examined them and said, "Are you sure?"

"Just calculations that I can reproduce."

The big man nodded and lit the first one, adding it to the pile of twigs. Soon they had a cheery fire, and everyone gathered close to the warmth except Bartholomew, who peered out the entrance. The smoke ascended, slithering into the low ceiling, and disappeared.

Kang nodded. "Some kind of natural chimney. Convenient."

The heavy rain continued, but the thunder seemed to have lessened. Celwyn joined Bartholomew by the entrance and asked, "What is wrong, my friend?"

Bartholomew glanced at the soggy but merry group by the fire as Sully took a pull from a flask and passed it to Ricardo.

"I also saw a gypsy shawl in the far corner. It isn't safe to be trapped in here." He took a few steps into the entrance. "I will scout the area."

"One moment and I will join you," Celwyn said. He hooked a finger at Kang. They left Kang guarding the mouth of the cave with a pistol he'd thoughtfully brought along. From the way he handled it, the magician suspected he had rarely used a firearm.

"Did you bring a pistol also?" Celwyn asked as they crouched low, shoulder to shoulder, peering through the curtain of rain out the opening of the cave.

"Yes. Our party may be trapped inside, but it would be suicide for an attacker to go in there." Bartholomew gestured behind them. "Kang would shoot."

"Or try to; he may shoot us by accident." Celwyn shrugged. "You were correct. I am hearing thoughts from strangers just to the north." He pointed. "Let us go south into the trees. Agreed?"

"Yes. I will cover you."

Celwyn ran, Bartholomew followed, but had only taken two steps before a rifle shot rang out, and he fell hard. Celwyn turned toward him. The big man raised an arm, waving him away. Through his teeth, he said, "I'll go back." He pulled himself back into the mouth of the cave. Another shot hit the heel of his boot before Kang pulled him all the way inside, swung around, and got off a shot of his own. The magician was pretty sure he hit a rock.

From a crouch in the trees, the magician called back in a low hiss, "How bad is he?"

A long moment went by, and Celwyn readied to ask his question louder when Kang hissed, "His shoulder. All the way through. What are we going to do, Jonas? The children are terrified."

The magician's expression turned grim.

The rain continued, but at least the thunder and lightning had stopped. Without fresh coal, the low rumble of the *Elizabeth's* engine in the distance had begun to die down. He had no trouble hearing internal chatter from their attackers from several directions, all in a Roma dialect. Celwyn assumed that besides rifles, they would have knives. Shots pelted the trees where he stood.

Celwyn's anger grew.

One by one, the magician uprooted the trees they hid behind, tossing them far up the hill. Small or large, he removed them, and as he did so, the chatter became audible. Colorful shirts and pants scrambled. An instant more, and he surrounded the attackers with the same trees, penning them into an area the size of a barn. They crouched behind the remaining bushes.

That won't help you, Celwyn thought. The magician lit the first bush on fire and enjoyed watching it burn as if the falling rain inflamed it. The voices grew afraid. Well aware the Roma were a superstitious lot; he lit more bushes nearer to the gypsies.

The magician looked skyward as the rain fell and inhaled the wet earthy smell around them. With a smile, he added a light ballad from a chorus of flutes that floated downward with the rain, covering everything, becoming louder and stronger. Trumpets synchronized, each blast a question and the next an answer, and the volume increased as the tinkling bells of a lone timpani joined them.

"Show yourselves!" Celwyn demanded and threw a large fireball into the midst of the gypsies.

"*Now!*" The music grew angry, and he removed the gypsies from the bushes, tossing them into the clearing before the mouth of the cave. The magician flung the firearms from their hands and elevated a few of them several feet into the air. From the rear of the bushes, one gypsy dressed all in black stepped forward, his swagger as pronounced as a panther.

"Please put them down, Jonas."

The magician turned: he had heard that voice long ago. As requested, he dropped the gypsies face-first into the mud as the gypsy in black approached him.

"I didn't know for sure it was you until I heard the music." A heavy beard covered the man's face, but the twinkling blue eyes seemed amused. "It is much prettier than I remembered it."

"Throw the rest of your weapons down." Celwyn told him, "And ask the woman to come out." He had heard her thoughts also a few minutes ago. Worrying about a child. He swiveled. From just inside the cave, Kang watched the tableau with his pistol trained on the gypsy in black.

When the gypsy issued orders, knives were thrown into the mud at his feet amid virulent cursing and fearful chatter.

"And the woman?" Celwyn asked.

"But of course," the man turned. "Reva, come out and meet Jonas Celwyn."

"Who are you?" the magician asked.

The gypsy faced the magician and studied him. "You must be of good stock; you have not changed in all these years. I'm not surprised you do not remember. I was a little boy when you helped my father, Dvancic. Where you fought the soldiers in the mountains." He bowed. "Sebastian, at your service."

In the gathering darkness, a diminutive woman emerged from the brush, walking toward them.

"Madam."

Celwyn bowed to her and turned to the man. "I remember your father well. But at the moment, I have a fragile young girl sheltering in that cave, and also my friends and crew. There is also the man you wounded whom I esteem very much. He will recover."

"My apologies," Sebastian said as the woman put her hand on his arm. "We will leave you in peace."

"Why did you shoot at us? To rob us?"

"No! Yes—" Sebastian retorted. "We are looking for medicine. We have sick children."

Celwyn rubbed his face. Kang was about to have an opportunity to nag him.

"Give me a moment." He went into the cave and straight to Bartholomew, where he lay on a rug Selkirk had thoughtfully brought along.

"Pain?"

"Yes," the big man said. "But I will—"

Celwyn waved a hand blocking them from the others as he laid a hand over the wound. "And now?"

Bartholomew smiled and said in a low voice, "Gone."

Celwyn nodded. "My price is that you take my mathematics tutoring for the rest of the week." He helped the big man sit up. "Can you walk?"

In seconds, the big man stood on his feet.

"Get everyone back to the train, please, and ready to resume our travels. The Professor and I will be back in an hour." He turned to Kang. "Please get your medical bag." The automat scrambled for it without a word, but his expression displayed all the anxiousness he was known for.

Before they left the cave, Celwyn stopped in front of Telly and softened his voice. "Everything is fine. Bartholomew will be sure it is. You will see the kitten soon and have your tea too." He patted her head and left her with more thoughts of her dolls and new dresses for them.

Once outside the cave, the magician and Kang approached Sebastian. "This is Professor Xiau Kang. Lead us to your children, please."

As they slogged through the mud, they approached a depression between the shallow hills where the forest thinned, revealing a ring of coaches and a pen of horses. Beside a now roaring stream, a central fire still burned under a make-shift overhang. Chickens ran underfoot and around several goats, and the aroma of roasted garlic permeated the air. Many of the coaches had tarp roofs, some were wooden. Silent children with dark, serious eyes peered at the newcomers from within the caravans as they walked past.

"Do you know what has made the children ill?" Kang asked as they stopped in front of the biggest of the coaches.

"Smallpox. We suspect." Sebastian helped Reba inside. "I will wait here. There isn't room for all of us."

Celwyn watched Kang as he examined the children, murmuring in a gentle voice. Both boys seemed to be about Zander's age, with masses of black curls and eyes too weak to be curious. He asked Reba a few more questions and then descended to the ground again.

From Kang's expression, Celwyn could see the news would not be good.

"It is smallpox." He handed Sebastian a piece of paper. "There is enough time to get this medicine from Wolkac. It is less than half an hour south of here. But you must hurry."

Celwyn handed Sebastian a pouch. "Send a fast rider. I'm going to leave the children with enough energy to fight this disease until they have the medicine. There are coins in this pouch to buy as much medicine as the rider can carry." When Sebastian began to protest, the magician slapped him on the back and said, "You must hurry."

Sebastian conferred with one of his men, who turned and ran to a horse. Sebastian watched him for several minutes, long after the man had ridden beyond where they could see. He wiped his eyes and turned to Celwyn.

The magician pointed to a coach at the end of the circle. "New blankets and clothes are in that wagon. Keep the children warm." He handed Sebastian another pouch of coins. "We must go. We also have a sick child, but her illness is not something medicine can fix. Be well, my friend."

"I cannot take this."

"Yes, you can, as a gesture of my respect for your father and for you."

Sebastian embraced him. Wordlessly, he bowed and shook Kang's hand.

By the time Kang and Celwyn reached the *Elizabeth,* the engine rumbled and belched smoke. Every light inside and out had been lit.

They found the big man in the classroom propped in a chair. He had been bandaged somewhat sloppily but bandaged. Bartholomew winked at them as he dealt cards to Annabelle, who had a tall stack of chips along with a glass of wine. The children sat in the corner with their books, giggling over the pictures.

As they approached, Kang raised a brow.

Celwyn looked at Annabelle and put it into words. "If your aunt could see you now, she'd shoot me."

Annabelle shrugged and eyed Bartholomew. "Raise you five." She regarded Celwyn down the end of her nose. "I hope you appreciate that I am foregoing having a cigarette." She threw in more chips. "I also just ruined my best boots out there, and my hair is still wet."

Celwyn didn't know exactly what to say. Kang maintained a blank expression.

"Jonas performed a miraculous repair on my shoulder. I raise," Bartholomew said as Kang moved closer, gently unwrapping the bandage on the big man's shoulder.

"You did an excellent job, Jonas." Kang rolled his eyes. "Amazingly, it is healing all by itself."

"You can't imagine how much I want a cigarette." Annabelle glanced at the children and then Bartholomew. "I think he's putting cards under his bandage." She threw chips into the pile. "Raise."

"Should the children see gambling?" the automat asked Celwyn in a murmur.

Celwyn said, "Probably not. But whatever they're reading has their attention." Yet, as he spoke, Telly put her book down and stared out the window.

With a jerk, the *Elizabeth* started forward again. Telly continued to stare out the window as the magician entered her thoughts. All appeared well.

"I swear." Annabelle threw down her cards.

The big man gathered in the pile of chips and said, "Jonas, I am well and can guard the train tonight." He tried to get up, but Kang blocked him.

"Relax until tomorrow," Kang told Bartholomew. "Don't worry. We'll send in a tray with your dinner, and be sure there are guards. Rest and bet big, my friend."

Chapter 30

THE *ELIZABETH* TRAVELED AT A GOOD pace across the valley and into the Bohemian Forest. As the last rays of the sun disappeared, the storm moved south, trailing the remnants of the clouds and rain. An hour later, they pulled into the train station at Bratislava.

The crew and passengers met in the dining car. Sully arrived, wiping his hands on his apron as Celwyn spoke.

"No one leaves the train tonight, and we replenish the coal as soon as possible. I want to be moving again at first light." Prince Leo looked like he wanted to object but stopped himself and sat quietly watching. There were murmurings, and then the conductor stepped up.

"We understand. But we would like to know: did you shoot the men who attacked us?"

"Not precisely," the magician replied. How to put it? "They only meant to rob us because they have sick children. It turns out that I knew their leader years ago. He regrets that Bartholomew was injured."

"I ... saw a flying tree outside the cave," Selkirk said.

"Strange things happen during storms. Can we load the coal this evening?"

———— ⌣ ————

Celwyn decided a nap was in order before dinner, but when he returned to his quarters, all he could see was the pianoforte. Calming and energizing, the soaring interplay of the notes brought joy. He sighed: if only all musical compositions included weather events of great magnitude. On the other side of the window, a few of the townspeople stood and listened. Yes, he would accept applause.

But all play must come to an end. When he returned to the dining car, he found a tableau. Kang had a pistol trained on Prince Leo with one hand and a whiskey in the other. Qing squawked at them from atop the bar.

"He tried to leave the train?" Celwyn asked.

Kang had turned to where the children couldn't see the pistol from where they sat at the dining table. He lowered it. "Yes, just now. I doubt he will run with you here. Also," he glanced at the little ones, "I don't think they need to see me shoot him."

Annabelle arrived in time to hear the exchange. With a frown for the magician, she held her skirts open and used them to shepherd the children like little ducklings ahead of her back to the classroom. "There is a new game I've been saving for you." They ran on ahead, emitting excited squeals.

"Why are you trying to get off the train?" Celwyn demanded of Prince Leo.

Tonight, the dwarf wore a suit of white with a pink handkerchief peeking from his breast pocket. His tie was a hideous brownish-green, similar to a decaying week-old dead frog, and he had trimmed his beard. He regarded Celwyn with deceptively friendly eyes. "I need to purchase my special tobacco. And I want a real beer. Beer is not served on your train."

The magician poured tea and collapsed into a club chair. "That's it?"

"Yes. I am not like you, Jonas. I sometimes have business interests that need my attention."

"You mean you need to know where the Russians are. Of course, you remember them? The ones who hunt you and will slit your throat with pleasure."

"Perhaps. I want to leave the train." Prince Leo shrugged. "Just for an hour."

Kang eyed him as he took the other chair. "I wonder what for."

"It is only an hour until dinner." Celwyn checked his pocket watch. "I'll accompany you into town." He gazed at Prince Leo. "You won't run from me."

The dwarf added a white hat and gold-tipped cane to his ensemble, and they exited the train. From across the square, church bells rang six times. As they walked, he explained in a helpful tone that the magician did not need to keep him company.

"But, of course I do," Celwyn said. "Ah, here is the tobacconist you mentioned." He held the door open for him.

The shop couldn't have measured more than fifteen feet square, but every shelf contained wooden boxes full of fine-looking tobacco. The counter displayed many types of pipes. One in carved burlwood caught the magician's eye.

"Smell this," Prince Leo said and held a box up. "It reminds me of Sheik Amon."

Celwyn obediently stooped and sniffed. "Interesting. But you'd better hurry if there are other shops you intend to visit."

"True." The dwarf made a purchase, and they walked to the inn next door, where he was unsuccessful in purchasing beer to take back to the *Elizabeth*. The bartender said he would be happy to pour him a glass if he intended to sit and stay awhile.

"No, thank you, we don't."

Celwyn steered Prince Leo outside and asked, "Now where?"

"The telegraph office," Prince Leo held up his hands. "No, no. There's nothing sinister with my request. You can watch everything I do."

However, when they arrived at the end of the street, the office windows had been shuttered. The dwarf frowned and began tapping his cane in frustration.

Celwyn said, "Let us revisit the bartender at the inn. We'll ask if he will send a message for you tomorrow morning after we've departed. Will that do?"

"Thank you, Jonas."

The next day, with breakfast a recent and unpleasant memory, Bartholomew, Kang, and Celwyn met in the magician's quarters. Qing fluttered his wings like a metallic windchime and soared around the room, celebrating their visit.

"The children are settled." Annabelle arrived and plopped into the overstuffed chair by the window. "Why meet here?"

"This ensures privacy from wiggling ears, such as Prince Leo's, and there is still the possibility that one of the crew is inhabited by Jax," Kang told her as he perched on the pianoforte bench.

Through the open window, a breeze weaved through fields of tall grasses under a hot sun. It seemed natural when the ground shimmered, and the magician saw a battlefield filled with bloodied soldiers and fallen horses that had become distinct and solid. Smoke drifted from funeral pyres, hovering like halos over the dead. The image dissipated when the conversation in the train resumed.

Annabelle blew out her breath and said, "I'd almost forgotten about Jax."

"That is wishful thinking," Bartholomew said.

"We will be in Prague by late tomorrow, and I thought it time to make some decisions," Kang said as the train blew her whistle and they rumbled across rough tracks. Over the next few minutes, the sunlight weakened as an army of fluffy clouds blew across the sky. Clusters of isolated houses and a smattering of outbuildings could be seen a short distance away. Some looked as if they'd been blasted with cannonballs or artillery.

"These are things we must talk about." Kang told Annabelle, "You probably aren't aware that your Uncle Celwyn has some particular talents, one of which he is using to help Telly."

Annabelle pushed errant curls off her forehead and glanced at Celwyn. "I know he performs unexplainable things. Is that what you are talking about?"

Qing chose that moment to fly off the top of the pianoforte and land on Celwyn's shoulder. The bird squeaked at Kang as the magician stepped around him. He nuzzled the magician's ear. To Celwyn, it may have been a sign of affection, but it felt like the backside of a tree rubbed his ear.

"One of my talents is the ability to enter the thoughts of someone, such as yourself." As he spoke, the magician did so, just a quick tour. He said a silent and quick hello.

Annabelle's mouth snapped open, and she glared at him. "How dare you!"

Kang controlled a smile and hurried to say, "Please do not be offended. Your uncle is discreet and discriminating with his, uh, talent."

"What did you ... you hear just now?" Annabelle demanded.

The magician shrugged. "Just a worry about Zander's schooling."

"Really? How is your rudeness helping Telly?"

Celwyn stood at the window, watching the verdant hills in the distance.

"Telly was traumatized, severely, by that monster Van Maskolc," Kang told her.

With less annoyance, Annabelle said, "I am aware of that, but she doesn't have wounds or scars."

"Your uncle healed her before you saw her. She had been burned and disfigured," Kang said. "The child went through, excuse me, hell."

"Oh no..." Annabelle blushed and bestowed a thankful look upon Celwyn. "Please forgive my temper."

"It is understandable."

"We believe Telly is having problems with what happened," Bartholomew said. "That is why Jonas is still helping her."

"She is reliving the horror, just as anyone would, and blaming herself, perhaps? We do not know." Kang held up his hands showing his indecision. "From the little I know of psychology; her experience may be too much for her to understand or confront."

"And she is so young," Bartholomew sighed.

Celwyn told Annabelle, "All I do is overlay the sad or horrible things she sees in her mind with pleasant images and thoughts." He made sure Annabelle was looking at him as he added, "It isn't enough."

"Why?"

"You will remember that we saw her crying as she ran into the avalanche a few days ago." Kang loosened his tie and frowned. "As you know, I got to her first, and what you didn't see or hear was her saying 'I want to die' before she went farther into the snow."

Annabelle's tears began. "And then more snow fell on her and buried her." She turned to Kang. "Thank god you saw where she was and dug her out."

"I agree." Celwyn left the window and sat down. "So, we have several problems: we need to find someone qualified to help Telly. We still face danger from Jax. And we also need to decide if the children should be given to a church and raised in their orphanage."

"Oh, no," Annabelle whispered and shook her head hard.

The automat nodded. "It isn't fair to them if we do not consider their safety when they are near us. You have seen how we attract danger. If that weren't the case, we wouldn't even consider the question at this point."

"There's more." The magician stood again and started pacing. "This goes to our most pressing concern. Once we reach Prague, do we stay together? There is no obligation for anyone to do so. But," he hesitated and met the gaze of each of them in turn, "I would prefer that we do. I've grown surprisingly fond of all of you."

Kang said, "I second what Jonas has said, with the exception of Prince Leo."

"I am more tolerant of him at the moment, but he bears watching." The magician stopped pacing and folded his arms.

"Because?" Annabelle asked Celwyn.

"His main occupation is stealing jewels and lying. He would throw his mother in front of a policeman to get away."

Bartholomew said, "No argument about him from here. As for the more important question, please count me as wishing to stay together when we reach Prague." He looked at Annabelle, trying to gauge her decision.

Qing flew to her. From a position at her feet, he tilted his head, perhaps considering a peck on her shin to hurry her up.

"He twists his head like that to show his admiration," Kang said.

"No. Now he is looking at my necklace." Annabelle made a face at Qing. "I don't trust that bird." She turned to the others. "But I do trust all of you. You have taken on the burden of protecting me, and I appreciate your efforts greatly." She studied them for a moment and added, "I would also like to stay together in Prague but reserve the right to change my mind later."

"When Patrick arrives?" Celwyn asked.

"You were in my mind again!" Annabelle sputtered. Tears threatened.

"No, just an educated guess," Celwyn said.

Kang patted the air with his hands. "Let's talk about the children."

"As I suggested earlier," Bartholomew pointed out, "I am willing and able to take them to a safe place and raise them. Because of my skin color and theirs, the plan would have extraordinary challenges.

However," he said a bit louder, "my vote is that they stay with us."

"I agree. I cannot picture being without them," Annabelle announced.

Kang handed her his handkerchief and said, "I expected what has been said and must be the voice of caution and perhaps discretion." He tossed Celwyn a look. "Trust me, Jonas certainly isn't."

The magician smiled. "Whatever do you mean?"

"Pffft. To go on, as the voice of caution: the children are likely to be in danger, at least initially, if they are near Jonas or myself. Jax is not our only enemy."

Annabelle threw the handkerchief back in Kang's lap. "Why was I not told?" Her face flushed in anger this time, not embarrassment. "I'm not a weak, hysterical woman!"

Kang said, "No. Not at all. We were more concerned that we protect you."

"*Protect me!*"

"And the children from being afraid." Bartholomew looked to Kang for help.

"Teach me to protect myself then!" She glared at them. "And from now on you must stop protecting me as if I am fragile. Do you understand?"

Bartholomew said, "I will do so. Please accept our apologies."

"Thank you," she said in a mollified voice but still maintained a glare for Kang and the magician. "What is the threat you spoke of?"

It wouldn't improve by waiting to tell her the news. Celwyn said, "Vampires."

Her mouth opened and closed, but her eyes said she had heard him.

"Yes, evil, sneaky, and deadly vampires. They are as nasty as a puss-filled cancerous boil." Celwyn had no problem reliving some of his past encounters with them.

Kang opened his hands. "Think, please, everyone. Can we protect the children against them?"

"I have an idea that will help," the magician said. "We can discuss it later. But for now, we must consider that everyone is in danger."

Silence settled over them while they digested thoughts of what could happen. The scraping sound of Qing chewing on a tassel from one of the pillows on the sofa seemed loud in the sudden quiet.

Celwyn growled, "Stop that." Qing eyed him and went back to chewing.

"All right. Three of us want to keep the children with us." Annabelle asked, "What about you, Uncle Celwyn?"

"There is no question that I do."

Annabelle's relief showed in her eyes. "Thank you."

"But we must also address Telly's unhappiness and fears. She is a danger to herself." He cued Kang. "There is a solution."

"Once we reach Prague tomorrow, I will telegraph several doctors I know to find one who can best ease her fears and restore her peace of mind." The Professor looked at each of them. "It is a new field. They are called psychologists and can heal her thoughts. But it will not be an easy task."

Bartholomew asked, "How long will it take?"

"Months, most likely. We will be vigilant and watch her. Jonas will continue to implant pleasant distractions in her thoughts." Kang turned to Annabelle. "We will want to be with her at the sessions to monitor progress and learn how we can help her."

"Yes, we will," she said thoughtfully as she moved her foot away from Qing and re-tied the lace of her boot.

"If we're to stay together, we will need a large home in Prague with specific amenities." Kang pulled out a paper from his pocket. "I have a list started."

"I would be honored to organize that," the big man offered.

"Thank you. We will need a staff also. With everyone's concurrence, I'll offer positions to the existing train crew, including Sully." Celwyn held up a hand. "But I will not offer him the chef position."

Several smiles accompanied nods of agreement and relief. The magician said, "Any one of them could be inhabited by Jax. We just don't know. But the Professor assumes that if that were so, he would have already attacked us."

"What about the train itself?" Bartholomew asked.

Celwyn said, "At least at first, we'll still live on the *Elizabeth*. I'll offer an attractive amount of funds to the conductor in appreciation for his services."

"Jimmy is his assistant. Perhaps he can help guard our new residence," Annabelle said.

"All to be determined. After we arrive, we'll make arrangements to park the *Elizabeth* for several weeks.

Everyone will need to be very careful once we reach Prague: I'm most concerned about the vampires."

Kang said, "I am more afraid of Jax, myself."

"Lovely." Annabelle rolled her eyes and stood up. The others did so also as courtesy demanded. "I must see to the children. We will probably need a nanny. Bartholomew and I will continue to be their main teachers?" She ended with a question to the big man.

"It is my honor to do so. For now, we have a great deal to do, and I will help prepare the children." Bartholomew pointed at Qing. The bird returned the look with the detached tassel hanging from its beak. "Jonas has another child to deal with."

PART III

Poetry, Music, and Justice

Chapter 31

THE *ELIZABETH* CHUGGED SLOWLY around a curve at the top of Mt. Kladno, which provided a stunning view of the city below. Hundreds of towers and church spires rose above the trees and miles of medieval streets, ornate houses, stately museums, and a multitude of parks spread out before them. The turrets of Prague Castle overlooked everything, and through it all snaked the Vltava River.

Zander and Telly pressed their faces to the train windows, giggling and pointing. As the train passed a shepherd with his sheep and a pair of horses, Zander announced, "Pony! I want a pony." Telly watched him with a small smile that didn't reach her eyes.

"What do you want?" Annabelle asked her with a hug.

"For you to sleep in my room," Telly said. "Every night."

As he listened to the exchange from a nearby chair, Celwyn winced. It wasn't what Telly had said as much as the heart-breaking pleading behind it: the child was not getting better. He put the travel guide of Prague in his lap and watched her. After a few moments, he said, "Telly, we love you, and we'll take care of you."

The little girl nodded at him gravely. Annabelle scooped her up and held her close. The girl waved at Celwyn as if to say she understood.

He regarded her a moment more and then looked at Bartholomew sitting in the next chair. "I hope we find a doctor for her soon."

"Agreed."

As they spoke, Zander began galloping in circles between the bar and map table, his imitation of riding a pony. Kang remarked, "We'll need to purchase a large carriage too, and horses, which means the residence requirements also include stables." Zander finally slowed to a stop and rolled on the floor.

"We have taken our time getting to Prague." Celwyn glanced at Prince Leo, who sat at the dining table working in a notebook. "We should assume any one of our enemies could be there waiting for us. Including his." The train braked, and as the answering screech resounded, they started rolling downhill.

"Have you spoken to the crew about staying on with us?" Annabelle asked. The dining car bumped and swayed as she took a seat on the sofa.

"Yes. This evening we will have dinner in town. When we return, the crew has promised to give us their answers. The conductor and Jimmy have agreed that they will stay as long as we're living on the train," the magician said.

"And then?" Bartholomew asked.

Kang handed him a drink. "Jimmy will most likely join us. The conductor prefers to travel onward to London."

"He is a brave and honorable man," the magician said. "But somewhat superstitious, for some reason."

Kang couldn't help a snort.

Ricardo arrived with a tray of cookies and milk. Prince Leo eyed the cookies as Ricardo sat the tray on the dining room table. Kang walked over and picked one up. He held it at arm's length. "Did Sully make the cookies?"

"No, Sir. I did." Ricardo's black eyes danced with good humor. "We've tasted his cookies. Too much flour."

Kang chewed with pleasure. "Excellent."

Nearly an hour passed before the *Elizabeth* arrived at the Prague train terminal. They chugged forward, directed to the main station.

"This train yard seems enormous, even compared to the one in Baghdad," Bartholomew commented.

"How much of a fee will there be?" Celwyn asked.

"Not too much." Kang paused at the door leading off the train. "We aren't part of a regular rail line, but they might be led to assume that we represent future business."

Celwyn nodded. The Professor had strong horse-trading abilities. He watched Kang approach the officials with their clipboards, and from the jovial expressions on their faces, it appeared that Kang's bribe for the *Elizabeth* was welcome in Prague. Minutes later, the automat handed the officials an envelope and asked another question as he pointed across the rail yard. The largest of the officials nodded several times and then indicated a different spot.

It took several more minutes of negotiations between Kang, the conductor, and train officials before they were directed off to one side and down a short stretch of track beside an abandoned field. On the other side of the *Elizabeth,* a narrow strip of ground separated them from a residential street and the commercial district.

Prince Leo settled into a chair next to Celwyn with a glass of wine. "What is the Professor doing?"

"He just finished bribing the railway officials properly. Are you joining us for dinner in town this evening?" Celwyn regarded Prince Leo's attire and assumed the peacock blue shirt and yellow cravat might be suited to a different activity. Perhaps a party on a beach.

"Thank you, but no. Can I assume I am no longer an unwanted prisoner aboard this train?"

"You may. But you are also welcome to continue to enjoy our hospitality."

The dwarf shook his head. "Thank you, but my trunks are packed."

"What about the Russians?"

"I will take my chances with those who pursue me. Unjustly, mind you."

"Of course."

Prince Leo sipped his drink and admired the well-appointed train car. "I do appreciate the accommodations, though. Mr. Sully is a nice chap, but I am fairly certain he is not really a chef."

Celwyn smiled. "Remember Podderman in Marseille?"

Prince Leo roared with laughter. "I do, most definitely." He sobered and added, "I appreciate your tolerance, Jonas."

"If you need our help, most likely we can be reached here or through messages left at the Opera House." The magician stood and offered his hand. "We will live on the *Elizabeth* for a while."

"It is pleasing that we are on good terms once more. Thank you for everything." He shook Celwyn's hand. "I'll be gone by the time you return from dinner."

Kang climbed back onto the *Elizabeth* with a satisfied expression.

"We have the use of track G for the next two weeks, and I have arranged for a carriage for tonight."

"Your efforts are appreciated."

Kang studied him. "You are distracted."

"That I am. You know, it has just become more difficult to guard the *Elizabeth* during the night: this city is big, with more curious individuals. And thieves." Celwyn inspected the crowd opposite the other trestle a hundred feet from the train. "Look at them. People talk, and we are of interest."

A cluster of busy men in top hats walked around a variety of beggars. Then came a pair of Turkish men in white ibises and a gaggle of women in elaborately embroidered dresses who stood and watched the train. A man in a clerical collar detoured around them while another, with a cart full of produce, stopped and stared at the train.

The magician continued, "There is a little bit of everyone here. I'll ask Jimmy and Ricardo to take the entrances to the train tonight. Bartholomew and I will relieve them about three in the morning."

"And I'll keep watch over Annabelle and the children." Kang rubbed his hands together. "I am famished. Where is Annabelle?"

"Primping and washing behind Zander's ears."

"Little boys are dirty. Where are we dining?" Kang asked.

The magician crossed to the table under the map and picked up a guidebook. "Baedecker's calls the *Golden Dandelion Inn* an "island of English tradition" in Prague. It will hopefully live up to its reputation." He waved a hand, and the aroma of braised lamb enveloped them. He waved again, and the smelled of baked pheasant became intoxicating. "Which do you prefer?"

Kang inhaled with a blissful expression and said, "Both."

"Here we are," Bartholomew announced as he held the door open for Annabelle and the children. "They are very hungry."

"Yes, we are. I could eat a bear!" Zander announced.

With a jingling of bells, a carriage pulled up in front of the train a few minutes later. The muscular horses wore plumes of feathers tall enough to rival some of Annabelle's hats. To Zander's delight, the Arabians snorted and stomped their feet while Telly hid behind Bartholomew's hefty leg and peeked at them.

"It is all right, young lady," Celwyn said. "They like to make noise, just like Zander. Later on, I have a carrot you can give them."

They rode through the streets of Prague past gas lights sitting atop ornate iron posts as high as the *Elizabeth*. Some of the streets remained in shadow, but the commercial district appeared as light as day. The further they traveled from the train yard, the more the citizens walked the cobblestones. Crowds formed in front of the ferry terminal for the riverboats, and even more waited in front of a theater.

"What does that say?" Zander pointed to a colorful poster of knights in combat pasted to the side of the theater.

Kang squinted. "The Meiningen Ensemble Presents *The Three Musketeers*." He said, "It is an adventure story you would like."

"So many people..." Telly murmured. Celwyn saw the worry in her eyes. She seemed to be searching for someone. Silently, he suggested to her that Van Maskolc was dead: he died, and she would never see him again. Not to be afraid.

"So many people!" Zander repeated. He glanced back in the direction of the train yard. "Why isn't Prince Leo with us?"

"Prince Leo said to tell all of you goodbye for now. He is on his way to his next destination." As Celwyn spoke, he hoped the man would exercise some common sense. Over the last few days, he'd come to forgive the dwarf's past behavior. Not to trust him. But forgive.

Zander's bottom lip protruded. "I wanted to play dominoes with him again."

"If you repeat that in English instead of Deutsch, I will play with you," Bartholomew told him.

After he had done so, Kang eyed Bartholomew and observed, "You don't understand Deutsch."

"I don't. But I recognized the word 'dominoes.'"

"Ah."

"Look!" Telly pointed beyond their carriage to a juggler in a red suit and bells on the next corner. He had attracted a modest crowd as coins landed in the case at his feet. She gripped Bartholomew's hand and giggled as she looked at the show. While they watched, a newsboy ran past them yelling, *"Young Turks Organize Against Sultan Hamid's Rule!"*

"Who is that?" Zander asked.

"He is an important man. We will talk about him tomorrow in class," Annabelle murmured as she inspected a dress in the window across the street.

The big man said, "Perhaps the day after? I hope we can choose the neighborhood for our new residence tomorrow. We will also need to shop for many things and obtain staff."

While they'd been talking, the juggler tossed the balls high. Celwyn sent them tenfold higher. The balls hovered and then, one by one, descended. The crowd clapped, delighted by what they saw. The juggler caught them and bowed as if the magician's helpfulness had been rehearsed. The clinking of coins into his case became a storm.

Their carriage rolled forward again with the juggler forgotten by everyone except Telly, who peered out the rear window until he was out of sight. Annabelle said, "I understand. We will have two bedtime stories tonight, one historical, and resume class the day after."

As they exited the coach in front of the *Golden Dandelion*, Celwyn noted another carriage pulled up a short distance behind them. The curtains of its windows were closed, and no one emerged to the sidewalk. The magician herded everyone inside and hung back to speak to the doorman. He waited several minutes more before joining their party inside.

Hours later, after kidney pie, succulent lamb, a fine claret, and an excellent trifle, Kang patted his stomach and said, "The children are yawning; they are so full. I believe I am, too."

As he clambered into the carriage, he handed a bottle to their driver and tipped his hat. Celwyn took his time climbing inside, adjusting his cuffs, and glancing to the rear. A different carriage sat there, and again with darkened windows. The driver appeared to be asleep in the box up top. Celwyn shrugged and scrambled inside. The carriage could be awaiting someone dining inside the Inn. Or not.

Telly promptly fell asleep in Celwyn's lap as they rolled forward. They passed sidewalks that teemed with couples and families on their evening strolls. Many wore coats and held umbrellas. At the moment, it wasn't quite raining, but the air swirled with a heavy mist.

"I've asked the driver to go slow and take the long way back to the train so we can see some of the city," Kang said.

"Could we stop at the Opera House, please?" Annabelle blushed just enough for Celwyn to notice. "I would like to see if there is any mail held for us."

"Patrick," Bartholomew said.

"Patrick," Celwyn agreed.

The blush won. "I can hope so."

Zander lifted his head off Kang's shoulder long enough to ask, "Who is Patrick?"

"Annabelle is sweet on him," the automat told him.

"She puts sugar on him?"

It took several minutes to find the exact phrasing and translate it so that Zander would understand. He frowned at Annabelle and said, "But you have us You don't need anyone else."

While Annabelle dealt with an explanation, Kang opened the glass and spoke to the driver. "The Opera House, please."

A few minutes more, and the dome of the Opera House came into view. Like an enormous snow globe lit with thousands of tiny lights, it stood bright against the night sky, the structure taking up the entire block. In front, people huddled in groups, still others walked briskly by, and the crowds thickened as their coach drew closer to the entrance. A long line of carriages disgorged exquisitely coiffed women in evening gowns and draped with furs. Men in tails and top hats escorted them inside as Zander's eyes widened even further.

"They are all dressed so fine," he said.

Bartholomew said, "I would be honored to buy you a new suit—"

"To wear to church," Annabelle inserted with a look at the others that said, "no arguing."

Kang shrugged and tapped the glass again. As he emerged from the cab, Celwyn handed a still sleeping Telly off to Annabelle and followed. He caught up with Kang at the base of the tall flight of marble stairs leading to the grand entrance and pulled Kang aside.

"Do you see the carriage fourth behind us? Don't stare."

Kang pretended to tie his boot and swiveled back again. "Yes."

"It followed us from dinner. Let's hurry." Celwyn darted up the stairs, with Kang close behind. They bypassed the crowd gathered in front of the gilded doors that stretched to the story above. "Quite the majestic entrance. I hear this is the first establishment in the city to have the new electric lights," Celwyn said. "Can you tell the difference?"

Kang studied the lights above the doorway as they walked inside and the lights from the magnificent chandelier overhanging the ballroom-sized foyer before them. "Yes. The light is clearer. No smell. It will take getting used to."

To their left lay the ticket booths, tables, and waiters servicing a full bar. Curtained cubicles lined the right wall. "What are we looking for?"

"There." Celwyn pointed straight ahead, and they approached the information desk.

When they emerged onto the street again, both the magician and Kang carried a box of correspondence. Dodging well-shod patrons, they started down the dozens of stairs.

"Good grief. I think Patrick wrote to her every day," Kang said as he shifted the box to his other arm.

"Damnation!" Celwyn exclaimed.

A most unwelcome tableau greeted them.

As she faced Mrs. Pearse in front of a gawking crowd of opera patrons, Annabelle railed at her in a full fury. Right behind her, Zander and Telly's faces were pressed to the windows of their carriage. Annabelle's voice reached them long before they arrived at the scene.

"No! I will not go with you," Annabelle fumed, her face far beyond the pale blush from a few minutes before. "I'm not a child!"

Standing in front of the carriage, unsuccessfully blocking the children's view, Bartholomew wore a confused and uncomfortable expression that said he clearly didn't know what to do. Annabelle continued to shout. "Those children are my wards. This—" she pulled Bartholomew forward, "—is my friend." She spied Kang and the magician. "And you remember Mr. Celwyn and the Professor? I can see you do." She took a breath and lowered her voice and grated, "I am in good company."

Mrs. Pearse's voice pierced the air like a knife sawing through a steel plate.

"I heard you were coming to Prague. I have every right to follow you." She turned to the magician, and her chin went up. "Oh. I see *you* are here." Swiveling back to Annabelle, she spat, "How can you associate with a criminal? He is a murderer."

Annabelle stepped forward, and Celwyn thought she would slap the other woman. He inserted himself between them and said, "It is wonderful to see you again too, Mrs. Pearse. I did not murder Colonel Gilliam. That is all you need to know."

While he spoke, the Professor herded a resisting Annabelle into the carriage, with a grateful Bartholomew close behind. Before Celwyn climbed in, he bowed and said, "Good evening, Madam."

Kang tapped on the glass, and they rolled away. Wide-eyed, Zander asked, "Who was that?" Kang handed him one of the boxes of letters. Celwyn handed the other to Telly.

"We'll talk about it later. Please pull out the letters with this." Celwyn pointed to the return address of Patrick. "Do you see it? Good. Hand them to Aunt Annabelle as you find them. Whoever finds the most gets an extra story tonight." The children dove into the boxes.

Bartholomew's face shone with sweat. "That was unpleasant."

"What happened?" the automat asked him, leaving a still incensed Annabelle alone with her thoughts.

"While we waited for you to return, there was a loud tapping on the window. It scared Telly, and she screamed. While I reassured her, that woman's face appeared in the window and scared her again."

"It would have scared me," Celwyn said.

Annabelle vibrated with anger. "I got out of the carriage and confronted her."

Kang frowned in thought. "I'm not surprised that she had enough time to reach Prague before us, but do not know how she knew we had changed our destination."

"Yes, we took our time. How did she know?" Celwyn rubbed his chin and said, "She probably bribed someone in Baghdad."

Annabelle tried to keep her voice steady and failed. "I don't care how she found us. She had better keep her distance." Zander handed her a dozen letters from his box. "Oh, thank you, sweetie." She kissed his forehead and visibly calmed down. She mouthed the words "Thank you" to the magician for the well-timed distraction.

"Here are mine, too," Telly said and received her kiss as well.

The magician almost looked forward to his three in the morning guard duty. It would be calm and without any pesky aunts in flowered dresses.

Chapter 32

A
N UNSHAVEN SULLY, WITH EYES AS blurry as a red snowstorm, served their breakfast instead of the porters.

"A mite early, isn't it, 'Gov'ner?" he said as he plopped a plate in front of Celwyn. "Me 'elpers are still sleepin' after guard duty. Me?" He placed Bartholomew's breakfast in front of him. "I haven't been to bed yet."

Kang looked at the unappetizing plate and said with a studiously serious face, "Thank you. We appreciate your dedication."

As Sully closed the door to the kitchen behind him, Bartholomew advised, "I wouldn't thank him until you taste the eggs."

Celwyn pointed out the window, "Look. It is a pony!" When everyone obediently searched for the pony, he waved a hand over the table, correcting spices, cooking, and adding a plate of perfectly prepared sausages.

Kang hadn't looked for the fictional pony, knowing the magician's penchant for ruses, and instead watched the transformation of the food on the table. "You have my deepest appreciation, Jonas," he said. "I do not see a pony."

"Who was that lady with Aunt Annabelle last night? She won't tell us," Telly asked as she poked a fork at her sausage.

Celwyn waited for Annabelle to explain.

"Just someone I know. Finish your breakfast, please. Our coach will be here soon."

As their carriage moved away from the *Elizabeth,* it picked up enough speed to rattle their teeth. Kang made a face. "The coach we buy will have shocks and cushioning. I hope Sully is awake and ready when the other carriage comes for him this afternoon. We need supplies for the larder."

"No worry," Celwyn replied. "The conductor has instructions to wake the old probate up when it is time."

At their first stop, they dropped off Bartholomew in front of an extensive complex of stables not too far from the train yards. As he stepped out of the carriage, it tilted with his weight and then settled again.

"I will need several hours here. Au revoir." With a doff of his hat, he walked toward the office.

"We will see you soon, my friend," the magician called out as they rumbled away. "What is our next destination?" he asked Kang.

"The maître'd last night suggested an agency on Havold Street for staff needs. It is a fair distance from here."

As they traveled along cobblestone streets lined with quaint brick buildings and baskets of flowers decorating the entrances, the sidewalks became increasingly populated with workers, shoppers, and foreigners of all nationalities. Telly licked her lips with a level of nervousness. Zander pointed out the horses he liked and any dogs he saw.

Annabelle stared out the window with a faraway look in her eyes. "I worry about Patrick's safety."

"When will he depart Agra?" the magician asked.

She shrugged. "I have only read four of his letters. They are quite lengthy. When we return to the train, I will finish the rest and know more."

Hours later, Kang thanked the proprietor of the Danlow agency and held an umbrella over Annabelle's hat as she climbed back inside the coach. A light rain pattered the trees as the carriage pulled away from the curb.

"Are you ready for my report?" Kang asked the magician. "I see you patronized a tobacconist in our absence."

"I did. Both you and Bartholomew will be pleased with my selections."

"Most likely." He eyed the package on the seat. "All right. Our first objective was a new chef, and they offered us one who will arrive in a few days," Kang reported. "We found two guards for night duty also." The carriage gained speed and then slowed again for a herd of shoppers blocking the street. Moments later, their coach had entered the heart of the commercial district full of wonderful sights and smells.

"*Schauen Sie hier*!" Zander bounced in his seat. "Toy store!"

Celwyn smiled. "And I spy a tea proprietor. We'll have to return here after lunch. For now, we must retrieve Bartholomew from the stables."

"We can get a pony!" Zander asked with childish determination.

"Not today," Annabelle said. "Do you think it will be long before we are able to move into a normal residence? Perhaps we should stop where I can commission furniture to be made."

"We hadn't thought of that," Kang said.

"And linens and dishes and cutlery." Annabelle added, "There are many things I'm sure we'll need."

"For the pony!"

Amid laughter, Celwyn said, "We do have a great deal to do." A general discussion of what they would immediately need ensued. "Ah, here are the stables."

A whiff of manure reached them as they traveled up the street. In front of the stables sat a large hansom painted a shiny black with a full team of dancing and snorting horses. The coachman wore a top hat and tails and appeared to be sober and clean. Bartholomew leaned against the carriage door wearing a satisfied smile.

"Oh my!" Annabelle exclaimed.

It took a while to transfer to the new carriage. As they did so, everyone was introduced to Edward Murphy, their new coachman. He appeared to be about forty years of age, muscular, and sported well-tended mustaches. As he solemnly shook Zander's hand, he said, "I will see you every day, Master Zander." He turned to Telly, bent his knee, and kissed her hand. "You too, Miss Telly." He received a tiny smile, a brave one, in return.

The boy ducked under the rear of one of the horses and said, "What are the horses' names?"

While they were introduced, Bartholomew said, "Edward will also function as a groomsman and handyman." He looked to see where Telly had gone. Satisfied that she also examined the horses and couldn't hear, he added, "Edward is also a crack shot and will help secure the train, and the new residence, as needed."

"Excellent," the magician said. "I also noted that he is of my height and build should we need any more subterfuge."

Kang agreed. "Dressed the same, he could pass as you. Except for his full whiskers."

"I wouldn't presume to ask him to shave his off. Therefore, I'll grow mine."

"No." Annabelle shook her head. "Just no."

Bartholomew saw Celwyn's mock surprise and laughed until he had tears.

Kang opened the coach door. "Onward, before the children tire out or I do. We have many stops." He tipped his hat at Edward. "Pleased to meet you." After the children scrambled inside the cab, he leaned toward Edward, saying, "Bartholomew will give you details, but please keep an eye out for anyone following us."

Celwyn scanned the street, seeing only stable hands and other horses out and about in the cloudy morning. He asked Edward, "Do you have a firearm handy?"

If the question was a test, Edward passed. He didn't ask why, just replied, "Not at the moment. When I move my things to the train, I will have one."

"We may need more. Let's make a firearm proprietor our first stop after lunch. Could you take us to a luncheon establishment, please?"

"Certainly."

Twenty minutes later, they descended from the carriage to the street again. The *Gelbe Brücke* had been painted bright blue with yellow shutters and sported wrought iron fencing. Wooden boxes of daisies lined the walk leading to the door.

"Would you care to join us, Edward?" Kang asked.

He tipped his hat. "Appreciate the offer, Professor. But I am going to stop home and get a start on my packing. My place is just a few blocks away."

"As you wish. We'll be ready by the time you return ... if the children don't dawdle." Celwyn watched the street, seeing only what could be expected: a variety of umbrellas, vendors pushing carts, and hurrying pedestrians.

The automat said, "I plan to dawdle if their wine is decent."

"How do you spell dawdle?" Zander asked Bartholomew.

"What does it mean?" Telly asked. Annabelle translated and explained. Telly said, "Don't dawdle," and gave Zander a little push.

Celwyn had just added a day's supply of distracting happy thoughts to the girl's mind. On the way here, he'd again caught a melancholy look in her eyes that seemed unfathomable.

"Edward, where is the nearest telegraph office?" he asked.

"Just down the block, Sir."

Bartholomew herded the children forward as he and Annabelle started up the walkway to the restaurant. To Kang, the magician said, "Do you have the contact information for your medical colleagues?" He lowered his voice, "Telly?"

"Yes." Kang watched the girl. "I noticed her expression also. I'll be right back."

Chapter 33

W HEN KANG RETURNED TO THE restaurant a few minutes later, he joined a merry party. The waiter had just presented Zander with a blue balloon shaped like a goose and Telly with a red one just like it. Celwyn sighed with relief that his customary good luck held: the animals hadn't been like the ones lining the horrific walls of Van Maskolc's mansion.

Kang picked up a menu and asked the waiter, "Is there fresh trout today?"

While he quizzed the waiter further, Bartholomew studied the street through the restaurant's lace-curtained windows. His voice tensed. "Please order some for me also, Professor. Excuse me."

Celwyn distracted the children as the big man wasted no time striding to the front door. "Make the goose walk please, Master Zander." The boy dutifully waddled the balloon to his sister's plate and back. By the time Bartholomew returned, Kang and the others had finished relating their order to their waiter.

Consternation and anger warred on the big man's face. Celwyn covered what the little ones could hear and said, "Go ahead."

Bartholomew kept his voice near a whisper. "I thought I saw Mrs. Pearse's carriage outside." He glanced at Annabelle, who looked ready to throw something. "I did see it. As I walked up to it, the coach quickly left."

"For now," Kang commented.

The big man nodded. "But there was something much more worrying out there. We should make another stop at the staffing agency and obtain more guards."

Celwyn felt a tightening in his stomach, knowing what Bartholomew was about to say.

"Mrs. Karras walked right by me in the street after Mrs. Pearse's carriage left. She wore a heavy veil, but I know her voice." He closed his eyes and said, "She told me to enjoy a nice luncheon."

"Oh, no." Annabelle looked at the children, and her brows drew together.

Celwyn growled, "We must warn Edward much sooner than we'd planned." Their food arrived. The magician waved a hand, and the children could hear their conversation again. "Please begin eating. We need to hurry."

"No dawdling!" Zander announced.

Nearly everyone had settled inside the carriage by the time Edward returned. Celwyn watched the street from the doorway next door. Mrs. Karras did not appear to be in the vicinity, but that didn't mean she hadn't seen them all, including the children. *Curse it*, he thought. *How did she find us already?*

"Edward, would you mind if I rode with you for a moment?" the magician asked. "We have encountered a situation that you should be aware of and the children shouldn't hear about."

"Certainly." He made room for Celwyn atop the cab in the driver's seat and picked up the reins. "Where to?"

Celwyn opened the glass behind them and asked Kang for the address of the staffing agency. To Edward, he said, "We need to hire guards for the train."

"Why didn't you say so, Sir?" From the fire in his eyes, Edward appeared to enjoy a bit of danger. "I can help you with that."

Celwyn said, "A most welcome offer, thank you." The magician assumed between the two guards they'd hired, Edward and themselves, they would be adequately guarded for tonight if they didn't make it back to the staffing agency. "In that case, please take us to our next stop on Vlaramir Street. Miss Annabelle needs to order furniture, and we need the services of an estate agent also. If we should pass by a gun proprietor, we need to stop there also."

Edward rubbed his chin in thought. "I believe right near Sheridan's Upholstery is an estate agent's office." He clicked his tongue at the horses, and they swerved into the traffic with the other carriages. "Mr. Bartholomew mentioned that you had a few enemies. Is that why we need more guards?"

It was the magician's turn to rub his chin. "Indeed we do. You seem a most level-headed gentleman, Edward."

Edward urged the horses forward, "I am."

"I hope so. We have attracted the attention of a vampire. She is especially annoyed with me."

The driver was silent so long that Celwyn prompted him, "A vampire. Perhaps more than one."

"I heard you, Sir," Edward said. "That pistol you mentioned probably won't do me any good now, will it?" He pulled up on the reins, slowing the horses for a turn.

"No, but it might be useful for other threats we face." Celwyn eyed him. "Are you still willing to work for us?"

"I'm thinking, Sir."

They passed under a medieval footbridge and rattled north toward a busier avenue, merging into a line with other carriages. As they rounded a corner, Celwyn faced the rear. "There doesn't appear to be anyone trailing us."

Edward nodded. "I am not one to run from a threat, Sir. In Beirut, I used to command a unit in her Majesty's Navy."

The magician sighed in relief. "We will make it worth your while. And we would be honored if you would be in charge of our security both on the train and at our new residence."

"Done. What does this vampire look like?" he asked as they pulled up in front of a brick building. The front of Smithy and Sons displayed painted posters of rifles, flying bullets, and fearful geese.

Celwyn jumped from the cab to the sidewalk. "She is about your age, extremely handsome, and extremely dangerous." He made a circular gesture at his chest. "She will try to distract you."

Their coachman nodded. "I will be on guard."

As he opened the coach door to let the others descend, Celwyn added, "One of the other situations we have encountered involves an elderly annoyance in a flowered dress who is bothering Miss Annabelle. Her aunt. No firearms are necessary. However, if you see anyone following our party, please inform us."

"Rightio." Edward began attaching feedbags to the horses' necks.

When everyone returned to the carriage, Bartholomew carried a box with a pistol. He informed Edward more pistols would be delivered to the train. Their driver nodded, and the carriage moved forward again at a good clip.

They had barely started a conversation about the kind of furniture they would need—Annabelle stayed firm on formal parlor furniture—before the carriage swerved to a stop in front of Frank and Son's Real Estate. Bartholomew bade them farewell and exited the carriage saying he would see them back at the train. With big eyes, Telly watched him disappear inside the building.

"What is he doing?"

Annabelle assured her, "He is finding a house for us to live in."

"But I like our classroom and our train," Telly said and started to tremble. "I do not like big houses."

Celwyn entered her thoughts and saw Van Maskolc's house on the hill as Telly remembered it: the tall windows where nothing could be seen, only imagined, and dark terrors. Flashes of the table she had been strapped to, then Van Maskolc's face hovering so close the magician could see the decay of his teeth and his leering rictus smile. Telly silently screamed as the bastard whispered at her.

The magician wiped that all away, at least for now, and replaced it with images of Zander and Bartholomew painting the doors of gingerbread houses with frosting and Annabelle planting lollipops in front of it. The increasing frequency of the horrible images in the little one's mind worried Celwyn the most. He turned to Kang and pointedly said, "We need to look for replies at the telegraph office on the way back to the train."

Annabelle said, "That is a good idea." She watched Telly, who had stopped trembling and just sat quietly. To Celwyn, she said, "Can I assume you just helped her?"

"I did. But it won't last."

She sent him a grateful nod and said to the children, "If you are good at the next shop, I will buy you fruit ices before we go back to the train."

Zander hugged his red balloon, and Telly declared, "We will be very good."

Chapter 34

LITTLE THINGS TRIGGERED OLD memories. Celwyn saw most clearly the sunset over Le Mont-Saint-Michel and the stormy sea rising below. He panted with exhaustion and realized he was fleeing the French Huguenots in 1593, running for the coast. At the time, he fought as a confederate for the wrong side of the conflict, judging from the bullet that whipped by his ear and the number of soldiers trying to kill him. A break in the storm clouds revealed the brilliant reds, pinks, and gold of the setting sun, bathing him in respite from the conflict.

What had triggered the memory? A comparison to the colors over Le Mont-Saint-Michel and disappointment at this moment. The colors of Prague's sunset couldn't be seen through the heavy sense of doom that gradually covered the train yard. Beyond the terminal buildings the streets still teemed with pedestrians, but few lights from the shops twinkled an invitation to visit. Even the *Elizabeth* seemed maudlin.

From his position in front of the dining car windows, Kang lowered his newspaper. "When will the new guards arrive?"

The magician consulted his pocket watch. "In about four hours, just after ten this evening. Edward will join them until he is satisfied that everything is secure. I'll also put a layer of protection between the sleeping cars and the rest of the train."

Kang took his empty glass to the bar and called, "Another?"

"Please." Celwyn watched as a carriage arrived in the yard, and Bartholomew got out. He paid the driver, crossed through the weeds, and climbed aboard. "Good afternoon, and welcome home. From your expression, it appears you have been successful."

Bartholomew removed his overcoat and said, "Yes, I think everyone will be pleased."

Kang handed him a glass of wine, and they sat on the sofa together. Celwyn couldn't imagine a more disparate pair, yet they meshed together like a bow and arrow.

"Before I start my report, I should tell you that I stopped at the telegraph office as requested." The big man handed a message to Kang.

Kang read it through twice and told them, "Good news. Doctor Ruttenberg will be in Prague in about two weeks. He will see Telly at that time. He is said to be an excellent psychologist."

"She is becoming more anxious by the day," Celwyn said.

Bartholomew nodded. "I will be with her any time Annabelle cannot." They remained silent for several minutes, each thinking about the situation until the big man said, "Perhaps this will bring our spirits up. We were successful at the real estate agent's office: there are two manors that meet our requirements. We can see them tomorrow."

Ricardo entered from the kitchen bearing a tray of water glasses. Celwyn stood, and said, "I'd better hurry Annabelle and the children along. It appears that dinner is almost ready."

With their meal over and a consensus that Sully could have done worse, Celwyn asked everyone to gather near the bar, leaving the children playing at the dining table and out of earshot.

He began by telling Annabelle about Doctor Ruttenberg's reply.

She nodded. "It can't be too soon. In Telly's dreams, she screams, and sometimes her legs move like she is running. Then she screams more."

Celwyn again cursed himself for not tearing Van Maskolc to pieces before killing him. He glanced at the children. "Our guards will arrive after the children are in bed, but we need to tell them about the guards in case they see them. We," he paused and looked at Telly, then Zander, "we need to instruct them not to open a window unless one of us is with them. Nor can they leave a window open more than a few inches."

"Why?" Annabelle asked.

"Because I do not want to find Mrs. Karras, or worse, standing by my bed watching me sleep."

Bartholomew said, "So, it is true that vampires can come in through a window?"

Kang answered, "They certainly can. Even a second or third-story window."

"I'll talk with the children now." Annabelle stood, causing the others to do so also.

Celwyn made a face. "I need to talk with Sully about this, too. If we can't be sure this instruction will be obeyed, we'll nail the windows shut."

As he spoke, Edward crossed the yard in front, arriving on foot with a large traveling bag. Kang held the door open for him. "Good evening."

Annabelle shook his hand. "It is good to have you join us. Please excuse me; I have children to look after." She hurried toward the cabins.

Celwyn asked, "Have you had dinner, Sir?"

Edward deposited his bag in a corner and took the chair Celwyn offered, refusing a drink.

"I'm fine, thank you. Got to keep sharp for a while yet. I'll stay with the guards until I'm sure they'll do."

"You met everyone earlier. Most of the sleeping cars and the children's classroom are through there," the magician gestured. "The only other entrance is the locomotive."

Edward hesitated and pulled on his mustaches thoughtfully. "So, I can assume there are vampires and that crazy old lady you described. Is there anyone else?"

"Just normal thieves and ruffians. And," Celwyn raised a brow at Bartholomew and Kang and received resigned nods, "we have another enemy who you should know about."

With an amused expression, Edward said, "My last employer is beginning to seem rather dull. If you'll excuse me, Mr. Celwyn, but you are a colorful bunch."

Bartholomew laughed. "We are also upstanding people. Just blessed with an overabundance of enemies."

"Our other enemy is not easy to recognize." Kang studied Edward as he said, "Do you believe in the supernatural? Or the occult?"

Although the man wanted to appear calm and able to take on anything, the automat's questions caused him to begin tapping the toe of his boot. Edward pursed his lips, and a fine sheen of perspiration appeared on his brow. After a moment, he said, "If you want to pay me as much as we discussed, I'll consider the extra monies as danger pay." He sat up straighter. "I'm not a coward. And it takes a great deal to frighten me."

Nothing like the present, the magician thought. Without touching it, he removed the glass from Kang's hand and sent it to the bar, where he refilled it. As the glass moved back to Kang, Edward swallowed several times but didn't say a word. The toe-tapping increased. Near the ceiling, a bright white light formed, thickening into a cloud, and from it, tiny crystal frogs cavorted before falling to the carpet. They bounced and rolled and then scattered.

"I am a magician, Edward." Celwyn waved, and the light faded. "By all accounts, I do more good than harm." He reached in his breast pocket and selected a peyote button. After he popped it into his mouth, he asked, "Do you like music?"

Edward looked at the carpet where the crystal frogs had dissolved. "For what I know about it, yes." His voice had the resolution of a man about to dive off a cliff.

Celwyn waved a finger, and a tinkling ballad from an unseen piano played a trill of Mozart.

Edward swallowed and said, "I especially enjoy Bach. Someday, you'll have to tell me how you do that."

The magician said, "I will try." He began to pace. "Back to our un-named enemy. Both the Professor and I know of him. Bartholomew and Annabelle have yet to encounter him. He is a despicable entity who is after either myself, or the science the Professor has developed. We're not sure which."

"He kills randomly as he follows us," Kang reported. "And because of that, we can't describe him to you."

Edward regarded them with a pained expression. "Why?"

"Allow me." Bartholomew held up a hand. "This is how it was described to me, and it might help you: we know the enemy as Jax. He assumes the body of an innocent person, and when he is done with them, he murders them and moves to a new body." The big man shook his head. "The problem is that it could be anyone he is inhabiting."

"I see."

Bartholomew said, "The best approach is to look for unusual and strange behavior in someone you know. Something out of character."

Edward's laugh had a metallic bounce to it. "Again, if you'll excuse me: this will be a challenge, but one I welcome."

Kang said, "We understand and do not take offense."

"I'll get used to it." Edward got to his feet. "The guards will be here soon, and I should stow my things and look at your perimeter."

Kang joined him. "I'll show you your room and where the lanterns are. We hope to be moving to a larger residence soon."

As the door closed behind them, the magician eyed Bartholomew. "We will need more than security guards when we move to the new residence."

"And you already have an idea of how to resolve this?"

"I do. But it will be rather delicate to arrange." The magician gazed out the window to the street, not really seeing anything. "I hesitate to go this route, but we have to fight our enemies with the kind of extraordinary terms that they understand."

Bartholomew regarded him with a spark of interest in his eyes. "That sounds interesting. What can I do?"

"When I have it set up, you will be in charge of the implementation." He checked for Kang and the others. "For now, discourage the Professor from following me." He was on his feet and moving. "Stay with everyone and protect them. I should be back within a few hours." He called back, "And if possible, the guards should be instructed not to shoot at me upon my return."

Chapter 35

THE MAGICIAN WASTED NO TIME hurrying across the yard. Striding to the nearest well-lit intersection, he looked for a hire carriage. The Staré Mêsto district lay at least five miles away, and he'd prefer this didn't take all night. Qing snuggled inside his coat, chewing on his collar. Celwyn sighed. He'd forgotten about him, but he didn't want to go back and face questions.

Several coaches went by, but none were for hire. He started north at a good pace, turning to scan the carriages every time he heard hoofbeats. As he crossed a street, Celwyn reminded himself he was due to implant more pleasant images with Telly before the evening was out.

Running footsteps approached from the rear. The magician whirled in a crouch, ready to fling whoever it was into the trees. Kang nearly ran into him.

Celwyn steadied the automat. "You didn't really need to—"

"Save the excuses, Jonas. I'm coming with you."

"What about protecting Annabelle and the children?"

"Good try. Bartholomew and Edward are doing so." He looked up the street and then down again. "Where were you going?"

Celwyn cursed his luck as he stood at the curb; this would go better without the automat. He scanned the street for a hire-coach and spied a theatre on the next block. "There's activity down there," he pointed. "We need a carriage. Our destination is a distance away." He started toward the theatre. "You should go back."

Kang kept up a steady trot and stayed with him. "Why?"

"Because the situation where I am going will be tricky, and I will stand a better chance of success if I'm not protecting you at the same time." He waved at a coach, which not only didn't stop but seemed to speed up. "How did you get away from Bartholomew?"

"I told him I heard Annabelle calling him, and he went to check."

"There's one!" Celwyn sprinted into the street in front of a carriage. Kang tumbled into the back while the magician relayed the address. The driver shook his head. Celwyn said, "The block before will do." He climbed inside before the driver could object further.

"You agree that we need extra help to guard against vampires and Jax?" he asked Kang.

"Yes." As they bumped high into the air over a trestle and then hit a pothole square on, the Professor noted, "It is unfortunate that this driver seems to dislike us." A police clarion drowned him out as it passed by in the other direction. "He seems a mite put upon."

The magician wasn't in the mood for little annoyances or having the automat along. "Circumstances make it necessary. We will be safe on the *Elizabeth* until we move, and the guards can watch the two train entrances. But we'll most likely have a much larger residence soon, with many doors and windows."

Kang added, "And larger staff that may not be as vigilant as we'd prefer."

Their carriage veered onto Naprstkova Street, and the gas lights that overhung the cobblestones appeared less as the darkness became pronounced. The buildings seemed older and more mysterious as their coach picked up speed as if the driver worried for his welfare.

At the end of the street, they spied a tall and thin building painted a deep blue that seemed to glow under the rising moon. The house favored gothic architecture, yet the roof sported red Spanish tiles. Pagan statues and yellow Moroccan tiles lined the steps leading to the door. Most noticeably, the entire house seemed to lean to the right.

As their carriage swerved to a stop at the corner, the driver flew out of his seat and had their door open before the wheels stopped turning.

"Get out, and give me my money!"

"But, Sir, we'll need a return trip. If you—"

The driver interrupted Kang, "No! Blast you. My money!"

Kang named an amount that made the man hesitate. "In gold. Come back in an hour, and it will be waiting for you." He handed the man double the fare.

The driver counted the coins and climbed back inside his cab. "I'll be on that corner," he pointed one block north, "In one hour." In Russian, he added, "God be with you two fools."

The automat and the magician watched the coach until it was out of sight and then turned to regard the house. Kang asked, "Who, or what, is in there?"

"A dozen years ago, it contained a notorious coven of the most adept witches on the continent." Celwyn smiled. "Judging from our driver's lack of nerve, it still does." He ascended the steps behind Kang, and the sound of their knock echoed: as if a great emptiness encompassed the house. Not even the squeak of a mouse could be heard.

Kang jumped when the door opened, and with it came a blast of bagpipes, the manic din from a brace of tin drums, and a soprano belting out a bawdy song. The tall red-headed woman holding the door screamed in delight and pulled Celwyn inside. Kang held onto the magician's coattails and was propelled forward before the door shut behind them.

"Jonas is back!"

Kang couldn't believe this many people could fit into a foyer, sitting room, and dining room. From the sound emanating from the kitchen, the musicians had taken over that room. He felt fairly sure he'd seen the yawning brass mouth of a tuba too. Dozens of women in flowing robes or thin chemises floated by or draped themselves across furniture. Occasionally men walked between the rooms, somewhat carefully, as they tended to have their rears pinched or attracted other more lascivious activity.

Some of the women couldn't have been any older than Annabelle, and others could easily have been cronies of Mrs. Pearse. Kang felt a distinct sense of unease and stayed as close as he could to Celwyn. All the while, he smiled as benignly as possible. He also found some of the inhabitants as fascinating as could be.

With a voice as clear as a mountain stream, one of the women began singing "The Last Rose of Summer." Others joined in as a wine bottle appeared in Kang's hand. He dutifully sipped and passed it along.

The red-headed woman embraced the magician, and kept him close, hip to hip, as she asked in a purr, "Where have you been?"

"Jonas, my love, don't speak to that witch." A diminutive dark-haired beauty approached and said, "Come sit with me instead." She inspected Kang from his toes to the top of his head. "You can bring your friend too." She tugged on the magician's hand.

"One moment, Martha. I'm looking for Francesca." Celwyn managed to say between the advances of the other witch.

"That cow? Upstairs." She pointed. "Come see me before you leave."

Celwyn disengaged himself from the red-headed witch. As they started up the steep steps to the next floor, he asked Kang, "If possible, can it be any noisier in here?" They detoured around an intertwined couple and a large black cat who refused to move out of their way. "It is amazing Jasper is still alive." The magician held out his fingers for the cat to smell. Jasper hissed. "And he still hates me."

They attained the landing, and Kang glanced over the bannister, seeing every nationality he knew and a few he did not. The woman in a kilt with extraordinarily hairy legs stood out, not because of her legs but the rings of tattoos on her naked back.

"Where do the witches come from?" Kang asked.

"Everywhere."

On the landing, they found another pair of witches, who eyed them speculatively. Whether with questionable intentions or other ideas, the magician didn't know. It had been relatively quiet for a moment, and then the bagpipes moaned, and the horns began to play. Kang shouted over them, "How do we know which room Francesca is in? I don't want any surprises."

"Good point. They do sometimes react." Celwyn approached the first door, knocked, and gently opened the door. A plate flew by his head and shattered against the opposite wall. He closed the door and approached a short man standing as still as a statue and wearing nothing except red long johns and thick eyeglasses.

"Excuse me." Celwyn bowed. "Could you direct us to Francesca? There are three other doors here."

The man didn't speak but pointed with his eyes to the staircase that led to the floor above. On the wall behind him, the hands of the clock moved backward. Kang began to feel off-center, not yet afraid, but close to it. Celwyn felt more irritated than anxious and started to climb the next set of stairs.

"I think you'll be safe while we're here, but don't eat or drink anything they offer."

Kang nodded and moved to the balustrade, where he could overlook the activity below. As the musicians played on, the couple on the stairs were still entwined—using every available limb—and the black cat had settled in for a nap. An Indian woman with enormous ears and arms disporting scores of gold bangles passed trays of food. The giggles and laughter following the trays reinforced Celwyn's warning. Kang counted. There were easily a hundred people below.

Celwyn passed a wall sconce that flickered on and off with his heartbeat. He'd noticed a spicy scent when they'd entered the house, and now it intensified, full of perfume and heat. This flight of stairs did not have kissing couples or inhospitable cats, and the landing contained no life on it at all. The music from below vibrated the floorboards.

Again the magician found four painted doors to choose from, and three of them stood open. He knocked on the fourth and went in. As the door closed behind him, the silence inside seemed as absolute as if he'd been atop a snowy peak. On the other side of the room, in front of a row of darkened windows, Francesca sat behind a monstrous desk. Dozens of ledgers had been stacked across the top, and a single Tiffany lamp illuminated her face in splotches of green and gold.

Celwyn crossed the room and took a seat in the lone chair. He leaned back and studied Francesca, seeing the same white-blonde hair piled high on her head and long earrings accentuating a graceful neck. Like a swan, and mean like one; the black eyes remained as annoyed as ever.

"What do you want, Jonas? I'm busy."

The magician opened his hands. "No greeting? No curiosity as to how I've been?"

"Please." Francesca regarded him like she would a bug on the floor. "We both know I'd pluck your eyes out if I could get away with it."

"In that case, I should tell you that I have a proposal that would benefit you."

Francesca leaned back in her chair. "Otherwise, you and that mechanical man can get out of my house before I turn him into a teapot."

Celwyn sighed. "Ever the eloquent business-woman, Francesca."

She threw down her pen, and ink splattered Celwyn's suit.

"Let's not pretend. I need money. These witches have no idea of what it takes to keep this house afloat in wine and blinis. What do you want?"

"I have a vampire problem." The magician stared at the ink on his best coat until it evaporated.

She threw back her head and laughed until tears rolled down her cheeks. When she finished, she dabbed her face, studied him, and said, "Why?

Knowing you, they couldn't sink a fang in your little finger."

"True. But I can't be in two places at once, and I have acquired responsibilities."

Francesca's smirk contained a high degree of malicious enjoyment. "Do tell. But make it quick. I'm busy."

"Children ... and others." Celwyn had no intention of letting Francesca into their lives any more than necessary, but enough to gain her sympathy and motherly instincts, if she had any. He doubted it.

"And the little tin man? You know that the wine he drank downstairs has a mushroom base."

"Not to worry," Celwyn replied, remembering Kang's internal receptacle that usually just held whiskey.

Qing poked his head out of the magician's coat. His eyes glittered when he saw Francesca's jewelry. "No." Celwyn pushed him back inside his coat and closed it.

"I'm not going to ask what that was."

"Probably for the best."

The witch opened a bottle of ink and refilled her pen. "So, you want my help with vampires."

"And there is also another entity not as easily dealt with," Celwyn told her about Jax.

"I can't guarantee a solution for this Jax, but we'll see." She made some notations on paper, scribbled more, and then named a price.

"It will be paid. My associate, Mr. Bartholomew, will bring your fee and our new address in a few days. Will that do?"

"Certainly."

"He will work with you concerning the details also."

Francesca asked, "Where will you be?"

"Hopefully immersed in music at the Opera House." He stood and kissed her hand, having to hunt for a spot without a large ring. "Thank you."

"You are charming, as usual. Don't thank me yet. If I have to rid the world of a few vampires, I will need more money to deal with the aftermath."

"Understood."

The door behind them opened, and a woman came in. As if on a string, Celwyn took a step toward her. Like a very satisfied cat, Francesca murmured, "Christina, may I present Mr. Jonas Celwyn. Jonas, this is my daughter."

Longer than it should have taken, and before Celwyn could speak, eyes as green as his own looked deep into him. They appeared beyond beautiful. His own were handsome, of course.

She had the white gold hair of her mother arranged down her back, and when she smiled, the magician felt himself teetering on the edge of a high cliff and beginning to slide off. He had to get out of there.

"Pleased to meet you. Excuse me." He bowed and ran out of the room.

Celwyn flew down the stairs and grabbed Kang by the arm. "Hurry!" He pulled Kang through the crowd of witches, consorts, other beings, and out the front door. They ran for the corner just as their hired carriage arrived. It was still moving as they piled in. The driver didn't argue and sped away up the street.

"What is wrong, Jonas?"

Celwyn caught his breath. "I was successful. We will have spells to protect the new residence from Jax and the vampires."

"Then what is the problem?" Kang held on as their carriage took a corner at high speed, nearly on two wheels.

Celwyn looked out the window and saw that they'd entered the old town commercial district. He tapped the glass and made a suggestion to the driver to slow down and take them to the train yard. Several miles away, the illuminated dome of the Opera House could be seen through the mist.

"I wanted to leave," Celwyn told Kang.

"It wasn't just that, my friend."

Minutes went by before Celwyn spoke.

"I fear I saw love again—and it terrifies me."

Chapter 36

AS THEY DEPARTED THE TRAIN YARD the next morning, Zander sat in Kang's lap to better see out the window. The new carriage felt cozy with all six of them inside.

"I want to sit up front with Edward. I like him," the boy said.

"We do too. You'll get a chance to ride up there soon," Bartholomew replied. To the others, he said, "Our first stop is not my favorite, but you should see it for comparison. The estate agent will meet us there."

Celwyn had relaxed since their adventure last night. Breakfast had come and gone without incident. Edward reported the guards would do fine without supervision and that they displayed a healthy respect for the generous amount of money they would be paid they would not let anyone pass by except one of their party or the crew. More good news: there had been no reports of voluptuous vampires. Perhaps

Mrs. Karras had given up, as Bartholomew had suggested. However, the magician doubted it.

"Will our new house have a classroom?" Zander asked.

Annabelle patted the pins in her hat, removed one, and replaced it again. "Yes. Would you like that too, Telly?"

The little girl sat across from the magician as they bounced along, and Celwyn regarded her. Although wearing a cheery yellow dress and ribbons, her cheeks appeared pale, and her hollowed eyes stayed down. He entered her thoughts and found exactly what he didn't want to see.

Everything was dark: no light, no hope. He went from room to room in her mind until he found one in the far back with a frail woman wearing a shawl and holding a little redheaded girl. She sang to the girl and held her close. It broke the magician's heart to know that this was the only memory Telly had of her mother. One by one, he filled the rooms with sunlight and vividly colored flowers. He added a treehouse full of dolls, a meadow of fairies, and a small unicorn.

Her expression brightened as she raised her eyes and nearly smiled. Celwyn hummed the tune he'd heard her mother singing and nodded at Kang to do the same. He sent a silent suggestion to Annabelle and Bartholomew to join in as well. Annabelle jumped, shot him an angry look, but began humming too.

Bartholomew didn't need urging, lending deep harmony to the others. Telly's tears poured down her cheeks, but they were happy tears over her smile.

She somehow seemed to know he had helped, for she crawled into Celwyn's lap and buried her face in his shoulder.

Bartholomew hummed the tune until they arrived in front of a very large manor in the middle of similar houses with extensive grounds. Celwyn frowned. Bartholomew had no way of knowing. Before Telly could turn around and see the ivy-covered walls—just like Van Maskolc's house—he removed all of the ivies.

Although a beautiful lawn lay in front of the house, the house didn't seem to welcome them. Kang regarded it, shook his head, and looked at Annabelle. She bit her lip, considering, and finally shook her head also.

"This is as I expected and hoped," Bartholomew said. "I'll ask the agent to follow us to the next house."

"May Telly and I go with you?" Zander asked.

Bartholomew held the door open. "Come along."

It took a bit of urging, but both children ran after him. When they were beyond hearing the conversation in the carriage, Annabelle glared at Celwyn. "If you *ever* go in my head again, unless there is an emergency, I will kick you where it hurts!"

Celwyn thought Kang enjoyed that ultimatum a bit too much. Kang saw his expression and smiled and smiled.

Throughout the drive to the next manor, a spark of happiness still lit up Telly's eyes as she gazed out the window with Zander, and they pointed out the dogs they saw. When Zander spied an organ grinder and his monkey, they both squealed and clapped.

"No monkeys," Annabelle told them. "They smell."

Celwyn sighed. The cycle seemed complete: Annabelle had settled into the role of mother completely. Necessary but depressing from his point of view. Bartholomew also cast a last wistful glance at the monkey's antics before saying, "This next house has most of what we want. I hope everyone likes it."

As they drove up the circular driveway to the front door, the magician enjoyed what he saw; tall towers, Georgian architecture with character, beautiful tall windows that sparkled. The manor house stood four stories high, plus a tower, and according to Bartholomew, it also had outbuildings and an ornate garden in back. He checked on Telly. Her eyes shone with delight as she inspected the house.

Kang asked, "Is the house empty?"

Bartholomew said, "It is supposed to be." He opened the door, and they filed inside.

Each room, from the kitchen to the salon, to the parlor and the conservatory, pleased Celwyn. The conservatory would most likely be his music room. A chattering estate agent joined them as they toured and began the climb to the upper floors. The children became more excited.

When they reached the second-floor landing, Zander ran from room to room. "Which is my room?" Telly followed him, comparing the rooms with her eyes.

Annabelle looked at the largest room and announced, "You can both have this room, and the one next door is our classroom. The playroom will be," she walked across the hallway and studied the room, "this one."

"Where is your room?" Telly asked with a small tremor they all heard.

"My room is going to be right next to yours, on the other side. And there is a door between the rooms." She pointed. "Look."

Telly dutifully walked back and forth. She nodded and seemed to calm down.

Kang said, "I believe mine must be upstairs."

"Mine also," Bartholomew added. "There is an office for you in the north tower, Professor."

"Excellent." Kang smiled. "I may spend my time gazing out the window instead of working."

"I'll occupy the conservatory downstairs if no one objects," Celwyn announced. Earlier, Kang and Bartholomew had agreed at least one of them should sleep on the first floor until the threats to them lessened.

Annabelle asked him, "Did you see the sunroom?

"I did. It would make a wonderful studio for Bartholomew."

The big man's jaw dropped open and he stared.

"Oils or pastels?" the magician asked, although he already knew.

Kang clapped Bartholomew on the back. "Don't fret about it. Just be glad he doesn't discover you want to be the emperor of Siam."

The magician dismissed the teasing with a smile. "We'll move in as soon as possible. Agreed?"

A chorus of agreement answered him, including the children's votes.

"What shall we call the new residence?" Celwyn asked.

Kang said, "I do not know. It is a bit German, hence the turrets, and Georgian with the recessed windows."

As they stood on the front porch of the new residence, Bartholomew said, "We need supplies, and I have other errands. Where should I meet you?"

Celwyn asked Edward for suggestions for luncheon.

"*Heißes Rindfleisch*. At the corner of Charles and Meigs. It has excellent fare. They have a butcher shop on the premises too."

"I'll be there by one o'clock." Bartholomew touched his hat and hurried east toward the market district.

Celwyn ushered everyone back into the carriage. As he did so, Kang pointed to a lone coach further down the street. He fished in his pocket for a coin.

"Heads—it is Jax," the magician said.

As Kang flipped the coin, he said, "Tails—it is Mrs. Pearse." The coin landed on the pavement. "Tails."

Celwyn wiggled a finger in the direction of the other coach, and its horses neighed. He raised a brow and said, "I wonder how superstitious the driver is." They watched as one of the horses turned toward its driver. When its lips curled back, they distinctly heard a deep and guttural sigh of "carrot." The driver jerked back in the seat and dropped the reins.

"Must you?" Kang complained but maintained a smile of amusement.

Again the horse turned to the driver. They couldn't hear what happened, but the driver bolted from the cab and ran up the street.

"The least you could do is provide the poor beast with a carrot," Kang said.

A bag of carrots appeared around both horses' necks.

Hours later, their carriage approached Charles Street rather slowly because the coach carried so many packages. Some lighter parcels had even been strapped to the back of one of the horses.

Annabelle watched the pedestrians. "It is interesting how they wear their hats here. A bit off-center. Hmm. I suppose it is attractive that way."

"Does this mean that you need to shop after luncheon?" Celwyn asked.

She sent him back a sarcastic look. "No. We need to arrange for so many things, and we haven't had a proper school lesson in days."

"I am very hungry, Uncle Jonas," Zander informed him.

Edward held the door as they exited the carriage. Kang asked him, "Will you join us?"

"I'd best watch the carriage. But *Heißes Rindfleisch* is known for their bratwurst if you care to bring me something for later."

The restaurant sported a glass front revealing dozens of patrons in both the main room and at the counter of the butcher shop next door. Carcasses hung in the window. Annabelle looked away in disgust. Telly walked up to the glass, cupping her hands to peer inside. Celwyn joined her. A half dozen white-coated butchers in blood-stained aprons moved between hanging carcasses, some of which still dripped blood. One of the men threw a cleaver at a carcass, embedding it to the hilt.

"Come along, Telly, this isn't appetizing," Celwyn steered her away, and Kang took her hand. Zander grabbed Celwyn's hand, and they entered the restaurant.

They were shown to a sizable table that Bartholomew had acquired. He greeted them with news of their moving arrangements and the likelihood that their new chef would join them soon.

"And I have surprises for both of you," he told the children. Celwyn enjoyed Zander's unrestrained curiosity and noticed Telly blinked several times with interest before her eyes turned dead again, and she looked away. The images he implanted seemed to last less and less each day. The magician provided new pictures of bunnies and puppies playing, and a smile touched her lips again.

"The visit with Dr. Ruttenberg can't occur too soon," he told Annabelle and Kang as Bartholomew teased Zander with hints about his surprise. "Look at her. She grows more morose by the day."

"We have to get her to understand that all is not lost. We love her, and we are her family," Kang said. "I'm sure Elizabeth will love her, too, when they meet."

Annabelle asked, "When will that be?"

"As soon as our enemies are gone."

The restaurant seemed to become even busier as the afternoon wore on. Patrons occupied every table, and most drank skeins of beer and enjoyed sandwiches piled high with ham and bratwurst. Polka music from a phonograph played in the background. The sights in the butcher shop next door could be responsible, but Telly refused to eat until Celwyn suggested that they have some soup together. Even with the fragrant broth in front of her, it took Annabelle a while to get her to try it.

When it was time for dessert, Annabelle asked Telly what she wanted.

"Perhaps the child does not want a dessert. So fattening."

The sultry voice came from over Celwyn's shoulder. He looked up and saw Mrs. Karras' bosom and then her face. As he began to react, Kang grabbed his wrist. "Children."

"Yes. Children. Such succulent little lambs," Mrs. Karras purred and touched Telly's hair with a gloved fingertip. "Who do we have here? My, what a beautiful child." A heavy diaphanous veil protected her against the afternoon sun, but the magician could see her features clearly—and the voracious gleam in her eyes.

"My name is Telly," the girl said as she looked at the jewelry the vampire wore. "Are you an evil queen?"

Throaty laughter met her question. "Of a sort." The vampire turned to Zander. "You seem to be an intelligent young man. With fire in your eye." She bent down until her lips were inches from his ear and whispered, "You suspect me of something?"

Bartholomew started to get up, but the magician motioned him to wait.

Zander's face grew red, and he reared back. "I know Uncle Jonas doesn't like you. You should leave."

"I suggest that you listen to him," the magician said. "Many things can happen without attracting attention." He stared at her earrings until the metal heated, becoming so hot the earrings began to melt.

The vampire batted at her ears and backed away. A second more, she hurried through the crowd and out the door.

"What is wrong with her?" Zander asked, trying to see where she went.

"A bee. A bee bit her, so she had to leave." Through the window, Celwyn watched with a broad smile as Mrs. Karras rushed by, pulling at her necklace, and throwing an earring in the air. "She is just someone we met on the train before we met you," the magician said. "Now, should we take our things home and pack for the new house?"

"Yes!" Zander said.

Annabelle still stared at where Mrs. Karras had run by and then gave a quick glance at the magician. "Yes. I have a couple more stops and so much to do. And I want to send a telegram. Patrick will be here soon."

As they approached their carriage, Kang handed Edward a packaged sandwich and said, "Did you see an attractive woman in red dress run out of the restaurant a few minutes ago?"

The driver sniffed his sandwich and said, "This smells as good as I remembered. Yes, she lit out of there like her feet were on fire."

"I'll try that next time." Celwyn regretted not going after her instead of finishing his luncheon. "That was one of the vampires we told you about." The magician couldn't help his amusement as he pictured Mrs. Karras in retreat. "Now you will be able to recognize her."

"Very interesting." Edward whistled. "I thought they'd look ugly or dirty. I'll be on guard."

Chapter 37

BY THE TIME THEY ARRIVED BACK AT the *Elizabeth*, the sun had set. Celwyn and Kang poured a set of whiskies with the expectation of a pleasant respite from the tiring day. Almost immediately, they heard the clash of pots from the kitchen, along with Sully bellowing.

"Should I assume from that racket that Sully has learned he will be our butler, not the chef, at Tellyhouse?" Kang inquired.

"I like that. Tellyhouse." Celwyn glanced at the kitchen door. "He didn't seem that unhappy when I told him. In fact, he said he'd be our coachmen if we needed him to." A pot hit the door and clattered to the floor.

"Excuse me." Kang crossed to the kitchen and opened the door slowly. When he returned, he said, "They are actually celebrating the move. Tossing the pots as they pack them."

"Indeed."

"Sully just can't see that well when he's aiming for the packing box. Every time he misses, he yells."

Celwyn considered his priorities and asked, "They're still making dinner later tonight and our breakfast tomorrow, I trust?"

"Breakfast will be oatmeal only." Kang sniffed the air. "I can't tell what dinner tonight will be, though. Should we be afraid?"

"I already am."

Bartholomew joined them and sat heavily in one of the club chairs. "I read a story to Telly and Zander. Telly seems to be all right, for the moment. Zander is so excited about moving he is ready to climb the walls."

Qing flew off Celwyn's shoulder to land on Bartholomew's arm and admire his gold chain. "This isn't yours," the big man told him.

"That won't stop him," Kang murmured, then yawned. "Do you know when our beds will arrive at the new residence?"

"Not soon." Bartholomew added, "We'll sleep here at least for the next two nights. But, the first load of our things will go over tomorrow. Some of the new sitting room furniture will be there by the afternoon."

"Staff?" Celwyn asked Kang.

"The message I received said the day after tomorrow." Kang smiled. "According to the agency, our new head housekeeper will make everyone sit up and behave. Perhaps even you, Jonas."

"Ha!"

"How are we going to explain the need for guards to her? Or about Jax?" Bartholomew asked.

"No clue. That reminds me." Celwyn fished in his coat, produced a piece of paper, and handed it to the big man. "That address is near the Staré Mêsto district. You won't find a carriage to take you all the way there. I'd suggest asking for as close as the driver dares to go. An acquaintance lives there that I've engaged to help us."

"How?"

Kang said as carefully as he could, "We need exterior protection, against vampires, on the new residence. The acquaintance is a witch, and she will help us."

Bartholomew gulped and turned to Celwyn.

"Francesca will supply a spell to guard the property. If you don't mind, you will be her contact." Celwyn's lips twitched. "She'll try to lay hands on you. She's a rather lusty witch." As he spoke, the magician blocked out thinking of Christina. He didn't need the distraction.

"A spell will keep the vampires away?"

"Yes. And perhaps more of them for Jax. I can do something similar on a magical level, but I have to be nearby to maintain it. With the spell, we are much more secure. We can come and go without worry. We can even have open windows without expecting to see something sitting on the sill and salivating over us."

"Edward may be able to help also," Bartholomew said.

"He isn't used to the strange goings-on yet," Kang objected.

Bartholomew looked at the kitchen and sniffed. "What is that *smell?*"

"Our dinner."

"It reminds me of cookouts in the Maasai Mara bush."

"What were you cooking?" Kang asked.

The big man shuddered. "During the droughts, nothing you'd ever want to eat."

In the distance, church bells cascaded in song, and through the train's windows, they could spy the top of the fourteenth-century buildings that lined the river.

"Prague is a most beautiful city," the Professor said.

Celwyn closed his eyes to reminisce. "It was the winter of 1708 the first time I saw those buildings. Some of the churches were built a bit later. A crazy tyrant ruled then, but he caused little harm. That is it!" The magician laughed.

"What is?" Kang inquired.

"That is who Prince Leo's costumes remind me of. Anyhow, Rákóczi's War of Independence between Rome and the Kurucs raged at the time, so I spent more time dodging soldiers than enjoying a summer afternoon lounging by the river in the charms of a woman." The magician drifted in a fond reverie until Kang spoke again.

"We don't know much about your coven of witches."

"What would you like to know? They have been in that house for a couple of hundred years and generally are left alone by the citizens of the city. They probably intentionally do a few unpleasant things periodically to insure their privacy."

"Oh." Bartholomew's brows drew together.

"Francesca has helped me before, as I have helped her." He smiled. "Most notably when her jilted lover built a bonfire in the woods and attempted to burn her to death."

"What happened?" Bartholomew asked.

Celwyn shrugged. "I killed him because he would have tried again. She is still angry with me for not letting her kill him. For spite, she arranged for me to be arrested."

"That seems to be a pattern with your acquaintances. But we'll have to finish the story another time." Kang drawled, "We have company."

The same small carriage they'd seen that morning drove along the path from the street and right up to the train. A different driver sat in the cab, and the open curtains revealed a very sour-looking Mrs. Pearse. She glowered at the train.

Celwyn threw back his drink. "It's been a long day."

"I'll inform Annabelle." Kang got to his feet.

Celwyn met the dowager at the steps leading to the dining car. As usual, she wore one of her flowered dresses and outlandish hats, but the fight seemed to have drained out of the old biddy. Like someone had poked a hole in her, she looked deflated and met his eye with a glare and a sigh.

"Mr. Celwyn, you have won. May I see my niece, please?"

Celwyn bowed. "Good evening. Please come inside." He took her arm and led her to the steps. With a glance over his shoulder, he added carrots to the bags around her horses' necks. After all, it neared the dinner hour.

The magician ushered the woman to the sofa as Annabelle and Bartholomew entered from the sleeping car. Annabelle's lips were set. She appeared pale as she approached. Mrs. Pearse stood again.

"Annabelle."

The younger woman got to the point. "Why are you here?"

The magician positioned himself next to Mrs. Pearse in case Annabelle lost control and decided to slap her after all. Kang remained on Annabelle's other side, close enough to grasp her arm. Bartholomew opted to stay out of the fray and had begun mixing drinks at the bar, half-turned to listen but far enough away to duck for cover if necessary.

It took a moment for Mrs. Pearse to answer, and her words surprised Celwyn. "I have decided to leave Prague and return to Philadelphia. You will be pleased to know that I will no longer try to arrange a proper marriage for you."

Bartholomew handed drinks around, and Celwyn again settled the older woman on the couch. She ignored the glass in her hand. Bartholomew took a chair next to Kang and frowned as Annabelle's color rose along with her words.

"That doesn't sound like you." Annabelle's eyes had developed enough heat to start a fire. "You have *never* listened to what I want."

"Since your parents died, you have been my responsibility." Mrs. Pearse's voice shrilled as her good behavior flew out the window. "How can you disgrace the family by living with these—these strangers? How can I present you as from a good family?"

Celwyn edged closer in the event Annabelle came out of her chair: it wasn't the time for magic that would have to be explained. Around them, the gloom of the evening had become complete. Even the stars couldn't penetrate the clouds. Mrs. Pearse's driver snoozed in his cab, hat over his eyes.

"They are my family," Annabelle ground out. "As are the children."

Mrs. Pearse fussed with her hat. "You don't know what you're doing."

"Yes, I do," Annabelle spoke clearly and held her temper. "The children need me."

"Where did you find them? What kind of parents did they have?"

When Annabelle would have answered, Kang interjected, "Bartholomew and Annabelle have done a splendid job with the children. We are also educating them."

The dowager gulped her drink and snorted, "That doesn't answer—"

"Would you like to meet them?" Celwyn asked. The question hung in the air as a true test of the woman's snobbery and humanity.

In a much less contentious voice, Mrs. Pearse bobbed her double chin and said, "Yes, I would. Thank you." To Annabelle, she added, "I would like to get to know them."

Annabelle's mouth opened and closed.

Celwyn stood. "I will bring them in. Please be aware that they are orphans who have been through trauma." As the magician walked toward the classroom, he congratulated himself. Perhaps he had a future as a diplomat instead of only being known for flinging ruffians into the air or off the top of churches.

Cold air met him as he opened the classroom door, and Qing screeched as he circled the room at high speed. The window stood wide open, and Zander leaned out of it.

"Telly, who is that?" The boy pointed. "He looks like a genie!"

In two strides, the magician was at the window. He illuminated the area revealing a horrific scene: Telly knelt in the dirt with a bloody knife in her hand, stabbing her stomach and crying softly. The vampire Delgado stood over her, whispering. He stopped when he saw Celwyn.

"Ah, Mr. Celwyn."

From his handsome head to his boots, Delgado looked the same, as if Celwyn had never seen him burn in Paris.

The vampire looked at the boy, turned to Celwyn, and said, "How adorable. Perhaps I will have him next." He sneered, "You can't stop me."

The magician's shock broke open. As he jumped to the ground, Celwyn flipped a hand, sending the vampire to the top of a tall tree. He knelt beside Telly and yelled to Zander, "Get the Professor!" At the same time, he directed a small explosion to the front of the train, intended to attract attention.

Bartholomew ran out, saw Celwyn, and came running.

"We must get her inside. Shield me."

The big man did so, and Celwyn stood again with Telly in his arms. But as he turned, he saw Delgado hopping off the last branch of the tree. The magician growled, and an iron cage surrounded the vampire. Edward came running, and the magician said, "Watch him."

As soon as he had seen her, Celwyn already knew the damage to Telly was more than he could fix, but he had to try. He laid her on the classroom floor as Kang slid to a stop on the other side of the girl. "Jonas, she's lost blood." He peeled back her bloodied shirt. "Too much blood. Can you help her?"

Celwyn had trouble seeing through the tears rolling down his face. "Not enough."

Kang saw Bartholomew. "Get my black bag from my room—" To Celwyn, "Can you at least stop the blood?"

Celwyn said, "I think so."

While the magician worked on Telly, Bartholomew returned with the bag. The automat muttered to himself again, "Too much blood." In a voice intended to encourage them, Kang said, "There is a procedure." He looked at the little girl's pale face and closed eyes. "We need to try."

Kang doused the big man's arm with alcohol and told Celwyn, "Leave that wound on her forearm open, and put this on it." He gave one end of a thin black tube to Bartholomew and the other to Celwyn. Working quickly, he sloshed alcohol on Bartholomew's hands and removed a flat tool from his bag. "Jonas... put a tourniquet on Bartholomew's arm. It will help this."

As he handed the tool to Bartholomew, he said, "Use that to hold back the skin if you need to. We're going to transfer your blood to Telly. Are you ready?"

"Yes."

Bartholomew grimaced as Kang cut into his arm and inserted the tube. While Celwyn held Telly, he put the other end into her open wound. "This isn't going to work," Kang told them. "Jonas, make the new blood go into her vein."

"I understand." The magician closed the wound around the tube in Telly's arm. He turned and did the same to Bartholomew's arm.

A sound like a dying cow came from the doorway as Mrs. Pearse swayed and then swooned. Annabelle had been right behind her and caught her. From the other side of the closed-door, Zander demanded to see Telly. Celwyn sent him a strong suggestion to calm down and that Telly would be all right. The pounding stopped.

With blood covering their arms and shirts, they sat in a ring around the little girl like distorted players in a horrific scene. Celwyn couldn't see any change in Telly: she still wasn't breathing, and the tint of her cheeks seemed to fade as he watched. "How long do we do this?" he asked Kang.

"Until the color comes back to her face. Were you able to repair her wounds?"

Bartholomew stroked her hair with his free hand. "Poor, poor Telly," he murmured and began to hum the lullaby he hummed before to her as a single tear escaped and ran down his cheek. From the doorway, Annabelle stood as still as a statue, unblinking and unmoving.

Celwyn said, "I repaired her wounds as much as I could. But nothing is working yet inside her—as it should. Will she live?" he asked Kang, who fussed with the connections to the tube.

"I think so."

"Then I'll be back in a moment." The magician was up and through the window in one leap.

Before he reached the cage where he had trapped Delgado, he could hear the metal rattling and roar of the vampire as he shook the cage hard. The cage door hung by one hinge, and at the sight of Celwyn, he snarled. Edward had his pistol trained on the vampire. Annabelle appeared at the window long enough to see what caused the noise and turned away.

The magician wrapped more iron bars around the cage and then raised it off the ground and twirled it so fast it blurred. The cage spun faster as it hovered above the trees. Edward yelled, and something jumped on Celwyn's back and scraped nails across his face. He shook Mrs. Karras off and kicked her far down the street. But she'd broken his concentration.

The cage crashed to the ground, and Delgado broke free. As he began to run, Celwyn slammed him down and kept slamming him until he felt Sully's hand on his arm.

"The Professor said to come back. Telly is dead."

Chapter 38

THE PAIN OF ANNABELLE'S WAILS echoed from the train.

When the magician ran back inside the hallway, he found Zander solemnly waiting by the classroom door like a little tin soldier. The boy's lips trembled as he tried not to cry. "That genie man told her to stab herself. Like the men at the restaurant did to the cows." Tears ran down his face. "He told her she would feel better if she did. He laughed... laughed as she did it."

Celwyn lifted him into his arms and hugged him close. For minutes Zander sobbed into his shoulder, and when he quieted, the magician motioned for Edward to take him. He closed the door softly behind him as he entered the classroom. Bartholomew still sat on the floor, covered in blood. He ripped the tube from his arm and threw it in the corner as he started to sob.

Next to him, Annabelle cradled Telly's body in her arms and wept. Kang patted her arm and turned a devastated face to the magician. Celwyn felt an unfathomable sadness at the deep despair in his friend and the anguish in Annabelle and the big man. He laid a hand on Kang's shoulder and, without touching him, wiped away the blood smear on his chin. His eyes met Bartholomew's, and they exchanged a silent sigh of grief.

Celwyn squatted in front of Annabelle and held her hand. "I'm so very sorry." She nodded and cried harder.

"What happened?" the magician asked.

Kang's voice was dead. "It didn't work. She died."

Celwyn inhaled and, when he could speak again, said, "Zander tells me that Delgado talked to Telly through the window." He had decided Annabelle needed to know the entire story so that there would be no argument about the moment when Delgado was punished. "Zander says that Delgado laughed when he told her to stab herself. I tell you this so that you'll understand when I dispose of him."

Annabelle nodded and sobbed.

"If Telly wasn't deep in despair, she would have resisted," Kang told Annabelle. "She knew you loved her."

Celwyn looked out the window. Delgado *would* pay. What happened was horrible, and he knew with certainty that the vampire would have just killed the child outright if he hadn't enjoyed manipulating her distress.

"Who—who is Delgado?" Mrs. Pearse asked.

The magician had forgotten the old woman. She sat in the corner, wringing her hands, looking like she had no idea what to do.

"A bad man. I chased him away," Celwyn said. "For now."

The police arrived before midnight. Kang handled the explanations and answered their questions. How he explained Telly's state of mind and how he kept the origins of their association secret, Celwyn didn't know.

Before the arrival of the *polizei,* Celwyn had decided there would be a better time and more appropriate place to deal with Delgado. Right now, all he could think of was Telly. He'd brought Edward back inside and dissolved the protective field encircling the vampire. Delgado had found himself on the sidewalk without restraint. In seconds he'd disappeared into the night.

A morose cloud of sadness had already settled over the train, smothering all joy and hope. As he stood talking to the police, Kang discounted the reports of the spinning cage and noise from the vampire. Annabelle's wails grew louder as the coroner's wagon left with the girl's body. When Kang returned to the dining room, Celwyn assessed his friend's mood: the automat seemed as solid as the logic they counted on but weary and resolute.

"We need to leave the train. We can't sleep here," Celwyn said as he drank, not sipped, whiskey and contemplated his glass.

Kang picked up the glass waiting for him and sat down with a deep sigh. Before the police arrived, Mrs. Pearse had been packed into her carriage by Bartholomew. Annabelle had embraced her before she took Zander's hand, and they walked back to the train. Now the boy sat with them at the dining room table, nibbling a sandwich, frightened eyes fixed on the door leading to the sleeping cars and classroom.

It had only taken seconds for Celwyn to clean the blood from the classroom, but he hadn't had the heart to remove Telly's dolls and toys. Would Zander's grief be worse with them there? Should they grieve and heal first, or was revenge a more appropriate response? Despite his earlier decision to wait, his hands flexed as he thought.

"Stop growling in your throat," Kang told him. "There will be time for that later." He nodded at Zander.

Celwyn agreed. He took a deep breath: there were questions he must ask while the memories were fresh. He looked at Zander. "Did the genie man come inside?"

Zander's lips moved several times before he spoke, "No. He danced outside and waved to us. Telly saw him, and she opened the window to talk to him."

Celwyn rubbed his face. He should have watched her more closely. More kittens, more birds, unicorns, and puppies. More flowers and dolls and fairies. It should have been enough. He winced, missing her little smile and the way she would hug his neck.

"We need to confer," Kang said with a look at Zander.

"We'll need the others too." The magician sent Edward, Sully, and the rest of the crew unheard suggestions to come to the dining room.

The conductor arrived wearing a nightcap and carrying a book. Sully and the porters approached them looking confused, and Ricardo's eyes bounced from side to side with fear. Celwyn assumed that all of them had probably seen or heard Delgado in the cage.

"Did someone want me here?" Sully rubbed his eyes. His shirt was only part-way tucked into his trousers. Celwyn finished the job for him and combed what remained of his hair.

"Edward, sit down, please," Celwyn said as he covered what Zander could hear. One of his books about farm animals appeared next to the boy's hand. Zander picked it up and managed a smile for Annabelle.

When everyone quieted, Celwyn spoke.

"You all heard the uproar here this evening."

"Yes, Sir," the conductor said. "We saw the police leaving."

Sully piped up. "And the Coroner's wagon."

The conductor shot him a look intended to stifle him. "Please go on, Sir."

"Telly died by her own hand a few hours ago," Celwyn told them.

Annabelle stifled a sob and whispered, "We will miss her very much."

"I am so sorry, Miss," Edward said.

Ricardo blinked away tears, and Selkirk stood at attention, watching Celwyn. Sully said, "Such a nice little girl. I'm very sorry."

"We all are," the conductor said. "How can we help?"

"As you know, we were moving into the city soon. Because of her death, we'll move sooner." He inhaled to try to control his anger which had returned. "There are two carts in the yard next to the train. Let's finish packing and go."

After more discussion, the crew left the room. When the door closed behind them, Bartholomew noted, "We do not have carts."

"We do now." Celwyn carried a sleeping Zander to the sofa and covered him with a blanket and deeper slumber. He glanced outside and back again. "Do you all agree that the boy shouldn't see where she died or the classroom again? If you do, we need to pack up the rest of the classroom and get him to the new residence before he wakes up again."

"I'll make sure he gets there safely," Edward and Bartholomew said together.

"Thank you," Annabelle murmured through her tears.

At the first light of dawn, Edward harnessed the horses to an overloaded cart. Toys poked out of boxes, and an empty birdcage balanced on top of a pile of trunks. Much of the packing had been courtesy of Celwyn's magic when the crew wasn't watching. As Edward pulled away toward Klouster Street, Ricardo sat beside him in the driver's perch and cast a nervous glance back at the train.

The Professor handed Celwyn a flask as they stood in the empty yard between the *Elizabeth* and the street.

"Coffee?" Celwyn asked, remembering other flasks Kang had offered him in the past. "It has been a horrible night."

Kang nodded. "You know, pounding the vampire into the pavement didn't kill him."

"It helped me," Celwyn grated and crushed the flask. Coffee dripped off his fingers. "I can't forgive myself for not seeing how distraught she was and what she would do." He raised his fists, and the entire train shook as the bar glasses started to fall.

"You'll wake the boy," Kang warned.

The train stopped shaking, but it took several moments before the magician spoke again.

"As soon as we're safely installed at Tellyhouse, I will find the vampires," Celwyn promised. "And this time, there will be no question that they will be gone."

"Is Delgado afraid of you?"

Celwyn didn't smile as he laughed. "He should be. Vampires are strong, but I can manipulate and evade most of them. And they know it." The magician again saw Telly's lifeless body on the floor of the classroom, and his own personal darkness descended. "So, they attack what I love. Do you know what Delgado did last night?"

Kang shook his head.

"Before Zander slept, I explored his memory. Delgado was in *our* yard, hovering outside the children's window."

Kang nodded. "Ah. That is why Zander says he saw a genie."

"Yes. Then Delgado talked Telly into opening the window and," Celwyn's voice grew colder, "he told Telly that he could make her feel better. He even helped her out the window."

"Did he give her the knife?"

Celwyn finished crushing the flask and threw it beyond the trees. "Yes, and he told her to use it like the man in the butcher shop did. Told her she could stop what scared her if she cut herself open and *let it out*!" Tears ran down the magician's face.

Kang put a hand on the magician's shoulder. "My friend, she would have done something like this sooner or later unless Doctor Ruttenberg was able to help her."

Celwyn took out his handkerchief and wiped his eyes. "Let us talk about what we will do now. What is the aftermath? The vampires will continue to buzz around us like nasty flies until I confront them again."

As they walked back inside the train, Kang asked, "Where is Bartholomew?" Celwyn held the door and followed Kang into the dining room. Zander still slept soundly on the sofa. The magician blinked and cleaned up the broken glass by the bar.

"He is on his way across the city with a purse of coins to visit Francesca. We'll need her protection spell sooner than expected." Celwyn almost smiled.

"She hates the light of dawn. He should be safe enough: he is personable and persuasive."

Kang shuddered. "I remember that coven well. I hope he can be quick when he has to be."

Celwyn's manner turned somber. "When you tried to give Telly blood, should it have saved her?"

"Yes. The process is experimental, but it should have worked."

"Yet, it did not."

"Even if it was the wrong kind of blood, she would have held on until we could switch to a different one." Kang frowned. "I couldn't use yours, for obvious reasons, but I would have tried the conductor's, or Annabelle's, next."

Celwyn sat down and put his head in his hands. Into the melancholy, Kang spoke softly, afraid Annabelle would hear if she walked in.

"Long ago, I felt the inevitability, the futility of Telly's distress. Like I said, she would have done this tomorrow, if not last night."

"You're trying to say that she would have done it even without Delgado's urging." Celwyn raised his face, again wet with tears. He looked outside, and with a flick of his hand, lightning exploded across the sky. "*Damn it!*"

"Don't let your rage blind you, or make you careless," Kang warned. "We need clear heads. Clear plans."

"I need music."

Moments later, from the rear of the train, the pianoforte disgorged a loud and angry torrent. Cascading marches of power and loss doubled on top of each other. Soon they were joined by a chorus of cymbals and thundering drums. Lightning lit up the sky again, and into the melee, a forlorn horn played a requiem for the dead.

Chapter 39

LONG BEFORE NOON, BARTHOLOMEW arrived at the rear of Tellyhouse smelling strongly of perfume but otherwise unharmed from his trip to the coven. He glanced at the stables, gazebo, and vast garden.

"I must say, it is in our favor that the witches dislike vampires. The spell will be in place by nightfall." The big man gazed at the third and fourth story windows of the new residence. "It will prevent entry, except through the front door at night. During the day, one of us will use the code word 'December' to disable the spell. At night, we use it backward, 'rebmeced' to turn the spell on again. The spell will only respond to the three of us."

"I don't want Annabelle to start thinking of the witches as another danger," Celwyn stated. "She needs to grieve in peace."

Before the arrival of the big man, Kang and the others took a break from unloading boxes to smoke. Celwyn lit his pipe as they stood in the back garden, watching the staff continue to unload another cart. Through an open window in the parlor, they observed Annabelle supervising the furniture delivery. Every so often, she would cross to the front windows and stare at nothing for several minutes.

"Telly would have loved these flowers." Bartholomew pointed to the tiered beds of hyacinths, roses, and daisies. Zander left off watching the unloading of the cart to join them. "Would you like to help me pick some of these?" the big man asked and handed him a basket. As they began picking flowers, Kang and Celwyn walked up the driveway where Zander couldn't hear them.

"I want to get everything back to normal as soon as possible." Celwyn glanced inside again to where Annabelle stood in a corner, again staring at nothing.

Kang nodded. "The staff will be here tomorrow at the latest, but I really wish—"

A carriage rattled to a stop in front of the house, and a coachman began unloading trunks and boxes.

"That isn't our carriage, and I don't recognize those trunks," Kang said.

After the driver finished unloading the trunks, he opened the carriage door.

One of the largest women Celwyn had ever seen alighted from the carriage in serviceable shoes and a plain woolen dress. The springs on the coach frame stretched, creaked, and then settled again. She stood well over six feet tall, with the shoulder breadth of a horse and a halo of chestnut curls surrounding her pleasant face.

"She looks sweet," Kang murmured as they approached.

"She could lift the coach with one hand," Celwyn murmured back as they reached the end of the driveway. "Which may prove useful."

"Good afternoon. Professor Kang?" her voice sounded as stern as a schoolmarm, yet melodious.

"Yes. Good afternoon, Mam." He bowed.

"To you also," she looked at the magician. "You must be Mr. Celwyn. I am Mrs. Polly Thomas, your new head housekeeper. You may call me Mrs. Thomas."

They heard the front door open behind them. Sully stood there, open-mouthed. As Kang introduced them, Celwyn enjoyed a brief respite from his grief. The top of Sully's head did not quite reach Mrs. Thomas' shoulder, putting him on eye level with her bosom. He struggled to look at her face as he addressed her.

"Angus Sully, at your service. I am the butler. Ricardo here," he pulled him forward by his collar, "is our footman and whatever is needed. Say hello to the nice Mrs. Thomas."

Ricardo did his best to bow and maintain the formal tone of the situation. "Pleased to meet you."

"And here is Selkirk. Say hello to Mrs. Thomas, boy," Sully motioned the other man forward.

Mrs. Thomas had stepped into the foyer and looked at them with a fixed smile. She ran a finger across the windowsill and frowned. To Kang, she said, "Sir, is this all the staff there is? A house this size will need two dozen or more staff."

The Professor stepped up, and his voice had a mix of persuasion and authority. "We're hoping that you'll contract the cleaning staff to come in and out but not reside at the house."

"I see." Her tone did not see.

While they spoke, Sully stared at Mrs. Thomas with the kind of fascination that said she might be the Virgin Mary ... but possibly a harlot. He picked up one of her trunks and, without taking his eyes off her, said, "Follow me, please." They stepped around Annabelle's furniture movers and down the hall.

"We don't have the beds yet," Bartholomew confided as they entered the parlor.

With a flip of his hand, Celwyn said, "I just took care of it for tonight." A phonograph appeared in the corner under the windows, and soft chamber music filled the parlor. "Who are your favorite composers?" he asked the big man and Kang.

New charcoal drawings of Mozart and Rachmaninoff appeared on the walls. Bartholomew looked at them, blinked, smiled, and didn't say a word.

"Bach. He thinks mathematically." The automat winked and lowered his voice. "I wonder how Mrs. Thomas will react to your, uh, talents, Jonas."

"Whatever do you mean?" The magician waved a hand, and twin ballerinas flitted across the ceiling, waltzing and twirling to Bach. One of them had Kang's face, and the other Bartholomew's.

After enjoying the performance for a moment, Bartholomew chuckled. "I dance very well. My, how tiny my shoes are." As they laughed, Kang monitored the door until the ballerinas faded again.

"We should find an establishment that will prepare a large meal for us to take back here. Annabelle is probably exhausted, and the kitchen has not been set up yet." Kang rubbed his stomach. "I'm thinking of a nice shepherd's pie."

"An excellent idea," Celwyn said.

"With a spice cake for dessert," the big man said.

Hours later, they sat at the dining table enjoying a hot meal. Mrs. Thomas wouldn't allow Sully, Edward, or the rest of the staff to join them, saying it wasn't proper even if the Professor and the others didn't know it. The housekeeper had a no-nonsense way of stating how things would be. She also made a point of not addressing Bartholomew directly as she served the post-dinner coffee.

After Zander had been excused to read in the parlor, Annabelle put down her cup and said, "Mrs. Thomas, have you ever been to America? Or Spain? Or countries other than England?"

The older woman replaced the coffee pot on the tray and said, "No, Miss. Just the area by Belgravia in London, and then here in Prague with my late mistress. Why?"

"It could be that you haven't noticed," Annabelle chose her words as carefully as if she were building a castle of eggshells, "But Mr. Bartholomew is an equal and integral part of our family. He is a dear friend and as brave as can be. His skin color is not important."

Kang said, "Please think of him as you do us."

Celwyn watched as a delicate pink crept up her neck and diffused Mrs. Thomas' face.

"I've never seen a colored man before," Mrs. Thomas told them and turned to the big man, addressing him directly this time, "No offense intended."

"At the risk of embarrassing him, Bartholomew is a very good man," Celwyn said. "Please take any problems to him as you would the rest of us."

"I will do that, Sir." She curtsied and marched out of the room.

Celwyn rubbed his hands together. "All right, shall we plan our errands for tomorrow? It is either that, or I spend the evening hunting vampires."

"Ever the clown, Jonas," Kang said.

Qing flew by from the parlor into the hallway and toward the kitchen. Kang jumped to his feet and ran after the bird.

For the first time since Telly died, Bartholomew laughed.

Kang called back, "I got him!"

The next morning, Celwyn escorted Annabelle down the steps of the porch and to the carriage. From above, Zander tapped on the window and waved.

"He only knows that I am bringing him a treat, not arranging Telly's funeral," Annabelle murmured as she gathered her skirts and stepped into the cab.

Celwyn settled on the seat opposite and said, "The Professor will entertain him, and I imagine there will be time for a wood carving lesson too."

Edward closed the carriage door behind Bartholomew, who got comfortable with a city map on his knee. The big man said, "After the funeral parlor, it would be best if I stop at the market and order things to be delivered. With luck, our chef will have arrived, and we will have a proper dinner this evening. It would be good for Zander to get into a routine again."

"Last night, he had a nightmare," Annabelle said.

"Do you want us to talk with him?" Kang asked as the carriage rolled forward down the driveway.

She pursed her lips. "Not yet. Let's see if it continues. This is all so horrible—" Her tears began again.

The rhythmic clopping of the horses' hooves became a soothing background as they traveled through the city. Their first stop was the Opera House, where they retrieved messages. Celwyn also left their new address for any future telegrams or messages. As the magician settled into the carriage again, with a smile, he handed a dozen envelopes to Annabelle. "Patrick certainly has time on his hands."

Annabelle's tears had dried, and she blushed prettily as she dug into the sheaf of papers. "He will be here soon."

"I will be glad to see him, but I wish it was under happier circumstances," Bartholomew said.

Annabelle's eyes clouded, and she forced cheer into her voice. "We'll do our best. Now that we have our house, will you be spending more time there or at the Opera House?" Annabelle asked Celwyn.

"I'm working on music that I hope to see produced there." The magician didn't directly answer her question. He must first eliminate the vampires, and he wasn't sure how long it would take. As he thought, a germ of an idea came to him, connecting everything that should be done and everything he wanted to do.

"I've heard the pianoforte at night, faintly," Bartholomew said.

Celwyn watched the street. "I doubt it is faint sounding for our neighbors, but I can make it tolerable for them. Ah," the carriage pulled to the curb, and he added, "Here is the flower shop. Telly always loved white flowers."

Moments later, the bell on the shop door tinkled as Celwyn closed it and turned.

Francesca's daughter, Christina, stood in front of him. She smiled and held a red rose to her nose. He couldn't stop staring, and he also couldn't help the hesitation before he found his voice and bowed.

"Good morning, Miss Christina. I trust your mother is well?"

She touched the rose to her lips, and Celwyn lost all other thoughts as he watched her, wondering if the petal was as soft as her lips, remembering the wisdom of the bard Shakespeare: *Women speak two languages—one of which is verbal.*

As they stared at each other, Christina murmured, "She is well, and I'm sure she sends her regards to Mr. Bartholomew." Annabelle and Bartholomew had joined them between the barrels of gladiolas and roses.

"My Uncle Celwyn seems a bit tongue-tied." Her lips twitched in amusement. "I am Annabelle Pearse Edmunds. Do I know your mother?"

Celwyn inserted, "This is my ward, Annabelle." He turned to her. "No, you do not."

With her own secret smile, Christina murmured, "Pleased to meet you." She glanced at the magician. "I assumed you were affianced to Mr. Celwyn."

The magician heard how Christina had spoken the word "affianced," and his emotions became even more confused.

Annabelle scoffed and repeated it. "Affianced? No, Uncle Celwyn and Bartholomew are my protectors. Along with the Professor, they are my friends." Her eyes lost their momentary luster. "Please excuse us. We're here to arrange flowers for a funeral."

Christina placed a hand on Annabelle's and said, "I know what it is like to lose someone. Please accept my condolences."

Chapter 40

WHEN THEIR CARRIAGE RETURNED to Tellyhouse hours later, Celwyn took the opportunity to observe the neighborhood, noting the placement of the other stately homes, the horses and carriages, impressive gardens, and the people out and about on the street. As their coach traveled up the circular drive and stopped in front of Tellyhouse, they saw Zander's face pressed against the second-story window.

"The little one knows we have returned." Bartholomew held a toy giraffe in his hands and a smile on his face.

Sully met them at the door in a new suit and gloves and pulled on the backside of his pleated pants. "Here, let me help you with those, Miss Annabelle." As he sat the packages on the hall table, he shot an irritated and furtive glance toward the kitchen like a squirrel who found his acorns stolen by a raccoon. Celwyn noted the man's whiskers had been trimmed, and he smelled like soap. Curious, he entered Sully's thoughts, hearing, "...*damn Frenchie ... thinks he's better than me ... damn Frenchie ... bloody* cachon..." And more of the same.

In an aside to Kang, the magician said, "I think our chef has arrived."

They walked halfway up the hall. Bartholomew stopped and sniffed. The others did, also, and exchanged hopeful looks.

"That smells heavenly!" Annabelle exclaimed.

"French onion soup!" Celwyn said.

"Fresh bread!" Kang added.

They rushed down the hall to the kitchen door. It opened, and Selkirk ran out, followed by a soup pot that bounced off the door.

"Out! Out, you cretin!"

Kang pushed the door open a few inches, and they peered inside. Behind sacks of flour and piles of vegetables, Mrs. Thomas loomed over a thin man with quick black eyes and very large ears. He saw them and grabbed a pot, ready to throw it. Mrs. Thomas caught his wrist and removed the pot. "Those are your employers."

"I do not care!"

"Please—"

"No one is allowed in my kitchen except you, Mon Cherie." The chef turned to Mrs. Thomas, kissing her hand, "Only you, Madam, can I allow here."

Celwyn sniffed the air again. Never had he smelled such heavenly soup. "Allow her to introduce us, at least."

Mrs. Thomas steered the man toward the door and said, "Miss Annabelle, Mr. Bartholomew, Mr. Celwyn, and Professor, allow me to present our chef, Monsieur Lucien, lately of Toulouse and Marseilles." Mrs. Thomas didn't tolerate disobedience. "Say 'hello.'"

"For you, I shall." The man made a quick bow, his long hair falling forward over his eyes. "I am pleased to meet you. Now, please get out of my kitchen. Luncheon will be served shortly."

As everyone trooped back up the hall and into the parlor, Mrs. Thomas followed. Zander met them at the door and hugged Kang, stopped for a kiss from Annabelle and Celwyn, and then jumped into Bartholomew's arms.

Mrs. Thomas put her hands on her hips and announced, "My apologies. Messr. Lucien is—excitable. He has taken a dislike to Selkirk but seems to tolerate Ricardo. It may be a few days until things are running smoothly."

"We trust your judgement, Mrs. Thomas," Kang assured her.

"For anything that involves the household staff, all details are in your capable hands, Mrs. Thomas." Celwyn thought again how very glad it was so.

She nodded. "Thank you. Miss Annabelle, I suggest that we hire a kitchen maid forthwith to help Ricardo. She will have a job scrubbing those ovens every day."

"As my Uncle said, whatever you suggest will be fine," Annabelle said. "What else can we help you with?"

"There are no beds in this house. I'm too old to sleep on the floor."

Celwyn winced. He had forgotten to reinforce the magic around the beds he'd temporarily provided. He sent a pointed look at Annabelle. She interpreted it and nodded.

"They arrive today, and the linens and other dry goods also," Annabelle assured her.

With a glare at the men, Mrs. Thomas said, "Thank goodness someone has some common sense. Is Mr. Sully available? Someone needs to help me with the rest of the shopping for the larder."

Kang sat down and tried to smile. "As long as he doesn't pick out the vegetables and meats." He glanced around at the box-filled room. "If you can wait a few days, we'll unpack, and you will be better able to determine what is still required."

"I understand." Mrs. Thomas folded her arms and looked down at them. "What is this I hear about a child passing away?"

Annabelle sniffed and reached for her handkerchief. Bartholomew threw a look of concern at her and said, "Our ward, Miss Telly, died a few days ago. Zander was very close to her."

"You poor thing." Mrs. Thomas embraced Annabelle and drew Zander into her arms. "Are you all right, honey?"

Zander's eyes displayed a layer of sadness, but he said, "Yes, Ma'am... I could use a cookie, though. It would make me feel better."

The housekeeper put him down and pretended to box his ears. "Go on with you. Maybe after your lunch." She turned to the magician. "Have you made arrangements for the delivery of milk? For coal or oil?"

They exchanged looks. "No."

"I'll assume that there hasn't been a bread delivery arranged either. I'd best get to work on these things." She marched out, wide hips swinging. As she reached the door, she stopped so fast the carpet under her feet curled. "What is *that*?"

Qing had chosen that moment to fly off the top of the armoire and circle the room. As he flew toward her, Mrs. Thomas screeched, threw up her apron, and ran.

In an instant, Annabelle was up and following her. "Do something about that damn bird," she called over her shoulder.

Zander and Bartholomew exchanged a look and began edging toward the door. Celwyn heard their thoughts and, when he stopped laughing, told Kang, "We'd better hope they find the baby snake they lost upstairs before Annabelle or Mrs. Thomas finds it."

"Or Qing gets it. He'd love to drop it down the front of Mrs. Thomas's dress."

"And then dive after it to retrieve it."

An hour later, Celwyn decided that he was participating in a true religious experience. Soft light bathed them as they sat at the dining table, with Ricardo serving and Mrs. Thomas at attention in the corner.

"This is our reward after what we endured on the train." Celwyn sipped soup, afraid the first taste had been only a cruel tease. But it remained wonderful.

"The bread is crusty, yeasty, and heavenly." Bartholomew savored a bite and chewed.

"Yes, it is," Annabelle agreed. "But the au jus is even more elegant."

Kang asked Mrs. Thomas, "Could you ask Chef to come in so that we may compliment him?"

She whirled and left. After a few moments, punctuated by the clatter of spoons and moans of bliss, Mrs. Thomas pushed a protesting Lucien into the room.

"Chef Lucien," Celwyn spoke with the reverence the man deserved, "we wanted to thank you. It is our honor to have you cook for us."

"But of course." Lucien took off his torque and straightened his white jacket. "And you should expect excellent meals from Lucien Pascal! Now, I must attend to dinner." He backed away, and Mrs. Thomas followed him out with a wary eye aimed at the top of the armoire.

Bartholomew asked, "Where is Qing?"

Celwyn opened his afternoon coat, "Here." Qing poked his head out and squeaked at Kang.

"I swear that bird enjoys playing games." Annabelle eyed him and continued to eat.

"We can't afford to lose Mrs. Thomas," Celwyn said. "And we have yet to tell her about our enemies."

"Please stop trying to ruin my luncheon, Jonas," Kang murmured. "I'd almost forgotten about the danger since we're used to it."

Zander stopped eating long enough to ask, "Who are our enemies?"

Annabelle regarded Bartholomew and the others. "Well? You three are in charge of that department."

Celwyn made sure he had Zander's complete attention before speaking. "If you ever see that genie man you saw the night Telly died, run away to us. If you can't find us, just run. Do you understand?" The boy nodded. "Don't talk to him. Run." He made this a strong suggestion in Zander's mind.

"There are also friends of the genie man." Bartholomew asked him, "Remember the woman with the big red lips at our dinner the other night? The one you didn't like?"

"The one who had bees in her ears?"

"Yes. She is a friend of the genie man. She is evil, too, and would hurt you. Any of the genie man's friends will hurt you." At his nod, Celwyn asked, "So, what will you do if you see them?"

"Run! To you!" Zander smiled. "No one will hurt me. I have you and my sword!"

"This is serious," Annabelle told him.

"Yes, Ma'am."

"Good grief, I feel old," she said.

Kang studied her for a moment and said, "We could invite your aunt to dinner now that we're off the train."

She hesitated and then said, "I don't know what to do about her." Ricardo arrived with the cheese tray as Mrs. Thomas brought in the coffee service cart. Annabelle made a selection from the tray. "I want to try to have a relationship again. I miss her."

"But?" Kang asked.

"She wouldn't understand about Uncle Celwyn's talents, and even less would she understand," she glanced at Zander, who'd been excused to play with the kitten, "the genie man." She looked at the armoire. "Can you imagine what she would do if she came face to face with that damn bird?"

Bartholomew said, "It would be safest if she did go back to Philadelphia, if you don't mind me saying so."

Annabelle patted his hand. "I never mind your suggestions. But..." she hesitated and then said nothing.

"This is your decision," Kang said. "I would like to bring Elizabeth here from Singapore but will not do so as long as our 'admirers' continue to bother us."

The magician stood. "Very well. Please excuse me. I'll be at the pianoforte the rest of the afternoon."

"And you," Annabelle called to Zander as he ran by with the kitten in pursuit, "will be in class. Bartholomew is ready with your geography."

"I'm still savoring our wonderful luncheon at the moment," Kang said. "However, I'll be there by three for the numbers lesson."

Chapter 41

HOURS LATER, CELWYN FINISHED A long run at the pianoforte with a flourish of cascading chords. He closed his eyes and savored the totality of the notes that still rang through his head, heart, and bones. The air in the room equalized back to the normal vibrations both seen and unseen, and he became aware of quiet noise from outside the house: the barking of a dog, the shrill complaining of the maid next door, and even more faintly, the clanking of pots in his own kitchen.

He stood and stretched. Up the stairs he climbed, still in a state of musical bliss. He bypassed the landing across from the classroom, choosing to not disturb Bartholomew's speech about the monks of Tibet and the temples in Chiang Rae. Zander's lessons were far more than just geography. The magician started up the next flight to visit the automat.

As he neared the third-floor landing, he glanced through the window, and a mature oak tree just outside blocked his view. He froze and turned to fully face the window.

A body hung from one of the high branches, swaying in the breeze, with a noose tied around its neck.

Celwyn shattered the window and straddled the sill. Glass tinkled to the paving stones far below as he jumped onto the branch and shimmied toward the body.

The magician reached the corpse, turning it to face him. He breathed again: it was a crude effigy of Kang, but it wasn't Kang.

A demonic cackle came from the branches above, and then another noose fell over his head. Celwyn reached to knock it off, but it tightened fast as Delgado jumped from the treetop down three stories to the ground. The momentum and change in weight yanked the magician to the top of the tree as he fought to remove the noose. He couldn't breathe. His vision blackened ... and he knew he was near passing out.

As the darkness rose up to meet him, Celwyn did the most expedient thing he could think of: he magically severed the rope and felt himself falling to the ground.

Kang shook him hard until Celwyn's eyes fluttered.

Bartholomew squatted next to him and leaned close.

"Is he going to live?"

Kang said, "Yes." He shook the magician again. "If he hadn't landed in this hedge, he'd be in even worse shape. Help me get the noose off of him, please."

Celwyn groaned and sat up. He removed the noose and opened his eyes. His left arm hung loose at an unnatural angle. He tried to flex the fingers on that hand and couldn't. "...my own fault."

"You don't say?" Kang asked with a relieved smile. "Exactly what happened?"

Bartholomew told Kang as he helped the magician stand, "I heard a noise and looked out the classroom window and saw Jonas fall out of the tree." Celwyn's left leg wobbled, and Kang steadied him.

"One moment," the magician requested. With a broad sweep of his good hand, he swiped the air from his head to his feet. He stood tall, flexing his leg. "Much better."

Celwyn looked to the top of the tree. "There was a body hanging from a noose in the tree, and I thought it was you." He looked at Kang. "When I climbed out on the branch, Delgado attacked."

"He pushed you?" Bartholomew asked.

"Not exactly. He got a noose around my neck and jumped out of the tree, effectively 'stringing me up' as the Americans say. When I started to lose consciousness, I cut the rope and fell."

Kang led them up the driveway to the side door of the house. The big man flanked Celwyn in case he wasn't as recovered as he appeared to be.

"You should know," Kang said, "when we arrived out here, Delgado stood over you. Edward rushed toward you and fired at him, but the bullets bounced off him. I'm not sure what the vampire planned to do, but when he saw the rest of us, he ran." The automat eyed Celwyn. "As you've told *me* before, it would be nice if you could be more circumspect, my friend."

Edward paced at the end of the driveway, his rifle at the ready.

Chapter 42

THE MORNING OF TELLY'S FUNERAL dawned as dreary as an ancient graveyard where tears flowed in rivers between the headstones.

The rain came softly at first, just a pattering on the leaves of the tall trees lining the avenue. The horses shook their heads, and the drops glistened like crystals on their plumes. Edward tapped their flanks, and the carriage rolled forward. Mrs. Thomas, Ricardo, and Selkirk stood on the portico of Tellyhouse as solemn as statues.

Annabelle stared at her hands as the silence in the carriage grew, overwhelming them with the memory of Telly. The horses maintained a sedate pace as many of their neighbors came out of their homes with servants holding umbrellas and standing at the curb. They touched their hats to acknowledge the coach as it rode by. As the rain fell harder and the horses splashed through puddles, the sound seemed louder and clearer than usual. Celwyn remembered Telly's smile. It would be a memory that never faded.

Zander looked out the window, pulling at the collar of his suit. He watched a flock of crows rise from a tree before them and follow the carriage in a dark cloud.

Ah. Celwyn saw them too. *Francesca has sent her representatives.*

Church bells rang in the distance as the carriage turned onto the cemetery drive. Even across the short distance, the earthy smell of freshly turned dirt reached them. Over the gravesite, a small tent had been erected, and underneath it, a collection of chairs awaited them, surrounded by tall vases of roses: the reminders of a brave little girl. A respectful distance away, the grave diggers leaned on their shovels and watched their party descend from the coach.

Celwyn took Annabelle's arm and escorted her across the grass as Kang and Bartholomew walked close behind with Zander.

"Do you wonder if Telly had other family?" Celwyn asked.

Annabelle said, "I do, but assumed if so, they would have taken care of her." Her steps slowed, and with aching in her voice asked, "What if we hadn't stopped the train in Pushkari that day, and you hadn't rescued her?" She buried her face in his jacket as Bartholomew patted her back. Beside them, Kang couldn't have looked any more miserable as he held on to Zander's hand.

Cascades of white blossoms lay across the top of a small coffin. Zander stared and licked his lips.

"Is Telly in there?"

Annabelle managed to say, "Yes. Let's sit down." She patted the seat beside her. The others took chairs on each side of them. To the right of the tent, the gravediggers straightened as a priest approached, his robes shining wet with the rain.

"Episcopalian?" Annabelle whispered to Celwyn.

"No, Turkish Orthodox. It was the best I could do since we aren't members of any churches." He added, "They generally do not like me."

"Don't ask why," Kang murmured.

The priest began speaking in a monotone, his words comforting and necessary. Celwyn decided to add something appropriate and necessary, also.

He blocked what the priest and gravediggers could see and hear as a transparent deep blue image of Telly appeared. She sat on top of the coffin and began to play with her jacks. As she threw the ball in the air, Zander's mouth fell open, and he would have run to her if Kang hadn't restrained him with a whispered, "Wait."

Annabelle's tears became a joyful remembrance, and her eyes shone as they watched Telly rise and come toward them. A light and spirited flute began to play. The priest hesitated and then resumed speaking. Telly reached Bartholomew and touched his hand. For each of them, she held their embrace and absorbed their sadness with her smile. When she reached Zander, she whispered in his ear and ruffled his hair. Then she turned back. With a final wave, she climbed atop the coffin.

The flute played softly as Telly faded into the misty rain and the priest's monotone reached a crescendo.

———{ }———

"That was beautiful," Kang commented as they clambered back into the coach. "I commend your imagination."

Celwyn looked at him. "How do you know it was my doing?"

Kang hesitated; his foot suspended above the running board. He finished scrambling inside.

"It could have been Telly just wanting to say goodbye to us." The magician straightened his cuffs and pointedly looked at his pocket watch.

Kang rolled his eyes and indicated Zander, who sat next to him. "We'll discuss it later."

"I asked Edward to take us down by the river. Telly had wanted to go there," Bartholomew said. "The ships on the river travel to Kiev and then Saint Petersburg." Bartholomew looked at Zander. "I wonder what is inside of the ships."

"Am I forgiven yet?" Celwyn asked the automat.

"Of course. But," he nodded at Zander, who had jumped into a conversation with Annabelle and Bartholomew about ships, "when he's a bit older, you will have to explain some of the things you do." He lowered his voice, "You also owe me. I had to tell Annabelle about your adventure in the tree yesterday. She was annoyed with you for putting yourself in danger. But she was pleased I shared what occurred with her."

"We're lucky Zander doesn't want to climb that tree, yet." The magician watched the traffic increase with more and more carriages joining the parade of vehicles to the river quay. "Yesterday, you mentioned bringing Elizabeth to Prague."

"I did." Kang eyed him and spoke slowly. "I plan to do so as soon as it is safe. Is there something I should know?"

Celwyn scanned the street. He thought he'd seen one of Delgado's lesser vampires, but apparently not. "Not quite yet. Do you see anyone we know there?" He pointed outside. Their carriage stopped, waiting in line for the others in front of them to move along.

"The man next to the apple seller looks like one of the men who delivered our parlor furniture."

"Oh!" Annabelle exclaimed. "We need to get back. The beds will arrive after lunch, and Mrs. Thomas and I have to get Zander's room ready."

Celwyn tapped on the glass and relayed the request to Edward. Zander did not look happy.

"We'll come see the boats tomorrow," Celwyn promised. As they turned away from the river, he noted that the man next to the apple cart still watched them. "How is Francesca's spell working?" he asked.

Bartholomew said, "Well enough." He studied the man by the apple cart. "I'll verify it when we return."

"What is a 'spell'?" Zander asked.

With a warning glare at Celwyn, Annabelle said, "It is a recipe. Used in making cookies."

"Cookies!"

Hours later, the movers had brought in the last of the beds, including a long and sturdy one for Mrs. Thomas. Last night she'd slept on the sofa and had not been happy about it.

The Tellyhouse parlor extended the length of the drawing-room and library combined and shared one wall of windows with the nearby sunroom. It was the room everyone seemed to gravitate to, including Zander, who had finished his lessons and played with the kitten in front of the fireplace. Qing watched them from the top of the armoire, probably wondering if the kitten wanted to play with him. Celwyn had noted the bird's interest from where he lay sprawled on the sofa and shook his head at Qing. He then resumed reading the newspaper and wondering how to refill his whiskey glass without getting up, and Zander noticing his movement.

Kang worked at the desk in the corner. His process required adding up figures, wadding up the piece of paper to throw at the trash bin, miss, and then doing it all again.

Each time, Celwyn put the ball of paper into the bin without Zander noticing. He yawned and asked a general question. "Do you think we should attend the revised production of *Swan Lake*? It begins next week at the Opera House. The production of *Werther* will debut in Prague soon also."

Bartholomew said, "I certainly would like to," as he came into the room and sat down. "Miss Annabelle has expressed interest in the story before, so she would probably like it, also."

"I've heard that the music is mesmerizing." Kang began a stroll around the room. "Yes, I would like to see it."

"It is good, but I'm not sure if 'mesmerizing' is an accurate description, though." Celwyn had found the music too stiff, too uninspired. He consulted his pocket watch. "Where is Annabelle?"

"She mentioned deadheading the roses after the movers completed their delivery," Kang said.

Noises of combat reached them from the kitchen. Dull thuds indicated something heavy hitting a wall. "That French onion soup is worth almost anything." Kang reminded them with a faraway look in his eyes.

"What do you think is happening?" the big man mused.

Celwyn yawned and said, "My vote is a temper outburst over a sauce."

"I think it has something to do with Sully and the affections of Mrs. Thomas," Kang announced with a twinkle in his eye.

"Why? Because Sully wishes he was still chef?" Bartholomew asked and shuddered at the memory.

"No, because he is wooing Mrs. Thomas." Kang smiled.

"Indeed." Celwyn thought about it. Households could be gossipy.

At that moment, Ricardo rushed into the room and stopped in front of them. "Excuse me—" he blurted and couldn't go on.

"What is it?" Kang asked.

Ricardo's eyes displayed the kind of fear that brought everyone to their feet. "Come. Please come with me—" He turned and ran.

Celwyn, and the others ran down the hall, through the side door, and outside into the weak sunlight. Once there, Ricardo veered right and sprinted for the rear yard. The gloom over the city seemed more pronounced, but Annabelle's white dress glowed in the remaining light as she knelt beside a dark shape under the roses.

Bartholomew reached her first and pulled her to her feet. She trembled and pointed.

Selkirk lay on his side with his throat slit open, eyes wide in terror. Mud covered his hair and face as if he had struggled with his attacker. Celwyn could clearly see the walnut stuffed into his mouth.

Kang removed the walnut, pocketing it. He stooped to get a closer look at the wound. "He was murdered no more than an hour ago. Probably much less. The body is still quite warm."

Celwyn thanked Ricardo, implanted calm thoughts, and assured him he would take care of the situation. As Ricardo backed away, the magician removed his memory of the murder of Selkirk.

Annabelle fainted. Bartholomew carried her inside past Zander, who rounded the corner running toward them. Kang intercepted him and led him back to the kitchen. "We're going to offer our services to help taste some cookies. Chef Lucien likes you, and I bet he will let us help him."

"But what—"

Kang held the back door open. "Come." Zander looked back over his shoulder, but by now, Celwyn had moved the body farther under the bushes. When Zander had gone inside, the magician wrapped the body in a tarp and lugged it to the stables. Edward saw him and assisted in pulling it inside.

"You appear to be a very direct man, Edward."

He scratched his head and looked at the tarp. "That I am. You look upset, Sir."

"That I am. Ricardo found Selkirk's body in the garden. He has been murdered." The magician pointed to the tarp. "Could you take his body to the church on Omari Street? They will be sure he is buried properly. I've made sure Ricardo will not remember this."

Without hesitation, Edward said, "Yes, Sir."

"Please be—evasive—about where you found the body."

Hours later, Annabelle still remained subdued, distracted, and only speaking when necessary. The discovery of a body was a traumatic event for any young woman, yet she did her best to carry on. Everyone kept their thoughts to themselves, remembering Selkirk, and uncomfortably aware there was a direct link from every one of them to his death. Celwyn went over each interaction with Selkirk, trying to determine why the man had been murdered. Had he been a repository for Jax ... or a witness to Jax?

"What is wrong?" Zander asked, worried eyes alighting on each of them.

"Finish your dinner, please," Annabelle said. Her hand shook as she reached for her water goblet.

As a distraction, what lay in front of them should have done nicely. The braised lamb, curried rice, apples, and salad Narcisse did not go without admiration from everyone at the table. As Celwyn savored a particularly succulent bite of lamb, he decided all efforts should be made to tolerate Lucien's artistic temperament. If he had to banish Sully to the stables, he would do so. In some respects, Edward would make a much more efficient footman and butler.

"I'm afraid I have lost my appetite," Annabelle said. "Please excuse me."

Bartholomew rumbled, "We understand."

They all stood as Zander pulled out her chair and she left the dining room. Through the open doorway, they viewed her progress up the stairs.

Mrs. Thomas also watched as she pushed the coffee and tea trolley into the room.

"Is the Miss well?"

Kang said, "She lost her appetite but should be all right. The food is marvelous." He chewed another bite of the lamb and eyed the cart. "Did you bring Darjeeling?"

"Pardon? Oh, yes, I did." The housekeeper still watched Annabelle as she reached the upper landing. "I'll just take her up some of it later."

"And cookies for me?" Zander asked with what was becoming a very hard-to-resist smile.

Mrs. Thomas ruffled his hair. "No. It is too late for cookies." As she cleared the table, she noted the preoccupied air. "Was there something else I can do for you, Mr. Celwyn?"

"An excellent dinner, Mrs. Thomas. Absolutely wonderful, as is the running of this house. You are to be commended."

Bartholomew said, "Everything is well organized."

"Thank you," she murmured, still waiting for an answer and wearing a suspicious frown.

"You should know that our footman Selkirk has resigned. He left this afternoon," Kang said.

Both Bartholomew and Celwyn, exchanging a glance, assessed his lie. It was a fair performance, as were their own bland expressions. Celwyn made a note to himself to be sure Annabelle could carry off the lie as well if asked.

At that moment there, was a knock, and Edward appeared in the open doorway.

"Excuse me, Mr. Celwyn, but I assume you'd want to know. Everything has been taken care of, per your instructions." He saw the remains of the lamb platter. "It looks like I'd best get to the kitchen if I want my dinner."

"Oh, go on with you," Mrs. Thomas said with a telltale blush.

Kang regarded Celwyn with a raised eyebrow. "The plot thickens."

"We'll get out of your way," Celwyn announced and stood. "Shall we? Zander, on upstairs with you. We will be up for bedtime stories soon."

Cigar smoke billowed in the parlor like clouds of steam from the *Elizabeth*. Kang coughed and said to Celwyn and Bartholomew, "Are you sure this is permissible?"

Celwyn puffed. "Per Mrs. Thomas, Annabelle isn't coming back downstairs, so we might as well enjoy ourselves while we can. And I told her we wouldn't require anything else this evening."

Bartholomew made a series of smoke rings in ascending size.

"You'll have to teach me how to do that," Celwyn said, and, with a quick check for the housekeeper, he added tiny red frogs perched on the edges of the rings as they rose to the ceiling. Bartholomew saw them and choked on his next ring as the frogs jumped down and scattered across the carpet. Qing squeaked in delight and swooped off the armoire in pursuit. In seconds, a metallic pecking on the wooden floor came from behind the sofa.

"As much as I'm enjoying this, we can't avoid our problem." Bartholomew asked, "What are we going to do? Selkirk was a good man who didn't deserve this."

"We're going to find Jax and avenge Selkirk. It may not happen tomorrow, but it will occur, my friend." Celwyn turned to Kang, "Where is your written description of the weapon you devised?"

"You are referring to what my brother wanted when we were on the ship?"

"Yes."

Kang pointed to the oil painting of Reichenbach Falls on the wall behind the dining room table. "In the wall safe. It should be secure since only the three of us know the combination."

"We should tell the combination to Annabelle, too," Celwyn remarked.

Bartholomew nodded and asked, "Is there still a danger that Jax will steal it?"

"In my opinion, yes," Kang said.

"We haven't really talked about Jax's calling card that we found in Selkirk's mouth." Celwyn sighed. "Another innocent death because of us." He vacillated between anger and sadness at the situation.

"It isn't our fault that Jax destroys lives around us." Kang's words belied his pained expression.

Bartholomew shook his head. "I agree. It may not be our fault directly, but we should stop him from hurting people. How can we do that?"

"I do not know." Kang frowned. "Have you wondered why Jax announced his presence?"

"Yes, and I have no answer. We should draw Jax out where we can get at him." Bartholomew smashed the butt of his cigar into the ashtray with more force than needed, then he mashed it again.

Kang suggested, "We could leave false papers sitting out. If that is what he wants, Jax could steal them and then leave."

"That would improve our safety but not stop him from killing," Bartholomew observed.

Imitating the big man, Celwyn blew two rings into the air and watched Qing dive off the top of the armoire and fly through them. "If you put out half of it, with embedded errors, and he took that, it would prove he is here in the house. It would guarantee that he would wait for the other half."

"I like that idea," Kang said.

The big man said, "So do I. Then we could destroy him."

"I could leave it there," Kang pointed to the large oak desk in the corner. "It would look as if I became tired and went to bed."

They nodded, and then Kang asked the magician, "Are you going out again tonight to look for Delgado?"

"Yes. I hesitate to leave you without extra protection against Jax, but in some respects, Delgado is more dangerous."

Kang said, "Jax is probably getting used to his new human vessel at this very moment."

Chapter 43

A FRESHLY PAINTED BLUE ZILLE called the *Blaue Kartoffel* chugged by the marshy area in front of the village of Husinec as it returned to Prague. The Vltava flowed slowly here, the water deep and nearly black in the lengthening shadows of dusk.

Miss Annabelle perched under the boat's canopy, wrapped in layers of furs, with Celwyn and Kang sitting on each side of her. The other passengers had gone inside the cabin to be warm: to them, a river ride was just a way to travel between the cities of Rez and Prague.

A few feet away, Zander leaned over the rail, watching the swans as the boat floated by them.

"I love this boat!"

"I do too." Bartholomew hugged him.

"It is still cold here and almost June," Celwyn remarked as they passed under the shadows of aged trees.

Kang said with a wink, "I wouldn't know."

Annabelle shivered and regarded him from under her wraps. "Really?"

Celwyn laughed. "I thought sarcasm was a gentleman's sport."

A road paralleled the river, and several horse-drawn carriages kicked up dust as they bounced along it, one of them managing more speed than their boat and passing two boys who trudged along carrying fishing poles. For more than a mile, the boat traveled by farmland until it reached the edge of the Král forest. The river curled again, and the top of the Opera House dome came into view in the distance.

"How is your music composition coming along?" Annabelle asked Celwyn.

"Very well, thank you." After verifying they were alone, he floated a sample across the water to them, just a quartet of light strings riding the wind. The magician loved the play of the notes with the gusts, inward and outward, then soaring again.

The music faded away as the boat prepared to dock. While the boat rocked with the current of the river, the crew used poles to steer the *Blaue Kartoffel* into her berth. Soon, the passengers gathered on deck, ready to disembark.

Behind them, the Opera House rose many stories high, its shadow reaching across the wide river. As the sun set, her lights flickered on, covering the dome and twinkling like thousands of fireflies.

Beyond the end of the dock, Edward leaned against the carriage door, smoking.

"Pleasant ride?" he touched his hat as they approached.

Kang said, "A very enjoyable excursion. The city of Rez is not as big as I expected, but their market area passed our inspection." He stowed packages in the boot of the carriage.

Bartholomew held up bags of fruit and vegetables. "I am hoping our chef will be pleased." He fished through one bag and handed Edward a pouch. "We found a tobacconist, too."

Edward poked his nose in the pouch. "Rich and strong. Thank you."

"Shall we?" Celwyn asked, feeling a chill as he tugged his coat closer and helped Annabelle into the coach. "It is nearly dark, and it would be best if we returned home." No one argued, well aware of the miasma of the vampires that hung in the air.

⁓

Sully held the front door of Tellyhouse open and greeted them as if his dog had just died. After everyone had crossed the threshold, Celwyn asked him, "Is there a problem?"

With a forlorn glance up the hall, Sully muttered, "Why are women so blasted hard to understand?"

Celwyn asked, with a studiously serious demeanor, "Such as Mrs. Thomas?"

"Yes." Sully closed the door behind them and cornered Celwyn between the potted fern and a pedestal holding a bust of the Queen. Kang and Bartholomew scampered away toward the kitchen, wearing smirks. "I told her I admired her, and she boxed my ears!"

With solemnity, Celwyn sympathized and suggested that when Sully next saw Kang, he ask him for his opinion, then slipped away to enter the parlor behind Annabelle.

Patrick, dressed in full uniform, arose from the sofa and walked toward them. "My darling!"

"What a surprise," Annabelle cried and rushed into his embrace. When they disengaged, she asked, "When did you arrive?"

"About noon. And who is this young man?" Patrick smiled as he knelt beside Zander. The boy stared at his medals, his face, and then Annabelle's smile of joy.

Zander bowed with a hand at his waist, as Celwyn had taught him, and said, "Pleased to meet you. I am Master Zander."

Patrick picked him up. "I am Patrick, and I've heard so much about you from Miss Annabelle."

Celwyn shook his free hand. "Congratulations on your return, my friend."

Kang and Bartholomew entered the room and lined up to do the same. Kang announced, "I say, this requires a toast." As he made the drinks, Bartholomew joined him at the bar, ferrying glasses to the others. Celwyn pulled on the cord by the door, and Ricardo appeared.

"Juice, please, for Master Zander."

A moment later, Mrs. Thomas brought the juice herself, saying Ricardo and the chef had reached a critical stage in the preparation of dinner. She looked at Celwyn. "And I know you and the others prefer to wait on yourselves usually and don't want a downstairs maid, but we will need to be adding to the staff now that Selkirk has left and we have another guest." She nodded at Patrick. "I had his bags taken up to the third floor." Her voice brooked no argument. "I've arranged for an upstairs maid to help Miss Annabelle during the day."

When she spoke, Annabelle and Patrick had sat side by side on the sofa, staring into each other's eyes. Kang walked Mrs. Thomas back to the kitchen, and when he returned, he lowered his voice as if he was imparting a state secret: "Beef Wellington."

Celwyn rubbed his hands together. He glanced at the love birds on the sofa. "Dinner will be glorious, but I doubt they'll notice." Patrick held Annabelle's hand. Zander sat on her lap, asking Patrick questions about India, monkeys, and elephants.

By the time she rose to dress for dinner, Zander had heard several stories, causing him to announce, "I am going fight in the cavalry. I will carry a sword and ride a pony!"

Annabelle tugged on his hand. "You need to bathe and dress for dinner first. Come along."

As soon as she left, Qing fluttered across the room and landed on the desk. He squawked.

"Nice of him to remind us of our trap for Jax," Bartholomew said.

"Is that chap still bothering you?" Patrick asked.

"Yes," Kang responded as he crossed to the desk and looked at the papers. "They may have been reviewed, but nothing is missing." He flipped through them again. "They are in sequence."

"It could be that Jax didn't have time to finish looking at them, or he may have been interrupted." Celwyn stared at the papers.

Bartholomew agreed. "Or he is waiting for the other half of them."

"I told Mrs. Thomas not to move any of the papers or allow the desk to be dusted by the cleaning crew," Kang said as he examined the rest of the desktop. A jar of pencils appeared undisturbed, as did the row of fountain pens and bottles of ink.

"I vote that we wait a few days more to see if Jax has actually looked at the papers. It could be that we've been wrong all along about his interest in them." Celwyn looked at Qing, and the bird flew over to him, nuzzled his chin, and burrowed into his jacket.

"From the beginning, Jax may not have been partnering with Talos and was just interested in us." Kang turned to the magician. "You know, Qing isn't really cold. He just likes you."

"How could he not?" Celwyn patted the bird.

"Your modesty is astounding."

Bartholomew hesitated and said, "Or Jax could have become alerted to the existence of the weapon described in those papers."

Celwyn stood and paced. "Although necessary, this discussion is not improving my appetite."

"Once before, we discussed Jax's intelligence," Kang reminded them. "I still believe Jax is not a deep thinker and that he is impulsive and opportunistic most of the time. Hence the dead bodies in very dis-coverable places, even when he isn't trying to throw suspicion on us."

Bartholomew mused, "If I remember correctly, we also couldn't decide which of you he was after."

Patrick spoke up. "I've been trying to follow all of this and can't. Could you please tell me what all has happened since I left you in Baghdad? Tell me about Zander and Telly, too. I deduced that you shielded Annabelle from some of the details."

"It wasn't just Zander's past troubles we kept from her," the magician said. When they had brought Patrick up to speed, his eyes brimmed with unshed tears. He began to weep when they told him how Telly had died.

"God damn Delgado! I'll kill him."

"Not if I get to him first," Celwyn promised him. The glasses on top of the bar began to vibrate.

Kang spoke up. "Let us talk of something more pleasant. On a brighter note, Annabelle has become a very good parent to the boy."

Bartholomew said, "Being a parent has had an effect on her. On myself also."

Patrick requested that they continue the story. Kang supplied the rest of the information, relating their adventures, suppositions, and fears. "Bartholomew can tell you about our new friends who have supplied protection for this house."

"Mafioso?" Patrick asked.

Kang laughed, and Celwyn snickered into his glass as Bartholomew shook his head. "Both Jonas and the Professor have a strange sense of humor."

"Because?"

"Because our new friends are witches. We're paying them for protection spells, and every time I consult with them, they try to seduce me. It is dangerous!"

Patrick pretended to understand the big man's dilemma but couldn't hide a smile. "I am very grateful that Annabelle has such good friends and protectors." The smile vanished. "And I'm very sorry she found Selkirk dead."

"She hasn't talked about it much," Kang said. "From what I can tell, Zander didn't see it. The poor little one has been through too much already."

"Agreed."

"Now is probably as good a time as any to tell you of some information I received from one of my telegrams." Kang regarded them. "It isn't wise to frighten Annabelle with it." He checked the door and glanced up the stairs, faintly hearing Annabelle lecturing Zander on where he put his dirty socks. Kang returned and said, "I asked my colleagues in San Francisco and other cities to look into the reports and activities of Jax. Any information was welcome."

"I hope this is good news," Patrick said.

"Yes and no. The reports say the unfortunate person who has become a host to Jax maintains the outward abilities, appearance, and mannerisms of that person. If they could play the piano before, they could continue to do so, but what isn't clear is whether or not Jax has access to their memory. Could Jax manipulate them to play a particular piece on the piano? Could he force them to commit a heinous act against their will? In both cases, the answer appears to be yes."

Celwyn asked, "Can the person Jax is inside of resist him? Refuse to cooperate?"

"That is unknown. You might ask, does he always kill the host he is leaving?" Kang shook his head. "Until someone witnesses these instances, no one knows. In other words, we do not know if he inhabited Selkirk, or if it is one of the cleaning crew hiding in a closet or the stables. Jax could have murdered Selkirk because he figured out who Jax is hiding inside of. We just don't know."

"The authorities just find the dead bodies," Bartholomew said.

"Where was Jax spotted before?" Patrick asked.

Kang consulted his notes. "London, 1798, is one confirmed place. Also, Madrid 1805, and Barcelona 1847. London again the next year. I saw him in Verona in 1851. Before you ask, when I saw him in 1839, he killed a corpulent man on the steps of the Vatican and disappeared. I never discovered what he really looks like."

"I worry about Annabelle and the boy." Patrick jumped to his feet and then sat again. "What should we do?"

"Be vigilant. Look for unexpected behavior: the host's voice will still sound the same, their actions and sometimes words will be the only difference." Kang studied the toes of his boots as he thought. "Whoever is hosting Jax may act perfectly normal."

Bartholomew said, "I think once we find what attracts Jax to us, we will be in a better position to deal with him." He gazed out the picture window as a flock of sparrows arrived, scattering across the lawn and pecking for their dinner.

"Solid reasoning," Celwyn agreed and then asked Kang, "Will you leave more of your false papers out tonight?"

"Yes."

Celwyn explained to Patrick, "We're hoping Jax takes them and leaves."

Patrick glanced at the door and lowered his voice, "Hopefully. On another and happier note, and in confidence, I intend to ask Annabelle to marry me. If she will have me."

Celwyn and Bartholomew said, "Congratulations!" at the same time.

Kang jumped to his feet and rummaged in the armoire until he found a cigar box. He passed it around. "Quick. Let us congratulate you before she returns."

"She does not have family close by." Patrick again watched the door as he tried to light a cigar.

"Her aunt, Mrs. Pearse, is in town," Celwyn said. "They are on better terms now. I believe she would be proud to give your marriage her blessing."

Patrick puffed on the cigar and verified the door again. "I wasn't expecting to raise a child so soon, but it would be my honor to be a part of Zander's life."

The magician saw the concern on Bartholomew's face and hurried to say, "We do, also. He will have the protection of us all." As he spoke, Mrs. Thomas arrived in a rustle of skirts. Her nose twitched as she pretended not to see the cigar smoke.

"Dinner is served. I'll run up and hurry Miss Annabelle along."

Patrick cut into his Beef Wellington and asked, "What church will young Master Zander be attending?"

While the magician looked at Bartholomew with his brows up, Kang said, "We hadn't discussed it yet."

Tonight's fare included herbed baby potatoes and asparagus with a delicate béarnaise sauce. Celwyn closed his eyes as he chewed and wished he could enjoy the meal several times over. It would be helpful to his culinary enjoyment if the dinner conversation only concerned non-controversial subjects.

"Roman Catholic is a possibility as is Buddhism, Episcopalian, or Muslim," Bartholomew speculated.

"Excuse me, please," Zander said. "I prefer the one with elephants and tigers."

The magician subscribed to no religion. He murmured, "Not my problem," and enjoyed another bite of potato.

Kang eyed the magician. "We will discuss it, definitely. Maybe we will consider monkeys, too." To Ricardo, who stood by, he asked, "What is the mood of Chef this evening?"

Ricardo, always direct and good-natured, said, "Fair." But he cast a nervous glance down the hall.

"Do you think he would come in so we could offer our compliments?"

"I will check."

After he left, Annabelle told Patrick, "Uncle Celwyn is working on a musical suite to be produced for the Opera House."

"What is it about?" he asked.

The magician cut a bite of his beef and chewed. "It will be a surprise. You will all be invited to the premiere."

"Where does it take place? Paris? Rome?" Bartholomew asked.

Celwyn shook his head. "Soon, I will supply details. It has been a very long time since my last performance at the Opera House."

"I'm not asking when that occurred," Kang said with a glance at the curious face of Zander.

"I have a list of things I need to pick up tomorrow." Annabelle fussed with the lace at her collar and eyed Patrick from under her lashes expectantly.

With a devoted puppy dog look, Patrick said, "I will accompany you."

"Master Zander and I have a long school session tomorrow." Bartholomew turned to the magician with a deadpan expression. "I believe it is Jonas' turn for the mathematics lesson."

"Don't even look at me, Jonas. I'm chaperoning the love birds," Kang said.

Annabelle objected. "We don't—"

"It is just for propriety's sake. I also wondered if we should send an invitation to your aunt for dinner." Kang sat back and waited for her decision.

For a moment, Annabelle pursed her lips, hesitated, and then said, "Of course. I will ask Mrs. Thomas to send the invitation for next week."

"Is that the lady I met when Telly died?" Zander asked in a low voice.

Bartholomew put his large hand across Zander's. "It is. She is a nice lady who wants to get to know you better."

The boy thought about it a moment and announced, "I will draw her a picture so she will like me!"

In a murmur he couldn't hear, Celwyn said, "I wish I'd thought of that on the *Zelda*."

Kang rolled his eyes. "Pffft. Shall we have our dessert now?"

Chapter 44

THE NEXT DAY, CELWYN WATCHED the street through the parlor window and sipped tea as Edward and the carriage drew to a stop in front. The magician noted that each day more roses bloomed across the front yard of Tellyhouse, and at the moment, they seemed especially vibrant in the dim light of the setting sun.

The pounding of Zander's feet running down the stairs could be heard, and then he rushed up the hall to greet Kang as he came inside, followed by Annabelle and Patrick. Bartholomew took his time coming down the stairs and headed to the parlor.

"Teaching is exhausting at times," the big man said as he sat down. The sofa creaked under his weight but held. Celwyn started for the bar, but Bartholomew shook his head. "Nothing for now."

Zander raced into the room and jumped in his lap. "Want to see my present?" He didn't wait for an answer and held up a stuffed bear that looked very life-like. "Captain Patrick gave it to me!"

"I hope you told him thank you," the magician said.

"I did!"

Patrick joined them and announced, "Annabelle is upstairs, changing for dinner." He regarded the boy. "She said that Master Zander was to go up for his bath in a half-hour."

Celwyn raised a brow. It could be just a coincidence, not a distraction, but Zander slid off Bartholomew's lap and approached Patrick to say, "We would have time for a game of dominoes before I have my bath."

From the bar, Kang poured a drink and watched Zander lead Patrick to the dining room table. Kang sat down next to Bartholomew and said in a low voice, "We had an incident today."

Celwyn wondered if it were only Zander that shouldn't hear what he had to say next.

Kang eyed the magician. "Please block them both from hearing, and the hallway, too, please."

Bartholomew sat forward, attempting to remain nonchalant, but his whole demeanor tensed like a drawn bow. Celwyn said, "Done. What happened?"

"It was after our third stop. Edward said he thought we were being followed but wasn't sure. I waited in the carriage." Kang sipped and said, "As Annabelle and Patrick came out of the tailor shop, a heavily veiled woman approached her. Patrick stepped between them and was flung half-way up the street. I came out of the carriage just as Edward leapt to the ground with his pistol."

Bartholomew inquired, "Was it Mrs. Karras?"

"Edward and I believe so," Kang responded. "She saw us and ran. And she is very fast. Patrick caught up to her first, and they fought. My god, that woman is vicious. The *policista* became involved, but I convinced them there was no need to arrest anyone. It was several minutes before we returned to the carriage in front of the tailor shop." Kang paused and glanced at Patrick. "Annabelle was gone."

"*Gone*?" Bartholomew repeated.

Kang said, "Yes. We looked inside the shop and were becoming extremely concerned when she approached us from the opposite direction carrying a package. She seemed surprised that we were looking for her. Patrick remonstrated with her strongly, as did I."

The big man said, "She is strong-willed."

"An understatement." Celwyn glanced at the domino players. He hated it when his premonitions came true. "I understand now why you thought Patrick didn't need to hear your report. He is too smitten to consider all of the possible facts."

Kang nodded. "After we talked with Annabelle, she agreed that it was foolhardy for her to have gone off like that and said it would not occur again."

"Do you believe her?" the magician asked.

After a thoughtful pause, he said, "I do not know."

"What was in the package?"

"Again, I do not know."

Footsteps sounded in the hallway, and Mrs. Thomas came into the room.

"Master Zander is wanted upstairs."

The gazebo at the rear of Tellyhouse had been painted a light yellow and built at the base of a small grassy hill. Beds of impatiens and tiny blue flowers lined the perimeter.

As they sat inside the structure enjoying the early morning buzzing of bees and fluttering butterflies, Celwyn said to Bartholomew, "Except for Annabelle's disappearance at the tailor shop, it has been an uneventful week." Celwyn swatted a fly off his nose. "Do you believe in premonitions?"

At the top of the hill, Kang, Annabelle, Patrick, and Zander played croquet and had reached the hole with a green flag.

"Look at the little one. He hits the ball very well." Bartholomew turned to the magician. "To answer your question, I do believe in *Vorahnung*, as they say in Deutsch. Also, I believe some people are more inclined to be receptive to suggestion. Such as what everyone else may or may not see." The croquet ball hit the side of the gazebo and bounced toward the driveway. "Or in your instance, circumstances are arranged to fit what fate has not already decreed."

Interesting observation, the magician thought.

"This lemonade is too tart." Celwyn made a face but continued sipping it, thinking that this should have been an idyllic morning, with the warm caress of sunshine, the graceful beauty of the butterflies, and profusion of flowers in the garden. Yet, he had a sense of an impending catastrophe that wouldn't go away. The magician scanned the area.

The view from the gazebo included the rear of the house, and frequently Ricardo would step out onto the back porch to curse in a torrent and smoke like an expectant father. Chef Lucian must be in a bit of a temper today.

Celwyn observed the croquet players. Kang prepared to hit the ball while Zander squatted at eye-level to the goal. A few feet away, Patrick and Annabelle held hands. Actually, there were three of them holding hands, if one included her oversized hat with its feathers, bows, and miniature birdcage on top. As he watched the lovers, the magician asked, "Have you had any problems with Francesca and the protection spells?"

"No."

"Then we can assume Jax is either inside one of our household, or someone who delivers to it. Kang reported that the rest of the false paperwork disappeared overnight. And as you said, the spell is in place. It couldn't have been a visitor."

"You have deduced that no one from the outside could have come in. Could it have been one of the cleaning staff?"

"Possibly."

Bartholomew put his glass down. His frown went deep. "This is unwelcome news."

"At least what was stolen was harmless."

"The danger is near and present." Bartholomew's voice took on a note of caution. "Zander is very excited about our outing tonight, but perhaps we should postpone it."

"Kang has already expressed the same reservations but wants to proceed."

"Indeed."

Celwyn wanted to proceed also. His unfulfilled revenge for Telly and the others rested heavily on his shoulders. "He is looking forward to our evening, as is Annabelle. She cannot decide what to wear."

The croquet game ended with Zander dancing in a circle and hugging Kang as they walked down the hill toward the gazebo.

Celwyn looked at Bartholomew. "Please bring your pistol tonight, and be prepared to use it." He sighed: there would be no going back. "I plan an alteration to the evening's entertainment. We should also expect to attract the attention of the vampires. In fact, I am counting on it. For once and for all, they will no longer bother us."

"I will enjoy watching him pay for what he did to Telly," Bartholomew promised him.

"I need to run some errands before this evening."

The magician stood, keeping a private smile private as part of a ritual before a well-crafted performance with or without a stage. Much of the preparations were in place, but there was one more task he needed to do: the most enjoyable task that he had saved for last.

Chapter 45

AFTER DAYS OF FOG AND DRIZZLING rain, tonight, thousands of stars paid homage to a full and pregnant moon. The evening displayed the crystal-clear air and feel of excitement that always heralded opening nights, and strong moonlight painted everything with a silvery brush. Edward pulled back on the reins, and they coasted to a stop in the line of waiting carriages. Across the street, the Vltava River surged swiftly by in the reflection of the lights from the Opera House.

"You look dashing, Professor," Annabelle said. "As do you, Uncle Celwyn. I've never seen you in a top hat and tails." She turned to Bartholomew. "You will be turning heads in yours also."

"Thank you. It fits very well, thanks to Jonas."

"Why are we stopping here?" the boy asked. The waiting coaches stretched the entire length of the block.

"We'll be the next carriage unloaded," Celwyn told Zander. "As you get older, you'll learn that the ladies enjoy inspecting each other's dresses, and tonight your Aunt Annabelle's will be greatly admired. Red is a fetching color." He reached across the seat and straightened Zander's tie. "Please remember that only whispers are allowed once we reach our seats."

"I will."

"And to not let go of Bartholomew or Aunt Annabelle's hand," the magician added.

Patrick spoke up, "I will be holding her other hand." He directed a wistful smile at Annabelle, much sweeter than any cake.

With a gloved hand, she touched his chin. "You, too, will be an object of admiration, especially with so many medals on your uniform. I may have to swat a few hands away."

Everyone laughed while they waited for their carriage to pull forward a few feet.

The tension rose as Celwyn cast an eye over the crowd, and Kang and Bartholomew patted the pistols in their pockets.

* * *

As they ascended dozens of steps to the grand foyer, they attracted respectful nods, stares, curtsies, and when Celwyn listened to their thoughts, a few snide comments. To the well-dressed patrons, their party did not represent aristocracy nor society and had made the supreme error of bringing a child to the Opera House. This appeared to be an even worse offense than including a black man as a full member of their family.

Celwyn controlled his reactions to the unheard comments: he had much to do and much on his mind. To complicate the situation, his earlier suspicion concerning Jax had grown legs and ran wild in his own mind, screaming for attention.

They walked across the waxed floor of the grand foyer, past the clusters of fur-wrapped matrons, the revealing gowns of the younger women, and the pot bellies and elegantly tailored suits of the men before reaching the far end of the rotunda. Celwyn admired a particularly well-cut dress coat and decided that when this was over, he would have to further explore the tailor shops of Prague.

They paused to avoid colliding with flocks of waiters who fluttered everywhere with trays of champagne flutes and tidbits to nibble upon. From an alcove in the north corner, a quartet played a ballad that reminded Celwyn of Suzanne. *How appropriately sad*, he thought. And how appropriate that tonight he would finally avenge her death.

"Jonas!" A diminutive man in an elaborate evening suit accosted them and smiled through a well-waxed mustache. Quick eyes under bushy eyebrows missed nothing as he pulled the magician aside. "I heard you were in Prague. What brought you here?"

Celwyn's mind centered on the evening's performance, Jax, and vampires. He didn't have time for this. "You old gossip, Jules. I'll meet you tomorrow. What hotel are you staying in?"

"Eh? You think you can get rid of me this easily? I'm at the Marlboro. We'll have luncheon." The older man started edging toward Kang and the others. Who are you with?"

Out of habit, Celwyn entered his friend's mind. As expected, he found colorful scenes of an undersea ship, a balloon that went around the world, and something about a cave leading to the center of the earth. As an author, his friend had a fine imagination. The magician couldn't help asking, "Do you still subscribe to the notion that much of fiction is truth?"

"Yes, Jonas. There is always a basis, if not actual occurrences, blended in. Do you remember—"

A gong sounded, calling the patrons to their seats. He slapped Verne on the back. "I'll meet you tomorrow." The magician had things to do. He whirled the man in the other direction, and when the author turned again, Celwyn and the others had left the area.

Minutes later, they were shown to their seats in one of the boxes overlooking the stage. Annabelle sat down, arranged her skirts, and regarded the other patrons.

"Did you notice that Zander is the only child here, and we're being whispered about?" she asked.

"I do," the magician said. As Zander stood up to look over the railing, he dropped their opera glasses. Celwyn caught them, making them invisible as he slipped them into Bartholomew's pocket. Zander blinked and peered over the rail. When no one reacted, he sat down and buried his face in his program.

Celwyn shrugged. "We couldn't leave him at the manor without knowing where Jax is—or trust the vampires—since they would know where we are."

"Are they here?" Annabelle asked with a nervous glance at Zander.

He smiled with grim satisfaction and pointed at a spot a few rows below them. "The vampires have followed us here." The magician made sure that Zander not only didn't hear him but that the boy continued to read his program.

"Where?" Bartholomew asked.

"Third row center, with Mrs. Karras exposing herself in fashionable indecency. Next to her is another one of her slimy escorts." Celwyn nodded at Zander. "Despite the distractions, I'm hoping he begins to enjoy the music and the pageantry of the opera." The magician allowed the clamor to reach Zander again and asked him, "What do you think of the stage below?"

"The orchestra is very big! Will they play the—" Zander consulted his program, "the Overture? It says that the royal court will be the first scene."

"They will. Does it say who wrote this opera and when?" Bartholomew asked him.

The boy flipped through the program until he saw the history details. "It was Chaikov in 1847."

"Very good. Your Uncle will have his own music produced here soon," Annabelle told him.

Celwyn agreed. Much sooner than everyone expected.

Kang arrived in the booth with a frown and plopped down.

"I walked through most of the building." Kang trained his opera glasses on the crowd below. "I do not see Delgado. There are a few of our enemies sitting below, about three rows from the stage."

"I can assure you, he is nearby," Celwyn said.

"Who is that?" Zander asked.

Kang said, "The genie man you saw. Can you tell us what this opera is about?"

While the boy summarized the story, the audience filled the theatre. It neared eight o'clock, and Act One drew near. Over the low murmur of the spectators, an oboe squeaked octave to octave, and the violins argued against the rumble of the bass.

Celwyn indicated the right side of the booth. "Annabelle and Patrick seem to be enjoying their evening out."

"If that is your tactful way of saying they're sitting too closely together and are oblivious to the rest of us, I agree." Kang nodded.

"It is helpful, actually," Celwyn told Bartholomew and Kang. "If you could lean in so we can speak in confidence, please." When they'd done so, he said, "I asked you to bring your pistols because they will be needed during, or after, the intermission. I do not wish to alarm Annabelle about the firearms. Or Patrick. He would feel obligated to either tell her, or act so nervously she would know there is impending danger."

"Understandable." Kang eyed Celwyn. "What will occur during intermission?"

The magician said, "I have planned a musical intermission, a presentation of sorts. And it also functions as a trap. Jax will most likely be there, along with the vampires." He looked at Bartholomew. "I do not know how Jax will behave, but be prepared, please. And do not be shocked."

"Bullets do not affect vampires." The big man frowned again. "They may not affect Jax."

"Silver bullets are effective on vampires." Kang fished in his pocket and handed some to him.

Keeping an eye on Zander and the lovebirds, Bartholomew turned aside, blocking their view with his massive back as he loaded his pistol. Kang began speaking as a ruse, in case one of them became curious about what the big man was doing.

"I have been working on the philosophy of what could be Jax's motivations. If we do find Jax, I'm hoping to have an opportunity to confirm my theory."

Celwyn expected that his friend would have that chance, but much depended on his own surmises. As usual, he considered his planning impeccable. The magician addressed Kang, "At intermission, please join me in front of the main entrance outside, but be careful. You, and any of our party, are targets." He lowered his voice. "It is very important that you hold on to Zander's hand and do not let go, no matter what happens."

"But Annabelle—"

"No. She is besotted and distracted. You are quick and determined and can anticipate danger. Make sure Zander knows to stay close before you go outside. I'll also put the idea strongly in his mind. I weighed the issue about his safety for tonight and believe he is safer in our company than in the house where he could be attacked because our enemies are well aware where we are tonight."

"Care to tell me what will happen?" Kang asked.

"We will be near the river. It is important that you act naturally, without any nervousness—which you would have if I answered your question."

Bartholomew asked, "Where will I be?"

"With me, with your pistol ready and on alert."

Chapter 46

A LIGHT BREEZE RUFFLED WAVES across the Vltava River as it ran dark and deep in the wide channel across from the Opera House. Celwyn and Bartholomew walked toward it, stretching their legs and stepping around vendors and waiting carriages. As they approached the river, the big man said, "Two of them are following us. Neither are Delgado."

"He is close by," Celwyn assured him. "I'm hoping that what happens here," he gestured at the river, "will draw Jax out. Please be certain that I am not interrupted by anyone for the next few minutes."

The fire in the magician's eyes began.

With a broad sweep of his hand, Celwyn lifted the surface of the river in front of them. The water glimmered and spread apart as it rose stories high, curling and opening like a book. The riverboats were pushed to each side as thick ice formed across the surface. Seconds more, and another layer of ice formed half-way across. The air shimmered, and the ice turned ghost-like, forming scores of crystalline figures. Dressed in finery, they held violins, flutes, horns, oboes, bassoons, and cellos. More of the ethereal musicians stood in front of drums and a glockenspiel. Off to the side, a lone harp faced them, its strings twinkling like a crystalline cobweb. The ghostly musicians arranged themselves on crystal chairs behind the instruments and began to play.

In the middle of the stage, a broad fissure formed in the ice, the cracking sound loud in the night as the ice opened wide, and an ornate pipe organ ascended from the river's depths. The instrument appeared much grander than one usually found in an orchestra: carved figures decorated the wood, the tall pipes reached for the sky, and the keys glowed silver and ebony under the moonlight.

Across the ice, in front of the spectral orchestra, hundreds of glass-like chairs spread out in row after row.

A commotion from the exiting crowds heralded intermission, and as the opera patrons poured out of the building and down the stairs, Celwyn's ethereal music played, drawing them closer. Kang, Patrick, and Annabelle led the procession across the street and onto the raised stage. Zander's eyes opened wide in wonder as he clutched Kang's hand, and they walked to the front and sat down beside the organ. Behind them, the crowd continued to flow across the street and approached as if the music itself pulled them onto the frozen stage. Underneath the ice, the river flowed dark and mysterious.

The clouds moved aside, and like thousands of floodlights had been lit, moonlight illuminated the scene. The violins bathed the audience with sweet music that silenced their chatter, covering everyone and everything. Celwyn stood in front of the orchestra, conducting with a crystal baton. When the violins quieted, the audience gasped as he turned, and with a smile, he separated into a second crystal image that walked to the organ. He flipped the tails of his coat back and sat down.

Into a moment of stillness, the first notes played, the same five notes that had resounded across the deck of the *Zelda* so many months before. Blending and cavorting, they soared high in a minor key and then plummeted into the majors, turning rich and full. Applause built from the audience as the music grew louder. A chorus of iridescent singers in flowing robes solidified above the river, their toes trailing through the water and onto the ice as they sang.

From beneath the organ, deep in the river, a light began to glow, growing stronger. The magician gestured, and the illumination blossomed and spread as the water became clear.

Audible gasps came from all directions as the audience saw the iron cage that lay on the riverbed. From inside the cage, Delgado raged, shaking the bars and bellowing. The music soared as the audience reacted, fascinated and repelled, unable to look away from the vampire's red eyes.

At the back of the audience, Mrs. Karras stood and pointed at Celwyn.

A dozen black-clad vampires ran toward the magician from different directions as Mrs. Karras streaked toward the stage. Bartholomew, pistol in hand, unwilling to fire and hit Celwyn, blocked them.

Celwyn spun around, flinging Mrs. Karras into the air and then high in the sky. She plunged into the water beyond the riverboats as one of the vampires ripped a claw across the magician's cheek. Celwyn gripped the vampire's face and twisted his head until he faced the other way. Languidly, the magician elevated above the converging vampires and opened his hand. A metallic net fell over them. As they thrashed and tore at the net, he tightened it into a large ball, lifting them above the stage.

"I love a good show at dawn, don't you?" Celwyn asked Kang, who had advanced to stand with him and Bartholomew. The magician pointed, and the net swung high above the crowd, spinning into a blur as he sent it across the street and to the top of the dome of the Opera House, where it dangled off the top of the spire.

Bartholomew smiled broadly.

The magician turned and lifted his baton. As the music began again, a few patrons edged away from the stage, but most couldn't help but watch Delgado strain at the cage under their feet. The citizens of Prague had a long and colorful history with vampires and did not scare easily.

The violins soloed, building to a crescendo as the French horns moaned and the music turned melancholy. Solidifying from the mist of the river, a parade of the dead approached them: it began with Selkirk, then Colonel Gilliam, McAllistar, and the rest of Jax's victims walked across the stage. Seconds more, and the magician's tribute to them dissolved.

From the other side of the stage, Suzanne's image solidified, crossing the ice to stand beside Celwyn as the music segued to a love ballad. The magician stared at her and began to cry, finally saying goodbye. She took his hand and kissed it. Telly stood with her, as solemn as only she could be. The magician kissed her forehead with trembling lips and gestured to the night sky as it turned white with flowers that rained across the river and then over all of Prague under the rising music of the violins. Suzanne and Telly dissolved into the mist once more.

It was done.

A woman in the crowd screamed.

Celwyn whirled.

With a knife to his throat, Annabelle dragged Zander from Kang's side, through the falling flowers, and onto the center of the stage. Patrick rose from his chair as Kang rushed forward. Annabelle dropped to her knees, pulling the child's head back by his hair.

"Enough of this spectacle. Enough waiting." She spoke in a deep, otherworldly, desiccated croak.

Kang's face was unreadable as he circled behind her. Celwyn remained on her right in a crouch.

Bartholomew stood directly in front of her with his pistol aimed at her face. His hand quivered.

"Had you ever heard Jax's voice before?" Celwyn asked Kang.

"Now I have," Kang replied, not taking his eyes off the knife in Annabelle's hand. Zander's eyes appeared unfocused, yet he breathed. "Have you blocked what he is seeing?" he asked the magician.

The magician walked to his right until the three of them surrounded Jax and said, "I have. He won't remember any of this."

Celwyn turned to Jax but saw Annabelle's profile. "Did you enter Annabelle the day you killed Selkirk in the garden?" he asked.

Low, guttural laughter escaped Annabelle's lips. Behind her, Patrick gripped the chair in front of him, staring at her in horror. Jax whirled and spat at him. "You simple man."

While they faced each other, the crowd murmured and edged back, finally frightened. Some of them ran for the street. Below the ice, Delgado still gyrated in fury and shook his cage. Jax watched him a moment. "He was supposed to participate tonight, and if he had, we would have killed you, Magician."

"I doubt that," Celwyn said with a sigh of finality. He turned and raised his baton.

Like a tangible, corporeal force, the violins began to play again. Five notes repeated, building and growing stronger, echoing across the water.

"What did you want?" Kang asked Jax. "After all this death, *what do you want?*"

Celwyn moved closer to Jax. Bartholomew cocked the hammer on his pistol and his tears flowed as he watched the knife at Zander's throat.

Jax's croak became angry.

"Do you think I didn't know those papers were fake, Professor?"

"Why Annabelle?" Patrick wailed.

Annabelle's face turned to him and back to Celwyn.

"What is important to you, Magician? I want into *you*, not some silly woman. Can you imagine the power I would have?" When Celwyn said nothing, Jax continued, "I tried before on the train, but it seems I must have your permission. Let me in." A low growl escaped Annabelle's perfect lips. "It is simple: I will let her go and let the boy go ... if you let me in." He rubbed the blade back and forth across the boy's neck in a caress.

Behind them, the crowd waited with the type of morbid fascination that immobilized those watching. Edward quick-stepped toward them from the street, rifle on his shoulder, aimed right at Annabelle's heart.

The five notes thundered. Celwyn looked down, clenching his fists.

"The boy first, then," Jax said. He drew the knife high, preparing to plunge it into Zander.

It was the moment the magician had been waiting for.

Without touching it, Celwyn yanked the knife out of Annabelle's hand, away from Zander's neck, and turned it on her, plunging the blade into her stomach and causing the crowd around them to erupt in screams. As Patrick rushed to her side, a thin stream of blue mist escaped Annabelle's lips and disappeared into the throng. Celwyn elevated himself trying to see where the entity Jax had gone and failed.

The ethereal music quieted while the audience's clamor grew.

With horror and sorrow, Patrick cradled Annabelle's head in his lap while Kang pushed everyone back.

Beside them, Bartholomew shook with anger. "You killed her!" he shouted at Celwyn.

"No—he did not!" Kang grabbed his arm and swung him around. "Think, man! Block the view of her while Jonas brings her back." He lowered his voice, "The wound was not intended to be fatal, only to scare Jax out of her."

Bartholomew's face contorted in relief.

As Kang spoke, Celwyn knelt and covered Annabelle with his cape. He removed the bloody knife and held a hand over the wound as he looked at the very tall and distraught black man beside him.

"My friend, I would never kill her. The Professor showed me where I could stab someone to cause the most blood flow, yet the wound is one that I could easily repair." He watched Bartholomew's face relax and turned back to study Annabelle a moment more. "There. Good as new. Patrick, if you could help her stand?"

Captain Swayne licked his lips and, with a trembling hand, brought Annabelle to her feet. As Patrick bent her over his arm and kissed her thoroughly, the audience applauded. The crowd may have cheered because a beautiful woman hadn't died or because she was embraced in the arms of a gallant military man.

"Much better than a performance of King Lear," Kang said, with a pointed look and smile at Celwyn. "I need to put a stop to all of this attention." He turned to the audience who had been sitting on the ice stage and raised his voice. "This performance has been brought to you as just that, a performance, an illusion that tells a story. We hope you enjoyed the show." He bowed. "Good night."

Beside him, Annabelle clung to Patrick and said in a thick drawl, "I *do* declare, I am so grateful that disgusting thing is gone." She watched Celwyn lift the boy into his arms. Her voice broke, "How is Zander?"

"He isn't aware of anything that happened." The situation reminded Celwyn of how, once before, they had rescued the orphan. With a raised brow at Bartholomew, he asked, "Are we good again, my friend?"

"Yes, Jonas. But please never scare me like that again!" The big man paced back and forth. "Good grief!"

Edward stepped up. "If you'll excuse me, I second that request." He lowered his rifle to his side. "I'll go get the carriage. I've had enough society, and drama, for the night."

Kang lowered his voice. "Jonas, you might want to wipe the blood off your face. And what about him?" he pointed to their feet. Through the water of the Vltava River, the vampire Delgado's red eyes still glowed from the bottom of the illuminated cage so clearly they could have touched him.

The killing of Telly and Suzanne came back to him, bringing the magician's sadness, too. It also brought the unseen spectral violins whose music surrounded them as the illusions on the edges of the stage began to fade. Celwyn said, "He is ready for the culmination of the evening."

"Are you sure?" Kang studied him as worry filled his eyes. "You are tiring now, correct?"

"Yes."

Bartholomew rejoined them and said, "As much as I want to see Delgado's demise, I'd best take everyone home. It is very late."

He took Zander from the magician's arms and herded the others off the frozen stage and toward the street. The automat pointed at the dome of the Opera House. "Will the net up there hold the rest of the vampires until dawn?"

"It is made of metal, and I'll be here to be sure it does." Celwyn smiled a hard smile of revenge. "It will be a very bright dawn, wouldn't you say?"

Kang patted him on the back. "I'll stay with you."

Moments went by as the crowd dispersed. They chattered in excited voices, entertained and unaware of the truth of what they'd witnessed. As soon as they cleared off the ice, heavy clouds rolled in overhead, obscuring the moon. An astute observer might wonder why the clouds waited until that moment.

"It doesn't appear that you brought your umbrella," Celwyn remarked as they gazed upward.

He produced a large one and handed it to Kang. "Join me for a moment, please." They walked away from the melting ice stage and onto the footpath paralleling the river.

Kang opened the umbrella and regarded the magician with an eyebrow up.

The magician turned, face upraised to the night sky.

The thunder began to the east, low and far away. Just a rumble, barely enough to notice. But, within a minute, it covered Prague, boom after boom, shaking the buildings to their foundations. The noise became deafening as the wind arose, competing with a joyous chorus of French horns announcing the arrival of the storm. The pedestrians in the street scattered as the heavens opened, and the rain poured down.

The electricity in the air sizzled, raising the hair on their scalps and arms. Even the automat Kang shivered in anticipation.

All of the emotion from Suzanne and Telly's deaths arrived, strengthening the magic, and Celwyn once more lifted his hands, sweeping them from side to side. Lightning illuminated the sky, turning night to day, seeming to crack the sky open. Directly overhead, one bolt separated from the rest, arcing high and coming down.

The smell of the electricity was overwhelming as the bolt went into the river, straight and sure into the cage holding Delgado. When it exploded, it sent waves of water flying upward. The lightning blossomed, unfolding like an enormous rose as it spread across the sky.

The music rejoiced as Celwyn opened his cape, letting Qing fly free into the night sky. The bird soared high and then dipped low over what remained of the ice on the river. He landed on the crystal pipe organ, pecking at the silver keys as they began to fade away.

Across the city, the spectral violins played forlornly, echoing triumphantly, in celebration of love, revenge, and ultimately music.

Out of the corner of his eye, the magician spied something white and diaphanous in the river. Horror gripped him. With the last of his strength, he plunged into the water, fighting the current as he swam to the bottom. He slowed, already knowing what he would find. In front of him, Christina's hair flowed in the current as if a light breeze blew through it. Her sightless eyes were open and her hands upraised, as if imploring him to save her.

Twin punctures decorated her neck.

Book Club Questions

1. Celwyn begins this journey based on a lie, but he finds companions and friendship along the way. What does this say about the nature of lies? Does it matter that Celwyn was tricked into this journey—once we see the experiences he has?

2. Celwyn is immortal, so he tries not to get too attached to the mortals around him. How does this distance affect him? Do you agree with the way he has been living?

3. Professor Kang is a long-lived automat, but he has learned to feel emotions like love and grief. Is his longevity part of the reason he and Celwyn are such fast friends? How can Celwyn learn from Kang and vice versa?

4. Professor Kang,an automat built hundreds of years ago who started life as a machine, is in love and happily married. Do you think machines can gain sentience and emotions over time?

5. Annabelle runs away from the life her aunt has planned for her, choosing uncertainty and adventure, and possibly love, over a life of predictability and security. What do you think of her decision?

6. Telly has signs of what we would call PTSD today, and though Celwyn tries to help her, in the end, he is unsuccessful. What do you think about the ways he tries to help her heal from her ordeal?

7. Charles Delgado seems determined to destroy everything Celwyn holds dear. What do you make of this villain?

8. Celwyn is smitten with Christina from their first meeting. What do you think about this connection?

9. Celwyn's power is closely connected to music. The magician can accomplish nearly anything with his magic. What do you think of his abilities? What would you do with such power?

10. This book transcends genre boundaries: fantasy, science fiction, steampunk, romance, horror, revenge. What elements did you enjoy the most? Why?

Author Bio

LOU'S EARLY WORK WAS HORROR AND suspense. Later, the work morphed into a combination of magical realism, mystery, and adventure painted with horrific elements as needed.

Lou is one of those writers who doesn't plan ahead; no outlines, no clue, and she sometimes writes herself into a corner. Atmospheric music in the background helps, "Black" by Pearl Jam especially.

More information is available at LouKemp.com. She'd love to hear from you and what you think of Celwyn, Bartholomew, and Professor Xiau Kang.

Milestones:

2009 The anthology story "Sherlock's Opera" appear in *Seattle Noir*, edited by Curt Colbert, Akashic Books. Available through Amazon or Barnes and

Noble online. Booklist publishes a favorable review of my contribution to the anthology.

2010 Her story, "In Memory of the Sibylline," is accepted into the best-selling MWA anthology *Crimes by Moonlight,* edited by Charlaine Harris. The immortal magician Celwyn makes his first appearance in print.

2018 The story, "The Violins Played before Junstan" is published in the MWA anthology *Odd Partners,* edited by Anne Perry. The Celwyn series begins.